Time Travel Tales

I0606748

Time Travel Tales

By
Jay Dubya

Published by
Jay Dubya
Hammonton, NJ 08037
3286_4H

Copyright © 2026 by Jay Dubya
All rights reserved. No part of this publication may be reproduced
or transmitted in any form or by any means, electronic or
mechanical, including photocopy, recording, or any information
storage and retrieval system, without permission in writing from the
copyright owner.

ISBN 978-1-58909-842-8

Printed in the United States of America

For Michelle and Steve

Other Books by Jay Dubya

Adult Fiction

Black Leather and Blue Denim, A '50s Novel
The Great Teen Fruit War, A 1960' Novel
Ron Coyote, Man of La Mangia
Frat' Brats, A '60s Novel
Pieces of Eight
Pieces of Eight, Part II
Pieces of Eight, Part III
Pieces of Eight, Part IV
The Wholly Book of Genesis
The Wholly Book of Exodus
The Wholly Book of Doo-Doo-Rot-on-Me
Thirteen Sick Tasteless Classics
Thirteen Sick Tasteless Classics, Part II
Thirteen Sick Tasteless Classics, Part III
Thirteen Sick Tasteless Classics, Part IV
Thirteen Sick Tasteless Classics, Part V
So Ya' Wanna' Be A Teacher!
Mauled Maimed Mangled Mutilated Mythology
Fractured Frazzled Folk Fables & Fairy Farces
FFFF & FF, Part II
Nine New Novellas
Nine New Novellas, Part II
Nine New Novellas, Part III
Nine New Novellas, Part IV
One Baker's Dozen
Two Baker's Dozen
RAM: Random Articles and Manuscripts
Modern Mythology
UFO: Utterly Fantastic Occurrences
Prime-Time Crime Time
Snake Eyes and Boxcars
Snake Eyes and Boxcars, Part II
The Psychic Dimension
The Psychic Dimension, Part II
Shakespeare: Slammed, Smeared, Savaged and Slaughtered
Shakespeare: S, S, S & S, Part II
First Person Stories
The Arcane Arcade

Thirteen Tantalizing Tales
PLOTS
PLOTS, Part II
THEMES
Hawthorne: Hacked, Shakespeare: Sacked, & Thurber: Thwacked
Hawthorne: Hazed, Hooked, Hammered and Hijacked
Suite 16
The FBI Inspector
Poe: Pelted, Pounded, Pummeled and Pulverized
Twain: Tattered, Trounced, Tortured and Traumatized
London: Lashed, Lacerated, Lampooned and Lambasted
O. Henry: Obscenely and Outrageously Obliterated
Homer's Odd Sea Odyssey
HOMER'S ILL ILIAD
Homer's Ill Iliad and Odd Sea Odyssey
The Timeless Time Machine
War of the Worlds
The Invisible Man
Parody Paradise
Parody Paradise, Part II
Parody Paradise, Part III
Parody Paradise, Part IV
A Christmas Carol
Bee 17, Short Stories
Bee 17, Part II, Short Stories
Bee 17, Part III, Short Stories
Bee 17, Part IV, Short Stories
Bee 17, Part V, Short Stories
Bee 17, Part VI, Short Stories

Young Adult Fantasy Novels and Stories

Pot of Gold
Enchanta
Space Bugs, Earth Invasion
The Eighteen Story Gingerbread House

Contents

The twenty-one novellas presented in *Time Travel Tales* are works of pure fiction. The stories' themes deal with movements, or shifts in time. Any character resemblance to any living person on planet Earth in this work is purely coincidental.

"The Music Disk"

Ever since his late '50s and early '60s glorious high school days Chad Elgin Elvins had an intense passion for early rock and roll music. The Hammonton, New Jersey man had over the past five decades amassed one of the largest vinyl 45s' collections around featuring such famed artists as Elvis Presley, Jerry Lee Lewis, Little Richard, Fats Domino and Buddy Holly from the nostalgic '50s, the Beatles, the Rolling Stones, the Kinks, the Supremes and the Four Seasons from the turbulent '60s and Fleetwood Mac, ABBA, Creedence Clearwater Revival, Chicago and the Eagles from the dynamic '70s. The man's extensive "hot wax collection" (with some duplications) amounted to a staggering total of over 25,000 '45s. And besides *that* colossal, numerical figure, the ceramic tile and marble-laying contractor's taped song collection also consisted of over 10,000 albums and his now-burgeoning CD library had expanded to 7,000 selections.

And the sentimental oldies' music fancier's mind was a virtual rock and roll encyclopedia of names of artists, songs, writers, music producers, record labels and chart-busters and Chad Elvins even cataloged in his computer-like mind's memory banks the exact month and year that a new title had been released, dating back to 1952. And the collector's brilliant oldies-oriented brain had classified thousands of titles by subjects and themes, too.

The dedicated record connoisseur had an admirable knowledge of all of the songs about "Days of the Week," all of the tunes that were written and sung about particular "Places", all of the titles with either "boys or girls' names," all of the more famous and least popular novelty numbers, all the songs with parts of the body mentioned in them like the 1958 hit "Willie and the Hand Jive" by the Johnny Otis Show, and even every existent popular and not-so-popular song about colors, animals and sundry food and drink items.

When Chad Elvins and his best buddy Jeremy Gibase weren't attending oldies revival concerts in Philadelphia, New York, Baltimore, Wildwood and Atlantic City, the inseparable pair would "cruise" downtown Hammonton in the music expert's 2002 dark blue *Toyota Camry* sedan and reminisce about '50s sock hops, ice cream parlors, DA haircuts, James Dean, pegged pants, poodle skirts, hot cars, local drive-in movies, teenage hangouts and especially recall and discuss the roots of rock and roll music.

"Do ya' remember when this three-block-long main drag used to have seven soda fountains and two movie theaters?" Chad rhetorically asked high school history teacher Jeremy Gibase as the two "cruised" south past Second Street on Hammonton's Bellevue Avenue. "The Fire Department used to be on your right in the center of town, Mark Press Men's Clothes, Miller's Department Store and Newberry's Five and Dime were situated over there on our left and even *Sears* and the *A&P* chain store were on our right. Times have really changed, haven't they Jeremy? Just look at this place now!" Chad Elvins emphatically pointed out. "It's eight p.m. Friday night July 29th, 2005 and Hammonton looks like a ghost town where even the most diehard spirits have abandoned it. Ya' know good buddy, we were lucky to grow up in the fabulous '50s, the best decade ever!"

"Ya' have that opinion right," Jeremy Gibase mechanically answered and nodded his head as his garrulous companion inhaled some much-needed oxygen to replenish his brain and vocal cords.

"Yeah, Jeremy. Friday night was really a blast and a half back in the mid and late fifties. Every hot car in town had enormous fins above its taillights, and either dice or a skull hanging from its rear-view mirror and spinners on its hubcaps," Chad fondly recalled and boasted. "And flat-head engines were still boss despite the popularity of overhead cam motors. And all the kids hung out in town on Friday and Saturday nights and waited on street corners for friends or dates to pick them up just to go cruisin'. Today anyone that's stupid enough to stay on a corner too long is a candidate to be molested or mugged."

"Ya' got that comment straight!" Jeremy concurred. "I used to love all those pretty girls wearin' saddle shoes, especially the Hammonton High cheerleaders! There was always something special about the way they looked, cute, innocent and vulnerable! Of course, we both married *HHS* '50s prom queens and we're both divorced and our kids are now adults with their own families to monitor. I suppose that's the principal reason we've remained such close chums," Gibase realized and stated. "And I do believe that our mutual affection for oldies' music has cemented our friendship over the years."

2

"If it wasn't for that ugly *Vietnam War,*" Elvins argued, "things might not have so drastically changed. Hippies and their rebellious protest caused young people to go from cigarettes to marijuana and from beer to cocaine."

"Ya' know Chad, sometimes you make more sense than anyone else I know or see babblin' away on television talk shows or on *Action News*," Gibase sincerely confirmed. "And isn't it a strange coincidence that we both like songs recorded by Chad and Jeremy since their names are also our official appellations printed on our birth certificates. Life in America is full of wonderful associations as well as loaded with unique surprises."

The two '50s enthusiasts' sustained their standard Friday night dialogue, exchanging fond memories of the now defunct Rivoli and Palace movie theaters, Dan's Record and Stationery Store, Godfrey's Drug Store and Soda Fountain, Augie's Hamburger Haven, K and H Auto Supply, the Sweet Shop, Kern's Drugstore and Ice Cream Parlor and last but not least the now-extinct Gem Restaurant on Central Avenue, a '50s teen hangout that was conveniently located a mere block east of yellow-brick Hammonton High School on Central between Peach and Vine Street.

"Back in the Elvis and Bill Haley Age, the Gem was the coolest place around before we had fast food franchise restaurants," Chad reminded his fascinated and wholly intrigued passenger. "We danced the jitterbug and the stroll with pretty girls in pony tails, ate delicious burgers and fries, and took or met our dates *there* for socializin'. And all the guys like you and me either wore our 'Big H' white and blue-trimmed Hammonton High letterman sweaters when we felt pleasant and congenial and had gorgeous dates, or we rebelliously donned our black leather motorcycle jackets, metal buckled engineer boots and blue denim jeans when we felt rough and tough because we were lookin' to meet some new women with looser morals," Elvins maintained. "The '50s and early '60s were the *Golden Years of Rock and Roll,* and also the golden years of our lives."

"You're again, a hundred percent on the money!" Jeremy automatically agreed. "Your logic is impeccable! Everything was clean, innocent and fresh back then. Like you said, there were cigarettes but no hardcore drugs around like cocaine or meth'. And kids, even the greaser tough guys that used to hang out in front of the Rivoli Theater and the Central Cafe all looked presentable in public and not like baggy pants ghetto derelicts and sad-sack losers as many teenagers often do today."

"And any guy caught wearin' an earring would've been shunned, ostracized or appropriately given the beatin' of his life!" Chad interrupted his normally reticent partner. "Kids today gotta' mimic every bit of trash produced by *Hollywood* and by the disgustin' rap music industry. And I don't know why rap is even considered music. It's got usually two very boring background sounds, a monotonous drumbeat or maybe some thug on drugs scratching the surface of a record. And the lyrics are absolutely pathetic, gross and anti-social, actually anti-civilization," Elvins confidently described and asserted. "Rap is to music what the devil is to human nature: a hellish threat to culture and its noble institutions! There's definitely a morality war in progress between the old and new generations, and it's all a mutation of the ugly '60s!"

Then, Jeremy Gibase reflected on reality for a moment and made a salient remark. "Say, Chad. Bruni's is too busy on Friday nights to order and swallow down an extra-thick pepperoni tomato and cheese pie. Since we're probably headin' out to Palace Pizza on the Black Horse Pike why don't ya' take the Weymouth Road shortcut. That route would be just like smartly takin' the hypotenuse of the triangle rather than takin' the longer base and height right angle to get there. We'll save three-miles in the process, too. See," Gibase verbally contributed, "all was not completely lost in my lackluster educational past. I learned some advanced geometry in high school and have remarkably remembered it, too. Say Chad, when are we gonna' drive out to Cleveland and visit the *Rock and Roll Hall of Fame?* We've been postponing that planned trip for over two years now."

"I still think the *Hall of Fame* should've been built in Philly' because Dick Clark's *American Bandstand* was originally televised from Billy Penn's *Quaker City,"* the driver objected. "But since Alan Freed coined the immortal term 'rock and roll' when he was a DJ in Cleveland, that's why the museum was built in Ohio and not close-by across the *Delaware* in Pennsy'. The way I feel right now we're never goin' out there to Ohio Jeremy. I still feel bitterness about the selection committee choosin' a remote primitive place like Cleveland over Philly'."

As Chad Elvins motored east on Egg Harbor Road past the Hammonton Lake Park Little League and Pony League complexes, the conversation switched to the driver's newly purchased Oldies

4

Music CD he had just received in the mail. The man behind the steering wheel commanded his riding companion to remove the plastic case from the glove compartment, take out the *Internet* acquired disk and then insert it into the *Toyota's* moderately powerful stereo CD player.

Jeremy Gibase anxiously and obediently complied with Chad Elvins' imperative, pressed a dashboard button and skillfully inserted the new music anthology into the projecting tray. The fellow riding shotgun was almost as euphoric about hearing the newly acquired compilation as was the all-too-ecstatic driver. But after shoving the CD tray back into the *Camry's* instrument panel no music was forthcoming.

"That's awfully strange!" a momentarily puzzled Gibase exclaimed. "The music isn't playing and the tray seems to be stuck and won't come out to be re-inserted. Something is undoubtedly amiss here! I hope I haven't broken a gear, a spindle, a sprocket or a weak spring inside."

"Japanese automobile technology in usually superior to that found in Detroit cars, and I admit it's all quite peculiar about the tray not workin' right!" Chad Elvins disgustedly replied. "*Toyota* products are usually good and dependable, pretty reliable and very durable. Are ya' sure you're pressing the correct button to eject the disk? These foreign cars are loaded with gadgetry and all kinds of cute features and stuff!"

"Yes!" Jeremy regretfully verified. "It's the same button I had pushed to get the empty tray to come out and then to go in while I was still holding the disk. What songs were on the anthology anyway?" Gibase curiously asked his traveling companion as the *Toyota* angled right at the Egg Harbor Road "Four-Way-Stop" red blinking light to turn right onto *County 559*, better known to area inhabitants as "Weymouth Road."

"I'm really disappointed, Jer'!" the driver indicated with a grim expression on his face. "The anthology I had bought over the *Internet* was a collection of '50s, '60s and '70s songs and the album's unique theme was 'Various Places'. I should've known better and purchased the item at Amazon.com."

"Hey, let me guess one of the songs!" Jeremy impetuously interrupted. "How about the 1977 smash hit 'Hotel California'? That song was more than just innovative! The tune's guitar arrangements were totally awesome and revolutionary! And I know you're a big

Don Henley, Glenn Frey and Joe Walsh *Eagles'* fan and I just gotta' reckon *that* particular creative number has to be on there!"

"You hit the bull's eye on that accurate guess!" Chad complimented his attentive buddy as the driver pounded the dashboard three times with his right fist, endeavoring to loosen up the annoying disk blockage inside. "And also from the rowdy seventies Jeremy is the '74 monster hit 'Sweet Home Alabama' by Lynyrd Skynyrd. That chart-buster has gotten to be one of your cherished favorites. It's definitely one of mine."

"What other '50s stuff do ya' have on the disk?" Gibase inquired as the *Toyota* sedan sped past Sunshine Fruit and Vegetable Farm's assorted corn, tomato and pepper fields, which were evident on both sides of the well-maintained two-lane county road. "I'm gonna' get mad if the disk you bought is defective and has somehow damaged your stereo system."

"That was goin' to be my big surprise!" Elvins woefully lamented. "As I already told ya', the general theme of the collection was different places, which could translate into the name of a city, town, island, peninsula, state, mountain or even the name of a river. From the year 1957 the album featured Patti Page singin' the ballad 'Old Cape Cod' and from the vintage year 1959 there is Wilbert Harrison's great rendition of 'Kansas City' and Freddy "Boom Boom' Cannon's lively creation 'Tallahassee Lassie.' I'm really ticked off and getting frustrated that this damned tray isn't rejectin' and the disk isn't playin' although it's inside the panel," the driver expressed his very apparent dissatisfaction. "I'll see if at least the radio is still workin'."

"That's not workin' either!" Jeremy revealed as he turned up the volume knob without achieving any positive effect. "This CD problem is really getting weirder by the second and has somehow affected your entire sound system! Now please tell me before I put my fist through your car's non-functionin' dash radio speaker, you must've had a samplin' of songs from the sixties on your new CD to finish out the album."

"Yes, and in chronological order if my memory serves me correctly, there was Johnny Horton's 1960 number 'North to Alaska', and then there was supposed to be the Dovell's blockbuster 'Bristol Stomp', which as you probably know was produced way back in '61 and was about the kids in Bristol, Pennsylvania, only forty miles from here. And exclusively keepin' with the places' theme I had mentioned," the driver proceeded, "the UK was represented with Jerry and the Pacemakers 1965 slow-dance-blast from the past 'Ferry Cross' the Mersey'. And from 1967 there was...."

"Hey, hold on a second Chad! Let me guess that one!" Gibase exuberantly begged while overtly demonstrating an excess of feigned emotion. "The 1967 big *place* song on the CD just has to be Scott McKenzie's haunting melody 'Going to San Francisco'! I loved the song but hated the hippie era!"

"The official title Jeremy was and still is 'San Francisco, Be Sure to Wear Some Flowers in Your Hair'!" the overly peeved driver academically emphasized. "And in addition, my good pal, now I'm really becomin' exceptionally irritated because Glen Campbell's dual 1969 hits 'Wichita Lineman' and 'Galveston' rounded out the *place* CD's terrific selections. I'm gonna' write Mr. Toyota a nasty letter of complaint, if there is such a guy with that name!"

There was a moment's pause as the blue *Camry* traveled over the Weymouth Road Bridge that arched above the busy *Atlantic City Expressway* and both occupants stared down at the hundreds of automobiles, limos' and casino buses zipping back and forth between Philadelphia and Atlantic City. Then Jeremy Gibase was inspired to ask Elvins a pertinent question that was dominating *his* rather confused mind.

"Well, Chad. aybe the disk is warped or something and that's why it's jammed inside the dashboard. What record outfit manufactures and distributes this inferior product with the tremendous selection by the original artists anyway? Ya' oughta' write them a nasty letter protestin' your bad experience with their shoddy malfunctionin' CD!" Gibase recommended as he examined and read the contents of the descriptive folder inside the plastic case.

"I believe I ordered the disk from a firm named Satin Record Corporation," Elvins related as the *Toyota* passed by the first section of fields belonging to the mammoth nine-hundred-acre Atlantic Blueberry Company Farm (Weymouth Division) on the left. "Yes, that's what its name is! Satin Record Corporation!" the livid and chagrined driver reiterated. "After I get done with Mr. Toyota, I'm gonna' also write Satin Records a critical letter fully describing their lousy merchandise if I learn that that freakin' disk has been improperly manufactured. It's really screwed up my entire stereo system!"

"Well, Chad!" Jeremy Gibase gasped in exasperation. "The company listed on *this* disk happens to be Satan Record Corporation and not Satin Records! Did you hear me Chad!" Jeremy exclaimed with concerned accentuation in his voice. "It's printed in small type right at the bottom of this little descriptive pamphlet' here, Satan and not Satin!"

"What?" bellowed the driver in a newly developed hoarse voice. "I knew you were walkin' over to my house to go cruisin' for some pizza and *Cokes* so when I strolled out to the mailbox and discovered the package inside I just hastily unwrapped it and tossed it into the glove compartment so that I could surprise you," Chad informed his equally perturbed passenger. "Instead, we're both bein' surprised with this oddball Satan Record Corporation nonsense. Kindly read the album's record titles to see if they're the same classic songs that we had just discussed. As a rule, I hate mysteries, but this particular mystery probably has more to do with a minimum waged shipping clerk's incompetence than it does with Lucifer."

Gibase quickly read off the list of titles that ironically were of "History Places" that had coincidentally been substituted for simply "Places." Jeremy's lips quivered as he quickly read off the litany: "Battle of New Orleans, 1959, Johnny Horton; Waterloo, 1959, Stonewall Jackson; Sink the Bismarck, 1960, Johnny Horton again; Battle Hymn of the Republic, no year given, Elvis Presley; El Paso, 1960, Marty Robbins; the *Vietnam War* classic Battle of the Green Berets, a '70s hit by Sergeant Barry Sadler; The Little Old Lady From Pasadena, 1964, by Jan and Dean," Jeremy reluctantly read as his hands began trembling in consort with his lips. "They ain't the same titles Chad!"

"Jeremy!" the driver shouted like a maniac about to go haywire. "What other songs appear on that crazy Satan Records' album?" the *Cambry's* navigator insisted on knowing. "My patience is approachin' the boilin' point!"

"Well, my illustrious colleague in strangeness," the rattled passenger continued in a distraught tone of voice, "there's Donovan's 1969 recording of Atlantis, Jerry Lee Lewis's Great Balls of Fire from '58, and finally, let's see, there's..."

At that precise moment, the *Toyota's* accelerator astonishingly mashed down to the floor without the driver's consent or volition. The vehicle's horn shrilly and eerily blasted away for five seconds and then remarkably ceased its clamor. And next both Chad and

Jeremy were totally shocked to observe that the vehicle was steering itself down the serpentine road at the incredible speed of one hundred miles an hour, going around bends in both lanes.

"The brakes don't work! The steering wheel's turning on its own!" the baffled *Toyota* driver shouted. And then suddenly all four of the late-model sedan's doors simultaneously locked on their' own. "And now we can't get out of this death trap! And the power windows won't go down either!"

"And look! There's an abnormal fog cloud up ahead right near the entrance to Atlantic Blueberry's packing house!" the history teacher alerted the already distressed and bewildered driver. "What's goin' on? This car's operatin' all by itself'! It's as if it's demonically possessed!"

Just as the *Camry* exited the Weymouth Road fog, the CD player ominously started whirring, and the recognizable introduction to Johnny Horton's unforgettable 1959 hit single "The Battle of New Orleans" came blasting through the foreign automobile's speakers. First Chad and then Jeremy attempted lowering the loud music's volume, but the radio dial failed to control or adjust the song distinctly being emanated.

"Chad!" the history teacher bellowed above the tune's extraordinarily loud decibels. "The asphalt road's disappeared and we're now speeding along on rugged terrain. And look! There's some sort of intense military battle happenin' up ahead. We're hostages inside some kind of queer anachronism goin' on here! I hope Chad it's just a mock re-creation of a post-colonial battle scene that wasn't too publicized in the local papers!"

"What in Earth's sacred name are ya' sayin'!" the totally shocked man sitting behind the wheel apprehensively shouted. "Speak plain and simple English, will ya'! It's a good thing we have our seat-belts on or else our heads would be rupturin' and warpin' the roof!"

"Holy *War' of 1812!*" the thoroughly amazed history' expert wildly exclaimed while unable to conceal his astonishment. "We're fantastically traveling at a hundred miles an hour right through the Battle of New Orleans! We're in Louisiana and not in New Jersey!"

"That's the song that Johnny Horton's singin'!" the ceramic tile contractor acknowledged and yelled back across the front seat. "Either this car's a nightmare fantasy in progress or it's been transformed into an honest-to-goodness time machine! Or should I say honest-to-badness time machine all caused by that diabolical

Satan Records disk we can't get out of the CD player!" Elvins persuasively continued. "And what's goin' on around us with all the cannons boomin' and the guys with white wigs in red coats runnin' around and shootin' their weird-lookin' muskets at us? Hey! Duck down Jeremy! Those deranged imbeciles are firin' away too close for comfort!"

As the dark blue car swiftly swerved and careened through a meadow dividing the assembled armies, the history mentor yelled to his perplexed associate that Louisiana had joined the United States in 1812 and the British were trying to still have their former American colonies back from the world-wide embarrassment the *Crown* had suffered in the 1776 *Revolutionary War*. Jeremy Gibase further explained to his bouncing and jolted cohort that General Andrew Jackson had fought the historic Battle of New Orleans at a place called "Chalmette" on January 8, 1815 and *he* furthermore related that the well-documented clash was also known as the "Needles Battle."

And when the unpredictable automobile zoomed by a very astounded General Andrew Jackson, Jeremy Gibase proceeded with his informative presentation. "Even though the Battle of New Orleans was the last skirmish of the *War of 1812,*" he prefaced, "it actually had occurred in 1815, so that's where we're now trapped in some sort of distorted excursion through a monumental moment in the past, presumably initiated by the song being played on your Satan Record Corporation CD!" Gibase theorized and remarked. "And also, Chad, since there weren't any modern-type communications back in 1815 a truce had already been signed across the *Atlantic*, but neither side knew about it!" the facts' expert academically conveyed to the very unnerved driver-non-driver. "In other words, Chad, this terrible event we're witnessin' was a battle that shouldn't have been fought in the first place! The peace treaty had been signed in the city of Ghent over in Europe, in Belgium I think, a full fifteen days before the battle ensued."

"Do ya' have any idea how many men are fightin' around us?" Chad yelled as the now "evil *Toyota*" swiftly passed through dense cannon smoke and heavy gunfire. "This whole thing is absolutely surreal!"

"Can't say for sure!" the history teacher demonstrably screamed back. "I believe the British had eight thousand soldiers that marched to capture New Orleans but were intercepted right here at Chalmette.

I know for a fact that over one-thousand-five-hundred redcoats were killed in this battle, mostly by Andrew Jackson's artillery and by his keen-eyed rifle shooters," Gibase added. "Fortunately, the American casualties were minimal and so Jackson decisively won a major battle that didn't need to be fought."

"I thought that Jackson was President of the United States?" Chad challenged as the gunfire between the opposing sides became more sporadic. "Isn't he the guy whose portrait is on the twenty-dollar bill?"

"Yeah!" Gibase boisterously responded as the very perceptible cannon fire diminished to only an occasional burst. "Andrew Jackson was a Democrat and became President in 1829 at age 61," Gibase pontificated as he continued bouncing up and down on the front seat. "He served for two terms until 1837 and then died at age 78 in 1845. I never thought these details I've memorized would ever be relevant to anything significant that's happenin' outside of my boring history classroom!"

While Chad and Jeremy were finally uncomfortably adjusting to their chaotic Louisiana environment, their *Toyota* entered into and was immediately enveloped by a dense fog cloud and as the CD format switched to the second song, silence momentarily prevailed inside the still-speeding vehicle. Then, the familiar rhythmic notes to Stonewall Jackson's 1959 classic hit "Waterloo" began throbbing through the car's stereo speakers. Soon the surrounding haze lifted and the inscrutable "mind of its own *Toyota*" was again smack dab in the middle of an enormous altercation being waged between determined armies on opposite sides of the dark blue *Camry*.

"Where are we now?" Chad yelled above the seemingly disconcerting loud music. "It doesn't look like Philly' or Pittsburgh or even Cleveland out there! We're definitely travelin' in another century! Say Jeremy! The damned key won't turn off the car!"

"It appears to be the Battle of Waterloo, located not far from Brussels, Belgium, which incidentally is not too far from Ghent," the thoroughly amazed history guru explained. "The conflict is being fought between the armies of Napoleon of France to our right and Wellington of England on our left. If I remember correctly Napoleon has the numerical advantage with 74,000 soldiers while Wellington has 67,000 troops. But a Prussian Army allied with England arrives just in time to reinforce Wellington's men, and that's how Napoleon met his Waterloo, so to speak!" Gibase editorialized. "If the short

French guy with the Napoleon complex had the wherewithal to attack a mere four-hours earlier, he could've defeated Wellington and the Prussian' armies separately, but the French dictator didn't advance on the British because the battlefield was soggy from a heavy rainfall the night before."

"Very fascinating stuff!" Chad Elvins sincerely exclaimed and admitted. "What year is it anyway? I don't see any calendars hanging anywhere!"

"That's what's so awesomely phenomenal about all of this!" the history buff hollered back across the front seat. "It's June 18, 1815, just five months after Andrew Jackson had defeated the British at Chalmette, but now we're speeding along in your *Camry* on another continent and watching the British take it to the French in an overwhelming victory. And coincidentally we've gone from Andrew Jackson at New Orleans to a vocalist who has dubbed himself' Stonewall Jackson singin' about 'Waterloo'!" Jeremy Gibase marveled and reported. "This whole experience not only goes beyond being bizarre; it actually transcends bizarre! Hey, Chad! Watch out for Napoleon wavin' at us up ahead! We're gonna' run the little runt over!"

The dark blue *Camry* (operating under some inexplicable intelligent force or dynamic supernatural energy) veered to the left avoiding a collision with the dumbstruck and very demonstrative little French general, who was wildly gesticulating and then scampering like crazy to escape the path of the motorized vehicle that quite naturally defied the science of *his* time.

As the dark blue automobile tested its shock absorbers and sped through the fierce fighting, the history authority related to the fellow sitting behind the wheel that Napoleon had lost forty thousand men in the intense confrontation and the British General Wellington (and the accompanying Prussians) approximately twenty-three thousand soldiers. "This Battle of Waterloo was an absolute crushing defeat for that midget-tyrant Napoleon and his *complex* ego!" Jeremy Gibase half-heartedly jested. "He deserved the fate that awaited him!"

"Holy smokes!" Chad Elvins incidentally boomed. "We're headin' directly into another low-flyin' cumulus just ahead! I suppose we're now off to *World War II* because Johnny Horton's comin' back on the Satan Record Corporation CD with his memorable version of 'Sink the Bismarck'! But how could we be in a sea battle if we're speeding at a hundred miles and hour in a car?"

"I guess we'll soon find out!" Jeremy bellowed back as the stirring starting notes of "Sink the Bismarck" began pulsating through the *Toyota's* stereo speakers. "I hope we aren't kept in a fog during the battle!" Gibase inadvertently articulated without any intention of being amusing. "This is one impressive naval contest I wouldn't want to miss."

"I thought that Bismarck was the capital of North Dakota?" Chad Elvins asked while indirectly requesting his traveling mate for clarification. "At least that's what I had learned in sixth grade Geography."

"There's a slight possibility that I might be mistaken but I believe that both the city and the famous battleship were named after the dignified Prussian nobleman Otto von Bismarck, who successfully unified the German states into one powerful empire in the late 1800s. That strong empire was eventually broken up after *World War I* but then it was cunningly reorganized by Adolph Hitler and his Nazi nationalism movement just prior to the start of *World War II.*"

"Very interesting, but very immaterial to us escaping the haunted confines of my accursed foreign automobile!" the aggravated driver answered. "I'd try smashin' my elbow through the window but I don't feel like squeezing out the opening I created goin' a hundred miles an hour. For all I know I might fall and land inside of *Mt. Vesuvius* when it was explodin' near Pompeii back in the days of ancient Rome."

"August 24th, 79 A.D!" Jeremy enunciated as several large shells shot from battleship gun turrets whizzed by the *Toyota* from opposite directions. "That's the date when *Vesuvius* erupted and eliminated Pompeii, a city with a population of around 25,000 panic-stricken people! Say Chad, do ya' think your CD player is tryin' to teach us some sort of demented moral lesson?"

Then, at that precise moment, one of the flying shells exploded near the car's chassis and the errant bomb rocked and vibrated the sedan circling above. "Great gods Chad! We're vulnerable to getting hit up here and we can't see a blessed thing because this low-driftin' vapor we're passin' into is as thick as *Campbell's Chunky Vegetable Soup*!"

Before Elvins could render a reply, the *Toyota* sedan exited the temporary fog and now the "demon car" was speeding in the air and flying over the *Atlantic* heading toward a massive sea battle being waged in the distance. And after approaching the notorious and formidable Nazi sea-juggernaut *Bismarck* (violating both logic and explanation), the charmed *Toyota* miraculously defied gravity and maintained its suspension while simultaneously circling above the ongoing conflict-in-progress between the infamous battleship and five British destroyers.

"We're now over the *Atlantic* about four hundred miles or so off the coast of France," Jeremy recollected and uttered from memorized language printed in his World History textbook. "The Nazi battleship was believed by many military analysts of the time to be virtually unsinkable. The *Bismarck* had eight 15-inch guns and the sea fortress was practically impervious to enemy attack," Gibase yelled to his now-petrified and mentally disheveled friend. "Its dense steel-plated exterior walls are the closest thing to impregnable that existed among battleships back in 1941."

"Well then, how did the British destroyers locate the *Bismarck* way out here in the middle of the *Atlantic?*" Elvins asked just before two potent shells exploded in the nearby sky and sent the suspended-in-air *Toyota* vacillating back and forth.

"According to my authoritative history text that I use to teach my apathetic seniors," Gibase nervously elaborated to his fellow time voyager, "the *Bismarck* had just sunk the British cruiser *Hood* off the coast of Greenland and then the English dispatched every available destroyer and battleship to go out in the ocean and effectively locate and destroy the legendary German war vessel. Remember Chad," Gibase haughtily disclosed, "the date is May 26, 1941 and the *Bismarck* was attempting to interfere with well-traveled shipping lanes between Europe and America. *Pearl Harbor* wasn't until December 7, 1941, almost seven months after what we're now witnessin'!"

"I see, so that's why there aren't any American ships blastin' away at the *Bismarck* down there!" Chad Elvins recognized and fully comprehended. "We're watchin' history in the making!" the tile and marble merchant and installer finally fathomed. "You know Jeremy we're comin' mighty close to bein' lambasted and slammed right into Kingdom-come! And that Satan Records CD is not a very good omen, either! Look Jeremy!" Elvins shrieked in pure terror. "We're comin' into British and German artillery range again while we're movin' towards that ominous-lookin' low-lyin' cloud!"

14

Johnny Horton's stirring patriotic song ended and the CD player was systematically switching to the next interesting anthology selection. The familiar instrumental introduction to Elvis Presley's emotionally inspirational interpretation of "The Battle Hymn of the Republic" was being played and the ceramic tile distributor sitting listlessly at the *Toyota's* helm felt motivated to ask his knowledgeable chum a question from the heart. "Do ya' suppose that we're seein' all this brutal warfare for some indecipherable divine purpose?" he philosophically related. "I mean Jeremy, is this some kind of ethical lesson we're being taught to have us change our errant ways of thinkin' and actin'? Do we have to repent for our sins? Is that what's happenin' inside this moral test tube we seem to be captured in? It's not our damned fault that history has been chronicled and documented as a series of needless belligerent wars!"

Before Jeremy could mentally construct and then verbalize a plausible response to his partner's erudite comments, the dark blue *Toyota* maneuvered out of the fog and found itself' bumpily speeding down a dale right in the middle of the chaotic *Battle of Gettysburg*. It didn't take the history scholar long to adequately perceive and interpret the fantastic particulars his senses were receiving.

"This Chad is July 3rd, 1863, the *Battle of Gettysburg,* the pivotal turning point of the *Civil War!*" the facts and dates' aficionado declaratively stated. "And there's General George E. Pickett on our right leading a charge of fifteen thousand men in a military formation up Cemetery Ridge. This maneuver we're witnessin' happened just after General Robert E. Lee ordered Pickett on what proved to be a crazy suicide mission amidst such a barrage of *Union* artillery and rifle fire. Only a few of Pickett's men actually reached the top of the ridge but they were only able to secure it for around a half hour," Gibase eloquently elucidated, "and then the *Confederate* vanguard had to relinquish control and retreat from their positions to save their lives. And General Lee lost twenty-thousand-men while attempting the bold advance and the South's Army would never recover from the overwhelmin' defeat it had received in this very crucial battle!"

"So, that's why Lincoln delivered the famous *Gettysburg Address* right here on this battlefield," Chad Elvins surmised and conveyed. "Plenty of good men on both sides were killed right here, and old Honest Abe' wanted to honor all of them because he still regarded himself as the President of the Southern States too! Now, it all makes perfectly good sense in spite of the insanity we're encounterin' in my crazy *Toyota*!"

Before Chad Elvins could ask additional salient questions pertaining to the *Civil War,* the *Toyota* (speeding parallel to Pickett's doomed men) bounced and banged along the rough combat-rutted ground and soon entered a thick nebulous-type mist as Elvis Presley's inimitable voice belted out the "Battle Hymn of the Republic's" final emotionally stirring lyrics, "Glory, glory hallelujah, His truth keeps marching on!"

"I've noticed that the events on the CD are not in chronological order, since the Civil War preceded World War II in time. Let's see, what's next on that despicable Satan album?" Jeremy asked the befuddled music collector. "I hope it's not AC/DC's 'Highway to Hell'!"

"Marty Robbins' 1960 tune El Paso!" the driver recalled from their earlier discussion, speaking in a monotone voice that made Elvins sound as if he were in a hypnotic trance. "I suppose we'll be driving right through the middle of a big western saloon brawl involvin' the narrator singin' the verses, and we'll see a jealous Mexican desperado named Jose."

And that's exactly what the two "time and space travelers" dually experienced, as the blue *Camry* kept rotating above and around the circumference of the "old West Texas town of El Paso." Their trip lasted for the song's duration, while the bandito Jose frantically chased after and vigorously pursued the timorous narrator, who had been caught flirting with the renegade's girlfriend inside the raucous-sounding saloon.

The recurring fog again appeared after the addictive-sounding song waned and finally expired, and soon, the *Toyota's* stereo began duplicating a steady drumbeat and Sergeant Barry Sadler began singing the familiar refrains to "The Battle of the Green Berets." Bombs and mortars were exploding on both sides of the self-guided *Camry* as Elvins and Gibase were undeniably involuntary participants in an incredulous beyond-their-control misadventure. The *Toyota* sped through a remote Southeast Asian village, almost ran over a dozen Vietnamese civilians and then zoomed past an arrow sign reading: "Da Nang, Ten Miles."

"We're navigatin' through the middle of the infamous *Vietnam War!*" Gibase concluded and yelled to the driver-non-driver seated on his left. "The time period is probably the late '60s or early '70s and either Lyndon Baines Johnson or Richard M. Nixon is President."

"Rock and Roll music was great up until around 1964," the man sitting in the "driver-non-driver's seat" opined in a trance-like hypnotic voice. "Then, with the numerous anti-war protests came drugs and the hippie movement, Jeremy, and the entire world changed and went helter-skelter, with violent demonstrations and torn communities, and feuding families all over America," Elvins shared. "Who could ever forget the emotional duress of those miserable pathetic late '60s?"

"Didn't you like the Beatles and the Stones?" Gibase argued, as powerful bombs were exploding, and napalm was burning all around the speeding *Toyota's* exterior. "I mean, there was some pretty decent music produced during that ugly era of turmoil, too!"

"To change the subject to something more realistic and life-threatening," the almost petrified driver-non-driver insisted, "what if we're injured or killed during this mysterious insanity journey we're now drivin' through against our wills! Will we be med-evaced by helicopter outa' here if we survive our sustained injuries or will we be buried here in one of these God-forsaken rice paddies if we're accidentally killed in combat? Jesus Christ, Jeremy! Are these lousy, hideous, curving Vietnam country dirt roads extremely bumpy, or what!"

"I hope your mind-of-its-own car is smart enough not to stop for those rifle toting Viet Cong standing in the road directly up ahead!" Gibase pointed out to his almost traumatized riding companion. "And look Chad! Plenty of American fighter jets are zoning in and strafing that area just in front of us! Thank God the Viet Cong gunmen are now all heading for cover!"

A large bomb that had been dropped detonated several-hundred-feet in front of the *Toyota*, which then fortunately entered the cloud of dark smoke that had resulted from the huge ordnance discharge. Before either the almost paralyzed driver-non-driver or his alarmed passenger could utter a word, the seemingly indestructible *Toyota* was speeding onward and accelerating on a paved surface that Gibase immediately identified as "Colorado Boulevard," which was quite consistent with the new song currently being played on the *Camry's* stereo system.

"That's Jan and Dean singing 'The Little Old Lady from Pasadena'!" Jeremy shouted to his virtually catatonic time-traveling mate. "She's racing us in that super-stock *Dodge* having California license plates! And the old bag can't keep her foot off the accelerator, just like the catchy lyrics suggest! At least this drag racing event is a trifle less dangerous than driving through a segment of the *Vietnam War!*" Gibase evaluated and stated to his almost numb companion. "You don't think that we're now going to be involved in some fun-like exploits, do you?"

"Not a chance, if Satan Record Corporation has anything to do with our agenda!" Chad Elvins answered in a robotic-type voice. "According to what *you* had read from the album's pamphlet, the next song on the anthology Jeremy is Donovan singing *Atlantis* from 1969. I'll bet my life's savings that we're gonna' wind-up somewhere on the Lost Continent."

"I'm surprised that Fess Parker's '50s hit *Davy Crockett* isn't on this CD, featuring various history events instead of the expected places that had been falsely advertised on the *Internet!*" Jeremy indicated to his addled and emotionless chum. "Then, we could've joined good old Davy, Jim Bowie, and Sam Houston gallantly fightin' Santa Anna's Mexican Army at the *Alamo!* Say, Chad. Where's your authentic Davy Crockett coonskin hat?"

"We were already almost executed by that berserk Mexican Jose back there in El Paso, Jeremy. That's all we need now is to be captured and placed before a firing squad by a fanatical Mexican general like Santa Anna," Elvins volleyed-back in a defeated tone of voice, as the Little Old Lady from Pasadena's supercharged *Dodge* began pulling ahead of the speeding *Toyota* just as both vehicles dangerously weaved in and out of city traffic. "Say, Jeremy! Thank goodness the song's almost over! Three cop cars are chasing after us," Chad reported after glancing into the rear-view mirror. "Believe me, this is one time I'd prefer getting a speeding ticket or goin' to jail, but the fuzz will never be able to catch-up to my possessed demonic *Toyota,*" Elvins lethargically stated.

Steam was shooting-up from a Colorado Boulevard manhole cover, and it quickly obscured all visibility seen through the *Camry's* windshield. The anthology selection then switched to Donovan's presentation of *Atlantis,* and before any specific interpretations could be exchanged between the automobile's occupants, the ostensibly invincible *Toyota* was again testing its shock absorbers, but this time along cobblestone streets inside a bizarre visual anachronism. Soon, an advanced ancient civilization was being swallowed up into the sea during a monstrous, tremendous, volcanic eruption accompanied by violent earthquakes.

Frightened people dressed in colorful tunics were scurrying in all directions in quest of shelter, the phenomenon occurring on both sides of the high-velocity dark blue sedan. Two-minutes into the song, a giant tidal wave was evident on the distant horizon and Jeremy and Chad both wished that their appalling dilemma could be more vicarious than visceral. Just before the legendary huge tsunami smashed into the fabulous fabled city and demolished it from earthly existence, smoke and ash from the erupting volcano obscured all windshield frontal vision and predictably, the *Toyota* escaped the devastating catastrophic explosions and it mystically zipped into a new terrifying dimension.

"That terrible danger was really too dramatically close for comfort!" evaluated and gasped Jeremy, who was too neurotic and torqued-up to even notice that his listener no longer seemed to care about anything. "I read a lot about the psychic Edgar Cayce's descriptions of *Atlantis* obtained while the prophet was under hypnosis, and I'll gladly share them with you when this nightmarish series of events is finally over," Gibase related to his now-tranquil colleague. "I just hope that the CD player doesn't get its command signals stuck, and we have to hear the anthology songs over and over again, until the damned stereo system finally breaks. Let's just hope that your dependable *Toyota* can run out of gas and finally stops itself! You say the ignition key doesn't work? Chad, are you in shock? Say something!"

"That's right my good friend," Chad bluntly confirmed. "I've tried turnin' the key at least a dozen times, but to no avail. We're victims to that satanic Satan Music Corporation's wicked anthology selection. I knew I should've bought a *Nissan Maxima* instead of this damned evil *Camry.*"

Soon, the now-filthy in-need-of-a-car-wash *Toyota* zipped out of the dirty volcanic smoke and ash, and the windshield wipers automatically activated, along with the windshield-wiper fluid jets. Some foul-smelling fumes and soot had entered the automobile's interior, and the coughing men suddenly sported begrimed faces. Jerry Lee Lewis's 1958 upbeat fast number "Great Balls of Fire" loudly resonated from the Japanese-made car's stereo speakers. A peculiar kaleidoscope of various changing shapes and patterns dominated the surrounding external environment as the dark blue

Toyota rambled forward to its next destination. Chad Elvins tried disguising his great anxiety.

"There's a Whole Lot of Shakin' Goin' On' out there, Jeremy," the driver-non-driver remarked as the very durable *Camry* passed through another unfathomable time portal and was immediately exposed to an abundance of great meteors and comets that were randomly falling from a dark cloud-covered sky. In the distance, one descending fireball crashed into the landmark *Statue of Liberty* as the self-propelled *Camry* increased its speedometer reading to a hundred and twenty. The vehicle was hectically speeding along a deserted New Jersey coastal highway. 'God, I wish I were back in good old 1957 or '58,' Chad solemnly prayed. 'Lord have mercy on us.'

"Let's hope the anthology music selections don't repeat themselves'!" Jeremy futilely reiterated to no one listening to his escalating paranoia. "I'm neurotic to begin with, and I've never traveled a hundred plus miles an hour for so long any previous time in my life! I'm just about at wits end, and my weak mind's rapidly approachin' both insanity and exhaustion in that exact order! Do you understand what I'm saying, Chad?"

"This ride's way beyond human reason and it's takin' us through the most disastrous scenarios imaginable," Chad Elvins stated like a dispassionate cyborg seated across the front seat as both the *Empire State Building* and the magnificent *Chrysler Building* were abominably hit by great balls of fire descending from the stratosphere and obliterating other emblematic New York City skyline edifices. "This is far worse than any nightmare I've ever had. It's an enormous tragedy of epic proportions that we're involved in. This ungodly itinerary makes me wonder if we're ready to meet our Maker."

Chad's cerebrum was reeling. "Say, Jeremy. I mean this sincerely when I tell you that this *Toyota* ride is absolutely more demonic than it is magical," Elvins apprehensively stated before another idea instantly entered his disorganized brain. "You never told me the last song on the Satan Record Corporation's anthology CD? What is it? I just got to know the title!"

Jeremy Gibase stared at Chad Elvins with seemingly penetrating pupils and with *his* mouth agape, and his eyes were bulging from their sunken sockets. Then, the passenger stoically divulged, "Skeeter Davis's '63 smash hit 'The End of the World.' Each man's heart, spirit, and doomed soul immediately slipped into a state of total despair.

"Batsto Village"

Usually on *Labor Day* weekend Frank Carletti would drive his wife Ginny and his six-year-old daughter Katie and seven-year-old son Sammy from their Hammonton, New Jersey middle-class home to Atlantic City, to Ocean City or to Wildwood, New Jersey and use the "last official weekend of summer" to enjoy the numerous junk food concessions, boardwalk novelty shops, game arcades and amusement piers and rides at the "Jersey Shore." But when September 3rd 2005 rolled around Frank decided it would be more judicious to avoid the boardwalk crowds and hoarse barkers, along with the hassle of heavy holiday traffic and visit historic Batsto Village, a local New Jersey pine-lands historic site that had been established during the George Washington/Ben Franklin colonial era.

"We can tour Batsto on Saturday the 3rd, relax on Sunday the 4th and have our standard hamburger and hotdog barbecue on Monday, September 5th," Frank suggested to Ginny the last Saturday in August. I haven't been to Batsto in at least fifteen years. It ought to be a nice pleasant change of venue for us and a really good academic experience just before the kids go back to school."

"But Katie and Sammy were looking forward to one last summer fling at the beach before the drudgery of classes starts," the wife countered. "I can understand the patio barbecue idea but it's going to be tough sledding convincing the kids to stay away from one of the area boardwalks. *Labor Day* at the shore has become both a habit and a tradition for them."

"We'll compromise and tell the kids the family will drive down to Wildwood the second weekend in September," Frank the-problem solver maintained. "The roads will be less congested and summer weather will still prevail. And we won't have to fight for parking spaces or stand in long lines to eat at tourist-trap restaurants. I'm sure the kids will trade September weekends and go to Batsto Village on Saturday the 3rd and then to fabulous Wildwood on Saturday, the 10th."

"You're so diplomatic Frank that you should've been an official at the *UN* rather than the best electrician in Hammonton," the wife commended. "Maybe this afternoon, I'll give the *Security Council* a call and set up an interview for you."

The children were quite amenable to the switching of September dates so on Saturday morning the family hopped into Frank's tan *Nissan Pathfinder SUV,* and five minutes later Carletti steered the vehicle across the *White Horse Pike* at the intersection of Central Avenue. The man behind the wheel then took winding Pleasant Mills Road northeast from Hammonton through Nesco past large blueberry farms and next motored past Sweetwater (on the scenic and tranquil *Mullica River*) to historic Batsto Village, a quaint "miniature *Williamsburg*" nicely nestled in the rustic New Jersey pine barrens.

"This little trip is going to be educational kids," Frank lectured his apathetic children in the back seat, "so just pretend it's your history class. We're going to see how people lived and worked two hundred and fifty years ago before we had cars, televisions, computers, custard stands, amusement rides, cell phones, video games and boardwalks. And if I remember correctly," the father recollected and emphasized, "they do sell ice cream and soda in the Batsto General Store. Just use your imaginations and pretend we're in a time machine and heading way back into the past."

"You're corny, Dad!" Sammy bluntly criticized. "My class went on a field trip to Batsto last year and they don't even have a Ferris Wheel or mini-roller coaster there, let alone a water slide or bumping cars. Next year take us to *Six Flags Great Adventure* instead! That's a really cool place!"

"Ginny, whatever happened to obedient and respectful kids?" Frank complained to his more tolerant go-with-the-flow wife. "Our children are spoiled rotten and are already making critical family decisions without their parents' essential advice or consent. At this rate, next *Labor Day* we'll have to get *their* permission to simply take them somewhere."

"Keep your eyes on the winding road," Ginny commanded her distracted spouse. "You never know when a drunk driver or a stray dog is just around the next bend. And as far as our children are concerned," the wife authoritatively argued, "they're far from being juvenile delinquents!"

After entering the Batsto Village parking lot, the family exited the *Pathfinder* and entered the "State-Operated Park." A costumed character dressed in a cumbersome *Jersey Devil* outfit handed Frank a brochure, which described how the State had purchased the *Wharton Forest* properties including the small community that is now listed on the New Jersey National Registry of Historic Places.

"Isn't that man hot in that silly *Jersey Devil* costume?" Sammy asked his parents. "He looks worse than *Santa Claus* or the *Easter Bunny,* fake as fake could be!"

"Quiet son, and listen up," Frank reprimanded his all-too-inquisitive and critical offspring. "It states in this brochure that Batsto Village dates back to 1766, ten years before the signing of the *Declaration of Independence.* Bog ore was mined from the banks of the narrow *Batsto River* and also from the *Mullica.* According to this pamphlet," the father lectured, "prior to the *Revolutionary War* the iron works made pots and kettles but during the *War* the mill produced cannon balls, cannons and other metal materials for George Washington's *Continental Army.* Isn't all this fascinating?"

"It's bad enough that I have to listen to that kind of boring book stuff in school," Sammy adamantly complained as Katie nodded her head in tacit agreement. "Why couldn't we have gone to *Great Adventure* instead?"

"Please act more polite and respectful," Ginny Carletti chastised her all-too-opinionated son. "I think we'll take the informal tour without paying for a guide Frank. Now children, this village is an important local historic site and in the 1800s the place was a glassblowing producing community for making windows, bottles, glasses and jars. We're going to see exactly how people lived and worked before there were any modern tools or appliances."

"That's right," the upbeat father interrupted. "According to this terrific pamphlet the wheelwright and blacksmith shops, several barns and the charcoal fueled iron furnace are the only original 1770s buildings still standing in the village. The piggery, the grist mill, Batsto Mansion, the General Store, the Post Office, the Sawmill, the Stone Barn, the Glass Works and the employees' cottages were all added in the 1800s. You kids will get a good idea of how people used to live in olden times and how hard it was to survive without modern machines and conveniences."

Eventually, the thoroughly bored children acclimated to their "academic environment" and enjoyed the pastures, the stables and the variety of animals on display including plow horses, goats, chickens, cows, sheep, wild turkeys and pigs. Batsto Village employees dressed in colonial garb demonstrated various colonial-era skills including horse hoofing, carriage wheel making, flyer printing, apothecary, tallow and soap making and carpentry, all trades practiced during the late 1700s and early 1800s.

On the early afternoon trek back to the dirt parking lot, Frank Carletti had an inspiration. 'It's definitely more desolate out here near Batsto than it is in the *Wharton Forest* fringe bordering Hammonton,' the father thought. 'I'm going to suggest to my friend Jimmy Distasio about not hanging out with the deer hunting club this December and mutually building a tree stand over on this side of Pleasant Mills Road. I think Jimmy's pretty level-headed and will go along with my intelligent idea.'

* * * * * * * * * * * *

After three lengthy telephone discussions, Frank Carletti finally convinced his best friend Jimmy Distasio to assist in building a tree stand independent of the Never There Gunning Club, which had half its membership debating to resign and change their new splinter club's name to the Ponderosa Deer Hunting and Recreation Lodge.

"I've had just about enough of the petty deer club politics," Frank told Jimmy one early October evening over the telephone. "Those guys are always partying, feasting, gossiping and getting drunk during deer week and none of them take the dying art of hunting too seriously any more. I say it's time for us to make a drastic change."

"I couldn't agree with you more," Jimmy loyally affirmed. "Last year I was sittin' next to an old geezer over at the Never There high on *Wild Turkey* and the word-slurrin' drunk was telling me that he could remember when the *Battleship Maine* was sunk in Havana, Harbor. Now Frank," Jimmy clarified and articulated, "the *Maine* was sunk to start the *Spanish-American War*, and as you know I'm an avid and devout student of history. That short *War* took place in 1898, so that lying old coot at the gunning club would have to be at least a hundred and twenty years old to be able to 'Remember the Maine' and tell me about it. That alone is reason enough to go buck huntin' on our own over near Batsto come the first week of December."

"Okay, Jimmy. I'm with you all the way," Frank confirmed. "And while that senile bald-headed curmudgeon was bending your ear about the *Spanish-American War,* another aged, whiskered codger was telling me all about how he remembered the John Philip Sousa concert at the Hammonton Lake Park Pavilion that was given the summer, right after the demented deer hunter had graduated from high school. I checked the records and that Sousa concert had to take place around 1920. Jimmy, how about you and me taking off next Friday, October 7th to build our own personal tree stand over near Batsto," Frank insisted. "I'll go over to the lumber company and pick up the necessary two by fours and the heavy-duty planks. I'll bring the ladder along too, but don't forget to take your hammer and nails. And also take along your .22 and some shells. We'll do a little shotgun target shooting after we construct our little secret tree platform."

"Perfectly fine with me, Frank," the ever-affable Jimmy Distasio wholeheartedly agreed. "I need a change of venue from my grueling and monotonous work routine. The tree stand task at hand should be no major challenge for a master carpenter such as myself'."

On the October 7th drive from Hammonton northeast on serpentine Pleasant Mills Road, heading toward Batsto Village, the men engaged in idle conversation about the most popular South Jersey legend that was reputed to inhabit and haunt the area. Frank brought the amusing subject up, and with Jimmy Distasio being a history and area myth buff, much to Carletti's amusement the *Pathfinder's* loquacious passenger had plenty of facts to contribute to the ongoing dialogue.

"The phantom *Jersey Devil* has certainly become the biggest New Jersey Pinelands' legend," Frank asserted to his best friend, who had introduced the topic of conversation. "He's been said to be terrorizing these parts for the past two and a half centuries goin' back to before the *Revolutionary War*. That's about all the background I know about the creature except the fact that the *New Jersey Devils* ice hockey team was named after the legendary diabolical beast."

"Well, Frank," Jimmy said while seizing the opportunity to expound on the seemingly ludicrous topic. "Over two-thousand sightings of the *Devil* have been reported since the story was first hatched. It all started with a Mrs. Shrouds of Leeds Point over near Chestnut Neck, you know, located near the mouth of the *Mullica*. Her thirteenth child was born deformed so she kept the ugly little brute sheltered in her house to avoid the displeasure of hearing neighbors' negative gossip," Jimmy vociferated. "Then one violent stormy night the creature flapped its arms and immediately grew wings, a horse's head, horns, hooves and a tail and then the hideous thing supernaturally escaped the house by flying up the chimney, never to be seen by any member of the Shrouds' family again. Ain't that story a crock and a half?"

"You say there've been over two-thousand eyewitness sightings?" Carletti marveled as he sped his *Pathfinder* through the somnolent hamlet of Nesco. "Sounds like mass paranoia to me, something like the Martians landing up in Grover Mills near Princeton during that infamous Orson Welles Halloween radio broadcast the old geezers over at the Never There keep talkin' about."

"That sensational radio show generated mass hysteria and some brain-dead people even committed suicide by jumping out of windows without ever thinking about turning the radio dial to verify the fictional account of invaders from *Mars* landing up there in Central Jersey," the long-winded Distasio added. "And I always thought that *I* was stupid!"

"Well, Jimmy. If there's such a grotesque-lookin' animal as the *Jersey Devil,* I'll trade in my *Pathfinder* for a Conestoga wagon and go and live with Daniel Boone and Davy Crockett in another century," Frank indulgently laughed. "People will believe the strangest things!"

"Don't be so amused!" Jimmy chided and cautioned. "The *Jersey Devil's* appearances have been well-documented. It will tenaciously hunt you down even in another state. In 1909 the monster was seen across the *Delaware* in Bristol, Pennsylvania causing havoc and chaos. The next morning its footprints, or should I say hoof prints were seen on both sides of the river in Bristol and also in Burlington. Posses and constables searched all over on opposite river shores but couldn't find any trace of the savage brute," Distasio proceeded without the benefit of taking a deep breath. "And nowadays people are afraid of being labeled lunatics so they never report *Jersey Devil* sightings out of fear of being shunned and ridiculed by their gossipy neighbors and fellow residents. But it's been reported in trustworthy newspaper accounts that the *Devil* has easily maimed and killed large domestic animals like fierce German shepherds and certain livestock up around Atsion Lake. And Frank," Jimmy said while feigning awe, "if the indigenous *Jersey Devil* has been around for over two and a half centuries as has been documented, ya' just gotta' believe the thing's immortal!"

"I'll leave all of this intellectual supposition stuff up to you," the driver answered his talkative companion while smiling and raising his eyebrows. "I'm more of a practical-oriented basic meat and potatoes type of guy. I don't like speculatin' about silly local legends."

"Okay, Frank. Have it your way as usual," Jimmy acceded. "But on the drive home, we can stop at Sweetwater Casino on the other side of the *Mullica*. Then, I could merrily chug down a few frosted mugs of brew and enjoy a good turkey club sandwich and some delicious ice cream cake roll with ample whipped cream and maraschino cherries on top for dessert. How do ya' like my suggestion?"

"Forget about food and the Jersey Devil, and say something relevant about hunting," Carletti sternly demanded. "You really get sidetracked sometimes, don't ya'! That's what this trip's all about!"

"You won't believe this story, Frank," Jimmy enthusiastically chortled. "But last week I was walkin' innocent-like in my back yard after fillin' the bird feeder and ambled by a majestic white pine I had planted as a seedling twelve-years-ago. I just happened to turn and my pupils glanced at eye-level at a low-hanging branch, and lo and behold," the excited passenger expressed with heightened emotion, "I see this really ugly fat groundhog sittin' on a limb and starin' me right in the face."

"I didn't know that groundhogs climbed trees!" Frank exclaimed in amazement. "What did you do? Faint and collapse on the ground?"

"I got scared and wished I had my trusty shotgun," Jimmy attested. "So then, I kept walkin' very carefully, pretendin' that no eye contact was ever made, until I completely evaded a scuffle with a clawed animal that I had at first thought was the infamous *Jersey Devil*. Hey Frank," the energetic-but-facetious passenger exhorted. "There's a trail leading into the woods up ahead. Let's go and scout out the perfect location for our secret deer stand. I can't wait to do some target practice after we get done our little buildin' project, and then we'll merrily head over to Sweetwater Casino for some suds and grub."

It was Indian summer with the temperature in the mid-seventies. Patches of golden-brown deciduous trees blended into the more abundant pine and cedar tree forest making for a most colorful and impressive-to-the-eye picturesque October 7th nature scene. Frank drove his tan *SUV* down the designated sandy trail for about a quarter mile and then halted at an intersection where another narrow dirt path in the woods crossed with the one *his Pathfinder* was on.

"We'll stop here and carry our boards, hammers, nails, and shotguns into the woods," Frank suggested. "I figure about a hundred feet into the forest ought to be sufficient. If we shoot a couple of bucks in early December from our soon-to-be-built tree stand, we'll be able to drag their carcasses out to this dirt road. We'll definitely have a few new trophies to keep the Hammonton taxidermists busy this winter."

"Good thinking!" Jimmy Distasio flattered. "We'll have to make two trips into the woods, because don't forget, we've got to take the aluminum ladder along, too. And I've brought along two cases of buckshot shells and a bag of tin cans to have a little target practice after we put that deer blind together."

"Now, all we gotta' do is select a clearing where we can bring some old rotten apples or sweet potatoes as deer bait a few days after *Thanksgiving,* and we'll be all set to get us some venison that we can share with the beer guzzlin' guys over at the Never There, and with the hard whiskey renegade fanatics over at the Ponderosa."

The men enthusiastically went about their enterprise, discovered a sturdy oak with thick limbs and then assiduously pursued their objective with Jimmy utilizing his carpentry talents to perform the more difficult tasks. In three hours, the observation platform had been completed and the close friends were contemplating their target shooting fun and then diligently consuming some "victuals and beer" over at the Sweetwater Casino and Marina Restaurant on the other side of the historic *Mullica River.*

"There's a shallow stream over to our left that feeds into the *Batsto River,*" Frank perceptively pointed-out. "Let's take a little ramble over there and see if there's any fish swimming' around. We might have just found ourselves a little secluded paradise to occasionally visit for fishin' purposes, too. Of course, Jimmy, you're divorced without any wife or kids to worry about," Carletti reminded his favorite hunting companion. "But in my case, I need a little escape from everyday family pressures and responsibilities where male-bonding is the best solution."

"No doubt about it Frank; hunting means escape from reality! What about the ladder?" Jimmy asked. "Should we put it back inside your *Pathfinder*?"

"It's not goin' to rust in the next fifteen-minutes, let alone in the next century!" Frank jested. "Not even the aluminum tabs on the soda and beer cans inside your brown paper bag will rust any time before *Y3K!*"

"I think this brook coming from the *Batsto* might empty into the *Mullica* a little to the south over near Crowley's Landing," Jimmy theorized and shared. "I estimate that the landing must be about a quarter of a mile from here situated right across this particular stretch of woods. Let's follow the brook so that we don't get lost and we can find a clearing where we can do a little impromptu tin can shootin'. My trigger finger is getting more than a trifle nervous!"

The men carried their shotguns and two brown paper bags containing empty soda and beer cans along with shell boxes to the vicinity of the pristine stream while temporarily leaving their hammers, saws, nails and ladder behind. Soon they passed between a pair of parallel cedars that reminded Frank of "football field goal posts" when suddenly a flash of light streaked between the evergreens and the men instantaneously felt a trifle shocked, apprehensive and unnerved. But both trekkers had too much pride to acknowledge or discuss any immediate trepidation.

After following the narrow strip of water for five minutes, the adventurers heard human activity ahead of them. Much to their bewilderment they spotted what Jimmy described as an "anachronism" and what Frank termed an "aberration or an illusion." Batsto Village was directly to their right, but it had fewer buildings than Frank had remembered from his *Labor Day* weekend visit with his family, and the settlement along with its human activity appeared much more authentic than it had the month before.

"What's goin' on?" Frank asked his befuddled partner. "Are we still in the twenty-first century or have we stumbled onto the set of some sort of movie bein' filmed?"

"Maybe we're livin' in the year 2005 but *they* certainly aren't!" Distasio exclaimed as he pointed to the burly village blacksmith and a pair of hardy-looking Batsto furnace workers conducting a three-way conversation a hundred feet ahead. "I know I watch a lot a science fiction on TV, which leads me to believe that we had passed through some kind of time portal back there when the sunlight flashed and flickered," Jimmy finally got the gumption to mention. "Let's pretend we're just a few itinerant travelers and lookin' for directions to Chestnut Neck."

As the two wanderers approached the hamlet's center, their presence was quickly scrutinized by the three villagers that had been conducting their conversation. All three men stood with their mouths agape staring at the new arrivals.

"Who are you gentlemen?" the tough-looking blacksmith curiously asked. "Are ye' patriots or Tories? Speak your peace men!"

"Er, we're patriots," Jimmy answered in a stammer. "My name's James Distasio and this fella' is my close friend and business associate, Frank Carletti."

"Well, I'm Nathaniel Dickinson," the blacksmith introduced himself, "and these two gentlemen are Joseph Bawl and Tom Hendricks that work the bog iron furnace."

"Ye' gentlemen don't appear to be Englishmen to me, whether ye' be patriots as ye' claim or Loyalists to the Crown!" Joseph Bawl perceptively observed and questioned. "Ye' seem to be foreigners, dark complexioned Italians or maybe even Spaniards runnin' away from justice."

"We're Italians all right!" Frank all-too-candidly responded. "We've coming from...."

Jimmy Distasio realized that Carletti was stuck for the name of an area town or village that had existed back during the *Revolutionary War* era. Then the carpenter/hunter remembered that the Borough of Berlin ten miles west of Hammonton had been established under another name with an inn and stagecoach depot in the year 1699.

"We're on our way from a place called Long-A-Coming and lookin' for transportation down the *Mullica* to Chestnut Neck," Jimmy explained and fibbed. "We understand that the British have come down from New York on warships and are plannin' a series of raids on certain privateers operatin' out of the Chestnut Neck settlement. The Redcoats are now just off the mainland in the *Atlantic* and getting ready to attack. We're originally coming from Philly', or, I mean Philadelphia," Distasio clarified, "and we've come to warn our brave men commandeering merchant vessels laden with makeshift cannons aboard. We have to get there and tell them that the ruthless Redcoats plan to plunder and then burn down the Chestnut Neck warehouses that are presently loaded with stolen goods."

"Well, that does make some weird sense even if you men talk with peculiar accents!" Nathaniel Dickinson admitted. "But where did you fellas' get those fancy clothes that you're wearin'?" the muscular soot-covered man asked while referring to the pair's blue denim jeans, cotton sweatshirts, gold band wristwatches and brown leather work shoes.

"Er, these are the latest fashions and haberdashery from New York, Philadelphia, Baltimore and Boston," Jimmy intelligently prevaricated. "You won't find-out about items like these, way out here in the Jersey wilderness for a couple of months or so; until some ambitious itinerant merchants finally arrive in a travelin' wagon and show them to you to buy."

"Well then," Joseph Bawl piped in, "where'd ye' get those crazy-lookin' muskets you're totin'? I ain't never seen any firearms like those before! They don't even have any bayonets on them!"

"Ya' see, Sir. These are the latest weapons developed in Italy that we wanna' show the pirates, er, I mean American privateers over at Chestnut Neck," Jimmy again lied. "We're honest importers settin' up our business in Philadelphia and have a ship comin' into port in about two weeks loaded with these new types of muskets called 'shotguns.' They have a much better range, and are more lethal from a distance than any weapons the Redcoats now have. These weapons will prove to be a big advantage during a battle and they'll easily win out over common muskets."

"Well, then strangers," a skeptical Tom Hendricks instinctively challenged. "Where are your horses or your stagecoach or wagon that brought you to these parts? I don't see no viable means of transportation anywhere! How'd you gentlemen get way out here to Batsto from Long-A-Coming?"

"Well, ya' see Mr. Hendricks," Frank said while stalling for the most appropriate explanation his mind could create. "We knew from a map that there was an iron bog village settlement in the area. We left our wagon and horses about a half-mile upstream and hiked the distance to here. Now that we found Batsto," Carletti aptly and persuasively added, "we'll be on our way because we got important business to attend to down at....."

"Chestnut Neck," Jimmy finished his best buddy's preposterous sentence. "We gotta' get there before the British ships do. Our new-fangled shotguns will help fight and defeat the enemy and bring freedom and independence to the colonies," Distasio embellished his false story.

"What ye' got in those brown bags?" Joseph Bawl inquired with a degree of suspicion evident in his tone of voice. "How come they aren't made out of cloth? Never seen any brown paper bags before!"

"Oh, just some things we shoot while aimin' and practicin' with our fancy muskets," Jimmy imaginatively fabricated. "Just a few personal items, I suppose."

"Well then, we're pleased to make your acquaintance and good luck on your vital smugglin' of weapons' mission," the burly blacksmith acknowledged while shaking the men's hands with a more-than-firm grip. "I believe Chestnut Neck is around seventeen-miles up-river, no exaggeratin'. Hope your horses are well rested for the remainder of your trip."

"They are," Jimmy again constructively equivocated. "We have a dedicated servant attendin' to them. They're in good hands, because the young man was a former stable boy over in Burlington City. Say, I've lost track of time since we left Philadelphia. What's the exact date?"

"October 7th," Tom Hendricks indicated with a look of suspicion seemingly welded on his grim face.

"October 7th, 1778?" Jimmy intrepidly asked, almost begging for verification.

"Exactly," Hendricks replied showing a bit of relief. "Ye' got *that* fact straight, anyway! Ye' good men ought to carry around a calendar or maybe even a copy of *Poor Richard's Almanac*, ha, ha, ha!"

The two disoriented time travelers departed the landmark village in total bewilderment, realizing that they indeed had been transported back to the colonial era, and that a definitive war of liberation was in progress. Carletti and Distasio retraced their steps back in the direction of where twenty-first century Crowley's Landing would have been located.

"This entire nightmare is impossible!" Frank evaluated in frustration. "We're a couple of transplanted *Rip Van Winkles* operatin' in reverse! How are we ever gonna' get back to the year 2005 where we rightfully belong?"

"I suspect we'll have to again pass between those two cedar trees you had joked were goal posts," Jimmy recollected and stated. "But first I want to follow this stream to the *Mullica,* just to see if there are any British warships anchored nearby. If my memory of local history serves me correctly," Distasio elaborated, "yesterday on October 6th the British burned the privateers' warehouses over at Chestnut Neck, along with ten ships that were being used by American confiscators up and down the Jersey coast. And on October 7th, 1778, which incidentally happens to be today in our current reality," Jimmy carefully elucidated, "the devious British command sent several warships up the river to destroy the Batsto iron works, since the village had been producin' cannons and cannon balls for the *Continental Army*. The British ship I believe was called the *Zebra!*" Then, a queer thought entered into Jimmy's very fertile mind. "Say

Frank. You don't suppose the dastardly *Jersey Devil* knows about that oddball cedar tree time portal we passed through, and uses it to move about the decades terrifyin' thousands of innocent people in different centuries? It just isn't moral or ethical for the supernatural to pick on and harass the natural, that's what I think!"

"After what's happened to us," Carletti answered while still being totally astounded from his recent experiences, "I'm inclined to believe anything either rational or illogical, including the crazy *Jersey Devil* story. I wouldn't be surprised one iota if we met George Washington, Alexander Hamilton, and Thomas Jefferson around the next bend in the stream."

"If we could have arrived a few years earlier," Jimmy noted, "we could've witnessed the signing of the *Declaration of Independence* on July, 4th, 1776."

The men followed the meandering brook in the direction of Crowley's Landing on the *Mullica,* carrying their shotguns and toting their boxes of shells safely tucked inside their brown paper bags, along with their target-practice tin cans. The wanderers exchanged expressions of disbelief and consternation along the way.

"I suppose we won't be seein' Sweetwater Casino across the river because of the two-and-a-half-century time differential," Frank cynically mentioned. "I'm afraid to go through that time portal again and wind-up being chased by prehistoric dinosaurs or maybe even hairy cavemen."

"Duck down!" Jimmy imperatively ordered. "Look out into the river to our left! There're two British ships anchored waiting for a more favorable tide. They're just biding their time for the water to rise to lower men onto landing boats, and then raid and pillage Batsto. Frank, we gotta' show some fortitude and intervene. There's the *H.M.S. Greenwich,* and the *H.M.S. Dependance.* The British flagship *Zebra* must be continuing its' wicked raidin' and plunderin' of the warehouses up near Chestnut Neck. It's time for us to act!"

"What do ya' have in mind?" Carletti anxiously asked his more audacious colleague. "I'm not about ready to die in the *Revolutionary War* nearly two centuries before I was born. This whole misadventure seems totally stranger than fiction! It actually seems totally stranger than science fiction!"

"Quiet!" Jimmy sternly whispered. "We'll load our shotguns and attempt woundin' a couple of the Redcoats on deck. That'll discourage them from comin' ashore because they'll realize they've been spotted and that more men with muskets might be on the way to defend Batsto. But remember Frank," Distasio indicated in a low voice, "our secret muskets will have a superior range and that reality should be enough to confuse and perplex the soldiers on board."

The men loaded their shotguns and had a surplus of shells available to effectively wage a small battle against their chosen adversaries. The errant deer hunters separately aimed their weapons at several British sentries patrolling the decks of the *H.M.S. Greenwich* and the *H.M.S. Dependance,* respectively. After hearing the shotgun blasts, the shocked sentinels fled for cover, not knowing from exactly where the aggressive gunfire was originating.

The two misplaced Americans had the advantage at the outset, and the British soldiers' muskets lacked the capability of firing their pellet balls the out-of-range distance into the defensive position the men had established behind several Crowley Landing pine trees. But then, two cannons aboard the British vessels boomed, and before Carletti and Distasio had precious time to worry or react, the branches from several fir trees in the vicinity came crashing-down to the ground. The two men were momentarily petrified.

"That was too close for comfort!" Frank gasped as he reloaded his shotgun. "Those cannons could do some serious permanent damage if they were a little more accurate! Here are two more shells, Jimmy!"

"Look!" Distasio yelled to his almost-delirious and now-hyperventilating hunting partner. "They're lifting their anchors and are set to sail up river back to Chestnut Neck. I can't believe it, Frank! We just thwarted the marauding of Batsto, and actually participated in an unrecorded *Revolutionary War* skirmish. Too bad there aren't any eyewitnesses or historians around to write-down and document what had actually just happened!"

"Maybe from now on I'll show more interest in history and more respect for other academic subjects I usually despise," Frank honestly confessed. "But now, we gotta' re-locate that time portal and get back to October, 7th 2005. Say, Jimmy. What if there're other bizarre time portals all over this remote part of the pine-barrens? I hate to sound too pessimistic, good buddy, but we might get trapped in another century and never be able to return to Hammonton!"

"That's a chance we have to take, and quite frankly, we really don't have too much of a choice in the matter, now do we?" Jimmy Distasio rationally argued. "And if we follow the stream back in the direction of the village, we'll eventually recognize the two cedar trees and then pass between them. That should get us back to your aluminum ladder and your *Pathfinder*."

As the men trudged along the shallow stream's bank, they traded random comments and remarks about their phenomenal "dual hallucinations". Frank Carletti was eager to return to familiar surroundings and people, while Jimmy Distasio was whimsically contemplating staying in the year 1778, gallantly and courageously fighting with the patriots against the British Redcoats. And then, after the *War,* settlingdown and living a simple, more-pastoral type of daily existence as a respected skilled carpenter in tranquil Batsto Village.

"Believe it or not, Jimmy, I can't wait to see Ginny and the kids again," Frank confided. "But I'll never tell them about our incredible October 7th adventure. That'll be our little secret for us to carry to our graves! What about you Jimmy? Are ya' excited about getting back to Hammonton?"

"I'm not attached to any wife or kids," Distasio regretted and admitted. "And I have half a mind to stay here in 1778 and help General Washington emerge victorious over King George the Third's minions. It's my grand opportunity to become a part of American history."

"You must be a little crazy beyond berserk!" Frank rankled and criticized. "You mean to say you'd barter all of your material comforts, your house and car, your 401K plan, and your rock music collection; and your fantastic plasma TV to live in a century without any modern technology or conveniences! It sounds more like suffering to me than it does like pleasure! What ever happened to the 'pursuit of happiness'?"

"To each his own!" Jimmy philosophically returned. "To each his own, Frank!" Distasio very deliberately exclaimed and reiterated.

"Okay, have it your way Jimmy, but I sincerely hope you change your mind," Frank added. "After I step through that mysterious time portal, I'll be turnin' around and wishin' you were right behind me. Just watch-out for that stealthy Jersey Devil, Jimmy!" Carletti sentimentally joked as he warmly shook Distasio's hand. "And don't forget, good buddy. You know where the time portal is, if ya' ever want to come back to the modern world."

The men shook hands, and then Frank hesitantly stepped between the dual cedars and successfully vanished into another time dimension. Jimmy stood his ground, wondering if he had all-too-impetuously made the wrong decision.

Two days later, the front-page headline of the *Atlantic City Press* read: "Man's Body Remains Found Near Batsto Village." The accompanying article described the gruesome and macabre details.

The mauled and mangled body of Hammonton, NJ resident Frank Carletti was found near the man's *SUV* that had been parked on a dirt trail inside Wharton State Forest, in the vicinity of historic Batsto Village. An aluminum ladder was located nearby, suggesting that Carletti had just completed construction of a deer stand, possibly with a Hammonton friend and companion, James Distasio, who is presently still missing and unaccounted for.

Carletti's badly mutilated body apparently had been ravaged by some wild animal, or animals, roaming around in the dense forest. A *State Police* forensics' team is currently conducting an intensive investigation, and more facts should be available for media dissemination within the next week.

"The victim's clothes were viciously torn and tattered," said Game Warden Michael Philips, who had made the terrible discovery while on patrol in his *Jeep*. "I immediately contacted the Atlantic County coroner's office and the *State Police* of the man's grisly fate. But in all my years as a New Jersey Forest Ranger, I've never seen anything quite as horrifying as this."

An all-out manhunt has been organized throughout the vicinity to find missing James Distasio. Anyone possessing any knowledge of his fate is asked to notify the appropriate state and local authorities, and a handsome reward of ten-thousand-dollars has been posted. More relevant information about this incident will be made public when it is available. Funeral service arrangements for Frank Carletti have not been finalized as of press time early this morning. However, a comprehensive obituary for the deceased is scheduled to appear in tomorrow's early morning edition.

"Parallel Developments"

Twin brothers Frank and Fred Davies were 1981 graduates of Hammonton High School, North Liberty Street, Hammonton, New Jersey 08037. From their early youth the twins were complete opposites both in demeanor and in physical prowess. Fred Davies was always an extrovert and a competitive athlete while his twin facsimile Frank had a shy personality genuinely punctuated with humility and modesty.

In June of 1987 Fred graduated from Philadelphia's *Temple University* with a law degree and Frank evolved out of New Brunswick's *Rutgers University* with a master's degree in biology research. In the fall of 1991 during a dual ceremony Frank and Fred ironically married twin sisters Lois and Eleanor Cataldi of Bridgeton, a large town situated twenty-four miles southwest of Hammonton.

In order to celebrate their fifteenth wedding anniversary Frank and Lois booked a Mediterranean vacation featuring two nights in Barcelona and a seven-day-cruise aboard the resplendent Regal Adventurer. Coincidentally, Fred and Eleanor (through the same travel agency) also made arrangements on a similar vacation aboard the Regal Adventurer, but the former couple's scheduled dates were Wednesday September 13th to Saturday the 20th while the latter pair's sailing dates were several weeks later from Wednesday, October 4th to Saturday October 11th.

"How come Fred and Eleanor aren't going to accompany us to Europe?" Lois asked her husband as they waited for the van to pick them up for the thirty-mile drive to *Philadelphia International Airport.* "Do we have leprosy or something?"

"Certainly not!" Frank politely answered. "My brother and I mutually agreed that we should take separate vacations touring Spain, the French Riviera and Italy. We thought it would be too confusing for everyone we met or communicated with by having two sets of identical twins. And besides Lois," Frank persuasively communicated, "you honestly don't get along too keenly with Fred and quite candidly I don't hit it off too well with my loudmouth sister-in-law, er, excuse me, with your twin sister. And I do believe Lois that the eight people we're traveling with will be more compatible with us than Fred and Eleanor will ever be. In the final analysis that's the bottom line!"

"I suppose I have to subscribe to the basic wisdom you've just expressed!" Lois confessed. "Here comes the van now zipping down the Pike approaching our driveway! Let's carry our four pieces of luggage from the front porch."

"And as you know, Lois, Fred and I have different sets of friends," the husband emphasized and clarified. "And as a matter of fact so do you and Eleanor. Warren and Melissa Mottola are much more mellow and gracious than Fred and Eleanor will ever be. And I want this trip to be as relaxing and comfortable as possible without those two garrulous nitwits ruining every meal and every sidebar excursion on our hectic itinerary!"

"Yes, my dear Husband!" Lois verified. "We seem to harmonize better with retired science teachers and their accountant wives than we do with relative lawyers and their flamboyant spouses. Warren is studious and academic just like you are," the wife maintained, "and Melissa is generally quiet and likeable. I guess it's because she's always concentrating with numbers and figures at work. That's why she and her soft-spoken husband aren't wild and crazy lunatics like Fred and Eleanor are!"

The cranberry-colored van pulled into the two-story gray colonial home's U-shaped driveway and halted right where the cement walk bordered the asphalt driveway. Immediately the driver hopped out of the vehicle and introduced himself.

"Hi, I'm Tom Dixon!" the man cheerfully greeted. "Why don't you two hop into the van and join your friends! I'll take care of loading your bags into the back storage compartment."

"Thanks!" Frank politely acknowledged. "You look trustworthy enough Tom! It's great to see that courtesy hasn't gone completely out of fashion! My wife and I appreciate your fine gesture!"

Frank and Lois were immediately welcomed by Warren and Melissa Mottola, who were seated near their pretty office manager daughter Lisa and her handsome fiancé David Winters, a young and serious corporate jet pilot. Other passengers in the enormous cranberry van were Jimmy and Joanne Valerio, a construction contractor and an accountant respectively with Joanne being employed in the same CPA's office as Lois. Rounding out the party of ten Europe-bound-Americans were Dr. Rose Jeffries (an infectious disease specialist at Camden's Cooper Hospital) and her new-found friend Judy Marks, a comptroller for a large automobile agency in Marlton, New Jersey. Soon after Tom Dixon had carefully arranged the new baggage in the van's rear, he re-entered the vehicle, slammed the door shut, fastened his seat-belt and casually started-up the engine.

The thirty-mile drive from Hammonton to Philadelphia was quite pleasant. The late summer scenery still displayed deciduous trees with ample green leaves about to assume their predictable autumnal hues. The men's conversation focused on the latest professional baseball and football scores and the rising stock market while the ladies preferred exchanging dialogue on the best clothes to take along on the trip and the various sights to be explored on the general itinerary. In a short forty-five minutes the van stopped in front of the *U.S. Airways* terminal in the newly renovated section of *Philadelphia International Airport*.

After paying Tom Dixon the appropriate fee and tip for his vital services, the ten passengers hired a skycap to transport their twenty pieces of luggage inside to the *U.S Airways* ticket counter. That particular procedure was conducted rather expeditiously and after the necessary passports and photo' ID's were officially checked, five minutes later the ten anxious travelers passed through the airport's tight security check.

"I hate being treated like a terrorist!" Lois complained. "But Frank, you're so mild-mannered that it's just like water off a duck's back to you."

"Why get upset with taking your shoes off and having them scanned along with your other personal belongings?" the husband passively accepted and stated. "Why become neurotic about what you can't change! And since everyone flying out of 'Philly has to go through the same process, it's perfectly tolerable! After all Lois, we're not being discriminated against!"

"Sometimes, you're so soberly philosophical!" the wife sincerely complimented. "That's one reason why I was so attracted to you when we first met at that wild party in Atlantic City! I really admired your calm disposition!"

"I'll try not to talk too much on the seven-hour flight to Barcelona!" the husband bantered tongue-in-cheek. "And I'll speak even less on the grueling eight-hour trip on the way back!"

"I can't believe we're actually going to Europe!" Lois jubilantly exclaimed. "I mean I've read about it in high school textbooks and in encyclopedias," the spouse marveled and said, "but now it's like a dream come true! Let's make the most of it! It might be a once in a lifetime opportunity!"

"Yeah, Honey!" the normally laconic husband readily concurred. "After going eight times to the Caribbean and twice to both San Diego and Las Vegas, this long jaunt sort of represents a departure from the ordinary. Outside of a cruise boat stop in Caracas, Venezuela, this is really only our second removal from the North American Continent. I hope we have a smooth flight!"

"I checked the forecast on the *Internet,*" Lois assured. "And it's going to be clear skies all the way to Barcelona except for an hour of mild turbulence. I can't wait to leave the New World for the Old! Maybe next time we can do Madrid, Paris, London and Berlin instead of Barcelona, Marseilles, Rome and Naples!"

"Anything you say, Lois! Anything you say!" the husband reiterated. "And just think! Thanks to modern-day airport security we only have to wait two hours before we finally board our wonderful airplane! We're scheduled to take off at 5:45 p.m. and then finally arrive in Spain at...."

"At approximately 7:45 a.m.!" Lois alertly finished Frank's sentence. "Already we're trapped in a time warp and soon destined to suffer significant jet-lag! But don't worry! We have the rest of our lives to recuperate!"

"You should do stand-up comedy, even when you're sitting down!" Frank mused and expressed. "Now let's interact with our eight friends before they receive the impression that we're both anti-social in addition to being extremely introverted!"

The seven-hour flight from Philadelphia to Barcelona was *not* interrupted with an hour of rough air pockets (as Lois had predicted from reading various weather reports) and a two-hour movie, random magazine scrutiny and a decent chicken and rice meal had sufficiently distracted the passengers from their lengthy confinement and overall travail. A weak drizzle awaited U.S. Airways Flight 948 when it finally touched-down and landed on its destination runway on Spain's eastern coast.

The passengers had to be transported by bus from the tarmac to the Immigration and Customs Terminal, an adventure *not* characteristic of most major big-city U.S. airports. *That* specific inconvenience was followed with an hour-long-delay while waiting for the passengers' baggage to arrive on the Barcelona terminal's luggage carousel.

"I hope that this isn't indicative of the remainder of our tour," the usually reticent Frank Davies remarked to Jimmy Valerio. "I suppose it's true that we Americans are quite spoiled and too used to instant gratification."

"Yeah, Frank!" Jimmy nodded and confirmed. "It could be said that Americans are like wristwatches, always thinking 'Get-there, get there,' while many Europeans are like grandfather clocks practicing the mantra 'Take your time, take your time!' Maybe we'd be happier with pacifiers in our mouths!"

"It's only 8:45 a.m.," an eavesdropping Warren Mottola reminded his male companions. "We have all day to squander if we ever escape this suitcase acquisition and retrieval area."

"You're absolutely right there, Warren!" Frank diplomatically commented. "But I insist that it's over three-hours too early for the old Spanish noon-to-three siesta tradition. And as you've so appropriately suggested Warren, let's act like amiable and cooperative tourists rather than as typical dissatisfied and ultra-critical picayune Americans."

At last, the luggage carousel was activated and the tired but now-rejuvenated Flight 948 new arrivals anxiously grabbed their suitcases from the rotating black belt slats. The multilingual Barcelona Customs personnel were friendly and professional in processing the several hundred folks through the initial security screening. After obtaining five luggage carts at the end of the "Immigration responsibility," the party of ten Americans hired a driver and a van to convey them to the Apsis Atrium Palace Hotel at 656 Gran Via de les Corts Catalanes, situated right in the heart of Barcelona's most elegant downtown shopping district. The twenty-five minute drive through the city allowed the ten Americans to view and evaluate the Spanish metropolis and compare it to certain American cities cataloged in their mental repertoires.

"They seem to have massive congestion gridlock, just like New York, L.A. and 'Philly!" Warren Mottola' observed and said. "But I'm especially impressed with their highway system and the use of tunnels. And everything, including the buildings and streets, seems to be well-maintained and really clean."

"I particularly like the architecture and how the four buildings at intersections are at catty-corners and not at right angles to the streets like they are in cities back in the States," Jimmy Valerio contributed to the conversation. "That unique construction pattern automatically makes each intersection more open and visible. Barcelona seems to be an urban paradise with lots of parks, fountains, monuments and museums," the observant building contractor added. "I do believe that the Europeans take more pride in their cities than Americans tend to do with theirs. Driver, what boulevard are we now on?"

"Las Ramblas!" the van chauffeur answered. "And that's the famous *Columbus Monument* we just passed! We're now only ten minutes from your cozy hotel."

"The sights are magnificent!" Joanne Valerio exclaimed. "We'll definitely have to take a double-decker bus tour and sit on top, weather permitting. I like the idea of open-air top-deck buses! I've already seen several dozen of them that were conducting tourists around this beautiful city!"

"And the shrubbery and flowers are really fantastic!" Lisa Mottola noted. "This part of the city is like one giant botanical garden! And they have lots of bougainvillea here just like we saw in..."

"In La Jolla and in residential San Diego!" corporate jet pilot David Winters remembered and finished. "And there's many sycamore trees along the boulevard too! Barcelona is very much like southern California except for the rain. I hope the sky clears up later today!"

"Yes, it will," the driver authoritatively replied. "And I suggest that you take a stroll down the Passeig de Gracia after you become settled in your hotel rooms. It's a terrific shopping area just two blocks away from the Apsis Atrium Palace. I highly recommend it and I guarantee that you won't be disappointed. It's rather exceptional!"

After the ten new arrivals checked into the hotel, a bellboy escorted Lois and Frank Davies to the elevator and then up to their second-floor room, which had a marvelous balcony view of the Gran Via de les Corts Catalanes. Frank was so happy to get to his room and take off his shoes that he gave the helpful attendant a generous five Euro tip.

"Hey, before you leave, how do we put the lights on?" Frank inquired. "These light switches don't seem to work!"

"Sorry, Sir. My mistake for not telling you!" the bellboy instantly apologized. "You have to place the plastic room key in this wall slot here just after you open the door. The key insertion makes the lights go on. It's a measure we use to conserve energy and electricity."

"I see! Pretty nifty and practical!" Lois earnestly admitted. "Maybe we Americans could learn something from other cultures if we cease being so independent and arrogant. Thanks for sharing that important information with us!"

After the hotel porter left the Davies to their own privacy, another minor crisis soon developed. Lois couldn't figure out how to flush the toilet.

"There's no flush handle!" Lois informed her equally puzzled husband. "There just has to be a handle somewhere! I feel so stupid and incompetent right now!"

After searching and experimenting for a full minute, Frank was surprised to discover the solution to the riddle. A flat rectangular silver metal wall plate (that appeared to be part of the bathroom's décor) served and functioned as a useful flush handle.

"Mystery solved!" Frank declared, pretending that he was a contemporary Sherlock Holmes. "I just wish the bellboy or the person at the desk would've explained that simple secret, or should I say *that* simple method to us! They just assume that we've been to Europe before and are familiar with the different habits and customs. Anyway, realistically speaking Lois, good old Yankee ingenuity and perseverance are difficult to stymie."

"Now, you're beginning to sound haughty just like your obnoxious twin brother!" Lois facetiously kidded. "Nothing can defeat or stifle Fred! And now your inflexible attitude is contrary to acceptable!"

"And now you're starting to sound a lot like *our* overbearing sister-in-law!" Frank creatively joked. "If the slightest deviation is not a calamity, then it most certainly is a disaster! What a mental case Eleanor is and always will be!"

"Let a smile be your umbrella is indeed *not* Eleanor's favorite maxim!" Lois diplomatically assessed. "That vicious sister of mine possesses the combined personalities of Lucretia Borgia and Medusa the Gorgon! Need I say more to support my premise and your analysis?"

That afternoon, the light drizzle subsided and the Davies took the airport van driver's recommendation and sauntered down the magnificent Passeig de Gracia, a splendid boulevard replete with spacious sidewalks, fabulous buildings, ritzy department stores and swanky fashion emporiums. The fascinating scenery was both overwhelming and breathtaking.

"This thoroughfare makes New York's Fifth Avenue look like an ordinary dump!" Frank sarcastically interpreted. "It's without a doubt the most excellent street I've ever walked along!"

"Now, you're again sounding exactly like your disgusting brother Fred!" Lois quipped and benignly chastised. "Stop acting like a ruthless uncivilized cynical American barbarian!"

"And you're again sounding just like Eleanor!" Frank asserted. "Stop chiding and reprimanding me as if I'm a five-year-old wet-behind-the-ears kid! Please Lois, kindly show me some more respect and consideration!"

"Well, to change the subject," Lois Davies astutely said, "many of the structures on this fantastic avenue were designed by Antoni Gaudi, a world-renowned Spanish architect."

"Probably, our English word 'gaudy' comes from the guy's name!" Frank deducted and articulated. "Everything on that building over there across the street seems exaggerated and garish!"

"I don't know about *that* uncharitable comment!" Lois replied. "But I had read about Gaudi in a brochure about Barcelona down in the hotel lobby while you were busy checking in. His work is still very popular here in Barcelona and actually the architectural genius has a huge reputation throughout Spain and Europe!"

"Look at that roof on the opposite side of the boulevard!" the mildly perturbed husband pointed out. "It looks like dragon scales accentuated with medieval fantasy towers. And that ostentatious apartment house on the corner looks like it belongs with the Flintstones back in prehistoric Bedrock! This Antoni Gaudi fellow was so out in left field that he's entirely out of the stadium!"

"You could never appreciate another person's artistic or personal expression!" Lois rankled. "Now your true feelings are fully exposed! Deep down inside Frank, you're an ingrate just like your hostile twin brother is!"

"And you're hostile and argumentative just like *my* vitriolic sister-in-law, who happens to look exactly like you!" Frank volleyed back.

"Well, at least my problem is not partially genetic like yours is!" the wife caustically lectured. "Both you and Fred need the services of several priests and a squad of psychiatrists!"

According to Spanish custom, supper was not served in the hotel dining room until 8 p.m. During the delicious dinner Frank (out-of-character) got entangled in a minor wrangle with Dr. Rose Jeffries, a political liberal.

"These Spaniard natives all seem rather cold and indifferent to Americans!" Frank generalized with a frown on his countenance. "They mostly seem apathetic, not to mention pathetic!"

"I've seen equally unconcerned dispassionate people, walking the streets of downtown 'Philly or New York!" Dr. Jeffries abruptly challenged. "I think you're being a little too judgmental!"

"You probably voted for John Kerry in the last Presidential election!" Davies vociferated. "I can tell by your tone and by your attitude that you're a devout left-wing liberal from the word 'go'!"

"How I vote is my own conscience," Dr. Rose Jeffries protested. "And I've learned from experience that nothing tangible can ever be achieved by debating either religion or politics! I suggest that *you* change the topic of discussion!"

"Why are you being so confrontational and belligerent?" Lois Davies disputed with her usually tranquil marital partner. "I'm becoming a trifle embarrassed with your new-found tirades and I don't condone them at all! It's all contrary to your general nature!"

"And I'm becoming pretty tired of *you* being non-supportive of your loyal husband!" Frank snidely affirmed. "Behind every man there's a woman, and that's exactly where she belongs!"

"Now you're proving that you're truly a right-wing male chauvinist!" Dr. Jeffries indicted her formerly mild-mannered philosophical opponent. "A dedicated conservative right-wing male chauvinist at that!"

"And Rose, you're probably a militant left-wing save-the-environment and an avid save-the-whales advocate!" Frank angrily responded. "All you left-wingers have some perverted idealistic agenda to pursue like valuing animals over humans! You're all on the brink of abandoning capitalism and adopting socialism as an honorable way of life! Your history heroes are probably Karl Marx and Vladimir Lenin!"

"I see no reason to prolong this regrettable verbal altercation!" Warren Mottola interrupted the argument. "We're all here in Europe to have fun and recreation and not to verbally assault and attack one another! Now let's all drink to our newly engaged couple, Lisa and David!"

"Yeah, David!" Frank unfortunately yelled while frivolously raising his glass in a mock salute. "The next time the *pilot* light on my basement hot water heater goes bonkers, I'll know exactly who to call!" Davies loudly said, deliberately insulting the young commercial jet operator.

* * * * * * * * * * * *

Day two of the European vacation was much more harmonious and favorable for the Davies than day one had been. Frank had attributed his recent aberrant behavior to being overly fatigued from the seven-hour-flight. The rain had ceased and a cloudy blue sky had appeared over Barcelona's delightful sixty-eight-degree temperature. After enjoying a hardy breakfast in the hotel's main restaurant, the party of ten purchased tickets for the "city bus tour," which originated on the Placa de Catalunya, only four blocks from the aforementioned Apsis Atrium Hotel. The twenty-five-mile bus excursion entailed twenty-eight stops where tourists could get off at their leisure, sight-see and next board another double-decker open-air bus on the grand circuit and then get off at another place of interest along the scenic itinerary.

"Look, Frank!" Lois indicated as the bus passed from the Passeig de Gracia onto Calle de Cerdena. "There's the La Sagrada Familia (the Sacred Family) Cathedral. The tour pamphlet says it was designed by the great Antoni Gaudi in 1882. It's still under construction although Gaudi died way back in 1926!"

"It's marvelously built!" Jimmy Valerio recognized and attested. "As you know I'm in the construction business but I've never before seen anything quite like this terrific architecture! It's a combination of both primitive and modern! Just look at those unbelievable spires or towers or whatever you want to call them! They're worthy of any person's admiration!"

Evidence of Antoni Gaudi's brilliance was very abundant all over the bustling city as the tour bus passed by the Pare Guell, the Museum of Catalunyan Art, the Pueblo Espanol, the city's main university campus, the Maritime Museum and the Picasso Gallery. Not far from the waterfront the touring party exited the bus on Las Ramblas and stepped in the direction of the Gothic Quarter, an alluring section of Barcelona with buildings and residences dating back to the Thirteenth Century.

"Let's stroll up this narrow alleyway!" Lois suggested to the less rambunctious members of the group. "It looks rather intriguing and adventurous!"

"And the natives probably don't have clothes dryers, because all of the laundry is hanging out of overhead windows!" Frank articulated, again finding fault with his environment. "Maybe they don't own washers either!"

"Regardless," Lois mildly countered, attempting to get the erratic exchange of words back on topic. "Let's see how far this alleyway extends! The walks on both sides are quite narrow and a compact car can barely squeeze by in the center!"

"That's why most of the people in this city have motor scooters and motorbikes!" Warren Mottola concluded and explained. "There's not too many large American SUVs speeding around town, that's for sure! And those new Mercedes Smart cars are now the vogue over here! Don't forget!" the science teacher elaborated. "Gasoline is around eight-dollars-a-gallon and is sold in liters just like Coke and Pepsi are back in the States. That's precisely why most conscientious Europeans must be frugal and economical."

"Why do they call them Smart cars?" David Winters asked. "Do they have artificial intelligence generated by an on-board computer?"

"No!" Warren laughed and corrected. "Smart stands for Small Mercedes Art car! At least that's what I overheard a tour-guide telling a curious tourist on the bus!"

The commercial ancient alleyway (that was dotted with small neighborhood grocery stores and bakeries) stretched for over a mile, and upon leaving the very historic medieval area, Warren perceptively spotted the Roman Arch, a brick copy of the famous Arch de Triumph in Paris.

"The edifice is made out of Roman bricks," Warren academically told his exhausted companions. "The flat brick is about half as wide as those currently used in the United States and it *was* standard building material throughout the ancient Roman World."

"I thought you were a science teacher?" Joanne Valerio asked. "You seem to be an expert on history too!"

"Yes, Warren," Judy Marks chimed-in. "You must study dictionaries and encyclopedias both day and night to have knowledge of a trivial fact like that! No wonder why kids are bored in school!"

"I majored in science, but minored in history at *Rutgers!*" Warren Mottola clarified. "But sometimes it's hard to divorce one subject from the other! For example," the erudite teacher elucidated, "architecture is a science that has a certain history! That's precisely when and where the two distinct disciplines integrate!"

"Barcelona is the most beautiful and most exquisite city I've ever toured and that includes Las Vegas and San Diego!" Lois Davies opined. "Even though the brochure I had read stated that it has a population of nearly two million, I haven't detected one slum or ghetto yet anywhere! It's truly unbelievable and exotic!"

The fatigued trekkers stepped into a small soda fountain and purchased Seven-Ups and Pepsi Colas to be drunk outside. Frank generously treated everyone to their beverages.

"You want to know something," the biology research specialist stated and complained, "they charge you extra if you drink the sodas outside. They sort of rent the table and chairs to you. It's a little different than how food merchants do business in the States!"

"Yes, it is!" Lois agreed. "In the States soda fountains don't have twenty outside tables and sixty outdoor chairs! That's what I consider one of the main differences between Barcelona and 'Philly!"

Day two of the European vacation trip elapsed without any major incidents occurring. The travelers were satisfactorily adjusting to the six-hour time differential and were indeed becoming more social and less irritable. All ten American tourists were highly anticipating the seven-day voyage on the Regal Adventurer, the highlight of the trip being less than twenty-four hours away. The New Jersey visitors readily agreed that certain aspects of life were full of gratifying moments.

* * * * * * * * * * * *

Saturday, September 16th arrived on the calendar, and at breakfast Judy Marks announced to the group that the ugly three-day weather pattern that had hovered over and near Barcelona was now drifting east towards Italy.

"That makes sense, Judy!" Frank acknowledged and commended. "Weather in the northern hemisphere moves from west to east and generally so does the jet stream."

"That's why our flight back to 'Philly will be eight hours, a full sixty-minutes longer than it took getting here!" Warren objectively added. "We'll be going against the headwind caused by the strong jet stream flow in the upper atmosphere!"

"Before we check-out of the hotel at noon and meet our pickup van driver," Lois mentioned to Frank, "I want to go to the Passeig de Gracia and view its splendor one final time, while I'll really be in

48

quest of purchasing some decent postcards to put into a new photo' album."

The Davies did walk the magnificent Passeig de Gracia and had only two brief hours to inspect marvelous sights that hadn't been observed and explored before. Frank seemed back to his quiet-disposition self but then remembered an unusual scene he had witnessed on the balcony the previous evening (at midnight) while Lois was taking her hot shower.

"While you were getting ready for bed, I stood on our suite's small terrace and was relishing the beauty of the Via de les Gran Corts Catalanes," Frank prefaced his observation. "The wide boulevard is really totally terrific when lit-up at night."

"Yes, and it's so wide that it takes a full minute to cross," Lois recalled and exaggerated. "I especially like the double-lanes on each side and the corresponding wide pedestrian walk paths next to them before the crosser finally gets to the four main lanes. The wonderful boulevards of Barcelona are not safe havens for careless jaywalkers, that's for sure!"

"Well, anyway," Frank continued as the pair finally reached a newspaper and souvenir stand. "While you were in the shower, I witnessed over three hundred midnight roller blade enthusiasts speeding by on the pedestrian walkway. It was pretty phenomenal! I counted each and every one of the three hundred and eleven of them. Instead of wild motorcycle gangs they must have roller-blade clubs here!" Frank humorously conjectured and revealed. "It's certainly less expensive than owning and driving gas-guzzling cars around Barcelona! Say, Honey. Here's a colorful book about the city to take home as a memento of our trip!"

"I don't want that one!" Lois emphatically disagreed. "I prefer this one!" she insisted as she handed the specific item to the souvenir stand proprietor.

"Allemagne!" the stand owner bellowed.

"He means the book's written in German and not English!" the husband recognized and interpreted.

"Entonces yo quiero uno en Engles, mismo eso uno!" Lois directed the salesman in broken stilted Spanish. "Then I want another one like the one I had selected in English!"

"Don't be ridiculous!" Frank strenuously objected. "The one I had wanted you to choose was all about the entire city and not just about the architectural works of Antoni Gaudi! Stop being so damned stubborn Lois!"

"You're again sounding like you're impersonating your rotten twin brother!" the aggravated wife steadfastly protested. "You're rapidly becoming the dispute king of American tourists! You've been far from hilarious lately!"

"And you're now evolving into a carbon-copy of that vicious viper, Eleanor!" Frank accused his spouse in a bellicose tone of voice. "I suspect that somebody evil and jealous is putting a heavy wicked curse on our relationship!"

The volatile couple hardly spoke to each other on the van trip from the Apsis Atrium Palace down the picturesque Via Laietana, which led to the Passeig de Colom and ultimately to the docked Regal Adventurer. All ten tourists seated in the vehicle transport took a final stare at the elaborate lengthy and wide gray paver-stone promenade that accentuated the incomparable Barcelona waterfront.

Obtaining the required Sea Passes was easily facilitated, once the ship's new passengers showed their passports and other relevant identifications to the courteous harbor terminal personnel. Everyone was allowed to board at 1 p.m. and the newcomers had six-full-hours to unpack and investigate all of the massive fourteen decks until the scheduled first seating supper in the Magic Carousel Dining Room at six-thirty (with the vessel's disembarking at 7 p.m. sharp).

In the grandly decorated Magic Carousel Dining Room, the waiter and assistant waiter introduced themselves to the ten American diners at their table. "Good evening, ladies and gentlemen! I'm Cem (pronounced Gem) and this is my very able assistant Tomas. I'm from Turkey and Tomas is from Czechoslovakia. We're here to cater to your every eating need!" Cem said in almost perfect unaccented English. "It will be our pleasure to serve you!"

Frank formally introduced everyone at the table to Cem and to Tomas and then ordered two bottles of Merlot for the assembled gourmets to enjoy. Soon the conversation turned to the other travelers aboard the ship after the well-trained waiters began attending to *their* individual duties.

In short time, Frank Davies' recently acquired Dr. Jekyll and Mr. Hyde alternating personality again unexpectedly surfaced. "You all must know, some of these Europeans aboard this vessel are quite rude!" Frank began his impromptu criticism. "I was standing in Line H inside the harbor terminal acquiring Lois's and my Sea Passes when this nasty grumpy elderly Spanish man tried to wriggle into a spot at the Line G counter and then pushed me out of his way!"

"What did you say or do to the impetuous old fellow?" Warren Mottola curiously asked. "I'd think that his aggressive behavior would've warranted at least a perfunctory 'Excuse me'!"

"Well, I quickly raised my left elbow and deflected the old ill-mannered coot directly out of my standing space!" Davies bluntly reported, much to his wife's utter humiliation. "And besides that scenario Warren, this afternoon at lunch up at the eleventh floor Quarterdeck Buffet, Lois and I were seated at a table for four when a Hispanic lady signaled to me with sign language if she and her mate could sit down. I suavely said 'Si! Hable Engles?' and the snobby witch answered 'Portuguese!' Then neither the woman, I'd say she was in her fifties, nor her self-centered husband ever once again glanced at Lois and me during their entire meal. It was as if we were lepers or convicts or inferior beings or something! The only friendly people on this boat are good old Americans! You can pick them out in a second by their cheerful and happy demeanors!"

"Frank, I think you'd better stop speaking so loudly!" Lois rebuked. "You never know when you're going to offend someone sitting at another table!"

"Well, let them sue me for all I care!" Frank automatically and indiscreetly returned. "Let them sue me, even if they're rude Europeans and not merely Sioux Indians!" the slightly intoxicated man awkwardly joked.

"Now, just wait a cotton-pickin' minute!" Dr. Rose Jeffries boldly challenged her philosophical adversary. "I strongly suggest that you stop making unsubstantiated prejudicial statements and unfounded gross discriminatory stereotypical generalizations!"

"You're sounding too much like a cowardly liberal again!" Frank yelled across the table at the now-flabbergasted infectious disease doctor. "You're always crusading for a dumb cause! Get a grip on reality, will ya'!"

"And you're sounding more and more just like your haughty obnoxious brother Fred again!" Lois aptly injected into the three-way exchange.

"And I think you're deliberately mimicking Mrs. Eleanor Davies!" the indignant husband snarled back. "She's a venomous viper if there ever was one!"

"Folks! This is supposed to be a happy occasion for all in attendance!" Warren Mottola adroitly interrupted, acting like both a referee and peacemaker. "I'd like to now propose a toast to officially honor my daughter Lisa and her fiancé David's engagement! Let's all sincerely drink to their future health, wealth and happiness!"

* * * * * * * * * * * *

At 6 a.m. on Sunday morning, Frank Davies opened the curtains to cabin suite 8322 and admired the superb view of the city of Marseilles. 'It's September 17th,' he thought. 'I vow to myself that I have to be more diplomatic and I must also stay away from initiating controversial subjects, especially with Lois and with that nasty despicable leftist Dr. Rose Jeffries.'

The passengers aboard the Regal Adventurer were given three separate tour options at each port-of-call. 'We could've toured Marseilles but instead Lois, Warren, Melissa and I have chosen the small fishing village of Cassis!' Frank reviewed in his now-somewhat remorseful mind. 'I'll try my best to make this day pleasant and enjoyable for all concerned! Wow!' Davies considered. 'There must be at least fifty tour buses lined up down there! You'd certainly need that many to accommodate the three-thousand four-hundred travelers aboard this super-mammoth ship!'

After a quick visit to the eleventh deck buffet for breakfast, Frank, Lois, Warren and Melissa assembled in the fourth floor Metropolitan Theater, were swiftly assigned to Bus #6, and then wearing small stick-on #6 badges, the four guests waited for their tour designation to be called.

"I think it's best if *we* hang around together on all five scheduled tours in France and in Italy," Warren privately suggested to Frank. "Lisa and David are lovebirds and only have romance on their minds and Dr. Rose and her roommate Judy tend to have radical political views that are diametrically opposed to ours. Otherwise, we'll have to be constantly defending our conservative viewpoints! Dr. Rose has already labeled you and me 'Neocons.' I believe that in this specific case Frank, distance from that militant Marxist is the best remedy in order to avoid conflict!"

"I totally agree with your recommendation!" Davies instinctively answered. "Prevention is always better than cure! Even Dr. Rose must realize *that* obvious medical truth!"

52

The ship had its own sophisticated security-check system and the passengers' Sea Passes served as viable substitutes for the customary passports and photo' IDs. Soon the four friends were on Bus #6 and heading through Marseilles traveling from the "New Port" to the "Old Port," which featured numerous scenic marinas loaded with local fishing boats, Mediterranean schooners and extravagant yachts owned by the rich and famous.

"Notice that the residences' principal rooms all have three sets of shuttered windows facing the street," the French female tour guide explained in English. "Notice too that the city is built in a semi-circle. Marseilles presently has a population of around one million people and it remains the second largest metropolitan area in France. On your left is the classic Byzantine Cathedral, a favorite of tourists from around the world. And up on that hill overlooking our proud city and the gateway to the Mediterranean stands the impressive Cathedral of Notre Dame de la Garde with its magnificent gold-leaf towers," the knowledgeable guide described. "And soon we'll be passing by our Theatre National de Marseille La Criee. This part of the city with its many fancy stores and cafes looks very much like Paris's Champs Elysees, which incidentally in English means the Elysian Fields! Looking out toward the sea," the upbeat woman loquaciously stated, "you'll notice a fort or prison situated on a small island. That's where the Count of Monte Cristo was held captive in the classic novel written by Alexandre Dumas, who as you know also wrote the book *The Three Musketeers*. And as we travel along the coast toward Cassis, please remember that the genius painter Vincent Van Gogh was often inspired by many of the area's olive groves and vineyards situated along that route!"

"This city is definitely beautiful, but in my humble opinion, I still like Barcelona better!" Lois whispered to Frank.

"Me too!" came his rather convivial reply. "Everything looked a bit newer and cleaner on the Passeig de Gracia and on Las Ramblas compared to what we're now seeing in Marseilles."

Tour Bus #6 left the main highway and the skilled driver slowly navigated the vehicle along steep winding roads above rugged jagged cliffs until it stopped at the summit of the white precipices overlooking gorgeous Cape Canaille, a full 1,300 feet above the placid Mediterranean.

"The guide said that this spectacular view is actually from a higher elevation than the one from the top of the White Cliffs of Dover! In fact, it's the highest cliff overlooking the sea anywhere in Europe!" Lois marveled and informed.

"It's truly sensational and breathtaking!" Frank confirmed. "Let's take some pictures of Melissa and Warren and then they can reciprocate! Just look at those fabulous homes with orange tiled roofs situated down there near the Mediterranean. I gotta' admit, it's all very enticing and extraordinary!"

The remainder of "Day 4" in Europe was inconsequential. The bus passengers were then taken with dispatch to the quaint fishing village of Cassis where they were left off on the outskirts of the town to be transported into the center while sitting in compartments of small trains on wheels pulled by cute diminutive locomotives of various colors. "The Mayor of Cassis insists that all tourists enter the village on these trams because of traffic congestion and pollution!" the tour guide explained.

"The City Mayor sounds like another radical left-wing liberal environmentalist, just like Dr. Rose Jeffries!" Frank complained to Lois. "He's probably an officer in Greenpeace and in PETA, too!"

"Now, now, Frank!" the amused wife giggled. "Let's not become cantankerous, and let's simply pretend that we're normal tourists out to sample the exquisite fishing village, peruse its leather shops and then take some pictures of us standing in front of the fine waterfront cafes and restaurants. This is no time to act like a bullheaded contentious American, now, is it?"

"I suppose you're right!" the husband reluctantly conceded. "This is no time to *harbor* any animosity!"

That evening, Cem and Tomas served the party of ten delicious suppers of surf and turf followed by large portions of baked Alaska for dessert. "I wonder how the chef could fit an entire state like Alaska in his oven!" Frank jested with even Dr. Rose getting a brief chuckle out of his somewhat witty comment. At 9 p.m. everyone enjoyed the lively show "Broadway Sights and Sounds" staged in the Metropolitan Theater, which was followed by an hour's social activity at the Anchor Bar's piano lounge and then by some casual gift shopping along the ship's expansive promenade.

"Thanks for not being so verbally combative today!" Lois praised her spouse. "You're again mastering the art of being civil!"

"I'm trying my best!" the husband solemnly pledged. "Believe me Lois. I'm attempting to be calm and tranquil! I'm really working on it! But for some remote reason I'm finding it quite difficult!"

* * * * * * * * * * * *

On the morning of "Day 5", Frank, Lois, Warren, and Melissa again stepped down the "gangplank" for the next stop on their wonderful sea odyssey. A "tender" would ferry two busloads of tourists to the mainland since Villefranche had no deep-water dock where the Regal Adventurer could moor and anchor.

"I always wanted to tour Monte Carlo," Lois began. "Because it's where Grace Kelly had married Prince Rainier in a fantasy-type storybook wedding! I can't wait to see the cathedral where the event took place!"

"We have to remember that Monte Carlo is the name of the casino in Monaco," Warren Mottola scholarly remarked and corrected. "People often get the two terms mixed-up and call one the other. Monaco and Monte Carlo are two different things!"

"It's too bad we had to make a choice between Monaco and either Nice or Cannes for our one-day shore excursion," Melissa piped-in and regretted. "Confidentially, I'd like to visit and explore all three places."

"You could do this exact same cruise again and see totally different things at every port!" Lois Davies concluded and shared. "Perhaps we can do it again before we're...."

"Before we're all in wheelchairs having dual oxygen tanks on the rear while gasping for our last breaths!" Frank said, while completing his wife's thought with terminology that showed a distinct insensitivity toward the handicapped. "I want my wheelchair to have chrome dual exhaust pipes!"

"That horrible statement was in poor taste, and I hope you think things out more in detail next time before you again say something off-color!" Lois disciplined her husband. "You're more tolerable and less miserable when you're being introspective with your mouth zipped shut!"

"I swear that both you and Dr. Rose have no sense of humor!" Frank argued in defense of his vulnerable ego. "Neither of you know the definition of the word 'amusement'."

"Let's act a little more aristocratic now that we're mingling with highbrow society here in the French Riviera, even though in reality, we're just middle-class Americans and not Counts or Countesses!" Warren intelligently intervened. "I really never aspired becoming a wealthy snobbish aristocrat anyway!"

Tour Bus #5 stopped on the Avenue St. Martin near the Monaco Oceanographic Museum, the institute where Jacques Cousteau had conducted much of his essential nautical research. Not far from the very excellent museum was the Prince's Palace situated atop Monaco Rock, where the thoroughly enchanted tourists observed the hourly changing of the guard.

"The tour guide said that if Monaco were ever attacked by an enemy, then France would come to its defense!" Frank related to Warren. "When's the last time France ever won a battle? Was it before or after Julius Caesar?"

Although several eavesdropping American tourists found levity in Davies' assertive remark, Lois certainly did not. "You're again being very sarcastic and offensive!" the wife reproached as she approached her opinionated husband. "Do I have to tell you exactly who you're reminding me of?"

"No *Eleanor!*" the husband intentionally wrangled. "I wasn't making a public speech! I was merely whispering something in private to Warren! Why does every little conversation that I have elicit scorn from your lips?"

"Well, your boisterous whispers sound like they're being shouted into a bullhorn let alone into a megaphone!" the wife passionately countered. "Right now, I believe that you're evilly transforming into your cavalier twin brother right before my very eyes!"

"Guys! Let's take a stroll over to the Cathedral where Princess Grace and Prince Rainier were married and are now buried!" Melissa Mottola wisely advised. "Then we can ramble over to the Monte Carlo Casino. We have two full hours to burn before we have to board the bus."

"The casino isn't open until this afternoon!" Warren recollected and quoted from a guidebook he had read. "And they charge you a ten Euros admission fee just to pass through the fancy doors! That's close to fifteen dollars! You're way behind even before you insert a coin into the first slot machine! I guess they want to keep all of the riffraff out!"

The foursome discovered a park located behind the city square that featured an array of colorful tropical plants, flowers and palm trees. Pictures were taken with digital cameras and then Warren noticed that all traffic in the square had been terminated to allow for the filming of a rap video in progress.

56

"Look, there's the famous rapper Bee_G being driven in that black Mercedes convertible. He's being chased by an anonymous villain in that gold and black Rolls Royce," Warren uttered in pure amazement. "This MTV video must be costing tens of thousands of dollars to film!"

"That lousy rap music is a scourge to America!" Frank opined. "It's corrupting the minds and hearts of our youth while it's eroding the very morality of society! And it's all done for the love of money! Bee_G doesn't care one iota about the damage he's doing to teenagers from Portland, Maine to Portland, Oregon. The hedonistic narcissist is a complete egomaniac. And the worst part about it is that rap music isn't even music!"

"Frank, please be quiet!" Lois simultaneously admonished and pleaded. "We're surrounded by Bee_G's film crew and several of his intimidating three-hundred-pound Titan bodyguards, and they're standing only twenty-feet away! Be more discreet! They might not savor what you're saying!"

"I'm tired of your perpetual, uncouth character assassinations!" Frank fiercely reacted. "You're not exactly the most supportive wife you know! I'm only trying to explain myself to Warren!"

"I just don't want to see you causing a scene with your ongoing diatribe!" the wife emoted. "And I want you to know that for the first time the word 'divorce' has entered my mind! I find your behavior ever since this trip began most abominable!"

"Look! There's an ice cream parlor over there on the corner!" Warren nervously indicated. "Let's all cool off with some tasty treats! Vanilla cones might just do the trick!"

"I'm lactate intolerant!" Lois answered. "I can only eat yogurt, and that's on a full stomach!"

"That's not all that's wrong with my fickle wife!" Frank condemned and divulged. "In fact, that's just the most minor flaw! Right *Eleanor!*" he alluded.

"You're mentally sick!" Lois yelled back. "You're a detestable disgrace to humanity!"

"At least, I'm human!" Frank hollered back, getting the immediate attention of Bee_G's formerly nonchalant, enormous bodyguards.

"It's going to be a long six-mile bus ride back to Villefranche," Melissa accurately predicted. "Let's all please learn to temper our tempers!"

That evening after supper, the normally compatible foursome attended a terrific one-man performance in the Metropolitan Theater starring Domenick Allen, a former member of the rock group Foreigner. All during the outstanding show, Lois and Frank sat mum and as still as statues. The Mottolas sensed and suspected that major conflict was about to erupt.

* * * * * * * * * * * **

"Day 6" of the European trip was Tuesday, September 19. As usual, Frank and Lois and Warren and Melissa met at the entrance of the Metropolitan Theater at 7:30 a.m. to await assignment to their designated tour bus and to obtain their associated bus badges.

"This was a really tough choice," Melissa began to test the waters and see if there was any apparent current riptide existing between Frank and Lois. "We could've gone to Florence but instead we selected Tuscany on the advice of our travel agent."

"Let's see what happens!" Lois blandly answered. "It's too late now to change horses in midstream."

"Tuscany's famous for Chianti wine, alabaster statue products, olive trees and excellent leather goods!" Frank said without any trace of rancor evident in his tone of voice.

"Yes, and I understand that many Renaissance painters found the Italian fertile valleys and the gentle sloping Tuscany hills as interesting backgrounds for their creative works," Lois Davies contributed. "And the weather's going to be eighty-two degrees, something between ideal and perfect!"

Tour Bus #8 traveled north from the port of Livorno along an elevated industrial highway stretching over several kilometers of marshland in the direction of Pisa. "I know many of you had desired to see the Leaning Tower and have elected to fore-go Florence to sight-see Tuscany. Believe me, you've made a wise decision and you won't be disappointed. Pisa and Florence are both located on the Arno River," their guide Maria said into her bus microphone, "which has over the centuries silted up. Thus Pisa, being situated inland, has over the years declined as a trading port and Livorno has risen. You'll all be totally enthralled and thrilled with both the medieval towns of Volterra and San Gimignano," Maria claimed. "Volterra even has some Roman ruins but actually during your short visit, you'll all feel like you're time-traveling back a thousand years into

58

the past as you shop in narrow streets that haven't changed too much in appearance in the last millennium."

Stellar high poplar and cypress trees randomly dotted the many vineyards and olive groves, as Tour Bus #8 was maneuvered around curvy bends while it ascended thirty-miles inland, going-up hill after hill on the gradual ascension to Volterra. Dreamy clouds wafted by in the valley below as the spellbound tourists feasted their eyes on the remarkable landscape. Frank, Lois, Warren, and Melissa all felt as if they had wondrously entered a magical fantasy realm.

Volterra, and later that morning San Gimignano, were true medieval-type anachronisms, highly regarded special places to behold. The couples bought several leather belts, handbags and wallets in each town without any incidents, problems, haggling or dilemmas occurring. Lois was contemplating Frank's severe vacillating Jekyll and Hyde personality swings, but then she dismissed them as 'signs of manic depression' and was indeed glad that her husband's deportment appeared being 'back to normal.'

Since the total tour lasted a full ten-hours, lunch was served at a remote farmhouse that specialized in tourist visitations. A full-scale three-course-meal was prepared and presented with the first dish being pasta, the second meat and vegetables and the third being dessert, all in small but very attractive servings. Chianti wine (grown and processed on the farm) was then poured into tall-stem glasses to complement the fine delicious food.

"The only negative feature of this country farm is that they only have two bathrooms, one in the adjoining room, and the other in the farm's office," Lois perceptively stated to her friends seated at the long country farmhouse table. "It's a little inconvenient for forty-eight touring adults with overactive kidneys. But then again, this is Italy and not New York."

"It sure beats the lavatory facilities back in Volterra," Frank uttered in a non-threatening voice. "A fat woman sat behind a table and charged us a half-Euro each to use the toilets. This is one distinct advantage of public bathroom accommodations in the States as opposed to here in Italy. At least the two patron bathrooms on this farm seem to have some degree of privacy."

"And we had to waste fifteen-minutes of our tour time standing single-file in a long bathroom line; at least the women did," Melissa Mottola remembered and offered. "What am I saying? It was a co-ed bathroom with a series of stalls! There were no gender designations!

But over here they call them W.C.'s or Water Closets and not Men's Rooms or Ladies Rooms!"

"At least, we haven't seen any holes in the floor with two feet painted on the cement showing the lavatory patrons where they have to stand," Frank pointed out to his listeners. "Several guys back in Jersey had told me that's what they had experienced at stops in certain parts of Italy. I'm glad we haven't discovered them yet!"

"Frank, I'm going outside to the farm's office to use the facilities," Warren judiciously hinted. "I'll beat the crowd, if ya' know what I mean!"

"Good idea. I'll go along and make sure you aren't molested by a savage poplar tree or by a demented chicken wandering around," Davies amusingly jested. "You might need my inexpensive personal protection."

After returning from the office's bathroom and then partaking of the delectable Tuscan meal, Frank and Warren were surprised to see that the farm's two "multi-functional" office secretaries had moved to the gift shop to wait on customers from behind the counter because the diners all had to exit the building/restaurant into the gift shop area in order to return to the bus.

That evening upon the cruise ship was "Dress-up night" and everyone eating in the Magic Carousel Dining Room had to wear formal apparel. After dinner the party of ten enjoyed the Russian duo of Tara and Alexandre performing their professional ice-skating skills in the ship's spacious Ice Arena and the show's stars had a cast of twelve very talented skaters accompany them in enacting their very complicated maneuvers.

"This colossal ship has almost everything!" Warren bragged to his favorite companion. "Even an ice-skating palace almost big enough for the Philadelphia Flyers to play an ice hockey game!"

"I had read where the Regal Adventurer is so huge that if you stood it vertically from stern to bow," Frank summarized and stressed without exaggeration, "the colossal ship would be as tall as the Empire State Building. Now that's what I call really thinking big! Hey Warren," the biology researcher related, "I can't wait to get out of this encumbering monkey suit!"

"Well, good Buddy. Glad to see that you're back on an even *keel!*" Warren Mottola merrily joked. "You had me a trifle worried there for a while, and that's the honest-to-God truth!"

             * * * * * * * * * * * * *

Wednesday, September 20th was "Day 7" for the fully acclimated Mediterranean tourists now cruising aboard the ultra-modern Regal Adventurer. Again, fifty-buses were lined-up at the dock at Civitavecchia, the modern-day gateway to Rome. Rosemarie, the gentle Bus #15 tour guide, was conscientiously explaining to her captive audience the overall layout of Rome. "The Vatican lies on the north side of the Tiber River, but on the south side is where the original Seven Hills of Rome are located along with the major shopping districts and ancient ruins. Our first exciting stop this morning will be the incomparable Vatican Museum."

The thirty-mile drive from Civitavecchia to Rome took an hour and a half, due to heavy traffic congestion first showing itself ten miles outside the city. "Subways and underground parking are nearly non-existent because every time a construction crew begins excavating somewhere," Rosemarie educated her receptive listeners, "important archeological ruins are usually uncovered and work must be halted. Therefore, as you might've presumed, there's little new construction going on in central Rome."

At the Spanish Steps, a second gray-haired tour guide named Luigi was picked up who, like most Italian men, was an incessant chronic cigarette smoker. But the veteran host was quite experienced at shuttling his tourists through the Vatican area and his presence was well-known to the various security guards and Vatican attendants.

"Today, the entrance line for the Vatican Museum is only four blocks long," Luigi mentioned to his assigned disciples, "but in another two hours it'll be eight blocks in length. Be happy that you've luckily arrived here at the most desirable time."

"I can't believe all of the beggars hanging around the outside wall trying to exploit the pilgrims and the visitors' good intentions," Frank suddenly criticized to his wife. "It's astounding how people will sometimes use religion to achieve their selfish devious ends!"

"These are poor homeless people that have probably somehow evaded the welfare safety net and have inadvertently fallen between the cracks," an irritated Lois replied after solidly nudging her husband in the ribs with her right elbow. "Now please stop acting so uncultured and give your undivided attention to Luigi."

"I know that some of you have with difficulty sacrificed seeing the Trevi Fountain, the Pantheon, the Castel Sant' Angelo and the

Forum for the sake of touring the Vatican and the Colosseum with me, but believe me when I say," Luigi appropriately pontificated and embellished with an Italian accent outside St. Peter's Basilica, "you haven't made the wrong decision. Perhaps sometime in the future you all can return to the Eternal City and see all that you've missed this first time around."

Luigi patiently distributed certain "Whisper Phones" to his assigned tourists so that they could place a plug into an ear and listen to his extensive narratives by turning up the volume. The lengthy line moved rather quickly and in forty-five minutes Luigi was conducting his "students" through the immense Vatican Museum, which exhibited long narrow galleries ornamented with huge wall tapestries and various invaluable marble statues. The highlight of the tour (beyond a doubt) was the incomparable Sistine Chapel, which possessed a tremendous arched ceiling displaying numerous paintings painstakingly created by the inimitable Renaissance genius Michelangelo.

"The frescoes were recently cleaned-up and they look as good as new," Luigi proudly explained to his tuned-in audience. "For your information Michelangelo also designed the uniforms for the Pope's Swiss Guards and in addition the Master had sculpted the famous Pieta, which you'll all see and admire later this afternoon inside St. Peter's Basilica."

"If they had Baptismal water basins in this church then it could be called the cistern chapel instead of the Sistine Chapel," Frank foolishly joked to his close male companion.

"Stop being so disrespectful and irreverent!" the eavesdropping Lois chastised her sardonic mate. "This is the Pope's favorite and most sacred chapel! Don't you have a conscience?"

"Shhhh!" two very stern-looking Vatican attendants reflexively implored, as they held their index fingers up to their lips, signifying the need for silence. "Shhhh!" they repeated.

"Sanctimonious Fools!" Frank uttered to Warren while effectively drowning out Luigi's voice on his Whisper Phone. "I wouldn't be surprised if God were to boot those snobbish 'Shhhh!' idiots right out of heaven!"

"Shhhh!" the Vatican attendants again reminded the talkative and impious tourists that were either standing or meandering about.

After leaving the awesome Sistine Chapel, a tour guide and his group discourteously cut in front of Luigi and immediately the two all-too-proud leaders became embroiled in a heated disagreement. Luigi began hitting the other guide with his Bus #15 lollipop sign while several security guards deliberately ignored the saber rattling and quickly paced away from the minor imbroglio.

"Hey, Pal. I'll give you a fat lip if you keep hassling my friend Luigi!" Frank yelled to the now-perplexed and flustered maverick tour guide. "Back off!"

"Frank, don't get involved!" Lois desperately pleaded. "You're behaving just like your lawyer brother Fred would in this situation!"

"Maybe I'm inheriting some of Fred's traits and he's getting some of mine!" Frank hypothesized and suggested.

"Don't be preposterous!" the perturbed wife answered. "That's totally absurd! I do believe that ever since this vacation began you're regressing in maturity instead of advancing! If you can't act your age, then please act your shoe size!"

"Shhh!" two Vatican foot patrol personnel very characteristically breathed-out from behind rigid index fingers. "Shhhhh!" they reiterated in animated fashion.

Two hours later, Frank Davies somewhat redeemed himself by performing a good deed on the opposite side of the Tiber outside the Colosseum. A young black girl wearing a "Detroit" sweatshirt was running to catch-up with several of her friends (who wanted to take a picture with three men posing and costumed in ancient Roman soldier uniforms) when she tripped over a slightly raised cobblestone and landed hard on her right elbow. Frank rushed over, asked the girl if she could move her arms and legs and then clasped his fingers around her waist and swiftly hoisted the still-in-shock victim to a standing position.

"At least you still have an ounce of decency in you!" Lois chided after Frank had executed his admirable humanitarian deed. "You might actually be the chivalrous Sir Walter Raleigh reincarnated! Helping others was one of your better qualities before we got married. Thank goodness you're once again a benefactor to society!"

"I'd do the same for you if you lost your balance," Frank retorted, showing a degree of rancor in his tone of voice. "I'm basically a gentleman and a Good Samaritan despite what *you* might think!"

"Thanks a lot!" an insulted Lois adamantly objected. "I would hope that you'd scurry over twice as fast for me! I guess I had just overestimated you!"

That sultry afternoon the passengers assigned aboard tour bus #15 devoured the traditional three course meal at an exclusive Rome hotel and then continued their tedious tour by returning to the Vatican for an inspection of St. Peter's Basilica.

"St. Peter must be a rich guy because he owns this vast structure plus hundreds of churches and schools all over the world!" Frank quipped. "He must be as wealthy as Bill Gates!"

"Frank, stop being so repugnant!" Lois disapproved, shrugging her shoulders. "You're rather repulsive and reprehensible at times!"

"Sometimes, I just got to be candid! That's why they call me Frank!" the husband stupidly joked.

"Your sense of humor leaves much to be desired and is none too amusing," the wife fired back. "You're even more bullheaded than ancient Greek mythology's Minotaur! At least *he* had a lame excuse for his stubbornness!"

"Guys, let's all politely listen to Luigi's lecture, even though it's now getting quite monotonous and boring!" Melissa Mottola proposed. "And just think. Tonight, in the Metropolitan Theater, the Regal Adventurer's multi-talented Singers and Dancers will be doing 'Hollywood in Motion.' Now that's something half-decent to be looking forward to."

At the first sitting dinner, neither Cem's sumptuous fillet mignon nor Tomas's scrumptious "sorbet delight" could adequately cheer-up Frank and Lois Davies from their mutual enmity and from their obvious dual emotional depressions.

* * * * * * * * * * * *

On "Day 8" of the comprehensive European trip ("Day 6" aboard the Regal Adventurer) Frank, Lois, Warren, Melissa, Dr. Rose Jeffries and Judy Marks were all assigned to Bus #13, which they obediently boarded on the Naples dock.

"Where are Lisa and David?" Dr. Rose innocently asked. "Those two infatuated and hypnotized lovebirds don't mingle too much! They're too focused on each other!"

"They're more ambitious and adventurous than we are!" Melissa Mottola explained. "They're touring downtown Naples, then taking a ferry to the Isle of Capri and next taking another one from Capri to Sorrento where they'll be gallivanting around. They promised to meet up with us in Pompeii."

64

"That sounds like a pretty rigorous and exhausting day!" Judy Marks remarked with a smile. "I hope Lisa and David can avoid the notorious pickpockets and purse snatchers constantly patrolling downtown Naples! Those crooks especially thrive on ripping-off vulnerable American tourists!"

"They'll both be so tired that they'll probably miss having sex tonight!" Frank uncouthly and distastefully theorized and said as the group stood in a circle waiting to climb aboard Bus #13.

"That last comment was rude and crude and totally unjustified!" Dr. Rose sternly protested and challenged. "You should rinse your mouth out with *Lysol*!"

"Either that, or learn to bite your tongue!" Lois verbally piled on. "I'm embarrassed to say that I'm married to you! You're becoming a pathetic excuse for a human being Frank!"

"I think you're all making mountains out of molehills!" Frank exclaimed like a true bona fide egomaniac. "Learn to lighten-up, will ya'!"

After everyone had clambered aboard Bus #13, Monica, the designated tour guide, diligently distributed the by-now-familiar Whisper Phones. "As the bus leaves the Port of Naples, which incidentally is famous for the invention of pizza, we'll be skirting the city and driving past Herculaneum and Pompeii, both towns that had been destroyed by the volcanic eruption of Mt. Vesuvius on August 24th, 79 A.D. to be exact. Then we'll be heading to Sorrento on the peninsula and taking the nearly forty mile scenic drive along the magnificent Amalfi Coast all the way down to Salerno," Monica expertly orated. "So just sit back and relax and be prepared for at least seven miles of walking before this invigorating ten-hour tour is completed."

The first stop just outside Sorrento was a local establishment called Miss Bellevue, a factory outlet that manufactured exquisite inlaid wood dining room tables with elaborate matching chairs, tea wagons and house furniture. The pieces exhibited in the showroom were quite intricately made and the tourists all marveled at the tremendous degree of craftsmanship that went into achieving the highly sophisticated-looking final products. Frank and Warren were tempted to purchase appealing double-pedestal dining room tables (and matching upholstered chairs) that were listed at 3,500 Euros.

"That's about the equivalent of $4,700.00," Warren smartly acknowledged after doing a quick arithmetical estimate in his head.

65

"That's what I call a bargain! You don't see stuff like this displayed at furniture stores back in the States!"

"But then you have to worry about shipping the set all the way across the Atlantic and who knows what condition it'll be in upon arrival back in Hammonton?" Frank objectively evaluated and maintained. "It's hard to return damaged goods when you're four-thousand or so miles away from the source!"

"Maybe, on our second trip to Italy, I'll have the courage to make the acquisition," Warren keenly answered.

"That's an un*warran*ted comment! You've never demonstrated a moment of courage since the day you were born!" Frank Davies arrogantly and caustically remarked. "You've been about as intrepid as an army deserter as long as I've known you!"

Warren Mottola abruptly left Frank's company to rejoin Melissa, who was preoccupied chatting with Lois, with Dr. Rose Jeffries and with Judy Marks, all concerned about Frank's annoying and insulting statements. A half hour had elapsed before the forty-eight tourists were instructed to again ascend the familiar steps into Bus #13.

"The classic song 'Come to Sorrento' was not a love melody," Monica matter-of-factly began her next memorized dissertation. "In fact, the lyrics are a political message, a past sincere appeal for certain lawmakers and officials to return to the city to organize a new government."

"Doesn't that obnoxious witch ever shut up?" Frank said to Lois. "She's giving me an intense headache that won't quit!"

"Here, swallow down a couple of aspirins!" the wife insisted as she frantically opened her purse to retrieve a small plastic container. "How am I going to enjoy all of the exotic bougainvillea sprinkled in with prickly pear cactus and the totally gorgeous array of other flowers when you're chronically complaining and finding fault with everything and anything? Haven't you noticed the majestic trees flourishing throughout Italy?"

"What about them?" Frank acerbically reacted. "What's so damned special about the trees? Trees are trees, aren't they?"

"In Tuscany, in Rome and all along this entrance to the marvelous Amalfi Drive," Lois explained, "the trees' limbs have been sheared off at the bottom and in the middle to form handsome canopies. I suppose it's been done to provide ample shade because they don't have nearly as many woods and forests here in Italy as we do have back in the States. That's the only suitable logical explanation I can think of!"

"Maybe, here in Italy, they have a surplus of unemployed lumberjacks!" Frank unrealistically and indiscriminately joked. "Unemployment abounds here because they have plenty of lazy non-industrious citizens! That's what the heck happens when you have a mostly socialistic type of government. Dr. Rose must feel right at home here in Italy! Most of the parasitic people in this country despise capitalism and free enterprise! That's why they'll never be as prosperous as we Americans are!"

"You're being absolutely implausible and irrational!" Lois profoundly protested. "I think I'll be sitting with Melissa for the remainder of the tour!"

"Now, you're again sounding like my bitchy sister-in-law!" the husband accused. "When we get back to Room 8322 be sure to check your passport and make certain that the name Eleanor Davies isn't printed on it! Better yet, examine your Sea Pass to determine whether or not your entire identity has been surreptitiously changed!"

"And closely check *your* passport and determine if the despised name Frederick Davies isn't typed on it!" the now emotionally disheveled wife snapped back. "You've become ruder than sin and cruder than petroleum!"

"We're now officially entering the world-famous Amalfi Drive!" Monica exuberantly announced into her trusty microphone. "Many rich Neapolitans maintain resort homes here! Notice that some residents use their concrete roofs as their garages because their homes are built on the sides of the mountains overlooking the sparkling blue sea. Those types of homes are usually the most expensive! There's nothing like this physical beauty anywhere else in the world!"

"It looks exactly like La Jolla along the California Coast just above San Diego!" Frank shouted and disagreed from his sixth-row seat, much to Lois's mortification.

"Thank you, Sir!" Monica cleverly and graciously responded. "I'll make a note of that fact and definitely mention it on future tours!"

The panoramic view of the mountainside town of Positano was quite outstanding, appearing as if it belonged on canvas in a masterpiece painting as it nobly lorded over the serene Mediterranean. Buildings and dwellings appeared terraced, one on top of another, in some instances fifteen structures high all the way up the mountainside. Only one main street passed through the entire town and security patrol personnel with communications' radios stopped traffic in one direction for a full half hour so that vehicles could smoothly travel in the opposite direction. Then the traffic monitors alternated the procedure for a full half hour to accommodate and alleviate northbound congestion.

"They need some Yankee ingenuity around here to build some decent highways!" Frank thought and then impulsively blurted out. "In the States this over-populated town would be referred to as a ghetto or a barrio!"

"How are they going to possibly build parallel roads on this mountainous coast?" Lois incisively questioned her husband. "It would be a bizarre undertaking, that's for sure!"

"We American capitalists can accomplish almost anything! That's why we're the envy of the entire world!" Frank egotistically boasted. "We're born entrepreneurs!"

"Please be quiet and listen to Monica!" Dr. Rose Jeffries commanded from her seat directly behind Frank. "Show some courtesy! Your unsavory opinions aren't exactly being relished or cherished by the other passengers!"

"Your totally silly politically correct nonsense is contrary to the operations of the objective adult mind!" Davies mercilessly ranted to Dr. Rose, much to her chagrin and humiliation. "It's a revolting social sickness that rivals any infectious disease!"

The somewhat-exhausted trekkers stopped in Amalfi (a large hillside town that resembled Positano in sublime appearance). The group ate the standard three-course lunch served at a posh hotel and then with renewed energy again boarded the tour bus for the anticipated trip to historic Pompeii.

"The traffic on this narrow street is quite horrendous, almost brutal!" Frank curtly mentioned to Monica. "And these people flying around the wicked curves on motor scooters are a definite hazard. This entire street is treacherous! How many turns did you say this winding road has?"

"Around two-thousand-five-hundred!" the effervescent tour guide recollected and confirmed. "Of course, that's an approximation!"

"That's about two-thousand four hundred and ninety-nine too many!" Frank negatively bellowed. "How do they get accident victims and emergency cases to the nearest hospital?" Davies relentlessly persisted. "This lengthy snake-like road is excessively dangerous!"

"By helicopter!" Monica replied.

"That makes sense because anyone in need of medical attention would otherwise die from traffic congestion let alone from lung congestion!" Frank condescendingly exhaled. "Where did you learn to speak English?"

"I spent three-years living in Brooklyn!" Monica patiently replied.

"Shut up!" Lois reprimanded as she gave her husband another healthy dig in the ribs with her sharp left elbow. "Shut up! Stop asking so many irrelevant annoying questions!" she angrily parroted.

"You're hysterically overreacting!" Davies fired back.

The archeological treasures of Pompeii were quite exceptional, ranging from the well-preserved gladiator practice arena to the antiquated amphitheater, where Greco-Roman plays were once performed. Then Monica led the tourists on a walking trip around the "resurrected city" that Mt. Vesuvius had violently buried under thirty-foot of volcanic ash.

"Notice the elevated rocks in the center of the street!" Monica indicated. "Residents would use the raised rocks to cross the road because raw sewage had used natural gravity to flow down the street from the higher ground to your left to the lower end of the city to your right!"

"The ancient Romans didn't know crap about crap!" Frank boisterously nitpicked. "I'll bet that the Italians have learned *that* particular tradition from their primitive ancestors! The E-*truss*-cans all had double hernias, especially the men!"

Monica just stared incredulously at Frank Davies while *his* disbelieving wife dragged him to the back of the crowd to avoid potential friction in public. "The people of Pompeii had a fascination, or should I say a special fixation with sex!" Monica pointed out to her remaining listeners. "Please observe this bit of graffiti drawn on this wall. Look closely! It's an exaggerated male reproductive organ!"

"It's homo erectus, even if the ancient Romans weren't gay!" Frank boomed for all to hear. "That graffiti was probably drawn by a *porn'* again Christian!"

Monica was stunned and at a complete loss for words at the speaker's general audacity and brazenness. Lois then pulled her

marital partner into an alley and again lectured him about his "total
lack of decorum."

"Lately, there's been nothing sentimental or commendable about
you Frank! You've managed to deride many people including your
good friend Warren on this supposedly wonderful tour!" Lois
screamed out of control. "You're an insult to your country and to
humanity!"

Frank intensely scrutinized his Sea Pass to verify his identity.
"Truthfully Lois, I'm not myself. Today I actually think and believe
I'm my ill-tempered brother Fred!"

* * * * * * * * * * * *

That evening, Frank and Lois dressed for supper and hesitantly
departed Cabin Room 8322. The couple remained non-verbal as they
entered the vacant elevator that promptly conducted them down to
the fifth deck Magic Carousel Dining Room. The emotionally
distraught feuding couple obstinately entered the ship's restaurant not
realizing that the whole place was virtually devoid of human activity.

When Frank and his peeved wife arrived at their familiar table,
they were appalled to see that Fred and Eleanor Davies were already
seated there. Frank was the first to comment on the weird parallel
coincidence.

"What are you two misfits doing here?" Davies exclaimed in
absolute astonishment. "This is more of an ugly aberration than a
blessed miracle!"

"Where are Warren and Melissa, Lisa, and David, Dr. Rose, and
Judy Marks?" the virtually mesmerized Lois Davies asked, almost in
a trance.

"This ugly encounter totally defies logic and reason!" Fred
incredulously replied. "You two are on this ship two weeks later than
you're supposed to be! This is supposed to be *our* European
vacation!"

"Something's mighty peculiar here!" Eleanor Davies stated from
her seat in a disconcerted tone of voice. "And I must admit that Fred
and I have been acting rather strange lately. He's been sounding like
you Frank and I've been sounding exactly like *you* Lois! *Our*
confused minds just couldn't account for those crazy anomalies!"

Just then, Cem and Tomas appeared to further complicate matters
on the already-bewildering scene. "Welcome folks for your final

70

dinner on the cruise!" Cem mysteriously began his odd-but-powerful discourse. "And today is Thursday, September 28th, 2006, what you four targeted passengers might consider a compromise date."

"You four dupes might think that Cem and I are working for the Regal Adventurer, but actually, we're delighted to report to *you* four honored people that we have another even more successful employer!" Tomas obscurely and cynically stated. "This ship, or should I say this heinous trap, happens to belong to someone *you* commonly allude to as Lucifer!"

"Yes, valued Guests, Tomas and I are shrewdly recruiting new clients and patrons for our awesome Master," Cem evilly informed.

"The terminology 'eternal slaves' would certainly represent and constitute more accurate language!" Tomas enlightened his rather astounded and appalled audience. "The four of you are now specimens, or should I say carefully selected participants in a new innovative *moral,* or should I say a new innovative *immoral* experiment involving the unique confluence of time and space. Congratulations Francis, Frederick, Lois, and Eleanor!" Tomas diabolically declared and snickered. "You're all about to be dishonorably inducted into a most premier organization!"

"Now, be ready to consume some delicious Deviled Clams for an appetizer, some Deviled Crab-meat for your main entrée and some Devil's Food Cake for your very palatable dessert," Cem confidently and confidentially related to his stunned prey. "You unfortunate nominees have no choice in this delicate awe-inspiring matter for indeed, all four of you naïve morons have just involuntarily surrendered your free wills!"

"No *Angel's Food* cake aboard Satan's favorite ship! Welcome to the enigmatic Prince of Darkness Regal Adventurer!" Tomas scrupulously clarified, much to the dismay and horror of his four victimized recruits. "Cem and I are greatly exuberant, way beyond *your* very limited human imaginations! This truly and undeniably is a most thrilling event! We've finally met our work quotas! We're now mercifully emancipated from perpetual drudgery! Freedom is finally ours! Thank you so much for *your* inadvertent cooperation!"

And then, with an absence of ceremony, both Cem and Tomas cryptically transformed into frightening zombies and next into incessantly laughing skeletons. In a matter of seconds, and without any indication of resistance, Frank, Lois, Fred and Eleanor obediently joined *their* un-illustrious and totally accursed damned company on a mysterious journey into infinity.

"Dual Events"

My wife and I had never been to Bermuda. Joanne and I had always previously vacationed at resorts on popular islands in the *Caribbean*. We had enjoyed week-long hiatuses on exotic isles like Barbados, Puerto Rico, Aruba and St. Thomas. We once took a *Cunard* cruise from San Juan to Venezuela, which featured scenic stops in Grenada, St. Lucia, St. Marten, St. John and St. Croix.

Joanne and I have always been warm-weather people. We prefer sunbathing and snorkeling to winter lodges, snowmobiles and skiing. Our travel agent had recommended Bermuda anytime from May to October to experience the best weather. My wife and I looked over some literature about the famous *Atlantic* paradise before boarding Flight #98 out of *Philadelphia International Airport*.

The takeoff from Philly' was smooth and easy. When the "Unfasten Your Seatbelts" light flashed on Joanne and I became engaged in a casual conversation. It felt good getting away from the mayhem and the myriad demanding routines of American mass society.

"It says in this excellent brochure that Bermuda is a British territory and only a mere two-hour flight from Philly'," my wife read out loud. "It takes us longer to drive from our South Jersey home to New York than to fly from the *Quaker City* to Bermuda."

"We'll probably spend more time going through customs in the *Bermuda International Airport* than we will on the plane," I cynically answered. "Let me take a gander at the map on the back of that pamphlet when you're through with it. I need to know exactly where everything is located in our new environment."

I immediately observed that Bermuda was not an island but actually a chain of about three hundred islands. I learned from my reading that nine of the coral masses are populated and they are connected by a series of well-designed drawbridges and causeways.

"Claire said at the travel agency that the island's capital Hamilton is a tourist's paradise," I recalled and shared. "It's remarkable that a cluster of tiny specks could be populated and yet so isolated in the *Atlantic* six hundred miles off the coast of North Carolina."

"I don't think the Wright Brothers would have made it from Kitty Hawk to Hamilton," my clever wife, a veteran middle school geography, English and history teacher laughed. "If I remember correctly their initial flight was just over a hundred feet."

"I read that the *Princess Hotel* has perhaps the finest accommodations on the main island," I casually added. "And just by coincidence that's our exotic destination. Actually, I can't wait until we land and get situated."

"It's pink, my favorite color," Joanne observed and related with a smile and a wink. "Just like my bikini and my nightgown."

The entire *Boeing 727* flight out of Philly' was as smooth as satin. My wife was perusing some more pertinent literature about Bermuda's various sites of interest while I was examining a small booklet that described in detail our choice of lodging. At that moment the entire Universe seemed tranquil and harmonious.

"Joanne, I gotta' admit the *Princess Hotel* is really gorgeous, in this advertising photo'," I said before taking another sip of my *Seagram's Seven* on the rocks. "It's situated on a scenic harbor, has both a salt-water and a fresh-water swimming pool and the facility has four splendid gourmet dining facilities. It even has fishing charters and glass bottom tour boats docked right on the harbor."

"And we also have beach privileges at the *Southampton Princess* on the other side of the harbor," my wife informed. "They have a ferry shuttle that transports guests between the sister hotels. I'm definitely going to check out the *Southampton* the first chance I get."

"Honey, that sounds really great," I amiably agreed, "and I just know that this hiatus is going to be a memorable vacation, I just know it. I'm glad we chose this hotel and this island. This is goin' to be an unforgettable adventure."

"Look here at this article describing our hotel," Joanne pointed out. "It states that Mark Twain used to stay at the *Hamilton Princess*. It says it was the author's favorite place on the island. If it's good enough for Samuel Langhorne Clemens," the social studies/language arts teacher told me. "Then, it oughta' be good enough for us."

It all seemed like a wonderful fantasy. There we were, escaping hectic work responsibilities and flying thirty-five thousand feet above the gleaming *Atlantic*, leaving the doldrums of jobs and home chores back in New Jersey. And Bermuda guaranteed us floral splendor and radiant sunshine. I looked at my watch to confirm reality. It was Monday, July 8. We were on a jet heading towards tropical leisure and elegance. I was at peace with the Universe.

I again glanced at my wristwatch that I had received as a college graduation present and noticed that the trade name was *Hamilton.* Then I realized a small coincidence, Hamilton, Bermuda and Hamilton wristwatch. My name is Hamilton Alexander, and remarkably, I did bear a strong resemblance to Alexander Hamilton's singular portrait engraved on the ten-dollar bill, but I refused to acknowledge *that* similarity when someone would insist that I looked like someone else.

I chuckled at the cute parallelism that my mind had coordinated. 'Life is full of such unique associations,' I mused and thought. It came to mind that my birthday was July 27, or 7/27, and we were flying southeast on a *Boeing 727.* I conveyed those subtle vignettes to Joanne, who indulgently laughed at my "absurd superstitious imagination."

I glimpsed across the jet's aisle in the midst of our merriment. My eyes scrupulously observed a dark-complexioned gentleman seemingly staring at Joanne and me. I suspiciously thought I had caught him peering at us several times before during the flight since we had left Philly'. At first, I mentally wrote the matter off as 'someone who disliked others that were a little loud and having a good time.' Instinctively though, I almost automatically loathed the stranger.

At that moment, bad vibrations pulsated down to the marrow in my bones. I turned and sipped the last ounce from my delicious rye whiskey on the rocks. My sixth sense perceived a bad chemistry existing between *him* and me. I whispered my secret feeling to my wife. Joanne casually dismissed my intuition as "an acute case of badly jangled nerves" and as "possessing a too-distrusting nature."

"Maybe you're right about my imagination and my twisted nerves," I answered as politely as I could. "I'm gonna' hit the lavatory and wash my face. That *Seagram's Seven* was supposed to tranquilize me, not activate my defense mechanisms along with my kidneys. Maybe I'll be a better evaluator of character when I return," I softly said to my wife, "but my sixth sense is seldom wrong when it comes to sensing another man's motives and his malicious intent."

I freshened-up in the small bathroom cubicle and then returned to my seat five minutes later. I was deeply disturbed seeing the sinister gentleman now sitting across the aisle engaged in polite conversation with my all-too-garrulous lovely wife. The new acquaintances were jovially exchanging anecdotes about freak accidents each had experienced on past vacations. Joanne introduced me to our fellow passenger but I must confess that I felt very uncomfortable and self-conscious in Nolan Phillips' presence.

'Nolan Phillips, where had I heard that name before?' I pondered as I briefly peered into the man's cold gray eyes. The name had a definite familiar ring. 'Something to do with history or literature,' I guessed. 'It has to be another bizarre coincidence like Hamilton and 727,' I surmised. 'Nolan Phillips seems to register some academic association but I can't exactly identity what it is.'

My natural audacity was tempted to ask Nolan and Joanne what person in history or literature shared Phillips' vaguely familiar name but I did not want to impress the stranger as being academically deficient in common cultural knowledge. As a rule I generally try avoiding public embarrassment or awkward situations at all costs.

'My mind must be really fatigued,' I determined in my defense. 'I need this *Princess Hotel* escape from the pressures of everyday reality,' I concluded. 'Joanne's right. I'm probably overacting to something that doesn't even warrant a second thought.'

Our new acquaintance tried his best to be affable. I was certain that the appellation Nolan Phillips my distrustful mind was considering was not a contemporary name but was somehow connected with the past, the remote past. As I intensely studied the man's very distinct facial features I believed his name might have been that of a former high school classmate or perhaps someone from twenty years ago from an old *Rutgers* college seminar. His name was like one of those trivial facts my high school teachers made me memorize only to be forgotten a week after the final exam' had been administered. It was there in my memory, yet it wasn't.

As Joanne and Nolan Phillips amused each other with broken elbow and sprained ankle stories, I promised myself that I would research the gentleman's name when I could find quiet sanctuary and sufficient time to fully analyze the situation in a Hamilton public library. There I could fully investigate the matter, if indeed it were a matter at all.

"Hamilton, Nolan would like to buy us drinks," Joanne informed me. I acceded to the stranger's friendly request simply to be cordial but I did not relish my wife socializing with Phillips. I was puzzled that she hadn't sensed the danger in him that my instincts had felt. Maybe it was my strict neo-Puritan childhood resurfacing. Joanne had always called me "a prude." 'Could it all be jealousy in

76

disguise?' I wondered. 'I don't even know this man,' I further thought. 'Why should every cell in my being instinctively hate him? He doesn't look like a criminal after all!'

After a pleasant blonde stewardess served us our particular drinks, much to my displeasure, Nolan Phillips disclosed that he would also be staying at the *Hamilton Princess Hotel*. The impertinent fellow then told me that I looked exactly like someone he had known in the past but he couldn't pin it down exactly who that anonymous person was. His observation rattled my consciousness. I felt that Phillips possessed the sixth sense, too.

"Nolan, everybody says that to me," I deceivingly answered, "and I do have a pretty standard-looking face. Today the *American Airlines* receptionist back in Philly' mentioned the exact same thing. But Nolan, unfortunately nobody seems to be able to tell me who my facsimile is," I responded as courteously as I could feign.

I conjectured what Nolan Phillips might have looked like wearing a white colonial wig or a tilted confederate hat. He too looked vaguely familiar but my rampant imagination couldn't pinpoint his identity if at that moment my life immediately depended on it.

"Well then, who do you think I look like?" I candidly challenged. "The President, the British Prime Minister, the Pope, Bill Gates?"

"I don't know," Nolan replied with an element of regret in his voice. "I can't seem to associate it right this minute. I've seen a portrait of you somewhere, perhaps in the *Guggenheim*, the *Metropolitan Museum of Art*, the *Louvre*, or maybe in the *Smithsonian*. But the mystery gentleman I have in mind has a long nose curved up at the end, just like yours!"

Joanne was amused with Nolan Phillips' insulting description but I was deeply mortified. 'Is he trying to harass and ridicule me in front of my wife? Does he have malicious intentions?' I reflected and fumed. 'If we had lived in olden days, I would probably be motivated to challenge him to a duel with swords or pistols,' I thought.

Much to my chagrin Joanne had not detected any malevolence in Nolan Phillips' disposition or in his graphic language. She considered his vile comment about my nose as being "cute and on-target."

'Maybe it's your strict upbringing that makes you skeptical of anyone that appears too convivial upon first contact,' I rationalized. 'It must be my *WASP*ish childhood, my jangled nerves and my fertile imagination,' I speculated. 'Learn to just get along!'

The *727* gently landed at *Bermuda International Airport* and the passengers eagerly disembarked. Inside the terminal courteous Customs Officials dressed in khaki Bermuda shorts thoroughly inspected the anxious tourists' luggage. The three long arrival lines moved forward at a fairly rapid pace.

My wife was talking up a storm with two lady passengers she had met before boarding the *727* in Philly' and Joanne was vividly relating her excitement about being there "in paradise." My nervous mind ignored her prattling and focused on getting our traveling credentials together for inspection. And to add to my quandary my brain was preoccupied with fears, doubts and suspicions concerning Nolan Phillips, and those turbulent thoughts were all rotating simultaneously in my mind like strange patterns inside a mental kaleidoscope turning in many directions.

Contrary to my ordinarily calm disposition, I angrily admonished Joanne about her apparent friendliness with Nolan Phillips. My wife indicated that she was tired of being embarrassed by my unwarranted "public hostility toward *friendly strangers*."

"Now, that's an oxymoron if I ever heard one," I criticized, "and I think your false observation about me is downright *pretty ugly*."

"Sometimes, you don't realize how cruel and offensive you can be," my wife flippantly snapped back, "and you must learn to control your nasty temper or seek psychiatric help. Did you hear me Hamilton?"

"You're possibly right," I guiltily acknowledged. "I'm sorry for overreacting like that. I'll be better tomorrow once I get acclimated to this new environment. You know Joanne, I have trouble adjusting to new places. I promise to treat you like a lady for the rest of our glorious stay here."

My spouse applied a big hug around my neck right in the center of the waiting line. Several other travelers smiled in recognition of her affectionate gesture. I looked behind me and saw Nolan Phillips snidely gazing in our direction, his evil eyes hidden behind thick dark sunglasses. I immediately felt antagonism toward his deliberate visual intrusion into our brief romantic interlude.

I felt compelled to go over and shatter his big protruding mandible into a dozen or more fragments. Fortunately, I resisted that very strong impulse and reason prevailed over reckless inclination. An attack of that nature would confirm to my wife that I was indeed paranoid and that I indeed lacked maturity and self-esteem.

Finally, much to my relief *Ginger* and I proceeded through Customs without incident or difficulty. A representative from the *Hamilton Princess Hotel* was holding a sign over his head to attract the resort's prospective guests around him. Soon the employee assembled an entourage of thirteen people. 'Thirteen is an unlucky number,' I automatically thought. 'If it weren't for the presence of Nolan Phillips, who was traveling alone, the number of people being transported would be a more acceptable dozen,' I reckoned. The hotel driver very efficiently loaded everyone's luggage inside the rear compartment of the large pink van and the excited tourists all found comfortable seats after clambering inside.

The trip from the airport on St. George's Island to downtown Hamilton on Bermuda Island was about six scenic miles. The vehicle passed merry tourists riding on mopeds, the basic means of transportation for the more courageous and independent-minded island visitors.

The driver courteously pointed out various places of interest on our splendid route. The hotel van traveled over a picturesque bridge and then it motored through the village of Flatts. Stately boats gently rocked back and forth in a majestic canal of crystal-clear aqua-green water. The driver stopped and told us to scan the canal for varicolored tropical fish flitting about in the shallows and we all claimed to have seen at least five apiece, even though I never saw even one during the "mass hallucination."

Fifteen minutes later, the large pink van pulled into the main entrance to the elegant *Hamilton Princess Hotel*. The edifice was truly worthy of its dignified royal name. It was a pastel pink castle enveloped in and abounding with lush green semi-tropical landscaping. The extremely beautiful palace regally lorded over placid *Hamilton Harbor*.

I sauntered-up to the mahogany registration counter, showed my reservation voucher to the desk attendant and then presented my *MasterCard*. I received prompt polite service from an attractive brunette hotel clerk who possessed a distinct British accent.

"Here are some terrific pamphlets on sites of interest you might want to visit or itineraries you might desire taking during your stay," the pretty young lady communicated. "Be sure not to miss the colorful military band parade on Front Street on Wednesday night at eight. It's a must. Be sure to take your camera."

"I understand you have a ferry that goes over to the *Southampton Princess*," I inquired. "That's quite a convenience for your guests."

"Yes, and they leave every two hours," the registration clerk said, "and don't forget the glass bottom boats that take you out to some really wonderful coral reefs," the young lady reminded me. "People often tell me they come back here just to see the beauty of it all over again."

I thanked the well-mannered obliging young woman for her assistance and then turned toward Joanne and was troubled to see Nolan Phillips standing several yards behind us in a parallel long registration line. I tried ignoring his presence but then my wife gave the ubiquitous annoyance a half-hearted wave. My concentration was interrupted by the voice of the charming brunette female clerk. "By the way Sir, I must tell you that you do have a very familiar face," she stated. "Have you ever been told about that resemblance before?"

I felt like screaming out, 'Look on a U.S. ten-dollar-bill, remove the guy's wig by placing your thumb over *his* head, and see if you could figure out the great mystery, you fool!' but I miraculously controlled myself along with my notorious volatile temper.

The young lady's question really pestered me because its timing coincided with the disquieting appearance of Nolan Phillips at the registration counter. I knew that the young lady's inquiry was purely innocent but nevertheless at the time, its utterance irritated me.

"I only wish I knew who my anonymous twin is," I answered the clerk's commentary. "You can't imagine how many people ask me that same question. I think I'm getting some sort of phobia over it," I added, "but somehow, I've managed to live with the vexing riddle."

A cheerful bellhop brought our four luggage pieces down the magnificent mahogany-paneled lobby that featured an exquisite pink marble floor. Expensive vases, paintings, wall tapestries and statues ornamented the stately corridor on both sides. Our room guide next conducted Joanne and me through several smaller hallways and then into the oldest section of the well-constructed palace. We were swiftly led across a verdant garden that featured hibiscus bushes and tall royal palm trees, which could have rivaled any that might have flourished in Eden. We finally arrived at our well-appointed suite situated in the newest section of the inimitable hotel.

Our accommodations overlooked the salt-water pool in the forefront and the calm waters of aqua-blue *Hamilton Harbor* in the serene background.

"This is no doubt the same view that Mark Twain enjoyed here at the *Princess,*" I theorized and reported to Joanne while feigning enthusiasm. "The guy had good taste and good eyesight too."

"We gotta' commend my favorite literary genius on his terrific selection of accommodations," my wife replied. "I'll have my Advanced English class read a selection of chapters from *Tom Sawyer* when I'm assigned my new teaching schedule in September."

Being in a blithe spirit, I gave a five-dollar tip to the appreciative bellboy. Joanne and I unpacked our suitcases and she put away her cosmetics in the bathroom vanity and I stored away our toiletries inside two matching bureaus. After getting the remainder of our things situated, we donned our bathing suits and scampered out to the salt-water pool as if we were a couple of carefree school kids.

A friendly employee advised me that beach towels could be obtained near the fresh water pool on the opposite side of the hotel's central promenade. Upon returning from my errand with the towels, I became angered when I noticed Nolan Phillips, in a tight-fitting French bathing suit, casually talking with my wife. Sensing that I was distraught with his presence, the bothersome fellow dismissed himself from *our* company before certain confrontation would ensue.

"I'm going to try a rum-swizzle at the hotel's Flamingo Bar," Phillips announced just before departing. "Care to join me for a few libations?"

"Maybe tomorrow, Nolan," I rankled, "because we're just getting used to the place. And besides, Joanne and I are still a little exhausted from the flight and from the long waiting lines in the airport and in the hotel."

When Nolan Phillips left our presence, I jealously interrogated my wife. "What did he talk to you about?" I demanded to Joanne. "And what was so amusing between you two? He must think our relationship is weak and vulnerable."

"Just wait a minute," my wife warned, "you're overreacting a bit, don't you' think?"

"Before this week's up that obnoxious creep's gonna' swallow his teeth!" I threatened. "All twelve of them," I sarcastically added.

"Please stop being so nasty, Hamilton," Joanne insisted. "Nolan seems like a very lonely man. He's just trying to be friendly. I can't understand for the life of me why *you* despise him so. You must have had an unhappy childhood and very few close friends!"

I had difficulty concealing the extreme animosity my total being felt for Nolan Phillips. "Maybe you're right, but I have my doubts about him having any honorable motives," I lectured Joanne like a modern-day Diogenes. "I just don't like how he boldly approaches you when I'm in the airplane's lavatory or when I'm off for forty seconds to pick up a pair of beach towels. I really trust you Honey," I confided, "but I don't trust Phillips as far as I can throw him. I guess I'm basically a very possessive husband."

That Monday evening Joanne and I had supper on the American Dinner Plan in the regal *Three Crowns Restaurant*. My emotions had finally adjusted back to an even keel from the afternoon's brief encounter with rather aggravating Nolan Phillips. From a small nearby lounge my wife and I heard a band playing a nostalgic medley of Frank Sinatra hit tunes.

After sumptuous dinners of shrimp and crab-meat delicacies, Joanne and I stepped to the romantic musical lounge where we were enjoying tropical rum-based cocktails. We intimately danced and romanced to the familiar powerful lyrics of "My Way."

"Ginger, I didn't mean to explode like I did at the pool today," I confessed and apologized. "I'm a little edgy being in a foreign place with so many strangers surrounding me."

"You always do things *your way* regardless of the circumstances," my spouse declared while alluding to the Sinatra song we were dancing to. "Give Nolan a chance to prove himself," Joanne objectively suggested. "He seems lonelier than you are, as hard as that is to believe. At least you have me to lean on."

The six-piece band took an intermission break. My wife and I made peace and strolled like two newly-weds hand-in-hand back to our secluded table. I glanced across the almost empty room and saw Nolan Phillips sitting all by his lonesome. Joanne followed a whim and suggested that I invite him over for a drink. I stubbornly refused.

Much to my astonishment my wife signaled for the reprehensible acquaintance to join our company. I was deeply distressed by Joanne's gesture of sympathy. Nolan Phillips casually strolled over to our cozy table. We ordered a round of tropical drinks and randomly talked about college fraternities, pro' football and the Venus and Mars natures of men and women. After we consumed a few more rounds of drinks Phillips didn't seem like such a bad fellow after all.

"Where did you go to college?" I inquired. "You have a North Jersey accent. I'll bet you attended either *Seton Hall* or *Fairleigh Dickinson*."

"*New York University,*" Phillips corrected. "I'm a prosecutor assigned to the Manhattan *DA's* office. What fraternity did you belong to?"

"Lambda Phi Sigma at *Glassboro State College,*" I said, "and then, I transferred to *Rutgers University* in New Brunswick and became a Kappa Phi, studied architecture and am now a builder. I also loyally serve as a Hammonton town councilman back in Jersey."

I volunteered to amble over to the bar and get a third round of tropical cocktails, since our waiter was nowhere in sight. The beleaguered bartender had trouble hearing my order because the band had returned from its break and started playing again and I had to loudly scream my requests above the catchy melody of "New York, New York."

As I turned around, my soul became infected with grief and inflamed with hate. I detected Nolan Phillips jitterbugging with Joanne. My next reaction was thinking that I did not want to cause a wild scene. 'Could this creep be so insanely stupid that he can't read my absolute contempt of him?' I wondered. 'When the time and place are right, I'll gladly read him the riot act for sure,' I thought.

When the two nimble dancers returned to our table, I told Joanne that I was experiencing a very vicious headache. I insisted that *we* should return to our luxury suite so that I could relax. Nolan noticed my sudden discomfort and sensing my enmity toward him the jerk diplomatically asked to be excused from our presence for the evening. As he nonchalantly walked away, I glared menacingly at his back like a mongoose scrutinizing a cobra.

On the return to our suite, Joanne and I stopped to converse at Adams Lounge, a large colonial hall of great grandeur inside the hotel. Our conversation, which centered upon Nolan Phillips, became a little too raucous for our fellow pedestrians to hear in *our* sophisticated public environment. The argument continued as we stepped briskly down the corridor to the privacy of our quarters. Inside I had to control myself from angrily slapping Joanne across her face. I recalled wishing that we had gone to the Bahamas instead.

"I never want to see you dancing with that lousy creep again, do you hear?" I wildly demanded. "He's up to no good! Can't you sense that in him?"

"You're a very vain, shallow and jealous man!" my wife shouted back. "You're an ingrate!"

"Maybe so, but I'm really going to hurt that idiot if he doesn't figure out which women he can't become aggressive with! He needs a good pulverizing!"

Tuesday morning, Joanne and I rented mopeds to further explore the city of Hamilton and its vicinity. It was great fun sightseeing the island and leisurely stopping at various unscheduled destinations. The warmth in our fragile relationship seemed to be rekindled.

At noon, we took a lunch break at a side-street fast food stand several miles outside Hamilton. A blue and white striped canopy covered a rear garden area where customers could eat in American picnic style, insulated from distracting highway noise. Joanne and I had hamburgers, French fries *Cokes* and some frank conversation.

After consuming the "American cuisine", we decided to ride our motorbikes over to Flatts Village to again enjoy the fantastic view the place provided. But then Joanne's moped refused to start. I was never mechanically inclined and my futile attempts at correcting the malfunction proved it. Then a very suspicious and repugnant thing happened.

Nolan Phillips climbed out of a nearby rented car and offered to transport Joanne's incapacitated bike in his trunk back to the *Princess Hotel* Rental Agency. I reluctantly agreed to *his* cavalier show of friendship. I didn't trust his intentions or his sincerity. I wondered how he had managed to show up right in the height of the motorbike crisis. Nolan Phillips was the last person in the world I wanted to owe a favor.

I hypothesized that Phillips had surreptitiously tampered with Joanne's motorbike, rendering it immobile so that the devious fellow could arrive on the scene and role-play "Mr. Messiah." I did not relish the notion that the obnoxious man had been keeping our private movements on the islands under close surveillance.

I drove Joanne to the *Hamilton Princess Hotel* with her riding on the back of my moped with her arms wrapped around my waist. I told her en route to Hamilton that it had been more than coincidental that Phillips showed-up at the exact same time as when the moped suddenly became inoperable. My wife saw matters differently.

"The guy's doing us a really big favor by taking my rented moped back to the hotel and now you're being totally vindictive and ungrateful for him helping us out," my wife chided. "You wouldn't be happy if you had a hundred-dollar-bill and were the only kid in a candy store."

Nolan Phillips had dropped Joanne's moped off at the Princess Rental Agency before Ginger and I got back to the Hamilton resort. I observed him standing next to the outdoor business counter smoking a cigarette and glancing nervously every now and then at his *Rolex* wristwatch.

At the counter, the rentals' manager gave my wife and me a twenty-dollar rebate for our "unfortunate inconvenience." The amiable man then said that I looked exactly like someone else. I became a little peeved and told him to mind his "own moped business."

"Sir, I didn't mean to offend or quarrel with you," the gentleman qualified, "and believe me when I say I don't want to pry into your personal life."

"You've been on Bermuda for too long and are suffering from a warm-climate version of cabin fever," I retorted to the congenial fellow living six hundred miles away from the nearest continent. "You probably also think that my wife looks like Miss Universe!"

"Now that you've mentioned it," the British gentleman responded. The moped manager then indulgently laughed while Joanne gave me a Medusa-like stare that should have turned me into stone.

I slowly walked-over to Nolan Phillips and reluctantly thanked him for his unexpected assistance. He very deliberately winked at Joanne and me and then said, "It was the least I could do Hamilton." I wondered what "the most" Phillips could do really might be.

That night, my wife and I again dined at the *Three Crowns*. I had filet mignon and Joanne raved throughout the meal about her "fantastic" shrimp, clams and mussels' combo'. I was happy to see that Nolan Phillips was not around to torment my sanity. "Thank God *he's* no-where in sight to further instigate me," I mentioned to my traveling mate.

"You're just envious because Nolan is acting like Superman or the Lone Ranger," my wife very effectively needled. "He always comes to the rescue right when we need him. He's a Johnny with spots everywhere to be standing on."

"I need him like I need three broken ribs and two massive, malignant brain tumors," I sneered like a true chauvinist pig. "That guy's trouble with a capital T!"

Wednesday morning, my wife and I had continental breakfast in our well-appointed suite. We donned our swim suits and took the early morning ferry across Hamilton Harbor to the *Southampton Princess*. We improved our rapport by frolicking in the surf, snorkeling and sleeping for an hour on the pink-sanded beach.

At noon, my pretty Italian wife and I enjoyed a sumptuous seafood buffet at the resort's Whaler Inn and then we rode the ferry back to the more conservative *Hamilton Princess Hotel*. Joanne and I took turns showering and decided to have room service deliver our dinners.

Just before dusk, Ginger and I dressed in typical tourist attire and strolled six blocks to downtown Hamilton for the Wednesday night military parade that the girl at the hotel's reception counter had strongly recommended for us to see. The colorful event celebrated the *British Empire's* glory days during the late-colonial Victorian era. I sensed Nolan Phillips' presence in the crowd of spectators, but thankfully I did not see him anywhere in the throng throughout the hour-long elaborate military march spectacle.

"Will you please learn to relax and become a cooperative tourist," my wife reprimanded me towards the end of the parade pomp and pageantry. "You're obsessed over nothing! Why do you keep turning around? You're going to need a chiropractor before this trip is done. You should only rubberneck back in the states where reality is more informal."

"He's here. I know he's here scrutinizing our every move," I sullenly replied. "I know he's spying on us, that uncouth uncivil intruder."

"I think you're developing agoraphobia, claustrophobia and Nolan Phillips' phobia all at the same time," Ginger smartly and spontaneously answered my paranoia. "You need to lie down on a psychiatrist's couch and tell the mind doctor everything you know about your mother!"

On Thursday morning, I ambled-down to the lobby's Registration Desk and purchased two glass bottom boat tickets for a late morning coral reef expedition. When the genteel male clerk handed me the tickets I checked the immediate vicinity to ascertain that Nolan Phillips was not stealthily observing my personal activity at the main desk.

Later that morning, Joanne and I boarded the ominous-sounding *Perils of Fate* and were standing near the stern of the glass bottom boat. I gritted my teeth when my keen eyes perceived Nolan Phillips sauntering down the long narrow dock ramp heading in the direction of the sightseeing boat. The rogue was the last passenger to board the *Perils of Fate,* which soon eased from its mooring and cruised into *Hamilton Harbor,* hardly leaving a wake.

The genial captain was knowledgeable and pointed-out various places of interest to his captivated all-tourist audience. Joanne gave Nolan Phillips a tentative wave. I gave him the absolute cold-shoulder treatment. I sensed that conflict was imminent but tried appearing generally civil and benign.

The *Perils of Fate* passed through an open drawbridge that connected two parts of Somerset Island, the last major link in the eastern Bermuda chain. The captain navigated his vessel to a rendezvous point about a quarter of a mile out to sea where *we* joined up with four other glass-bottom boats originating from other hotels and marinas, forming what my erratic mind synthesized as a "sightseeing armada." The ship's pilot explained over the intercom speakers that the five boats would motor out to the coral reef and view the spectacle one ship at a time in a "caravan on water" so that the sea animals below would not be disturbed in their natural habitat.

While the captain was addressing his alert enchanted passengers over the intercom, I overheard Ginger chatting with the same ladies that had been on our flight from Philly'. The gossipers were exchanging ideas about different merchandise and clothing bargains available on Front Street. In the meantime, I was involved in deeply thinking about how to resolve certain negotiations of my own.

I decided to define some basic terms with my assumed adversary. I figured it was time to let Nolan Phillips know my exact sentiments about his constant intrusions. I approached the agitator's position on the other side of the glass bottom boat. The scoundrel leech was looking-down at the colorful coral reef, admiring its beauty.

"I'll level with you, Phillips," I diplomatically began, "I would like to be on friendly terms with you for the remainder of my vacation here. I'm a very jealous man," I strongly maintained, "and I would appreciate it if you would stay away from my wife. That means keeping your eyes and hands off of her, is that perfectly clear?"

"Look here, Hamilton, I'm not trying to make time with your wife if that's what you're implying!" Phillips defensively stated with a florid face. "Your wife reminds me of an attractive girl I used to date in Manhattan. Joanne brings back pleasant memories of Cindy."

"That's a very unimaginative and completely lackluster excuse," I curtly answered. "But I'm warning you, Nolan; lay off or there's going to be big trouble in paradise. Stop stalking my wife like you're some kind of predator!"

The captain's voice came over the intercom's speakers and he instructed all passengers to report to the "below deck." He then maneuvered the *Perils of Fate* to a favorable position directly above a marvelous array of tropical fish, thick vegetation and coral resplendence. Soon everyone was below and partaking of the real-life visual fantasy, that is, everyone except Nolan Phillips and me. I wanted to continue our disagreement in private.

"Look, Phillips. It's not my fault Joanne looks like an old flame of yours," I emphasized. "Just remember pal, she's still *my* wife regardless of how your warped mind associates her with your past! I'm not going to allow *your* past to interfere with *my* present!"

"Ya' know, Hamilton. Your mind contrives situations that don't really exist. You're always trying to reinvent reality and then define it in your own neurotic terms," Phillips assertively accused, "and I seriously do believe, if I may add, that you need professional psychological help!"

"Tell me the truth," I adamantly insisted. "Did you follow us to the luncheonette outside Hamilton the other day and tamper with Joanne's moped while we were eating? Did you stoop to committing that kind of vile sabotage?"

"You've really gone off the deep end!" Phillips hollered while losing his temper. "You're crazy! Neurotic! Psychotic! You need the services of a competent shrink quick!"

I roughly grabbed Nolan's arm to indicate my seriousness. He attempted escaping my tight grasp. We violently wrestled against the railing above the boat's stern. Phillips frantically swung his clenched right fist twice at my jaw. I blocked his first punch but his third blow caught me solidly in the chest. We fiercely grappled some more, as the captain monotonously continued his loud lecture into his microphone, his voice being amplified over the boat's speakers.

I managed to get my right hand free from my tormentor's grasp and savagely smashed Phillips with an uppercut to his chin. It was a lucky clean shot I had delivered that stunned him in his tracks. The lummox staggered backwards from my blow's force. We had

88

degenerated into two desperate animals, primitively struggling for survival. Danger was not a concern. The laws of civilization had been abandoned. We were strenuously battling for dominance in a two-man jungle.

I wrapped my hands around Phillips' throat and squeezed firmly with all my might. My heart wanted to strangle the man in the worst possible way in order to achieve my ultimate victory. We were both desperately gasping for air, panting like two lung cancer patients. Adrenaline rushed through my arteries and veins, giving me extra strength. I twisted all my weight to the left and maniacally shoved Nolan Phillips over the boat's stern. My ears heard a loud splash. Thirty seconds went by on my *Hamilton* wristwatch. Nolan Phillips did not surface.

My obstinate ego defensively justified to my conscience that my extreme violence had been performed in self-defense. I considered leaping into the *Atlantic* but I instantly thought that the salvaging of *his* life wasn't sufficient motivation to convert me into a Good Samaritan exercising self-sacrifice. '*He* wouldn't do the same for me if our roles were reversed,' I selfishly speculated. 'I will live to enjoy the rest of my life at Nolan Phillips' expense,' I decided.

My pupils again intensely scanned the azure-emerald water below, searching for some evidence of the despicable brute, but there was no sign of his body. 'He's drowned and good riddance,' I thought. 'He's hit his head against the coral rock, went unconscious and drowned,' my stubborn mind concluded.

My lungs inhaled and exhaled ten deep breaths to help me regain my composure and my sanity. I tucked my light blue cotton shirt inside my blue denim jeans and then pretending that everything was normal, I furtively descended the black metal steps to listen to the captain's drab narration. Everyone standing in a circle below deck was preoccupied, visually appreciating the magnificent coral reef. No one ever noticed my stealthy arrival.

Joanne was still intermittently gossiping with her lady tourist friends, and did not observe my quiet return below deck. My conscience was now saturated with guilt but my heart felt little sorrow for Nolan Phillips' demise. My mind truly believed that I had vanquished a terrible foe. Phillips had been bent on wooing my wife and then destroying me in the process. I observed that the other more docile tourists were content staring down at the fabulous reef through the boat's glass bottom, so I pretended to do likewise in order to cunningly conceal the atrocious felony I had recently committed.

"If you'll all direct your attention to the direction of the bow," the captain suggested, "you'll see some really splendid tropical fish. Those two yellow ones are known as long-nosed butterflies. Those multicolored ones are queen angelfish. Look at those lobsters crawling near the center of the reef next to that impressive white brain coral."

The other tourists' eyes keenly focused on the underwater enchantment. I still was breathing heavily and perspiring from my traumatic ordeal that incidentally had exhausted most of my energy. My mind was spinning in a quandary as the captain continued his boring monologue.

"Have you ever seen such beauty anywhere before?" the boat's official narrator rhetorically asked. "There's a spotted goat fish to your right and that mean-looking critter over there is called a Nassau grouper."

The captain's glib presentation was rudely interrupted by an elderly woman's horrendous shriek. The startled lady pointed her forefinger to the right side of the glass bottom's underwater coral reef view. Everyone reflexively turned to witness the source of her terror. Soon there were numerous cries of shock and loud exclamations of disbelief.

Nolan Phillips' rigid body was seen floating beneath the boat, face down, slowly drifting toward the ridge of coral rock. His forehead banged into the coral reef and everyone aboard the vessel cringed except me. The impact turned his corpse sideways, facing the boat's bottom. Nolan's eyeballs were bulging out of their sockets. Screams of terror echoed throughout the cluster of shock-stricken passengers. The captain pleaded with the crowd to "quiet down, please don't panic!" But much to his dismay the mass hysteria continued.

Everyone else observing the gruesome phenomenon gasped, as Phillips' remains continued drifting with the current underneath the *Perils of Fate*, eventually wedging between the boat's hull and the immovable coral formation. Blood seeped out of the corpse's forehead and traces floated upwards from his mouth. The red water plume then filtered outward in the direction of the boat's glass bottomed pane. The stressed-out captain ineffectively commanded for his now-delirious passengers to climb up to the main deck.

90

The Harbor Police were notified of the tragedy. They sent an expert *SCUBA* team down and soon located and successfully removed Nolan Phillips' body from the sea, and the victim was immediately taken to the Hamilton Hospital Morgue.

That afternoon, I was visited in my hotel suite by a team of very intelligent detectives conducting a "routine investigation." The chief inspector believed Nolan's death "an apparent suicide" rather than a homicide. "Nolan Phillips had confided to me that he had been despondent, lonely and depressed," I divulged to the investigators. "He was in a total state of anxiety, sort of bipolar if you know what I mean," I clarified and continued. "I believe he was psychotic or perhaps even paranoid. When finally alone, I suspect that Nolan surrendered to his death wish and decided to abandon this cruel world once and for all."

Joanne related to the authorities that Nolan Phillips was "a lonely sort of man." Our corroborative statements were accepted as depositions to be presented during the coroner's inquest. The team of officers thanked us for our "cooperative, helpful observations and comments."

"His body does have a broken jaw," the chief inspector noted. "We know *that* fact even before any autopsy has been performed. Do you know anything about how that injury might have happened?"

"I saw his chin hit up against the coral reef as his head drifted below the glass bottom boat," I calmly testified under duress. The policemen conscientiously jotted-down my testimony on their report pads. I wisely hid the sore knuckles of my right hand behind my back while I was providing the examiners with the false information.

"Unless there's some radical change in venue," the chief inspector said, "you won't be detained on Bermuda for further questioning. I think you've both satisfied all our immediate concerns."

Friday was our last scheduled day on the heavenly main isle. Joanne wanted to purchase some souvenirs for our two nephews and niece. We agreed to separate and then meet again an hour later in front of the *Atlantic,* a huge tourist ship out of New York docked along Front Street.

I casually walked the pavement, strolling past a strip of shop window displays colorfully designed to lure American and European tourists inside. I glanced into a novelty photography store that took old time black and white pictures of vacationers dressed in "authentic historical period costumes." I stepped inside the cheerfully decorated establishment out of sheer curiosity. I must honestly confess that some mysterious psychic force seemed to attract my attention and then magnetically draw me into the store.

My eyes perceptively surveyed the wide variety of outfits on exhibit from different periods in history and I observed that the apparel was hanging on long display racks. I decided to try on a colonial costume along with an accompanying white wig. My fancy thought that Joanne would be delighted with a photo' of me attired in eighteenth century garb. 'She desperately needs me to show her something amusing so that she'll think I still possess a sense of humor,' I reckoned. My hands eagerly put on my chosen ensemble. A sprite British sales clerk assisted me with maneuvering into my complementing silk long-tailed coat. My blue eyes examined and appreciated my stellar appearance in a full-length mirror.

"Sir, if I may say so, you look just like that chap on the American ten-dollar-bill," the salesman alertly observed and stated. "Hamilton, I believe the man's name was. Never made it to President, did he?"

"No," I said. "He was assassinated before he could ever attain that high office."

The genial salesman was elated when I ordered ten reproductions of the original photo' he had taken of me dressed in the colonial haberdashery. I paid the affable gent in fifty and twenty-dollar denominations. I did not want to give him a ten-dollar bill and have him meticulously compare the portrait to my profile and I certainly didn't wish to give him my *MasterCard* with my name "Hamilton Alexander" on it standing out in bold relief.

At that odd moment, I was grateful that I didn't have to explain those particular details to the cheerful man, who was delightedly preoccupied making arrangements to send the ten duplicate photos to my New Jersey residence. I then asked for and received directions from the blithe salesman to the Hamilton Library. I told him I was a visiting college professor who needed to study an "important academic matter."

At the library, I located *Encyclopedia Britannica* H. I avidly read the biographical account of Alexander Hamilton. My interest was impressed that he had been the first U.S. Secretary of the Treasury and that he and Benjamin Franklin were the only two "non-presidents" honored by having their portraits engraved on American paper currency. The informative article further stated that Hamilton had been killed in a pistol duel with Aaron Burr in Weehawken, New

Jersey on July 11, 1804. 'July 11!' I thought in amazement. 'That was yesterday, the same day that Nolan Phillips had met his demise! What a weird coincidence!'

I rushed to grab *Encyclopedia Britannica* N. I thumbed through the pages and found the information for Philip Nolan, the coincidental name reversal of my deceased former enemy. Next to the listing was the instruction "See Edward Everett Hale." I directed my attention back to Encyclopedia H and leafed through the pages with great anticipation. My research yielded some satisfactory-staggering results.

Edward Everett Hale (1822-1909) was a distinguished clergyman, editor, humanitarian, and noteworthy author. He is most remembered for his popular novella *Man without a Country*. The tale, the encyclopedia explained, was about a young officer named Philip Nolan, who had exclaimed during a court martial hearing, "I never want to hear of the United States again." Nolan was placed on a warship and his commanding officers were instructed that no one would be permitted to provide the prisoner with any relevant news about the United States until *his* death. Philip Nolan was the notorious *Man without a Country*.

The article further indicated that Nolan had been court martialed by the Army because he had been suspected of being a disciple of Aaron Burr, a former maverick United States Vice President under Thomas Jefferson. The encyclopedia description detailed that according to Edward Everett Hale's story, Burr desired to carve out a new independent territory for aristocrats and Federalists in the American frontier. The article finished by clarifying that Philip Nolan was actually a fictitious character but that the story *Man without a Country* had been written in the style of a factual account and the famous tale was designed to muster Northern patriotism during the *Civil War*.

'Philip Nolan, a fictional character,' I pensively thought. My inquisitiveness had reached its ultimate peak. I found *Britannica Encyclopedia* B and frantically flipped through its pages until I located "Aaron Burr." I felt a trifle dizzy and giddy when I examined his portrait. The dimensions of the library room seemed to expand and contract several times during my intense scrutiny. Aaron Burr's documented portrait looked identical to the Nolan Phillips that I had briefly known on my Bermuda vacation.

Burr had murdered Alexander Hamilton in a gun duel on July 11, 1804. I looked very much like Hamilton. Nolan Phillips looked almost identical to Aaron Burr. I had been responsible for Nolan Phillips' death on July 11. The incredible 'dual events' were really 'duel events.'

'I've gotten revenge for a spectacular pistol duel that had occurred back in 1804,' I thought and considered while sitting inside the stone silent library. But quite confidentially, I felt no particular guilt or remorse for performing my evil deed aboard the ironically named *Perils of Fate*. After all, according to the infallible *Encyclopedia Britannica's* text, Philip Nolan was a fictitious character. Nolan Phillips had to be a reincarnation of that same fictitious character. I've objectively concluded that I did not murder Nolan Phillips. Let me be completely rational about this entire matter. It is absolutely impossible to kill a recycled imaginary fictional character from American literature. I must be genuinely specific in my astute analysis. 'Only a crazy person would think otherwise,' I intelligently evaluated and concluded.

"O. Bush, G. Alter & B. Sawyer"

I was driving my metallic blue *Buick LeSabre* towards Atlantic City, New Jersey on congested *Route 30* on a Saturday morning in March 2000. My destination was *Harrah's Casino* to try my luck at blackjack and to play an additional hundred-dollars-worth of video poker. On the way driving east on the *White Horse Pike,* I figured I would stop in at Hammonton's Silver Coin Diner to eat a decent hardy breakfast. I remember logically thinking, 'I have all day to lose my hard-earned money at the casino so what's the rush?'

After entering the bustling establishment, which was packed with mostly town patrons, I noticed that there was an end seat vacant at the busy counter. I sat down to the left of an acne-faced teenager, who seemed disinterested in my arrival while he concentrated his attention on devouring his breakfast of toast, ham and eggs.

I had learned in my college sociology class back in the mid-'60s that it is wrong to judge anyone by his or her appearance even though the personal stereotype is probably correct ninety percent of the time. Civilized people know that it is improper and downright discourteous to be presumptuous. "Prejudice is when you *pre-judge* someone," I remembered a discriminating professor had once lectured.

So, what if the kid had four fake silver chains and a bronze medallion dangling down from his dirty neck! So what if he wore baggy pants and sported an unkempt long shaggy hairstyle that looked like it could feed a colony of lice! 'I should not do the unthinkable and stereotype the young fellow,' I perceptively thought. I reckoned I would show some basic decency and strike up a casual conversation with the young man just to demonstrate that I was a friendly sort of guy. I wanted to show my young fellow-breakfast diner that I was an open-minded civil American citizen that respected everyone's sacred *Constitutional* rights.

"How ya' doin' there, amigo," I said in a very contrived friendly salutation. "I used to teach at the local high school; that is, before I intelligently retired two years ago. But I don't seem to remember you as being a student there. Are you from out of town?"

"Sort of," the kid succinctly mumbled with a gross amount of food and saliva spilling out from the corners of his enormous mouth. "I'm just passin' through the area and heading for Philly' for some recreation. I come around these parts once or twice a year."

"Where ya' from?" I persisted with my amiable interrogation. I figured the lad would say something like Berlin, Atco, Pleasantville, Folsom, Egg Harbor, Medford, or Atlantic City.

"I'm actually a time traveler from the year 2085," the teenager calmly answered. "I don't really stay in one place all too long."

"Sure, and I'm the nefarious Sheriff of Nottingham and I'm here in this diner looking for Robin Hood, Friar Tuck and Little John," I laughed. "I must say, young man, you have quite an active imagination. You wouldn't have any idea where the exotic-looking Maid Marian is, would you? I live just around the corner in the center of Sherwood Forest."

The thin teenager stared at me with a nasty scowl that seemed to exaggerate his strange-looking facial features. "Alright, don't believe me when I tell you I'm from the future; the future you'll never live to see!" the kid testily challenged. "See if I really care!"

I didn't desire to appear as rude as I had really been, so I humbly apologized for what *he* had perceived as a rather sarcastic remark. Strangers often misinterpret that I am anti-social but actually, I am usually very shy and reserved upon first contact. 'I oughta' humor this spoiled super-sensitive kid,' I thought. 'Then I can go home and look him up on the Sci-fi cable channel.'

"Tell me young man," I suavely stated to deftly disguise my very abundant skepticism. "Is your great-grandmother Chelsey Clinton?"

"Who in *Andromeda* is she?" he replied. "Does she live up on the space station? I remember a Dorothy Clinton from my third-grade astronomy class, but no Chelsey Clinton. Who is Chelsey Clinton anyway?"

"Former President Bill Clinton's daughter," I accurately clarified. "Never mind about her," I declared, truly believing that my new acquaintance was probably not a conscientious student of current events. "Well, who is the President of the United States in 2085?"

"Obadiah Bush," the kid casually responded quite matter-of-factly while munching away on his slightly burnt toast. "Obadiah Bush is President of the United States," he repeated with his mouth completely full. "And I didn't vote for the guy in my high school's mock election, either!"

"Is Obadiah Bush George W. Bush's grandson?" I innocently asked.

"Naw," the kid muttered as the wise-guy chewed another disgusting mouthful of his slightly burnt toast. "I think I read in a telebook somewhere that he's some long-gone politician named Jeb Bush's great-grandson."

A polite waitress exited the diner's swinging kitchen doors and approached the busy counter. She applied her pencil to her check pad and jotted down my simple order of pancakes, coffee, orange juice bacon and eggs. After the waitress rushed back through the swinging doors into the Silver Coin Diner's busy kitchen I realized that I had become rather intrigued by the laconic teenager's overall nonchalance regarding my questions about the future president. I decided to extend our conversation to the vital domestic and international issue arenas. I asked the lad what types of social problems plagued the USA in the year 2085.

"None," the kid tersely replied. "There aren't any major problems like there are in your time. President Obadiah Bush took care of all that stuff. Many people regard him as a born genius."

"How is that possible?" I insisted on knowing. "You must be gravely mistaken. There will always be wars and recessions. Everyone with half a brain knows that."

The enigmatic kid then explained that President Obadiah Bush had used his great influence to pass a very critical bill through Congress during his initial term as the nation's "CEO." All high school students were expected to graduate with honors and after age eighteen, a law mandated that every student was required to either serve four years in the military or an equivalent number of years performing vital social service. Then after demonstrating their patriotic dedication the young men and women of the future had earned *the right* to attend college. The twenty-two year-olds then would have a greater sense of maturity and responsibility upon entering universities. They would not goof off, would not frivolously join fraternities and sororities, would not party all the time, would not make having sex and orgies their avocations, and finally would not waste their parents' hard-earned money drinking beer and vodka. Everything seemed plausible.

"Wow!" I exclaimed. "That's a terrific idea you just described. Going into the military or doing four years' community service work delays adulthood," I marveled and uttered. I paused for a second to capture my next fleeting thought. "Then students will not graduate *Princeton* or *Michigan* until they're around twenty-six. College grads will finally be mature enough to enter the competitive job market place. That terrific plan you mentioned sounds very practical."

I proceeded to ask the kid about hot-button social problems such as teen pregnancies and abortions. The young man informed me that Dr. Gene Alter, a renowned *Nobel Prize* recipient from *Harvard,* had perfected a formula that effectively delays the onset of puberty until age thirty. Congress had passed a law in 2082 mandating that every infant had to be inoculated with the secret chemical solution right after his or her first birthday. The program was an important part of their required vaccination schedules.

"No teenage girls get pregnant anymore because of that amazing formula," I stated. "And stupid sexual urges are put on hold until well-after high school, and the onset of puberty is delayed well-after military training or mandatory social service and subsequent college attendance are under students' belts. Without destructive hormones interfering with essential brain functions," I continued my analysis, "college students could engage in very serious career pursuits. They could for the first time in history actually be bona fide college *students*. This creative story of yours is absolutely phenomenal!"

"Unfortunately," the kid said, "I'm still a virgin because of Dr. Alter's stupid research. That's one reason I often come back to your wonderful immoral time period, so that I can be with non-virgins. Nine out of ten kids that live in your time are innocent non-virgins, did you know that?"

"Don't feel badly and take it to heart," I sympathized with elementary compassion, "but I really like the idea that science is actively involved in prevention and in intervention. In the future kids' minds and instincts are no longer controlled by dumb biological impulses and temptations," I said to the adolescent above the din inside the diner.

I was wondering how the United States Congress managed to pass such controversial bills with the great philosophical divide separating Republicans and Democrats. "How did the Republicans ever push through such strong laws with the likes of the *ACLU*, the *NAACP* and *NOW* activists out there?" I curiously asked.

"There are no longer any robotic-like Republicans or Democrats," the young man indicated before burping loudly. "Only Republicrats and Demlicans exist in the future. President Obadiah Bush shrewdly made both parties learn to agree so much on all things. That's why there's little or no difference between them."

'This kid sitting next to me is either Nostradamus reincarnated, or an absolute fraud possessing a very rampant imagination,' I thought.

98

I wondered what had been done in 2085 in the area of ecology, so I requested clarification from the vernal guru, who incidentally appeared too knowledgeable to be believed. I wanted to know exactly what the time voyager had to say about the future world's environment now that Obadiah Bush had solved the country's fundamental educational and teenage delinquency crises and Dr. Gene Alter had effectively remedied the very formidable teenage pregnancy and abortion dilemmas. I was becoming more and more interested in the kid's past, which would naturally be my grandson's future. My inquisitive mind needed more explanations.

"What has the government done about preserving and conserving the environment?" I instinctively inquired. "Has air pollution been controlled? Have all the world's forests been restored?"

The unkempt-looking boy's response was very enlightening. He described in detail the remarkable sage Professor Branche Sawyer, who taught "Science and Forest Destruction" at *Waterloo University*. The remarkable genius was instrumental in developing two dynamic special waste-conversion machines. The first apparatus ingeniously manufactured oxygen and nitrogen from garbage, and the second amazing device produced carbon dioxide from raw sewage. According to my new acquaintance, President Obadiah Bush signed a law that every American household's residents must have their garbage disposal units and toilets and sinks hooked-up to the two wondrous inventions or else ten more years of military or social service was required of the wasteful non-law-abiding violators.

"That's great!" I observed and praised. "No more trash collection and expensive recycling of paper, metals and plastic rubbish. Those machines Professor Branche Sawyer invented can easily recycle nature without any need to have trees, rain forests and plants doing the job. You don't need any more 'Save the environment' campaigns or fancy catchy slogans," I declared. "You don't need people and animals exchanging oxygen and carbon dioxide with plants and bushes any more to keep the complicated life cycles going."

"That's basically correct," the young man readily agreed, "and all the trees on the Earth have just about been chopped down and it really doesn't matter too much whether we have them or not. I mean, who really cares about toothpicks or splinters when you have plenty of garbage and waste?" the lad rhetorically asked. "But when ya' need toothpicks or sawdust, ya' gotta' have a few of those stupid forests around to knock down."

I began to place some credence in the young man's insistent claim that the human enigma was indeed a genuine time traveler. I suddenly converted into my greed-mode and thought that I might materially profit from *our* chance encounter. "How about some good stock tips?" I pleaded. "And please tell me, who's gonna' win the next *World Series* and the next *Super Bowl*? If you could just tell me those simple things, you can stop here at this diner every Saturday morning and I promise I'll buy you breakfast."

"Forget it, you self-centered moocher," the youthful Silver Coin Diner customer criticized. "Spend all your dough while it's still worth something. The *Greater Second Stock Market Crash* will happen on December 23, 2030. You have just a few more years to lose all you've got before you *will* definitely lose all you've got."

"Wow! The winter solstice," I acknowledged. "But on December 21, 2012 the world's supposed to end! Just like the ancient Mayan calendar predicted. Disaster and doom are scheduled to happen on *that* dangerous date. Those Mayan priests really knew every *Aztec aspect* of their astrology!" I wholeheartedly joked.

The future boy wonder was not-at-all impressed with any aspect of the Aztec or Mayan calendars. He switched subjects and related that he was on his merry way to an *N*Sync* concert at Philadelphia's *First Union Center*. "If I drop out of high school," the kid explained, "the law states that I'd have to be trained by the government to work in a factory or do boiler-room telemarketing to recruit more lazy people into the Army or Navy. What a horrible punishment! I'd much rather be here sittin' and talkin' with you!"

"Well then," I said. "If you're under so much pressure to succeed in the year 2085, why are you sitting here in this diner eating breakfast right now? Shouldn't you be home studying your subjects? If you flunk out of high school, you'll then qualify for the government's cruel and unusual rehab' punishment programs."

"I need some recreation time, real bad," the boy declared. "My high school curriculum is really intense. I like going to *N*Sync* concerts because Oldies music tends to calm my nerves. Once in a while I also check out the *Back Street Boys,* too."

I dared not ask the youth what the music of the year 2085 sounded like when today's rap and hip-hop songs sound so much like maniacal urban dissonance. Before I could proceed with our extraordinary discussion the unpredictable kid pulled out a shiny metallic object from his jacket's left pocket. I mentally examined the

100

queer-looking item as he held it in his hand and generally described the instrument's very unique functions.

Four designations were on the metallic object's top segment: a Pound Key, a Star Key, and buttons P (Place) and T (Time). The rest of the exquisite "Time Calculator's" surface contained red-colored buttons labeled zero through nine. The boy continued showing me his fantastic "Space/Time Pocket Coordinator" device as he identified its various fascinating features. To tell the truth, the casing looked authentic and it appeared that it very possibly could perform all the fantastic capabilities that the kid claimed it possessed.

"This sophisticated transporter is my own personal molecular atomic space/time/matter compressor and re-materializer," he casually explained, "and it can transport me to any desired location in any specific time period."

"Sort of like Scotty doing his beaming-up thing on *Star Trek,*" I smartly added.

"Who the heck is Scotty?" my fellow customer asked. "Is he your dog?"

My eyes glanced down at the young man's notepad that had been placed between us on the diner's front counter. On it were scribbled nine numbers, which I attempted to memorize their arrangement. Without any warning or clue, the young fellow said "See ya'!" He grabbed his notepad, pressed a sequence of buttons on his magical calculator and then instantly disappeared in a flash into thin air.

My eyes looked-around the crowded diner, and all of the other patrons were preoccupied chattering and kibitzing, completely oblivious to the futuristic *N*Sync* fan's hasty-but-impressive departure. My next instinct was to search under the counter. I was still in a stupor about the boy's incredible testimonies regarding his future world when the harried waitress approached carrying my breakfast order.

I volunteered to pay for the boy's meal and politely instructed the diner employee to simply add his $4.98 tab to my bill. 'His company was worth the small additional expense,' I thought. 'If he was a fraud, he was indeed a very intriguing fraud.'

The next morning, I awoke at 8 a.m. with an inspiration. I would call the eight-digit number the kid had scribbled at the diner on his note-pad's front cover. I anxiously lifted a pen and jotted down the numbers I had recalled from the Silver Coin. I wanted to know if the oddball juvenile had been a terrible hoax and I also wanted to know exactly where he lived. I slowly and carefully dialed the number and I was happy to hear the voice of the youthful *N*Sync* fan on the other end of the line.

At first, he was not-too-thrilled to be hearing from me because where he was, it was five o'clock in the morning. Gradually I got the kid to come to his senses and he stopped being so grumpy and defiant over the telephone.

After I apologized for my waking him up, we amiably talked for over an hour. I didn't learn too much more about the year 2085 because all the kid really wanted to talk about was N*Sync, Britney Spears, Madonna, Fleetwood Mac and the Back Street Boys.

Yesterday, I stepped out to my mailbox and picked up my long-distance phone bill. After re-entering the house, I opened the envelope and then inspected the list of long distance calls I was being charged for. One particular number had been billed for the incredible sum of $987.52. I angrily lifted my living room phone from its cradle and promptly dialed my long distance company.

"Hello," a pleasant female voice greeted, "how may I help you?"

"Look, I just received my monthly phone statement," I hollered like a maniac, "and one call is erroneously listed here for the amount of $987.52! There's gotta' be some gross error here! I'm not paying for your company's negligence in keeping accurate records."

The well-trained operator suavely instructed me to patiently wait on the line while she did her due diligence and professionally conducted her competent investigation into my inquiry. In the meantime, I was able to harness my emotions and simmer down a bit.

The woman's soothing cordial voice returned. She skillfully read the appropriate relevant information off of her computer screen. "Sir, you had spoken for one hour after calling San Diego," she aptly stated.

"That's right," I admitted and confirmed. "And I did speak with someone in San Diego, a teenager I believe."

"The San Diego call was a 900 number. The cost of the service was over sixteen dollars a minute. Wow sir, that's a pretty expensive 900 number you were calling!"

"What!" I very nastily shouted. "You must be joking! That's impossible! The first numbers on the billing are 1-999 and not 1-900! I had called a 999 number and not a 900 number."

"Sir," the operator eloquently interrupted my wild rant. "Apparently, they have run out of 900 numbers out in California just like they had run out of 1-800 numbers all over the country. You could easily solve this kind of problem by not making any *future 900* or *999* phone calls."

My right hand slammed my green living room telephone down into its cradle. I grabbed the sheet of paper upon which I had scribbled the young man's futuristic San Diego phone number. I hastily ripped the paper to shreds and then promptly threw the tiny flakes into my kitchen garbage compactor. I cared less that in the year 2085 vital oxygen would be efficiently made out of common household rubbish.

"The Attic Television"

On *New Year's Eve,* December 31, 2001, John Peter Walker was celebrating his forty-eighth birthday with a bottle of his favorite scotch, *Johnny Walker Red.* The brand name of his most preferred whiskey had been chosen for consumption as equally by coincidence as it had by design. When on required business trips *Johnny Walker Red* was the introverted tycoon's most requested "on the rocks" drink in bars from Miami Beach to Honolulu. The tycoon was certainly addicted to that specific brand of whiskey.

John P. Walker was the richest man in Hammonton, and perhaps the wealthiest investor and entrepreneur in all of southern New Jersey. His good fortune all started with the acquisition of the family's road-paving materials' patent, which eventually led to lucrative contracts and enormous royalties from other area, national and international asphalt contractors. John's deceased father had acquired and owned the road sealant patent, but since the company founder had focused his energies on the day-to-day operations of his business the elder Walker never pursued the exclusive formula's economic potential. By 1990, John Peter Walker had taken over the firm and had amassed sufficient capital to finance a small army of equipment to honor major road-surfacing contracts all over the tri-state *Delaware Valley* region.

'Dad would have been mighty proud of my accomplishments,' Walker thought about his deceased benefactor as he liberally poured several ounces of premium scotch over a glass containing four ice cubes. 'I've parlayed my father's small paving business into a financial monster having no serious rival firms within a thirty-mile radius of Hammonton. It's too bad you and mom didn't live to see *my* great success,' John P. Walker lamented as he raised his glass to his lips, respectfully saluting an oil portrait of his deceased parents on the mansion's den wall. Then the highway-paving mogul slowly sipped the rich whiskey, savoring its unique taste. 'Yes Dad and Mom,' the young man sincerely acknowledged, 'I'm grateful for my inheritance and I promise I'll be diligently pursuing the company's excellent reputation until the day I die!'

A rapping at the walnut-paneled den's door was followed by the entrance of Giles pulling a handle and Hillary pushing the rear of a metal squeaky-wheeled cart having an ancient table-model television on its top.

"Where should we leave it, Mr. John?" Giles Wood, Walker's faithful butler politely asked his rather eccentric and presently apathetic employer.

"Next to that far wall near the electrical socket," Walker pointed and answered rather imperatively. "Right in front of that shelf of rare books."

"Don't tell me, Sir, that you plan on watching this old rather obsolete contraption?" Hillary Wood, the loyal Walker' maid jested. "This thing is as old as *you* are. In fact, it *is* exactly as old as you are!"

"You don't say," John P. Walker lazily replied. "Then, that bulky museum piece would've had to be manufactured in or around the remarkable year 1954," he added realizing the unique parallel.

"That is correct," Giles affirmed with absolute certainty. "It was manufactured the same year *you* were born, exactly forty-eight years ago. What a curious coincidence! But I'm afraid that this antique has seen better days."

"They don't make *Emersons* anymore," Walker seriously interrupted. "If I recall from my childhood this particular unit was one of *that* company's most popular items. It has a twenty-one-inch bowed screen with a control panel on the left," the mansion owner recollected and related. "And I still vividly remember this relic from when I was a kid sitting on my Daddy's knee. My God Giles and Hillary, time marches on, doesn't it?"

"Many brand names have gone out of business since then in the television market," Giles recollected and mentioned. "Besides *Emerson,* I remember TV sets with extinct names like *Muntz, Philcoo, DuMont,* and *Admiral.* Those TV products have all gone the way of the *Edsel, the Hudson,* and the *Packard* in the post *World War II* automobile industry."

The very wealthy man contemplated his fleet of thirteen classic cars parked in a huge garage recently added onto his impressive mansion, one of which was a mint-condition '54 brown *Packard.* His reverie was interrupted as the conversation continued.

"And Mr. Walker," the maid courteously stated. "It was very kind of you to donate this exquisite *Emerson* television to the Hammonton Historical Society Museum. It's indeed a real collectors' item," Hillary Wood continued, "and it was only gathering a pound of dust up in the attic. My husband and I thoroughly cleaned it up from top to bottom before we carefully transported it to your den.”

“That will be all for now,” John P. Walker thanked his servants before gulping down another mouthful of his favorite scotch. “Giles and I will take it over to the historical society on Wednesday. Tomorrow’s *New Year’s Day* and I guarantee you no one will be there to accept this noteworthy treasure from the ‘50s. Giles,” Walker continued his reminiscence, “do you remember us watching shows like *Ed Sullivan, Jackie Gleason, Milton Berle, Jack Benny,* and *I Love Lucy* on this splendid device?”

“I most certainly do, Sir,” the straightlaced butler recalled. “And if my failing memory serves me correctly, we also had viewed many episodes of *Howdy Doody, Dragnet, The Life of Riley, American Bandstand,* and *Ozzie and Harriet,* too.”

“*Ozzie and Harriet,*” Walker indulgently laughed. “The perfect ‘50s American family. If only life today was as simple and laid back as it had been back in the nifty fifties. Of course,” the multimillionaire continued prattling, “I’ve become filthy rich over the last dozen years,” the road-paving baron boasted. “So, I guess I can trade a little complicated existence and aggravation for a modern huge bank account. In the final analysis,” Mr. John Peter Walker assessed, “the prospect of a prosperous and profitable 2002 doesn’t seem that bad after all. Cheers to the *New Year!”* the wealthy fellow said as he lifted his glass.

“Anything you say Mr. Walker,” Giles quite amiably agreed. “I must congratulate you! You must be a very intelligent man since you’ve made many clever strategic money decisions to expand the family’ business in the last decade.”

“Actually, Giles, my decisions involved more luck than intellect,” Walker reluctantly acknowledged to his butler. “It was more like being in the right place at the right time than anything else. But I want to thank you both for finding and bringing in this archeological artifact,” the happy resident related. “Stop by after midnight and we’ll celebrate the *New Year* by polishing-off the remainder of this fine bottle of scotch. See you both in about an hour right before the grandfather clock chimes strike twelve. And Giles,” Walker said with a smile. “Don’t forget to grease those squeaky wheels on that metal cart.”

"Thank you, Sir, and I promise you I won't forget," Giles pleasantly answered. Then the butler and his accommodating wife jointly exited the luxurious den.

John P. Walker was a self-confirmed recluse. He shied away from having close friends, thinking that they would be more interested in his prolific *Merrill Lynch Cash Management Account* than in the distrustful man's true companionship. There were hundreds of acquaintances in his computer e-mail address book, but his dependable friends could be counted twice on a thumb-less hand. 'A secret is only a secret when it belongs to me,' the slightly paranoid man reckoned. 'As soon as it is shared with one other person it's a secret in jeopardy.'

The self-made businessman poured another glass of delicious scotch and sat back on his cranberry-colored soft leather sofa. 'Materialism is great,' he thought. John P. Walker was tempted to grab his remote control and activate his large-screen television featuring stereo sound, but suddenly the middle-age gentleman felt a temptation to get up and casually saunter over to the early '50s *Emerson* set that was still situated on top of the squeaky-wheeled metal cart.

Then, Walker chuckled as he had an inspiration. 'I'm going to plug this baby in to see if I could get more than static on the screen,' he laughed, placing his scotch drink on top of the convenient TV cabinet. 'I wonder if this antiquated thing still conducts electricity after sitting idle up in the attic for over forty years. I suppose I'll soon find that out!'

John P. Walker reached around the set and soon found the device's electric plug. Then he inserted the two-pronged object into the wall socket, meticulously turned the "ON/OFF" knob inside the control panel, adjusted the "rabbit ears" and impatiently waited to see if anything would happen.

In ten seconds, the vintage *Emerson* TV's picture tube illuminated. John rotated the station selector to 1, noticing that the old set had thirteen channels on its dial. To Walker's delight and amazement, a news broadcaster appeared on the black and white picture tube. The mildly astonished man increased the set's volume on the control panel, lifted his scotch on the rocks from the top of the television cabinet and then returned to his soft cranberry-leather sofa.

"Why that's Douglas Edwards sitting behind a studio desk, doing his nightly news program!" John P. Walker marveled and uttered.

"This must be a '50s television rerun special or something," the viewer theorized and softly expressed. "That news show went off the air maybe thirty-five years ago, and Douglas Edwards is certainly now deader than a doornail, no doubt about it. Gee, nostalgia is a wonderful thing!" he said to no one but himself'. "Let's see what good old deceased Douglas Edwards has to report."

"In January news," Douglas Edwards began his broadcast, "the highly motivated Michigan State Spartans defeated the UCLA Bruins in the annual *Rose Bowl Game* by a score of 28-10. The football extravaganza was played before a capacity crowd in Pasadena, California. Now moving on to some favorable economic news," Douglas Edwards said and paused as his hands shuffled to the next page, "*General Motors* has announced that the giant corporation is planning a one billion dollar retooling and expansion to its popular line of automobiles, which includes *Chevrolet, Pontiac, Oldsmobile, Buick,* and *Cadillac.* In other jobs-related news," the serious-faced Douglas Edwards remarked, "on January 19th, the Senate will approve construction of the *St. Lawrence Seaway*. The new project is designed to..."

John P. Walker reckoned he would step to the fascinating television set and perform an experiment by manually changing the channel. Returning to his soft leather sofa, the successful entrepreneur was more than surprised to notice that Douglas Edwards was also doing the news on Channel 2 as he had been presenting on Channel 1. Walker could not believe his eyes and his ears upon contemplating the bizarre phenomenon. The wealthy fellow settled into his comfortable seat, poured another generous measure of *Johnny Walker Red* onto the shrunken ice cubes in his glass, and started to imbibe more of the potent alcohol as he again scrutinized the black and white TV screen.

"On February 2nd of this year, President Eisenhower officially disclosed for the record that the first hydrogen bomb had been detonated back in 1952 at Eniwetok Atoll in the Pacific," Douglas Edwards reported. "The bomb was extremely powerful, according to sources, and it..."

John P. Walker had again risen from the sofa and changed back to Channel 1 to test a theory that was swimming-around inside his half-intoxicated mind. The results of his effort proved rather disconcerting to his sense of rationality because the aforementioned Douglas Edwards broadcast was still in progress.

"In a special message to Congress," Douglas Edwards read from his teleprompter, which apparently was now functioning properly, "President Eisenhower today urged widespread modifications to the much-maligned Taft-Hartley labor law. It should be noted that our chief executive has staunchly advocated a return to flexible farm price supports."

The bewildered viewer switched back to Channel 2. Douglas Edwards was calmly reporting another pertinent event to his faithful American audience. "On February 23rd, Dr. Jonas Salk, the developer of a breakthrough serum against polio, administered injections of the vaccine to Pittsburgh school children. The inoculations are scheduled to continue for the remainder of the month and then the results will be evaluated throughout the course of the year," the news sole anchorman disclosed. "And now on the entertainment scene, *The Confidential Clerk,* a popular play by celebrated writer T.S. Eliot opened at New York City's Morosco Theater. The new *Broadway* production stars Claude Rains and Ina Claire as..."

'This is absolutely incredible!' John P. Walker imagined. 'Each channel seems to correspond to a different month in 1954. Channel 1 was January and Channel 2 is February. If my crazy theory is correct, Channel 3 will be March.' The man's head was dizzy from the shock of his stark observation and from the accumulative potency of the scotch whiskey.

Sure enough, Channel 3 was featuring the March 1954 news, so John Peter Walker tried twisting his neck first left and then right to shake out the loose cobwebs and to sober up a bit. Being thoroughly intrigued by the surreal mystery his eyes and mind had been interpreting, the extremely puzzled fellow returned to the comfort of his fine leather sofa.

"On March 1st," Douglas Edwards professionally indicated, "five Congressmen were shot by Puerto Rican Nationalists on the floor of the *House of Representatives.* All five are recovering from their gunshot wounds. In sports," Edwards conveyed, "Tom Gola led the *LaSalle Explorers* of Philadelphia to the NCAA Basketball Championship in a spectacular and impressive 92-76 win over *Bradley.* And on March 25th," the broadcaster continued in his standard monotone voice, "an *Academy Award* was presented to *From Here to Eternity* as the best motion picture of 1953 and an *Oscar* was earned by William Holden for his best actor performance in *Stalag 17.* Switching back to domestic and international events," the news' personality very deliberately proceeded, "on March 25th President Eisenhower revealed that a hydrogen bomb explosion in the Marshall Islands had exceeded all military estimates and government expectations. The blast definitively proved that the United States is ahead of Russia in the nuclear arms research and development race."

Being absolutely captivated with what his' mind was processing, John P. Walker again stepped to the very extraordinary *Emerson* television and abruptly twisted the selector dial to Channel 4. The perplexed man poured another few ounces of *Johnny Walker* and mechanically chugged the whiskey down the hatch. 'Douglas Edwards was on the air even before Walter Cronkite!' Walker marveled and evaluated. 'This whole weird thing is some sort of exceptional paranormal experience. It's too fantastic to be a clever prank or a practical joke!'

"On April 16th," Douglas Edwards announced with a stoic expression on his now-familiar countenance, "the *Detroit Red Wings* defeated the *Montreal Canadiens* in the Stanley Cup finals, four games to three. *Motor City* ice hockey fans enthusiastically celebrated the team's victory by..."

John Walker had again risen from his soft leather sofa and aggressively flicked the dial to the left back to Channel 3 to determine if the March of '54 news was still in progress. "On March 10th," Douglas Edwards said, "federal officials divulged that the Atomic Energy Commission approved plans for the *Duquesne Power Company* of Pittsburgh to construct the first nuclear power electric generating plant. The new facility is scheduled to go from drawing board to..."

The now-inebriated viewer hastily flicked the channel rotator forward from position three to four, or from March to April. John P. Walker staggered back to his seat very confounded by what his normally reliable five senses had been receiving and the astounded viewer was quite perplexed by what his' confused mind had been comprehending and reviewing. His common sense told him to deny all that was being perceived.

"Congress has authorized the construction of the *United States Air Force Academy*," Douglas Edwards confidently reported, "and it will be a first-class institution that will rival similar military academies at West Point and at Annapolis. The site of the new school will be somewhere in Colorado, but the exact location will not be made public by the federal government until two months from now in early June."

The now-drunk and annoyed tycoon got up and switched to Channel 5 and then slowly trudged back to his comfortable leather den couch. He incredulously glanced at his quart bottle of *Johnny Walker Red,* which was now only half' full. The peeved and neurotic observer once again plopped down into the soft center cushion of his cranberry-colored sofa. The mentally disheveled fellow again reached over and filled his glass with whiskey and then blankly stared at the classic television situated directly before his eyes.

Douglas Edwards was peering into the camera at his loyal 1954 nightly television audience. "The big news in May is that the U.S. Supreme Court in a landmark decision declared that racial segregation is unconstitutional in the nation's public schools. The practice of 'separate but equal', prevalent mostly in the American South up to the present time, will no longer be a viable argument to prevent the creation of racial integration into our nation's public schools." The famous anchorman cleared his throat and then resumed his long-winded recitation. "Most of you viewers already know that the 80th running of the *Kentucky Derby* was won by *Determine* in a time of two minutes and three seconds. Jockey Ray York was aboard the victorious thoroughbred as it triumphantly made its way to the *Churchill Downs* Winner's Circle. *Determine* will now attempt to achieve horse racing's most coveted honor, the *Triple Crown.* The next difficult challenge after the *Derby* will be the *Preakness,* which later in June will be followed by the ever-popular *Belmont Stakes.*"

Wholly intoxicated, John Peter Walker awkwardly stood and clumsily approached the ancient electronic mechanism. The annoyed gentleman anxiously turned the selector to Channel 6. "Well, now. I'll review some more ancient history," he slurred and stated to himself. "It all seemed so damned important back in 1954 but now it all seems so terribly haunting, so ugly and eerie. I always suspected that Douglas Edwards was a stern charlatan back when I was a kid. Now I realize the idiot must be an evil sorcerer. What on Earth has happened to sanity?"

The befuddled and distraught asphalt merchant slowly shuffled back to his familiar soft leather sofa. He instinctively imbibed another mouthful of scotch as the 1954 June news appeared on the *Emerson* television screen.

112

"According to *Air Force* Secretary Harold E. Talbott," Douglas Edwards aptly stated, "the site of the new highly anticipated *Air Force Academy* will be Colorado Springs, Colorado. Elated government official gathered today, June 6th to officially make the public announcement before..."

John P. Walker predictably rose and rushed to the fifties' table-model television perched on top of the metal cart. He roughly rotated the knob counterclockwise to May. On Channel 5, Douglas Edwards blandly declared, "The 38th *Memorial Day Indianapolis 500 Auto Race* was won by Bill Vukovich, who achieved an admirable average speed of 130.8 miles per hour. It was Vukovich's second consecutive *Indy'* triumph. Congratulations Bill from all across America! And now on to some regular news."

The very groggy viewer still standing in front of the *Emerson* shook his head in total disbelief. A puzzled look remained on his face and his fingers quickly gripped and advanced the dial ahead to Channel 7 to review some of July's relevant events. Walker slowly sipped his glass without ever thinking about adding fresh ice cubes, which had all partially melted inside of an opened metal ice bucket disguised as a medieval knight's helmet. In disgust, Walker slammed the ice bucket's knight visor shut.

Douglas Edwards' grim face and penetrating eyes nearly filled the black and white television screen and presently occupied the full attention of its somewhat hypnotized viewer.

"The '50s were a time of black and white," Walker mumbled and maintained to himself'. "Sneakers were black and white, television screens were black and white, camera pictures were black and white, newspapers were black and white and segregation was black and white. What the hell is going on here? Devil, show yourself!"

"On July 13th," the grim-faced news commentator prefaced his narrative, "the Gross National Product for 1953 was officially announced. The Department of Commerce indicated that the *GNP* was put at 365-billion-dollars and that this hefty statistic illustrates the prosperity of a growing and thriving American economic system. On the sports scene," the highly rated announcer read from his teleprompter, "the world tennis championships at *Wimbledon* are scheduled to resume today in merry old England. Vic Seixas and Maureen Connally are the men's and women's' favorites respectively. The annual tournament is a highlight of each summer, and participants are honored to enthusiastically compete in the prestigious classic each..."

The addled disbelieving viewer again habitually rose from his comfortable sofa and stubbornly twisted his wrist to the left back to Channel 6. "The June calendar is highlighted by the annual running of the *Belmont Stakes,"* Douglas Edwards matter-of-factly articulated, "and *High Gun* won the highly-contested event with jockey Eric Guerin proudly escorting his champion steed to the Winner's Circle. *High Gun* dramatically won the racing contest with an impressive time of two minutes and..."

John P. Walker desperately switched ahead to Channel 8 to investigate into 1954 August news. The perplexed viewer's patience and prudence were eroding as rapidly as his fading sobriety. He stood slumped over, awkwardly leaning against the metal cart that held the now despicable obnoxious-sounding heirloom *Emerson* table-model television.

"On August 9th," the famous '50s news broadcaster asserted, "Cooperstown's *Baseball Hall of Fame* inducted nine new members. Topping the list of new inductees was..."

Walker disgustedly and vigorously changed the station to Channel 9. He dejectedly reentered his spot on the still comfortable leather sofa and sank down into the cranberry-dyed central cushion. His heart, mind and soul were in a total quandary. 'This whole damned thing reeks of evil,' Walker thought, 'and I don't have the will or the strength to fight it. I'm a hapless victim and nothing more,' the afflicted fellow concluded as he instinctively swallowed down another quantity of scotch.

"Back on September 6th, Vic Seixas and Doris Hart respectively had won the men's and women's' divisions *of The U.S. Lawn Tennis Association Tournament,"* Douglas Edwards reported and reminded the nation's viewers on Channel 9. "And today September 24, the *United Steel Workers of America* banned all communists, fascists and card-carrying members of the *Ku Klux Klan* from its ranks. In other national news," the commentator competently continued, "the *U.S.S. Nautilus,"* the first atomic powered submarine is slated to be commissioned at Groton, Connecticut. On hand for the momentous occasion will be..."

John P. Walker had just enough strength to wobble across the palatial den to the *Emerson* table-model television and savagely advance the selector to Channel 10. He leaned against the metal cart to support his almost limp anatomy with his left hand while holding his half-full glass of scotch with his right.

"Our news department has recently learned that on October 13th, the much-heralded B-58, our nation's first supersonic bomber was ordered into production by the *Air Force,*" the commentator related. "And yesterday, October 15th, *Hurricane Hazel* ravaged the eastern coastline causing widespread devastation and loss of life. The most violent hurricane in decades has killed ninety-nine persons in the U.S. and another two hundred and forty-nine in Canada. Combined North American property losses are estimated at over a hundred million dollars," Douglas Edwards glibly disclosed. "And finally, in the dynamic publishing world, the literary community is looking forward to this year's *Nobel Prize for Literature.* The leading candidate for the coveted award is reputed to be Ernest Hemingway, whose most renown literary contributions were the novels *The Sun Also Rises, A Farewell to Arms* and *For Whom the Bell Tolls.* The announcement will be made October 28th at the *Nobel Prize* headquarters in..."

The now totally inebriated American "new money aristocrat" stooped down and rotated the channel dial one notch to the right. "I still remember hearing about that damned destructive *Hurricane Hazel,*" the TV viewer muttered to his scotch glass. "It blew the roof off of almost every flimsy house in the Hammonton area. And that overrated author Hemingway was nothing more than a mentally sick perverted alcoholic."

"In the November 2nd national elections," Douglas Edwards austerely articulated, "the Democrats gained a valuable additional seat in the *Senate* for a narrow-but-important 48-47 majority over the Republicans. Meanwhile, in the *House of Representatives,* on-a-mission Democrats gained twenty-one seats to establish a 232-203 majority. President Eisenhower expressed his disappointment at the outcome of this year's...."

"Who cares about damned 1954 politics?" John P. Walker angrily exclaimed. "It's as dumb an activity as religion is, and both subjects are unworthy of public discussion or debate," the intoxicated man mumbled as he emphatically twisted the television knob to the left back to Channel 10. "I already know what happened in 1954," the disgusted viewer mumbled and complained, again slurring his words.

"The fifty-first *World Series'* best of seven games was decisively won in a surprising four games to none victory by the *New York*

Giants, who easily vanquished the favored *American League Cleveland Indians* despite Cleveland's supposedly superior and invincible pitching staff consisting of veterans Bob Feller, Mike Garcia, Early Wynne and Bob…"

The road paving *CEO* managed to regain his equilibrium, traipse to the "haunted" television and switch the selector ahead to Channel 11, where the November 1954 news was still being delivered. Walker gawked down at the television set with his mouth agape.

"Yesterday November 4th," stern-faced Douglas Edwards formally announced, "the much-acclaimed musical *Fanny* opened on *Broadway*. S. N. Behrman and Joshua Logan have written the show, which is expected to draw…"

Realizing that the ongoing phenomenon he was witnessing had been verified by checking and re-checking the monthly events on various channels, John P. Walker frantically rotated the television knob to Channel 12. The now-apprehensive skeptic retreated to his soft cranberry-colored leather sofa and with a trembling hand poured the remaining contents of the *Johnny Walker Red* bottle into his ice-less crystal glass.

"Now it's finally December of '54," the asphalt contractor neurotically stammered. "This ought to be interesting. It's the month I was born, exactly ten minutes before midnight of the *New Year*. In fact the exact time is right now," Walker observed as he reflexively glanced at the handsome gold-gilded clock positioned on the den's stone fireplace's Canadian oak mantel. 'Let's see what materializes!'

But then the all-too-worried mogul felt nauseous in his stomach. "I feel like vomiting," Walker realized and admitted as he stared at the empty quart of *Johnny Walker Red* and then peered at his empty crystal glass, both now situated on an adjacent den table. "I was a fool to drink so much scotch just because of this bogus bothersome television set," the multimillionaire confessed to himself.

Douglas Edwards seemed to be waiting for John P. Walker's undivided attention. Then the news broadcaster proceeded with the irrelevant December of '54 news items. "Senator Joseph McCarthy of Wisconsin was condemned by his colleagues in a special session for his misconduct during *Senate* committee meetings over the last several years. The flamboyant Republican *Senator* had no remarks to make to the press concerning his recent formal reprimanding. In military news," Douglas Edwards proceeded, *"the U.S.S. Forrestal,"* the largest warship ever built at almost sixty thousand tons, was christened and launched at the famous Newport News, Virginia shipyard."

At the sight of a champagne bottle being broken to officially launch the *Forrestal,"* the mere thought of any type of alcoholic beverage made John P. Walker up-chuck sour stomach juices from his upper digestive tract, which he sloppily wiped from his mouth. Nothing could now distract his eyes and the man's total concentration, all of which were intensely focused on the 'evil 1954 *Emerson* television screen.'

"On December 26th," Douglas Edwards matter-of-factly stated, "the *Cleveland Browns* convincingly defeated the *Detroit Lions* in the *NFL Championship* game, thus giving the Ohio city a much-anticipated sports' championship that had eluded the baseball *Cleveland Indians* in the recent October *World Series* extravaganza. *Browns* owner..."

Suddenly, the Emerson television screen went blank and then showed a series of alternating and fluttering horizontal and vertical lines. "What's goin' on?" John P. Walker moaned in his stupor. "This old set can't quit before it gets to my birthday! What about December 31st?" he mocked as his troubled eyes witnessed the incessant flickering. "Come on you damned thing! What's next? Don't give up now!"

An image appeared on the television monitor but it wasn't the countenance of newscaster Douglas Edwards. Instead, a familiar voice from the past resonated from the *Emerson's* primitive speaker. "Hello, this is John Cameron Swayze bringing you the *Camel News Caravan,* brought to you by *Camel* cigarettes. I'd walk a mile for a *Camel,"* Douglas Edwards' contemporary rival news commentator remarked.

John P. Walker foamed from his mouth as more sour stomach digestive liquid spewed-up from his esophagus. The millionaire was in shock as his form slouched-down in his comfortable couch and his ears half-heartedly listened to the new anchorman's enunciation.

"Our news program is coming to you tonight over Channel 13," John Cameron Swayze related to his almost incoherent audience of one. "Just before midnight tonight, December 31st, 1954, a deformed baby showing signs of mental retardation was born to Joseph and Louise Walker at the Atlantic City Hospital," the anchorman reported with little emotion.

"That's impossible!" John P. Walker hiccupped. "As you can plainly see, John Cameron Swayze, I'm perfectly fine! Hic! Don't try demeaning me! Hic!"

"Upon being taken home, the imperfect infant was immediately switched with the baby of Giles and Hillary Wood, loyal employees of Joseph and Louise Walker," Swayze reported. "As a result, Giles and Hillary Wood are the biological parents of John Peter Walker, and slow-learner' stable-boy Johnny Wood happens to be the sole legitimate son and heir of the now-deceased Joseph and Louise Walker, the former owners of the lucrative Walker Asphalt and Tar Company of Hammonton, New Jersey."

"What!" John P. Walker balked at what he considered false news reporting. "My butler and my maid are my parents?" he gasped. "This terrible secret has been kept from me for almost forty-eight years!" he vociferously screamed at the ancient Emerson TV. "And my poor mentally challenged lame stable-boy Johnny Wood is really supposed to be me, the original John P. Walker!"

John Cameron Swayze's all-too-sober black and white appearance then instantly dissolved upon the television screen. A moment of static and vertical and horizontal fluttering followed. Then the set mysteriously turned itself off.

At three minutes before midnight Giles and Hillary Wood entered the mansion's spacious den. Giles was carrying a bottle of vintage champagne to officially celebrate the arrival of the *New Year*. The pair immediately rushed to John Peter Walker's aid when they noticed his limp form slumped down upon the cranberry-colored soft leather sofa.

"My God Giles! What in the world has happened to him?" the maid yelled.

"There's no pulse! Hillary, there's no pulse I say!" Giles Wood shouted as he desperately felt his employer's wrists and throat. "He's dead! My God Hillary! I think he's dead!" Giles panted. "Either he had a massive heart attack or had choked on his own vomit! My God Hillary! He drank an entire quart of scotch!"

"Our son is dead! Giles! Our son is dead!" Hillary deliriously shrieked.

"Yes, and we have both kept this ugly secret for too many years. Hillary, did you hear what I said?" Giles anxiously asked. "We've kept this terrible secret for too many years! We had promised *his* parents never to tell it. And now this family tragedy has ended it all!"

118

"I'll call the rescue squad. Perhaps they can revive him," Hillary Wood suggested to her all-too-formal husband. "Maybe *he* is in such a drunken state that it seems like his heart isn't beating!"

"No, Hillary, not yet. Don't call the paramedics just yet!" Giles insisted. "I first have something I feel I must do. Our future deserves to be secure after all we've been through!"

Giles Wood swiftly paced out of the luxurious room, down the majestic wood-paneled corridor to the mansion's mammoth library. He swiveled a portrait of Mr. Joseph Walker to the right, exposing the combination knob to a huge wall safe. Putting on his clean white gloves, the knowledgeable butler repeated the combination he had memorized over the years, "Thirteen-left, thirteen-right, and now thirteen left."

"Giles, what on Earth are you doing?" flustered Hillary Wood demanded. "You're committing grand theft when *we* should be calling the rescue squad!"

"Hillary, all these pathetic years we've sacrificed and toiled for absolutely nothing," Giles ranted like a madman. "Our own son, our own flesh and blood, has paid us shoddy minimum wages to be *his* exploited butler and *his* private domestic maid. At least his substitute parents showed us kindness and generosity in helping us send *their* physically impaired and mentally deficient son to special schools," the butler argued. "And all these years *we* have not been justly and fairly compensated for raising *their* lovable *Johnny* in the servant's cottage. And for the past thirteen years *we've* had to labor for the selfish whims of *our* own son, this pathetic egotistical dolt, who treated *us* as if we were illegal aliens or common area indigents."

"Giles, what *you* are doing is evil!" Hillary screamed, revealing a trace of her own guilty conscience. "Put the money back, I tell you. Giles, please put the money back in the safe!"

"The perfect crime!" Giles cackled as his hands held the stacks of hundred-dollar-bills that had been cached away in the concealed safe. "This is our retirement, Hillary. Our honestly earned retirement ticket to tropical climates, do you hear?" Giles laughed deliriously. "This is finally our just compensation for what the diabolical Walker family has done to our lives this past half-century!"

"What should I do?" Hillary begged her husband. "Should I call the authorities now?"

"Wait another ten-minutes, until I hide this cash in the servant's quarters," Giles cunningly advised his wife. "Then, you can notify the rescue squad of Mr. Walker's untimely-but-warranted and propitious demise!"

"You mean of *our son's* demise," Hillary Wood sobbed.

"No Hillary. I meant fraudulent Mr. Walker's demise!" Giles maintained. "No decent son would ever treat his parents like John Peter Walker has treated us these past, miserable forty-eight years!"

"The Timeless Sports Car"

Henry Johnson was very content with his station in life. The man was a successful lawyer in his hometown of Hammonton, New Jersey and was looking forward to early retirement. Johnson had married his high school sweetheart Lois and the couple had three grown sons, Howard, Harry and Hugh. 'Howard is now ready to take over the family law firm,' Henry Johnson thought as he stepped out onto the Bellevue Avenue/Horton Street pavement from *his* Attorney Office, 'and Harry is a prominent doctor at *Jefferson University Hospital* in Philly. And young Hugh is a prominent real estate developer in Saddle Brook up in North Jersey. What more could a 59-year-old man wish for?'

Once a month Henry Johnson would meet two cousins Charles "Chickie" Sceia and John Fallucca for lunch at a different pre-determined area restaurant. The three "paisans" would traditionally converge on a familiar convenient eatery on the third Thursday and enjoy each other's company over burgers and frosted mugs of thirst-quenching draught beer.

'Last month's cousins' engagement was at the *Mill Street Pub* over in Mays Landing,' Henry thought, 'and today's lunch is at the *Great American Grille and Pub* in Hamilton Township,' the lawyer reminded himself as he sauntered to his tan *Lexus* parked around the corner on Horton Street. 'This time was *my* choice in the rotation so I know exactly where the restaurant is located. I can't wait to see Chickie and Johnny and discuss and solve the world's perplexing problems,' Johnson mused as he clicked the remote-control mechanism unlocking his luxury automobile's driver-side door. 'I actually look forward to these once-a-month get-togethers.'

Henry Johnson steered his expensive car down Horton, made a right onto Orchard and then another right onto North Third Street. He stopped at the red traffic signal and proceeded straight ahead across Bellevue, and where Third merged with Central Avenue at the yellow-brick *Hammonton Middle School,* the driver then took Central to *Route 30,* the *White Horse Pike.* In another five minutes the suave sociable lawyer was on Weymouth Road heading toward *Route 322,* the *Black Horse Pike.* 'I've ridden this highway at least three thousand times and know every inch of it,' Johnson mused.

Fifteen-miles east on "the Pike" toward Atlantic City was a shopping center across from the newly constructed ultra-modern *Hamilton Mall*, and in that shopping center were various shops and stores all having the same attractive red brick façade, with one of the larger establishments being the aforementioned *Great American Grille and Pub.*

'Today we're scheduled to get together at 3:15,' Henry thought as he inserted a music disc into his dashboard panel and then listened to the *Billboard Top Rock 'n' Roll Hits of 1956.* '1956,' Henry imagined with a nostalgic smile. 'What a wonderful year! And what a horribly tragic year it was also!' the lawyer recalled.

The tan *Lexus* cruised past the huge *Atlantic Blueberry Company Farm, Mays Landing Division* on the right, and just before the sentimental '56 oldies *CD* finished playing its last selection, Henry maneuvered his well-equipped vehicle right off of *Route 322.* Then the hungry man made a sharp left turn and next drove behind an *I-hop,* a *McDonald's* and a *KFC* franchise. Soon Johnson was in the designated shopping center that featured a fine mixture of brick-façade stores, supermarkets and shops.

Henry checked his wristwatch and compared the time to the clock inside his fabulous car. '3:05,' he thought. 'I'll sit and wait here until Chickie or Johnny arrives. They're both usually pretty punctual, actually more punctual than pretty,' the good-humored fellow mused and chuckled.

It was a warm April 24 day, and as Henry listened to his '50s music and adjusted his air-conditioning a few degrees cooler, he recollected the significance of the particular date. 'Lois and I were married on April 24th,' Johnson fondly remembered, 'and then there was that tragedy, that terrible tragedy that I don't want to think about ever again.'

The fastidious lawyer raised the volume to his 1956 oldies' *CD* and then after recollecting the horrible catastrophe that had occurred on April 24th of that same unforgettable year, Henry Johnson quickly switched the CD mode to a more contemporary John Fogerty album, *Premonition.*

Henry again checked his watch (impatiently awaiting the arrival of either Charles "Chickie" Sceia or Johnny Fallucca) in a nervous reflexive response to alleviate his temporary emotional anxiety. It was now 3:15, and neither cousin's vehicle had entered the parking lot facing the designated *Great American Grille and Pub.*

'It's very unlike either of them to miss our monthly appointment,' Henry reckoned as he attempted to make himself more comfortable in his light brown leather driver's seat. 'My cousins are both dependable fellas'. Something is definitely wrong here! But I'm not going to panic!'

Afternoon shoppers pulled into and others exited parking spaces to the left and right of Johnson, who now wondered what was keeping his cousins from promptly showing up. 'I'll wait here until 3:20 and then enter the restaurant,' Henry considered. 'They might already be seated inside enjoying cold draughts. But where are their cars? Maybe they came together in a new car I'm not familiar with?' Henry hypothesized. 'And in the past, we've always had the courtesy of waiting outside in our autos' so that all three of us could enter together!'

Five more minutes elapsed, and Henry was now feeling more than a bit apprehensive. He climbed out of his tan *Lexus*, paced across the asphalt and soon stepped onto the shopping center's sidewalk. The slightly concerned man opened the front door to the popular restaurant but only two patrons were seated at the bar and other customers were occupying only three out of the four-dozen tables in the dining room. After glancing around the pub's interior several times, Henry felt awkward when he suddenly noticed the bartender and a curious waitress staring at him, so without initiating a conversation Johnson quickly abandoned the premises and shuffled back to the security of *his* tan *Lexus*.

'I'll wait here until 3:45,' Henry confided to his image in the rear-view mirror. 'It's so unlike either Chickie or Johnny to forget about our habitual monthly luncheon,' Johnson thought as he double-checked the date carefully written inside his monthly calendar book. 'I feel so stupid every time I call to remind them about the monthly late-lunch session. And Chickie and Johnny always tell me to remind my clients about court appointments and depositions and not to lecture *them* about honoring *our* monthly restaurant luncheons.'

3:45 arrived, but cousins Chickie and Johnny had not. Henry Johnson reluctantly fired-up the tan *Lexus* sedan's engine, backed out of his parking space and soon was heading west on the *Black Horse Pike* back toward Hammonton. As Henry approached the landmark *Palace Diner* on the left, he was struck with a sudden inspiration. 'I'll call cousin Johnny on *his* cell phone and give him a good friendly reprimand for failing to remember the *Great American Grille* lunch engagement. I got to get this weird anomaly out of my mind so that I can think straight. I hope that nothing unexpected happened to them!'

The somewhat distraught driver punched in the appropriate telephone number on his cell phone, touched the "Send" button and waited through three rings. Johnny Fallucca answered his portable cell phone on the fourth ring.

"Hello!" said the call's recipient.

"Johnny," Henry began in an imperative tone. "Where the heck were you? I was parked outside the *Great American Grille* from 3:05 until 3:45, and neither you nor cousin Chickie showed up!" Johnson admonished. "I had always thought that you guys were supposed to be reliable mature adults!"

"Henry," Johnny replied with a degree of astonishment, "Chickie and I are sitting at the bar in the *Great American* Grille right now still waiting for *you* to show up. We're now feeling pretty happy nursing down *our* fourth frosted mugs. We were beginning to worry about you. From where are you calling? *Outer Space?"* Fallucca mildly chastised.

"That's impossible!" Henry ranted into his cell phone's specially installed overhead microphone attached to the driver's side sun-visor. "What time did *you* get there? And how long have you two clowns been sitting there?"

"Cousin Henny," Johnny amiably replied. "We've both been sitting here at the bar since 3 p.m. waiting for you. Are you trying to pull some sinister trick on us? I think you're a little old to be playing silly high school pranks!" Johnny Fallucca joked. "Now what's the story from your end?"

"Believe me, Johnny. I had entered the restaurant; looked all around, but only saw the lady bartender talking to two old gents that looked nothing like either you or Chickie," Henry maintained. "And there were only three tables occupied in the dining area, and neither you nor Chickie were in there. Did you guys ever get up and step to the *Men's Room* by any chance?"

"No! Never! Our kidneys are still in good condition," Johnny facetiously replied. "We were at the bar all the time and nowhere else. We figured we'd spot you right when you entered. You were right about one thing," Johnny told Henry. "There *were* two old geezers flirting with the woman bartender on the opposite side and she didn't like it one bit."

"Is this some sort of weird practical joke you two guys are playing?" Henry interrogated like the prosecutor he often was. "If so, it's not-too-funny and it's now very impractical and has worn out its impact!"

"Honest, Henny. We're all mature grown men, related by common relative's blood and not inclined to play stupid juvenile pranks on one another," Johnny Fallucca declared as his voice shifted into a more serious tone. "Maybe it's time for *you* to visit your optometrist?"

"I'm sorry, Johnny, if I've falsely accused you," Henry diplomatically apologized. "But where were your cars? They certainly weren't in the parking lot, or if they were," Johnson defensively continued, "I surely would've recognized them!"

"That's a mystery for sure," his cousin conceded. "They're parked in the lot as sure as Chickie and I are sitting and drinking at the bar right now!"

"Perhaps I really do need to have my eyes examined," Henry Johnson admitted to his honest and trustworthy cousin. "I'll schedule an appointment for early next week. I'm heading back toward Hammonton now and will see you fellas' Wednesday, May 22nd at 3:15 p.m. for a late lunch at *Sweetwater Casino* on the *Mullica River*. It's still *my* choice! And let's not mess this one up! Write it down right now!"

"Okay, I'll tell Chickie," Johnny lustily laughed. "Sweetwater Casino, Wednesday, May 22nd at 3:15 as usual. But why don't you just turn around and head back to the restaurant? It's no big deal, ya' know!"

"Thanks, Johnny, but it's also my wedding anniversary and tonight I'm taking Lois and the three sons out to *Venice Plaza* over in Berlin to celebrate!" Johnson mentioned. "The place has a great gourmet chef so maybe it's a blessing in disguise for my delicate intestines that I'm missing a delicious lunch. I certainly don't want to over-exert my sensitive digestive system! Maybe a rain-check with you guys is in good order."

"All right, Henny," Johnny chuckled. "Go out with the family and have a terrific time. I'll tell Chickie here your very strange-but-entertaining story. And please tell Lois and the boys we said 'hi', and don't forget about May 22nd, 3:15 p.m. at Sweetwater. Don't mess up this time! See ya' cousin!"

"Bye, Johnny. And tell that occasional alcoholic Chickie I said 'hi'," Johnson jested and answered while shaking his head in disbelief at the very weird non-meeting that had recently been discussed over the phone.

Just as Henry Johnson pressed *End* on his car phone, the driver realized that he had gone straight in the fork in the road, and instead of veering off left, taking County Road 559 toward Hammonton, he was now en route to the village of Elwood.

"Oh well, I guess a minor detour is just what I need to top-off a rather peculiar afternoon," Henry said to his aging silver-haired reflection in the rear-view mirror. "Maybe the hamlet of Elwood has blossomed into a major metropolis since the last time that I've been there," the driver snickered. "I haven't traveled this back country hick road in many years even though it's only eleven or so miles from Hammonton."

The rather disgusted fellow tapped the dashboard *CD* indicator to change his music preference from John Fogerty's *Premonition* album back to the *Billboard Top Rock 'n' Roll Hits of 1956.* Dark storm clouds were observable to the west toward Philadelphia along with occasional lightning flashes and peals of thunder rumbling in the distance. Johnson raised the volume to his '50s music to escape his present emotional perplexity and then he mentally navigated back to the year 1956.

'I seldom take this remote road,' Henry thought. 'In fact I can't recall the last time I had, possibly it *was* as far back as 1956. Oh well, and I guess I just have to accept the inevitability of occasional April showers.'

The tan *Lexus* rounded a bend on the right and the first object that came into Henry Johnson's view was a magnificent white 1956 *Thunderbird* convertible with a splendid *Continental* wheel cover on its back. The impressive shiny classic sports car was situated on the front lawn of an old white bungalow that was in desperate need of several coats of paint, appearing to have been built during the *WWII* era.

"What a rare beauty!" Henry gasped as he slammed on the brakes. "It's got red interior just like the one I had wanted back in '56, but Dad quickly put an end to my fantasy by making me drive his black '53 *Pontiac* around Hammonton."

Henry carefully backed-up his tan *Lexus* in order to gain a better inspection of the marvelous white vintage automobile that appeared to be in mint condition. A handwritten poster attached under the left windshield wiper blade read "Like New: Only $20,000.00!"

The clever lawyer clambered out of his luxury vehicle to admire the white relic from *his* past. 'I've got to have this baby!' the examiner covetously thought as he stuck his fingers inside the convertible's interior and touched the well-preserved red leather upholstery. 'I couldn't own it back in '56 but I sure have the means to acquire this great roadster now!'

An old farmer in a checkered red and black flannel shirt and grimy blue jeans came ambling-out to greet the prospective customer. "Howdy, Mister!" the elderly whiskered gentleman said. "I'm Brent Wagner, the owner of this here perfectly reconditioned *T-bird*. Isn't it a beauty!"

"Sure is!" Henry marveled and concurred. "I really wanted one of these bad when I was a rambunctious teenager. Trouble was that my dad was a very frugal practical man, even though he could've easily afforded to purchase one for me. I'm not quite as economical as my Pop was."

"Well son, if you're that interested, ya' can have it for a mere twenty thousand," the old farmer stated. "And that's a real bargain, yes sir-eeee it is! This honey is only got seventy-three-thousand original miles on it. Belonged to my brother-in-law who left it to me in *his* will," Brent Wagner emphasized. "Now I have no use for this classy toy, so I figured I'd convert it into quick cash to spruce-up my dilapidated bungalow a bit."

Henry walked back to his tan *Lexus,* reached inside, and shut-off its engine. His desire was to negotiate a lower selling price to claim his heart's desire. 'I'm going to buy this *T-bird* if it's the last thing I do!' the man mentally promised his greedy eyes. 'Maybe I can haggle the old gent down a bit!'

The elderly man pulled a toothpick from his toothless mouth and uttered, "Say stranger, I'm gonna' start the engine up, and you'll notice that this here baby purrs like a happy kitten. Still got a lot of zip, too, I must admit!"

"I'll give you eighteen-thousand-dollars for it right now!" Henry offered. "I'll gladly write you out a check for that amount right this minute! I always pay everything by check for obvious income tax purposes. That's why, Mr. Wagner, I always have my checkbook readily available."

"Wait a minute!" the shrewd old codger replied. "I wanted cash on the barrel-head, not a damned check! The *IRS* will take me to the cleaners with a check, yes, they will!" Brent Wagner argued. "If ya' want to pay by check, the price is twenty-five thousand to allow for federal taxes."

"If it will start and can be driven, I'll give you twenty-five thousand," Henry reluctantly responded with a trace of regret in his voice for compromising *his* already set purchasing price. But in his heart, Johnson aptly knew that money was no object in realizing his fondest and grandest teenage dream come true.

The old gentleman entered the car, reached into his pocket and removed a set of keys on a ring, one of which he inserted into the ignition. With one twist of his right wrist, the white *Thunderbird* started up and sounded as good as new.

"I'll take it!" Henry enthusiastically consented as he watched lightning flashing and heard thunder rolling to the west in the direction of Philadelphia. "You certainly drive a hard bargain Mr. Wagner! I must say!"

"How do I know that this here check you're gonna' cut me isn't gonna' bounce?" the old man challenged. "I've been burned several times before with lesser amounts!"

"Because I'm a lawyer in Hammonton, and I have a family name and a good personal reputation to maintain!" the attorney argued. "I can't afford to write a bogus check, because then my last name would be Mud instead of Johnson."

"Johnson? Hammonton lawyer! I've heard of you," the old farmer acknowledged with a forced grin. "Ya' do have a good name around these parts; I'll admit to that. Show me your driver's license with your name and address on it and then I'll reluctantly sell this here precious jewel to ya'!"

Henry Johnson showed old Brent Wagner *his* bona fide New Jersey driver's license, which matched the identity the lawyer had originally claimed to be. The elated old backwoods resident stuck his head inside the sports car and opened the passenger side hatch and inserted a second key into the T-bird's glove compartment and then he removed the automobile's "Bill of Sale." "I was comin' out here to shut the windows just when ya' stopped because it looks like rain coming this way!" Brent Wagner informed Henry.

Henry Johnson was quite familiar with the transition of a standard car ownership document, and after the men signed the required signatures in the appropriate places, the deal had been officially consummated. Henry then wrote out a check for the prescribed amount to the now-ecstatic Brent Wagner, and the two men shook hands to recognize and verify the transaction.

"Ya' gonna' come back and pick it up?" the seller asked his euphoric new-found customer.

"Why yes," Henry confidently indicated. "I'll return later this afternoon with one of my sons, and we'll pick it up and take it back to Hammonton. It'll be a glorious anniversary surprise for my wife, Lois."

Henry eagerly walked the fifteen feet to his tan *Lexus,* opened the driver's side door and entered his distinctive automobile. Upon turning the ignition key, for some remote reason, the electrical system did not respond. Henry tried five times to start the engine but his efforts were to no avail.

The dismayed lawyer exited his auto' and noticed that Brent Wagner was still watching him. "These new cars and their sophisticated computer systems," Henry moaned to the backwoods shack owner. "Sometimes, I think that modern technology is actually going backwards."

"I know exactly what ya' mean!" Brent Wagner attested. "Give me a four-barrel carburetor with a *V-8* engine any day over this here fancy fuel-injection *V-6* stuff! I ain't never had no problem with this here *T-bird* nor with my '53 *Chevy* parked behind the house. Say Mister," Brent continued, "how would ya' like to leave your *Lexus* parked on my lawn and drive the *T-Bird* home. Then you and a mechanic can return here and tow your fancy machine back to Hammonton."

"Terrific idea," agreed Henry. "I'll be able to skirt the thunderstorms because I'll be heading northwest toward Elwood while the thunder and lightning seem to be going southeast toward Williamstown."

Brent Wagner neatly folded the twenty-five-thousand-dollar check in half and gingerly placed it in the upper-left-pocket of his red and black checkered flannel shirt. The two men then pushed the tan *Lexus* onto the weed-infested, unkempt front lawn, as Henry Johnson guided its forward progress by vigorously turning the steering wheel to the right.

After the *Lexus* had been moved a safe distance off the country road and onto the unkempt lawn, the two men again shook hands.

Johnson forgot all about his disabled *Lexus*, opened the *T-bird's* door and eagerly leaped inside. The now-mobile-again lawyer waved "goodbye" to the grateful old fellow as *he* pulled away heading northwest toward the hamlet of Elwood.

'This fabulous *T-bird* is timeless!' Henry thought as he watched the seemingly accurate speedometer needle rise up to fifty. 'It's just as beautiful and graceful in 2002 as it had been back in '56. I'll be the envy of everyone in town!'

Henry casually turned the sports car's radio knob to determine if the device still worked. He was both rewarded and shocked when his ears perceived the familiar voice of a Philadelphia *DJ* from the past, *his* past. Joe Niagra's baritone said, "Thanks for listening to *WIBG*, Philly's top rock and roll radio station, and the only boss sound in town. This rockin' bird is about to fly. Now here's a blast from the past, a knocked-out Niagara nifty! Here comes Bill Haley and the Comets singing and playing the teen *National Anthem,* 'Rock Around the Clock'."

'This has got to be a commercial or a cruisin' record promo' of some sorts!' Henry Johnson imagined. His eyes briefly glanced at the radio and observed that the dial was set on *AM 99*, the exact position of *WIBG,* Philadelphia back in the nifty '50s. 'This just *has* to be a flashback commercial,' *his* naturally skeptical mind again thought.

In total amazement, the baffled driver turned the radio knob and found a news broadcast in progress. "And in entertainment news," the baritone-voiced announcer declared, "*My Fair Lady*, a smash hit musical by Alan Jay Lerner and Frederick Lowe is proving to be a fantastic box-office attraction at the *Mark Hellinger Theater* in New York. The popular *Broadway* play is based on George Bernard Shaw's classic story *Pygmalion,* and the terrific new musical features talented stage stars Rex Harrison and Julie Andrews. In other national entertainment news, …"

Henry Johnson turned the radio dial and momentarily heard Carl Perkins singing *his* famous rendition of "Blue Suede Shoes", and then the disbelieving driver quickly rotated the knob to another news broadcast. "The *Marine Corps* has finally finished investigating the drowning of six recruits at Parris Island, South Carolina while a platoon was on a so-called 'disciplinary march. Sergeant Matthew C. McKeon has been convicted of drinking on duty and found guilty of negligent homicide. His rank has been reduced to *Private*. In other news," the radio announcer continued, "the *New York Coliseum* is scheduled to open on April 28th. The new *Coliseum* will indeed be the world's largest exhibition building, covering over nine acres at a phenomenal cost of over 35 million dollars. In other current news, Victor Riesel was blinded when…"

Henry neurotically turned the radio dial back to *WIBG Radio 99* and heard Joe Niagara gleefully shout, "And now here's Elvis Presley's smash-hit recording of the classic rhythm and blues number Heartbreak Hotel!" Henry listened to the song's familiar intro', and then turned the *T-bird's* dial to "OFF."

'This is impossible!' the highly alarmed driver evaluated. 'I must be caught in some kind of time vacuum, a puzzling time warp! There's definitely one way I can prove that my theory is correct and I'm going to test my idea.'

Henry drove his new white *Ford Thunderbird* convertible (with the top down) into downtown Hammonton, which to his astonishment was downtown Hammonton, vintage 1956. 'Oh my God!' Henry thought. 'There's *Godfrey's Drugstore* on the corner. That business disappeared in the early sixties, and over there is *J.J. Newberry's* five and ten, and *Miller's Department Store*, and all of the soda fountains I used to enjoy so much as a kid. And look, the *Rivoli Theater's* marquee is visible down the street, and *Fire Company #1* is still in the middle of town and not out on Lincoln and Passmore Avenues! And all of the cars on Bellevue Avenue are 1956 models and earlier.'

The astonished driver steered his handsome *Thunderbird* to the right and onto Central Avenue. He parked his 'wheels' on the street outside of *Olivo's Supermarket* and ambled across Central to his favorite teenage hangout, the *Gem Burger Palace*. Seated inside booths and at the counter were carefree *Hammonton High School* students' eating burgers, chatting the latest gossip and listening to jukebox tunes. The boys were wearing their white and blue trimmed lettermen's sweaters and most of the girls were costumed in blue and white cheerleader uniforms with black and white saddle shoes while other looser and tougher-looking young females were wearing pink and black *Poodle* skirts.

As Henry's eyes scanned the very active teen' scene he noticed his future wife Lois gossiping with *his* best friend, Tommy Davidson and *her* best friend, head cheerleader Candy Taylor. And also congregated inside the hangout were Bob Simpson, Chet Douglas, Dave Jensen and Jim Parker, all teammates of Henry's on the fearsome *Hammonton High School* 1956 football team, but none of them recognized their good friend's bearded face and silver-haired middle-age appearance.

Henry's mind was in a state of complete bewilderment as he approached the main counter where several of his old chums were sitting on stools discussing various topics. Mr. Clyde Dawkins, the gem's proprietor asked Johnson where he had gotten the "strange light blue jeans" *he* was wearing.

"Oh," Henry said with a smile and a blush on his cheeks, "my mom put them in the washing machine and they faded when she used too much bleach. Maybe I'm starting a new fad?" he joked. "What do ya' think?"

"You're still living with your mother?" Mr. Dawkins inquired and criticized shaking his head in mock disgust. "Why Mister, I think *you* look like you're about sixty years old!"

Henry heard his former high school friends Bob Simpson and Chet Douglas laughing on their main counter stools in response to Mr. Clyde Dawkins' typical sarcasm. Feeling embarrassed and a bit disoriented, Henry Johnson rushed out of the establishment and hopped into his newly acquired *Thunderbird* as he heard Jim Lowe's "The Green Door" blasting from the *Gem's* jukebox speakers.

"I need more verification of my new reality!" the mentally-disheveled driver said to himself. "Either I'm cracking-up in a major mental meltdown or I *have* already cracked-up!" The time-traveler turned on the ignition and motored around the block to another familiar old Hammonton haunt where he had bought dozens of automobile magazines and comic books in his youth.

Henry parked his *T-bird* outside of *Dan's Stationery Store*, which in 2002 had the designation *Tapper's Stationery*. He briskly stepped inside the establishment and checked the date on the newspapers, and it was indeed April 24th, 1956. Johnson glanced at the saleswoman behind the counter and at a customer purchasing a pack of *Lucky Strike* cigarettes. "That will be thirty cents Mr. Flemming," the woman politely informed.

'Why that's Mr. Flemming the local electrician buying the cigarettes and the lady behind the counter is Mrs. Martha Merlino, Lois's aunt! Those people died in the 1970s! I even attended Mr. Flemming's and Aunt Martha's funerals!' Henry remembered. 'I really *am* back in 1956!'

Johnson exited *Dan's Stationery Store* in a hurry. The date April 24th, 1956 was now a nagging nightmare that had been lingering in the back of the man's now-boggled mind. Henry's father, Dennis Johnson had been killed at precisely 5:30 on that date on Moss Mill Road while changing a tire. He had been struck by a speeding tractor-trailer that had veered off the roadway. 'If everything else is correct in this inexplicable time warp, I have more than enough time to make it to Moss Mill Road and save Dad!' the time traveler reckoned while intensely scrutinizing his wristwatch.

The driver of the '56 *Thunderbird* sped around the corner to Egg Harbor Road, briefly stopped and then turned left. Henry's new old car zoomed past *Hammonton Lake Park* where a *Little League* game was in progress and then turned left again onto Moss Mill Road. Soon Johnson had crossed the *White Horse Pike* (which now in 1956 had a 'Stop Sign' and no traffic light) and was instantly heading east toward Egg Harbor City.

When the auto's speedometer registered fifty-six miles an hour, the dashboard lights automatically and mysteriously flicked on and the time clock coincidentally indicated that it was nearly five p.m. 'I still have a half-hour to rescue Dad!' Johnson hypothesized. 'If I act quickly, I can save *his* life! I *will* save his life!'

Henry mashed his foot down on the accelerator, and the *T-bird* responded with a swift burst of power. The driver recalled the year 1956, and a newsreel of events paraded through his unsettled mind as he sped east. Besides his father's accidental death, Henry had graduated *Hammonton High School* and had been accepted at the *University of Pennsylvania's School of Law*. He had been aggressively dating Lois Morgano and the two had expected to be married in April of 1960.

'I still have plenty of time to prevent the accident,' the owner of the marvelous time-vehicle evaluated. 'I want to get the tire changed before that tractor-trailer arrives or before that thunderstorm on the western horizon hits Moss Mill Road.'

As Henry Johnson nervously drove further down the two-lane county highway, the lawyer recalled that Dennis Johnson had only been thirty-eight years of age when *he* had met *his* tragic death. 'Dad would be eighty-four if he were still alive,' the determined son concluded. 'I'll make sure that *he* lives to see that age!'

Up ahead on the right, a black '53 *Pontiac* sedan was situated on Moss Mill Road's right-hand shoulder. A middle-aged gentleman in a dark blue business suit was preoccupied jacking up the left rear-wheel. Henry halted his immaculate white *Thunderbird,* shut off the motor and got out to render his benign assistance. Saving his father's life was paramount in the time-traveler's mind.

"Hello," Henry greeted his beleaguered father. "I'll help you get that tire changed in a jiffy. You're in a business suit and I'm sure you don't want to get any grease or grime on it!"

"Why thank you, Sir," Dennis Johnson answered, not recognizing his oldest son sporting a beard, mustache, and a distinguished middle-aged appearance. "My oldest son wants a white *T-bird* just like yours," Mr. Johnson related. "I don't think he's quite ready to have such a fancy car yet, if ya' know what I mean. I don't want to spoil any of my sons by giving them what they can't actually afford to buy on their own!"

"I understand completely," Henry stated. "I had to work long and hard to get the money to purchase *my* new car. Tell your son it's well-worth having and saving for."

Henry picked-up the lug-wrench off of the ground and loosened the nuts holding the tire to the wheel. Then, the Good Samaritan methodically jacked the black *Pontiac* up to the desired height, removed the rim's lug nuts and pulled the deflated tire off the wheel.

"Ya' sure know what you're doing," Dennis Johnson sincerely complimented. "I hope that all three of my sons grow up to be just as helpful and as courteous as you are!"

"One thing's for sure," Henry joked. "A flat tire's only flat on the bottom. But I'm sure your sons will grow-up to be fine outstanding citizens," Henry assured his appreciative listener. "Apples and acorns don't fall far from the family tree! Are you on your way to a business meeting?"

"Yes, as a matter of fact I am," Mr. Dennis Johnson answered. "I'm goin' to Egg Harbor City for the *Atlantic County Bar Association's* annual dinner meeting. My wife has a *Civic Association* meeting over in Hammonton, so I'm goin' alone. Good thing she's missed all this flat tire aggravation! All because of one lousy misplaced nail I suppose!"

Soon, Henry had the spare tire (that his father had already taken out of the trunk) onto the rear wheel. He placed and then tightened the new rim's lug nuts onto the corresponding protruding bolt threads and after lowering the black *Pontiac* to the road's shoulder, he finished tightening up the lug-nuts using the tire iron.

Severe lightning began flashing to the west over downtown Hammonton, so Dennis Johnson figured he'd lift the damaged tire and deposit it inside the automobile's trunk.

Suddenly, a speeding tractor-trailer came loudly rumbling around the bend and Dennis Johnson yelled for the helpful middle-age citizen to "Get out of the way!" The driver of the gigantic truck blasted *his* air-horn and heavily applied the brakes. The enormous rig's tires screeched on the highway's asphalt as its air brakes locked.

Henry Johnson stood petrified for a moment and then attempted jumping out of the path of the oncoming monstrosity. The tractor-trailer's right front fender clipped the victim, and then hurtled him over the black *Pontiac,* where he landed twelve-feet away inside the fringe of a pine forest.

A Hammonton ambulance arrived twenty minutes later, and transported the unfortunate highway helper to *Atlantic City Hospital.* The victim was pronounced dead, and the attending doctors on duty reported to newspaper journalists that the man had sustained multiple injuries that had caused massive internal bleeding.

* * * * * * * * * * * *

On April 24th, 2002, Dennis Johnson, an eighty-four-year-old retired attorney made a wrong turn after leaving the *Black Horse Pike,* not far from a traffic light adjacent to *Palace Diner*.

"Dennis," his wife said. "You should've turned left at the fork and gone back to Hammonton. Now you're going to wind-up in Elwood."

"Big deal, Lois!" the stubborn elderly man gruffly replied. "So what, if I missed the hypotenuse of the old right triangle! We'll just detour five-miles out of our way, Lois. I seldom travel this back road. That's all we'll have to do to get to Elwood, and then we'll take *Route 30* west to Hammonton. Anyway, my dear wife. I really enjoy driving my new tan *Lexus*. Ya' know, Lois," Dennis Johnson proceeded to say. "We don't have many more years left on this Earth to relish the wonderful material comforts life has to offer."

"You're so philosophical," the wife observed and commended. "You've always been that way, even in high school. I think that's one reason I married you!"

A mile ahead, old Dennis Johnson observed a white '56 *Thunderbird* convertible with red interior parked on an unkempt lawn in front of an old wooden-frame country bungalow. The elderly driver immediately applied the brakes.

"Why are you stopping?" Lois Johnson asked her suddenly rejuvenated husband.

"Lois, our oldest son always wanted a white '56 *Thunderbird,* but I was too stubborn to buy one for him. And once a stranger stopped on this very day in 1956 and helped me change a tire over on Moss Mill Road. The poor man was killed when he was hit by an out-of-control tractor-trailer just before a terrible thunderstorm hit. I'll never forget that violent accident, Lois, and I'll never forget that horrible afternoon!"

"You never told me about a man being killed!" the wife returned.

"I was so upset that I never found out his name from the police and never even called *his* family or attended *his* funeral," the elderly man informed his wife. "And I've felt guilty ever since that day."

"Then, you're going to buy that beautiful white car?" the wife asked in a very surprised tone of voice.

"I sure am, Lois," Dennis Johnson verified. "I sure am!"

"Time Vigilantes"

Michael Daniels stood erect before the austere-looking judge and next to his state appointed defense attorney in the crowded *Camden County Courthouse*. A solemn-but-confused expression ornamented Daniels small facial features. The bailiff stood at attention left of the elevated seat on the judge's platform. The black robed New Jersey public official austerely stared down at the accused through thick bifocals resting on the bridge of his nose.

"Michael Daniels, raise your right hand and place your left palm over the *Holy Bible!*" instructed the bailiff. "Now, do you swear to tell the truth, the whole truth and nothing but the absolute truth so help you, God!"

"Yes sir," came the almost inaudible reply.

"Michael Daniels, how do you plead?" Judge Matthew Dixon asked.

"I think not guilty," the shy young man answered in a low hoarse voice.

"Are you certain?" the seemingly inflexible courtroom judge adamantly asked. "Could you speak a little louder and repeat your plea for everyone present to hear. And please don't say the word *think*. It's a subjective word that suggests uncertainty. Now Mr. Daniels, you should either plead guilty or not guilty!"

"I plead not guilty!" the defendant accused of first-degree murder firmly stated.

"Counselor, have you adequately advised the defendant of his *Constitutional Rights* and of the possibility of a lesser voluntary manslaughter plea bargain should he have instead pleaded 'guilty'?" the by the book judicial authority asked the tall lean defense attorney.

"Yes, Your Honor," Attorney Mark Brookes respectfully replied. "The defendant is very obstinate in that particular matter, insisting that he was unaware of any malicious intent on *his* part upon committing the alleged act."

"But Counselor, must I remind you that twenty-one other highly suspicious deaths had occurred at the *Echelon Mall* on the evening of May 20, 2002! Twenty-two people, many of them children, teenagers and perfectly healthy adults suddenly collapsed and died for no apparent reason. If convicted," Judge Dixon continued, "Michael

Daniels might also be implicated in the other twenty-one bizarre mysterious deaths."

"In all due respect Your Honor," Attorney Mark Brookes slowly indicated, "my client claims to know nothing about the other twenty-one inexplicable deaths that had transpired at the *Echelon Mall* on the night of Monday, May 20, 2002. The county's *Medical Examiner* and the best forensics' professionals in New Jersey haven't a clue as to a satisfactory logical explanation for the exact cause of the other twenty-one deaths other than cessation of vital signs," the gaunt-looking defense lawyer nobly stated. "The cause is a baffling enigma to the state's most expert investigators. The exact cause is too difficult to discern for even the most sophisticated and knowledgeable experts to identify."

"Very well then, Counselor," the dignified judge sanctimoniously replied as he now sat still as a statue in his elevated black leather chair. "Do you have anything else to disclose before I direct the witness to take the stand and ask the prosecutor to proceed with his opening statement?"

"Yes, Your Honor, for the record," Attorney Mark Brookes elaborated, "I would like to have it entered that the identity of the victim remains unknown. The deceased had no wallet, no credentials, no *Social Security* card, no driver's license and no credit cards in his possession. The only things *he* had in his pocket were ten-and-twenty-dollar bills, four hundred and seventy dollars total cash. The fingerprints on the bills matched none on record anywhere. The victim was shopping alone at the time of his demise, and no one in the mall knew his name. And," the State Appointed Counsel proceeded, "my client believes that the murder victim had possibly been involved in the killing of the twenty-one other victims at the *Echelon Mall* and that the anonymous murder victim possibly had an accomplice in performing those nefarious criminal acts."

"Is *Exhibit A* the device believed to be the murder weapon?" the judge prudently asked the county prosecutor. "I'd like to examine it when the questioning commences."

"Yes, Your Honor," the chief Camden County District Attorney responded. "If you'll notice," Jeffrey Jensen suggested holding the unique object up to the judge while wearing sheer plastic surgical gloves, "our chief investigators believe that this instrument is some ingenious multi-functional weapon, some sort of organic tissue disintegrator," the county prosecutor expounded. "When pointed at a

138

person, we believe it activates a distinct invisible death ray that instantly makes heart, liver and kidneys stop functioning. Our forensics' experts experimented with this device at the *SPCA* and satisfactorily demonstrated its properties by killing three dogs and two cats that were about to be put to sleep."

A roar broke out from the huge audience seated in the crammed courthouse. Judge Matthew Dixon pounded his gavel on his elevated desk-podium yelling, "Order in this court! Order in this court! Any further gallery outbursts will result in immediate removal, and I hereby instruct the bailiff and the other court security officers on duty of my intent!"

After absolute silence had been re-established Judge Dixon again addressed the accused. "Michael Daniels, before I accept your earnest plea, clarify one thing for me. Did *you* know that the object in the prosecutor's hands was a murder weapon at the time of the alleged murder incident?"

"No, Your Honor. I didn't!" the defendant emphatically answered. "It looks rather peculiar, doesn't it, sort of like a microphone with a flashlight head at one end, with three strange switches in the middle. That's really all I know about the thing, other than it was only in my hands for about ten seconds."

"Very well then, Mr. Daniels," Judge Matthew Dixon assented. "The court accepts your plea of *Not Guilty*. We shall now hear opening statements and relevant arguments for Case Number 2943, State of New Jersey, County of Camden versus Michael Anthony Daniels."

* * * * * * * * * * * * *

In the year 2370, the *Democratic* and *Republican* parties had become extinct because their political persuasions no longer met the changing socio-economic needs of American society. The fledgling *Neo-Puritan Party* came into power in the United States in 2376 following a bloody and devastating thirteen-year civil war between the radical left-wing *Libertarians* and the conservative right-wing *New Age Moralists*. Within a year stringent elements were set into motion to prevent a repeat of, or a continuation of, the horrible national catastrophe that had been courageously fought between cities *(Libertarians)* and rural towns *(New Age Moralists)* all over the nation.

In 2377, *District Military SWAT* squads were authorized to dispatch "moral vigilantes" to patrol city streets, slums, ghettos and drug-infested middle-class urban neighborhoods. Those "behavioral reformers" were not only assigned to enforce the nation's new laws but also to monitor the accepted practice of America's customs, traditions and favorable social habits. When law and "social order" had been forcibly re-established throughout the land, "moral vigilantes" were then delegated in teams of two to time-travel to the past. Their assigned objective was to punish "ancestral violators" that did not conform to the "high moral standards" based on "common sense" that constituted the rigid principles of the newly implemented *Neo-Puritan* philosophy.

Zentar and Grel were veteran "moral vigilantes" who had been working together for seven years since the quelling of the last significant *Libertarian* upheaval. The two highly decorated time-warriors ambled to the designated "Year 2002 Locker Room" to change into light-dyed blue denim jeans, black tee-shirts and spring denim jackets to simulate the clothing worn by males of the era that they would soon be visiting.

"What's your assignment?" Zentar asked Grel. "Or is it the usual search and destroy mission? I'm glad we both have only ten more years until retirement."

Grel opened a sealed envelope that contained his "Vital Instructions." "It says," the Time Vigilante read aloud, "proceed to *Echelon Mall,* Voorhees, New Jersey, May 20, 2002 from seven to eight p.m. Grel, you are hereby delegated and elevated to the distinguished *Non-Smoking in Public Places Patrol.* Efficiently eliminate anyone you find smoking in public. Feel free Officer Grel to exercise your judgment when it comes down to life-or-death situations."

"That's only right," Zentar agreed with the new edict formulated by the *District Moral Code Commander.* "People should be more considerate of those that don't smoke. I mean," Zentar momentarily paused to organize his justification, "I mean, Grel, it's bad enough that people are so stupid destroying their own lungs and bodies with hungry cancer cells. But if the lunatics are so addicted to nicotine, then the violators should be smart enough to only smoke cigars and cigarettes in the privacy of their own homes. People should have the decency to not inhale and exhale contaminated toxic fumes in public places and jeopardize the health of other human beings."

"You're right on the money," Grel concurred with his loyal partner in moral law and social values' enforcement. "If people are ignorant enough to abuse the health of others by expelling quantities of smoke into the air," the time vigilante haughtily hypothesized and opined, "then Zentar, those stupid people must face the severe consequences without the expense of court appearances, police reports and jail incarceration. We just zap them with our *Internal Organ Destabilizers,*" Grel said as the time policeman examined his splendid weapon that looked somewhat like a black microphone with a flashlight head attached on the front end.

"Aren't you going to ask me what my special assignment is?" Zentar coaxed as he ripped open his "Confidential Orders" envelope. "You know, Grel. We both spent an entire week studying the speech patterns and mannerisms of these year 2002 freaks and I feel no compunction about killing the defective units."

"Okay, you're my partner," Grel admitted to Zentar. "So naturally, you're heading to a place called the *Echelon Mall* with me. But what specific detail must *you* home in on? Are you going to kill the passive smokers inhaling the nicotine and tar from the active puffers?"

"Ha, ha, ha," Zentar bellowed in a rare display of emotion. "I've been assigned to the *Elite No Kissing in Public Patrol.* Anyone caught showing affection in public is to be executed on the spot. Grel, everyone knows that showing affection in public breeds self-centered spoiled, bratty children and makes infatuated adults such repulsive ingrates that they're then instinctively governed by hormones and not by reason. Hey Grel," Zentar expounded. "Tell me how many people you've killed this year while on *Vigilante Patrol?* Have you kept a record?"

"Why, yes," Grel acknowledged and confirmed. "I've killed three hundred and fifty-six in the past twelve-months while on 'Affection Stakeout' and a thousand seven hundred and fifty-three total for all of my various *Vigilante Patrol* assignments."

"Wow! You're several hundred executions ahead of me!" Zentar exclaimed with admiration. "I'll have to accelerate my eradicator button on this particular expedition," the moral crusader seriously stated as he made a last-minute adjustment to a side dial on his very lethal weapon. "I have some serious catching-up to do. Ya' know Grel," Zentar concluded and stated, "I like these blue denim jeans I have on a lot better than our soft-plastic uniforms we have to wear.

Maybe I'll stay a while, retire and live out my life as a freelance assassin in the year 2002!"

"Don't become too corrupted by the crime and moral decay of the year 2002," Grel sincerely warned, "or I might soon be assigned by the *District Commander* to exterminate you! Make sure you have the five-hundred dollars in 2002 cash for us to buy food and merchandise with!"

Zentar and Grel believed in the importance and the necessity of their assigned "morality enforcement patrols." In their briefing from Captain Dorn, they had learned that Year 2002 Americans were reprehensibly egotistical, so despicable, so unappreciative and also so completely and intolerably aberrant of the fundamentals of social organization. Moral Patrols were often officially commissioned to journey to the past and assassinate individuals caught smoking, kissing, loitering in public places, cursing or spitting on public sidewalks or acting uncouth, boisterous and obnoxious inside public areas and squares. The Time Vigilantes' actions were justified from their point of view because both men had been wholly indoctrinated into a strict moral discipline code that made each hunter think unilaterally in identical idea-interpretation-reaction patterns. Both Grel and Zentar behaved and obeyed like similar well-synchronized murder machines.

"I particularly enjoy exterminating fat people," Grel proudly boasted. "There's no satisfactory reason or explanation for anyone weighing three hundred pounds and walking around a shopping mall eating a triple-scooped chocolate ice cream sugar-cone. When I see a person like that, I deviate from my prescribed orders and zap that lousy violator right on the spot."

"Now you're talking my language," Zentar related and agreed. "*Neo-Puritans* have the right idea and I'm glad they emerged victorious from the war and totally vanquished the major opposition parties. Fat people, invalids, ugly people and cripples all carry bad genes," the cyber-policeman confidently maintained. "Eliminate them as the *Internal Security Council* has intelligently mandated and big expensive *future* drains on our fine government and on our now strong economy have been swiftly excised out. Cancel-out problems in the past to ensure a moral and prosperous future, that's my philosophy along with the *Internal Security Council's* positive thinking too."

"Just remember," Grel reminded his cold heart hell-bent-for-leather comrade, "you've been delegated by the government to kill violators kissing in public. Zentar, as a general rule you're not allowed to terminate corpulent, lame, ugly or feeble wheel-chaired senior citizens at random on this specific scouting foray into enemy territory. You're to only kill those kinds of idiots if you don't come across a lot of inconsiderate public kissers. And above all else," Grel joked while showing little conscience, "don't kill any smokers. That's *my* personal responsibility on this mission."

America in the year 2380 AD was a tranquil civilization devoid of the ravages of "frustrating social diseases." The ultra-right-wing *Neo-Puritans* had transformed men, women and children into "Reverse Transcendentalists," or a society that valued thinking over feeling. The edicts and mandates coming out of Washington had maintained "Man is a rational, intellectual creature capable of learning, discovering, analyzing, studying and inventing." Expression of emotions while in public areas was regarded by the government as an extension of "overt animal monkey behavior."

Expressions of feelings and emotions were not only at first discouraged but after the "moral revolution" were later suppressed. *Neo-Puritan* government officials both despised and deplored demonstrations of affection in public. And when violators were caught on tape by spy cameras located at every city intersection and at every town traffic light across the continental United States, then the "criminals" were apprehended by "Storm Police" and then put into stocks and placed on public display in the center of town or in a city square to be publicly scorned and ridiculed. The "immoral criminals" were then mocked, spit upon, slapped and humiliated by amused bystanders and by righteous passing citizens.

Zentar and Grel were both aware that all aspects of life had to be logical and rational, including law, morality, behavior and even death. Everything had a scientific explanation and had been transmitted as "basic educational truth" to the public via schools and via the government-controlled mass media. The entire society was functioning in a precise manner like a well-oiled machine.

According to the *Neo-Puritan Party* leadership, the elimination of "animalistic emotional behavior" would make the achievement of "rational reality" more readily attainable. Scientific principles such as "cause and effect" were taught as factors that govern human behavior as well as being prevalent elements in technology also, so if a "criminal" committed a public fault, then his or her action was pragmatically judged to be the "cause" of a predictable "effect" (punishment and public ridicule). The inflexible codes of the *new* social sciences were shrewdly molded and elevated to be exact sciences similar to chemistry and physics, and psychology, religion and sociology were banned subjects in all of the nation's colleges and universities. Such were the narrow-minded but extremely effective teachings and practices of the stern-faced *Neo-Puritans*.

"Are you ready to enforce social justice upon idiotic fools and insane hypocrites in the year 2002?" Grel asked his highly motivated companion.

"Our beam transmitters are pre-programmed to the Men's Room just outside the Food Court at the *Echelon Mall,* Voorhees, New Jersey. Check your gauge coordinates," Zentar advised his vigilante colleague. "It's almost time to initiate our essential mission to eradicate future decadence!"

"Everything is desirable!" Grel alerted. "Let's synchronize our time-space alteration beams."

"All right, contact and away we go!" Zentar directed. "Let's have a blast into the past!"

* * * * * * * * * * * *

Three men were washing their hands in sinks and a boy was combing his hair as Zentar and Grel suddenly crystallized behind them in the men's lavatory mirror's reflection. The two futuristic space-time visitors immediately turned right and stepped out of the *Echelon Mall's* tidy Men's Room in a well-disciplined military cadence as if nothing extraordinary had ever happened.

The four bewildered individuals looked at one another with astonished expressions on their faces, all sharing the same "mass hallucination" and "group illusion," shrugging their shoulders in disbelief at what their eyes had just perceived but what their minds desired not to recognize.

Inside the "Food Court Pavilion", Zentar and Grel decided it was time to split up, promising to rendezvous again at 8 p.m. in the same tidy Men's Room for the return passage to Precinct Headquarters, 837 Arch Street, Philadelphia, Pennsylvania, year 2380.

"See you in an hour," Zentar predicted to his very efficient comrade. "Don't get lost in any lingerie departments!" the Time Vigilante facetiously added.

"Make sure you don't expire any smokers," Grel reminded his determined patriotic colleague. "And don't be a maverick. Only focus on and zap kissers with your *Internal Organ Destabilizer* and leave the nasty despicable smokers to me."

"You do have a propensity for manufacturing your own brand of propaganda," Zentar volleyed back. "You'd make a damned good politician now that lawyers have been made illegal!"

Grel meandered to his left at the *Echelon Mall* Food Court's crowded custard and ice cream concession and Zentar remained stationary inside the colorful "Food Court Pavilion" searching for potential recipients of his formidable death ray. 'This isn't exactly random killing,' the well-trained assassin thought. 'Random means to kill anybody violating the country's future moral codes, but I'm especially in quest of people showing excessive affection in public at the wrong time and at the wrong place,' Zentar rationalized and considered. 'I'm not governed by any narrow time schedule or by any specified itinerary to perform my vital service. I only have an agenda that will make future generations more cerebral and less animalistic and emotional. Raw emotions are merely extensions of the basic animal state of existence.'

Zentar alertly observed a young couple embracing in a long customer line in front of the *Food Court's* pizza concession. 'They must be low-mentality teenagers infatuated with one another's *animal magnetism*,' Zentar speculated and concluded. 'Married couples usually are tired of each other after a month of sex and don't care to show public affection like these unfortunate adolescent imbeciles are about to.'

Predictably, the acne-faced high school students' mouths came close together, and in another three seconds, their lips met. Soon the young lovers were engaged in an extended kiss. The futuristic commando was very adroit at his chosen trade and without even raising his deadly weapon to his eyes, he easily extinguished the two young students of *Cupid* with two instantaneous waist-high invisible laser jets pulsating from his remarkable weapon.

No one milling around the *Food Court Pavilion* noticed Zentar's efficient evil executions, which had indeed been performed very stealthily and very deftly. Two youthful bodies collapsed to the tan-tiled mall floor and then a chorus of hysterical screams permeated throughout that corner sector of *the Food Court Pavilion.*

The successful time traveler assassin casually sauntered in the direction of the custard and ice cream station situated in the middle of the *Echelon Mall* Food Court adjacent to the colossal double-decked indoor shopping center's main traffic corridor. 'Grel and I will be out of here is less than an hour once we meet our quotas,' the confident killer reckoned, 'and the incompetent police won't be able to coordinate mall camera pictures from all of the selective assassinations for over two hours. Even if the moronic cops cordon off all entrances and exits to the mall,' Zentar slyly concluded, 'we'll both easily escape *their* wimpy dragnet by simply disappearing into *time* while shrewdly eluding being trapped in *space.*'

In front of the *Pretzel and Donut Factory,* Zentar spotted a male and a female passionately kissing. It didn't matter if they were husband and wife or simply an engaged couple about to be married. Public affection was a taboo that had to be purged from the Year 2002 to guarantee society's future health in the Year 2380. Zentar wasted little time reacting to the capricious display rather promptly and effectively.

'Silly, frivolous fools!' Zentar evaluated. 'They ought to know better and have more consideration for the public that has to be unnecessarily exposed to *their* juvenile antics. *They* should know that in the future, television shows, movies and soap operas aren't allowed to have kissing scenes in them. Dumb subhuman cretins!' Zentar imagined. 'In the future, people simply *like* each other and are compelled by law to *like* everyone in their society. *Love* is too strong of a word to use in 2380 AD. *Love* is just an ideal, a distant longing for a girl or for a woman, like *Don Quixote* had felt in literature for *Dulcinea*,' Zentar mentally assessed. 'That's what *love* should really be in the Year 2002, but the word *like* is exactly how the abstraction *love* is described in 2380, and *like* never involves affection!'

As Zentar reached into his jacket to wrap his fingers around his trusty "violators' zapper," the futuristic visitor wondered what it would be like to actually kiss a woman. Realizing the folly of his rampant imagination, the dedicated space-time patrolman squeezed the side of his awesome weapon, and in five brief seconds a pair of invisible death rays had "destroyed" the "two human examples" lying motionless on the tile floor.

146

The very dangerous time commando scanned the area above the store facades for mall surveillance cameras. After completing *his* cursory camera inspection thirty feet away from the fallen affection victims, Zentar strolled to another section of the mall, pretending to be one of many apathetic eyewitnesses that wanted nothing to do with the travails and fates of the already dead mall patrons. Shouts and gasps were heard as alarmed and appalled shoppers rushed to the scene to view the macabre charred spectacles lying on the elaborate brown-tiled floor designs.

Pacing three-hundred-feet down the busy mall corridor, Zentar encountered two gay women holding hands. Lesbian behavior was regarded as "an abomination" by the rigid-morals' *Neo-Puritan Party,* which staunchly condemned all forms of homosexual activity. 'They don't even have to kiss each other for me to be motivated to kill them,' the time visitor wickedly thought. 'This human vermin disgusts me and turns my stomach sour. I can even taste the foul putrid digestive juice pumping its way up to my mouth! I hate scummy queers even more than I despise public affection!' the futuristic soldier's twisted mind diabolically decided. 'I can't wait to zap these scurrilous licentious violators!'

In another ten-seconds, two female corpses lay prone on the brown-tile floor amidst yells, hollers and shouts from exasperated mall shoppers that happened to be in the vicinity. Zentar chuckled to himself' as he slyly feigned looking inside a glass partition of an exclusive men's store, coyly studying several pair of fancy-dress-shoes. 'Don't need those suckers!' he thought with a wide smirk on his face. 'I'll take combat boots any day,' the Time Vigilante grinned as his eyes glanced down at the brown penny loafers on *his* feet.

Two very distraught security guards, followed by three anxious Voorhees Township policemen, sprinted by the shoe display in the opposite direction, all racing toward the crime scene. Zentar nonchalantly shuffled his way toward the expansive entrance to a prominent department store. 'Those ugly female faggots got what they deserved,' he mentally reviewed with great satisfaction. 'If they want to be lesbians, then the damned perverts should be lesbians outside of public scrutiny in the privacy of their own homes. In the year 2380,' Zentar mused, 'even popular songs don't mention the words' kiss, affection or love, and I'm exclusively thinking about heterosexual relationships. Those female freaks are on their way to *Hell* right now, and that's exactly where the lecherous sinners belong! The *Devil* already owned their souls before I punctually eliminated them from this Earth!'

Zentar then stepped inside the enormous well-stocked department store and advanced through the perfume, jewelry and panty hose departments. In front of the dual ascending and descending escalators the callous human automaton witnessed a young kindergarten age girl dashing up to an elderly woman yelling "Grandma', Grandma!" The affectionate young girl gave her grandmother a massive kiss on her lips and the elderly woman wholeheartedly reciprocated.

'There's no depth to their simple childish minds,' the enraged observer concluded. 'All the two dolts know how to do is express shallow ideas of a need for security to each other!' Zentar angrily imagined with his eyes blazing red. 'They'll be executed on the basis of lacking mental depth and of showing a lack of regard for others in this public environment.'

The unbridled exhibition of genuine natural affection caused animosity to well-up inside Zentar's consciousness and ten seconds later, two still bodies lay dead on the department store floor amidst resounding screams from horrified mall customers and completely stunned sales personnel.

Zentar next entered and then took the elevator up to the second floor and exited into the gigantic store's sporting goods department. Immediately, the Time Vigilante's perceptive eyes detected and focused on a mother loudly smooching her baby's face and the overt sound of exaggerated affection and loud cooing only intensified the time assassin's rage. 'Stupid frivolous asinine behavior!' the commando's mind criticized. 'That foolish woman doesn't realize that true happiness comes from achieving, from producing, from inventing, from thinking and from exploring the limits of human intelligence. That kid will never be able to have the patience and discipline to write a book or to accomplish anything great in life that requires a lot of thought,' Zentar mentally criticized and analyzed. 'That mother doesn't realize that true happiness results from satisfaction being derived from success. A kid who is too secure is afraid to fail, and failure is necessary to build character and integrity,' Zentar convinced himself as his mind reiterated certain moral axioms that military instructors had incessantly inculcated into *his* very complex thought patterns. 'What ever happened to parent-centered families? Child-centered families breed demanding doltish offspring that are lazy, contented, egocentric and that are falsely

148

praised for just existing and that are undeservedly doted on for not achieving anything special in life or for that matter, ever achieving anything mediocre!'

Before the highly trained Time Vigilante administered his fatal death ray, some other negative thoughts swam through his very upset mind. 'Lazy spoiled brats are the result of this silly ridiculous affectionate behavior mental sickness! Instead of children imitating mature parents, parents in this derelict socially chaotic age of 2002 are absurdly imitating immature children and acting like two-year-olds themselves! Whatever happened to the notion that children should be seen and not heard or touched?'

A minute later, the mother and her infant lay dead in front of the sporting goods department's pyramid baseball bat display. After a sales clerk desperately yelled for assistance, a crowd of delirious and hysterical curiosity seekers gathered around the helpless victims, who both would soon be riding in local coroner's hearses rather than in hospital ambulances.

The very proficient time-travel murderer paced to the front of the department store where seven beleaguered police officers rushed by *his* slow methodical gait. 'Life in my future time might be cold, calculating and analytical,' Zentar reckoned, 'but it's certainly more objective and rational than in 2002. Little is subjective and emotional in 2380, and I *like* it that way. Everything makes sense. It bothers me when adults act like children when parents and grandparents should be setting models of mature behavior for youngsters to imitate,' Zentar reasoned and justified. 'The people of this peculiar age are so primitive and so un-evolved. The parents slobber all over and delight in licking their babies' faces much the same as primitive apes do with their young. It looks so sloppy and it sounds so awful when they suck on each other as if the mother and kid were lollipops. It sounds and looks like mother monkeys licking and sucking their helpless chimpanzee offspring. That's exactly what it looks like and what it sounds like,' the Time Vigilante thought as turmoil and confusion abounded around him. 'These damned mentally underdeveloped humans of 2002 haven't yet evolved beyond the gorilla level of existence! Human intelligence must ultimately triumph over animalistic feelings!'

Zentar's cruel heart lusted for more homicides, so the human killing machine entered the mall's *McDonald's* and sat down at a booth without ordering anything. According to schedule, in fifteen minutes he would be meeting Grel, who had been creating *his* own premeditated havoc with unwary smokers all over the panic-stricken mall.

Glancing to his right, the conscience-less time slayer from the future observed two small children across the aisle. The moral vigilante surreptitiously suspected the two were brother and sister as they were innocently and voluntarily kissing one another. As usual, the toddlers' parents were preoccupied chatting and they and their pristine children were oblivious to the killing machine's cunning scrutiny.

'What's wrong with the people of this wretched era?' Zentar wondered. 'They all seem to want to be targets of my wrath and they all appear to have definite death' wishes. Don't they know that they're exchanging millions and millions of germs and spreading infection with their slimy tongues and wet mouths constantly licking each other?' the crazed highly-disciplined homicide enforcer remembered from one of his military indoctrination lectures.

Then, the moral vigilante's temper escalated to an even higher level. 'Affection merely breeds complacency and a false sense of security,' he thought and truly believed. 'It never leads to suspicion and the enactment of intelligent survival behavior. That's why lions rule the grasslands and antelopes don't. The lion is more intelligent than the antelope. The lion is the hunter and the antelope the prey. Don't these stupid people understand that only intelligent and wary creatures survive in a world fraught with competition and struggle! Too much security will lead to societal decay and to cultural decline!' Zentar vengefully imagined. 'These disturbing entitlement-oriented kids will never enjoy the much more meaningful abstractions in life such as honor, happiness from achievement, justice, courage, courtesy, beauty and truth. All these spoiled conditioned brats know is security resulting from affection, and too much security is evil and will eventually lead to *Western Civilization's* decline!' concluded the brainwashed moral vigilante to his very receptive will and *Neo-Puritan* value system.

Zentar instinctively reached into his denim jacket's pocket and removed the power source for his deadly death ray *Internal Organ and Tissue Disintegrator*. His first impulse was to warily gaze to his left to ascertain that his villainous act would not be observable to any normally inattentive *McDonald's* diners.

Much to *his* utter astonishment Zentar's eyes recognized Darf, a member of the *Libertarian Party's* Stealth Secret Police, aiming *his* death ray gun directly at the enemy he had readily identified and had been astutely stalking inside the *Echelon Mall*.

The thought of 'Survival' dominated Zentar's machine-like precision mind and as he quickly ducked down under the booth's table, Darf's ray blast flashed across and above the intended victim's head. Ironically, Darf had performed Zentar's duty by inadvertently and unintentionally killing the little boy and his sister affectionately kissing one another in the adjacent *McDonald's* booth.

Seeing an opportunity for escape, Zentar slid out of his smooth green leather booth, crawled a distance of ten feet on the floor, rose to his knees and then hustled as fast as his legs could carry him out of the fast food establishment. In his haste to safety, the distressed Time Vigilante had accidentally left his extraordinary zap disintegrator behind during all of the mass confusion.

Michael Daniels, a mentally challenged but dependable *McDonald's Restaurant* employee, recognized that Zentar had left his personal property on the light green leather seat. Daniels ceased wiping down the top of a neighboring table, ignored the delirious exclamations of shock and fright around him, picked up the strange alien weapon and instinctively pursued its owner into the main mall shopping area.

"Sir, Sir, you left this inside the store!" Michael Daniels shouted at the top of his lungs. "Please stop and let me give it to you!"

A young child broke away from his mother's grasp and wobbled directly into Michael Daniel's path. The mentally challenged high school special needs student leaped into the air to hurtle over the toddler, and when the teenager's right wrist made contact with the brown rectangular tiled floor, the weapon was activated. An invisible deadly ray was discharged and immediately paralyzed the fleeing Zentar, who immediately dropped to the floor and was dead in ten seconds.

* * * * * * * * * * * *

Judge Matthew Dixon carefully studied Michael Daniel's pallid face and asked Camden County Prosecutor Jeffrey Jensen to remove *his* surgical gloves and hand them to him, so that the court official could closely examine the "alleged murder weapon."

"May I remind the judge that the defendant Michael Daniels is a mentally challenged high school student working part time at *McDonald's* on a special state-sponsored school work program," Defense Attorney Mark Brookes glibly interrupted.

Judge Matthew Dixon carefully inspected the alien lethal ray expeller. His thumb accidentally slid against an inconspicuous side-control as coincidentally the "flashlight head" had been pointing straight into the judge's face. A secondary ray was emitted and Judge Dixon instantaneously vanished from sight.

The flabbergasted bailiff and the amazed police guards on courtroom duty rushed forward with drawn revolvers. The shocked courtroom audience was unaware that Judge Matthew Dixon had accidentally teleported himself' to the year 2380 where his "good workable mind" would be thoroughly infiltrated and indoctrinated to become a member-in-training of the "Honorable Neo-Puritan Moral Vigilante Police Patrol."

"The Hotel Delaware"

Superstitious people believe and attest that strange incidents often occur on February 29 of every *Leap Year*. I had never placed too much credence in that unscientific claim until Tuesday, February 29, 2004, which unfortunately is a date I will certainly remember forever. Let me fully explain my accursed dilemma so that all will comprehend the true nature of my misery. The courtesy of another person's sympathy and understanding will be greatly appreciated. I realize that my tale will seem both illogical and incredible to anyone interpreting it, yet I believe I must share its veracity.

A *Leap Year* has three hundred and sixty-six days on the annual calendar, one more twenty-four hour interval than that which exists in a normal year. Greenwich, England scientists and concerned astronomers have adjusted the mechanics of the moon and months to interface with the Earth's revolution around the sun because a quarter of a day is lost each normal year when coordinating those particular solar system relationships. To accurately adjust for the quarter-day time discrepancy in the Earth's elliptical orbit around the sun, February 29 was created on the post medieval *Gregorian Calendar* (developed in the 1580s by Pope Gregory), which we still honor today after the old Julian Calendar (developed in 46 B.C. under the reign of Julius Caesar) had been discarded.

Some *Leap Years* are unluckier than others. Every year divisible by the number four (lets' say the year 2004 or 2008) is generally regarded in common knowledge as a legitimate bona fide *Leap Year*. No problem! So far so good! But every "century year" divisible by a hundred is *not* a *Leap Year* unless that particular year is also divisible by four hundred; then it is still defined as a legitimate, bona fide *Leap Year*. For example, the years 1800, 1900, 2100 and 2200 AD are *not Leap Years* because they can't be divided by four hundred. Conversely, the Year 2000 *was* recognized as a legitimate, bona fide *Leap Year* because it *was* divisible by four hundred.

A person born on this planet Earth has a one in 1,506 chance of being born on February 29 of a *Leap Year,* but nevertheless 4.1 million individuals living around the globe have made their official grand appearance on that weird day and of that large number, 188,000 of them live in the United States. Before February 29, 2004, I had always felt sorry for people born on February 29 because their birthdays arrive only once every four years. Now I feel sorry for myself' for not staying at home on that ill-starred date. Allow me to fully explain my dilemma.

Some humans residing on this remarkable planet have attempted to conceal the bad omens that are associated with *Leap Year*. For example, *Sadie Hawkins Day* is celebrated on February 29 when single women once every four years are permitted to abandon traditional courting practice and chase after or propose marriage to men, thus attempting to make the "unlucky aspects" of that ominous day appear less threatening and more tolerable to the human race. But I can earnestly assert from my own personal experience that February 29, 2004 is a day I feel compelled to remember for all eternity. Soon you'll learn why.

I had made an appointment for Tuesday, February 29, 2004 to meet the book editor of a small publishing company at eleven a.m. at the *Regal Restaurant,* Baltimore Avenue, at the southern end of Ocean City, Maryland. I had been an arcade owner and operator of *Dealers Choice Games* at 410 South Boardwalk, Ocean City, Maryland, from 1967-'81. So naturally I was quite familiar with the city and with the reputable *Regal Restaurant*, which was one of my favorite breakfast and lunch haunts when I had been an industrious summer boardwalk businessman in that popular resort city. From a nostalgia point of view, I was really looking forward to making the business/pleasure trip down to the Maryland shore.

The editor's publishing firm was located in Annapolis, Maryland, and so Ocean City was a convenient halfway destination for us to rendezvous to discuss my book submission that had attracted David Evans' attention. A contract had been signed by me and mailed to the publishing company. All I had to do was drive seventy-miles from my Hammonton, New Jersey home to Cape May, catch the 7:30 a.m. ferry across *Delaware Bay* to Lewes, Delaware, and then drive another hour down the Atlantic Coast to Ocean City, Maryland. My only regret at the time was that the very busy editor had scheduled our "brunch engagement" at 11 a.m. on the very inauspicious date, February 29, 2004.

My wife wanted to borrow my merlot-colored *Nissan Maxima* to impress some of her friends with *our* new driving machine, so I had to settle driving her light brown *Nissan Altima* from Hammonton seventy-miles south down to Cape May, New Jersey. I left my home at six a.m., figuring I had more than sufficient time to make my easy connection with the *Cape May-Lewes Ferry,* since I had conducted similar trips hundreds of times before from 1967-1981.

Driving down Bellevue Avenue in Hammonton, I accidentally ran over a board lying in the street that had nails protruding face-up. I felt the *Altima's* steering wheel wobble when I drove another three miles to the *Atlantic City Expressway* entrance. Five miles in the direction of Atlantic City I frantically veered my wife's brown automobile into the *Frank Farley Rest Area* and quickly inflated the hissing tire with air.

Speeding down the *Expressway* at eighty-miles an hour, I thought I had had a hallucination of sorts. I had an uncanny sensation that I had skidded off the right shoulder of the highly traveled highway and that the light brown *Nissan Altima* had entered a pine barrens' forest and had then slammed into a tree, knocking me unconscious. 'I really didn't get a good night's sleep!' I remember thinking after surviving the rather surreal manifestation that seemingly featured a very real impact. 'I must get to the ferry before this confounded front tire goes flat. Then I will have really *missed the boat!"* my mind mused. 'I mustn't disappoint the editor by having a real collision. That accident was merely a wild figment of my imagination!'

In my wandering mind the same "air injection" of the affected tire was duplicated fifteen-miles down the *Expressway* when I exited the toll thoroughfare at Pleasantville and then I again anxiously repeated the nerve-racking inflation procedure. After taking the *Expressway* to the *Garden State Parkway* I had to again stop at a *Parkway Service Area* and fill the tire with air and then desperately continue my extremely harrowing journey south. At Cape May, I anxiously drove into a gas station and repeated the left front tire inflation a fourth time until I finally and gratefully made it to the ferry dock at 7:20. My mind was in a very paranoid state from all of the duress that had converted a supposedly pleasant ride into a living nightmare.

When I pulled-up to the *Cape May-Lewes Ferry* tollbooth, I turned-up the volume on the *Altima's* stereo radio, and then paid the unwary grim-faced female collector the exact amount for crossing the bay. She never heard the air hissing and sizzling out of my left front tire. I was too arrogant and proud to understand that the tire traumas were seemingly attempting to warn me not to cross the *Delaware Bay.*

I drove the light brown *Altima* forward, boarded the ferry, and at the time, I felt haughty and confident that I had cleverly outsmarted a major obstacle (by fooling the apathetic toll collector) caused by unlucky February 29, 2004. The ferry's entrance ramp was raised, the ship's loud horns sounded, and next, I perceived that the huge one-hundred-twenty-vehicle capacity boat had gently slid out of its daily mooring.

I smugly sat in my wife's car, speculating that I would exit it a half-hour later and report my flat tire predicament to the captain when the ferry was halfway across *Delaware Bay*. 'The captain will get several of his crew-members to go down with a can of air-sealant and inflate my front tire so that I can safely make it down to Ocean City without further incident,' I cleverly imagined. 'I've outsmarted the ferry personnel by making my tire problem *their* tire problem to solve! I can always buy a brand-new tire and have it mounted at a service station in Ocean City.'

A half-hour finally elapsed on my watch. I casually got out of the *Altima*, inspected the front tire and immediately ascertained that it had indeed gone flat. 'Tires are only flat on the bottom!' I recollect humoring myself' with a familiar overused joke.

My eyes glanced around and extraordinarily observed that the light brown *Altima* was the only car on the ferry, which (as I have mentioned) could easily carry and transport over a hundred similar-sized vehicles across the bay. Furthermore, after ascending the white metal steps to the top-deck, I detected that the ferry was enveloped in a very dense fog. I could barely see the landmark partially sunken concrete ship situated in the distance off of Cape May Point, but the famous *Cape May Lighthouse* was completely shrouded by the heavy veil of dense atmospheric haze that had descended on *Delaware Bay*.

Looking ahead south in the direction of the Delaware shoreline, I couldn't see any signs of land or of man-made structures. 'The fog's as thick as pasta sauce!' I evaluated. 'It's a good thing this ship has an adequate radar system!' I thankfully considered in an effort to allay my heightened anxiety.

Upon entering the main concession area, I immediately recognized that something was very abnormal. 'Where are all the other passengers? I'm the only one in the entire room! Where are the waitresses and the food attendants? Nobody's on this cursed ship except me!' I quickly realized.

I wildly clambered up metal stairs to the captain's deck and attempted to open the door to his control room but the doorknob would not turn and the windowless white metal object would not budge. 'This is stranger than peculiar!' I nervously thought. 'This popular ferry has transformed into a mysterious ghost ship of some kind! Damned February 29!' I neurotically blamed that date. "Damned February 29, 2004!" I lustily screamed out into the apathetic dense *Delaware Bay* fog.

I investigated the entire ship and found no evidence of any other human being aboard. I anxiously searched in the Men's Room; in the lounge area; in the engine rooms, and even had the audacity to enter the forbidden "Ladies Room". But much to my disappointment and dismay, apparently I was the only person making the 'supernatural passage.' I recall wishing 'Please Lord, if only I could locate just one petrified passenger to provide me some semblance of comfort from my overwhelming apprehension. Then I'll feel a whole lot better,' I solemnly prayed.

My feet stepped to the ship's bow and I futilely held my left-hand up to my sweaty forehead, endeavoring to get a glimpse of some remote familiar landmark, or perhaps hear a common *Delaware Bay* oil tanker's horn blasting. 'I've taken this ferry ride at least five-hundred-times between 1967 and '81 transporting merchandise from family boardwalk stores in Ocean City, Maryland, Rehoboth Beach, Delaware and Atlantic City, New Jersey,' I remember thinking and analyzing. 'But this misadventure has got to be the most frightening seventeen mile crossing above and beyond any nightmare or seasickness I could ever have experienced!' I concluded as my body trembled and my knees knocked together. 'There just has to be some feasible explanation!'

The ferry's eerie foghorn blew three times, and as I stared-off into the distance, my eyes finally were able to identify a nebulous-looking familiar object, the first of two parallel jetties that had been constructed about a mile into the *Delaware Bay* on the Lewes, Delaware side. 'At last, something I know and recognize in this crazy horrifying mental jigsaw puzzle! Now, I have some hope! Those jetties had been built to prevent beach erosion,' I recalled.

The captain-less ship then strangely deviated from its normal course (that I had memorized in my head) and slowly cutting through the very palpable fog, it turned left and then entered the channel between the two jetties instead of continuing straight ahead past them to the Lewes, Delaware dock. The vessel was now nearer to Cape Henlopen than to its appointed destination, the Lewes, Delaware terminal.

I felt an intense chill circulating throughout my stunned body. The combination of an overall sinister atmosphere, along with an accompanying damp mist was comparable in my mind to imagining *me* traveling to a close friend's funeral aboard a mysterious lost ghost ship adrift at sea. At least, that was the odd-type of sensation or perception that my consciousness had been rationalizing.

The ferry sounded its loud foghorn one final time and then effortlessly glided and slowly eased into a berth (that was unfamiliar to me) on the Delaware shore. I was quite perturbed and distraught with my heart filled with distinct trepidation, not knowing whether my crazy misadventure was an actual experience or a fantastic arcane delusion. Overhead gears threaded with thick chains suddenly began rotating and next the exit ramp for cars and passengers squeakily descended. 'We've landed near Cape Henlopen and not near Lewes, the ferry's destination,' I recollect thinking. 'This is definitely not where *we're* supposed to be! Something's certainly amiss here!'

My pupils steadfastly gazed through the persistent dense fog and saw a vague illumination directly ahead. A dim light shone from a hand-held lantern, and a shadowy figure was silhouetted behind the weak glow. As if my body and spirit had suddenly been magnetized, my legs reflexively began walking in the direction of the obscure figure who was holding the morbid-looking lantern.

My mind was still aware of the light brown *Nissan Altima* parked near the ferry's bow, but my heart and body could not resist the inexplicable potent force that was deliberately pulling and dragging me like an invisible tractor-beam to the ominous figure holding the ancient-looking lantern.

"Welcome to the *Hotel Delaware!*" the old, white-bearded ghoul greeted. "Do not be afraid. I'm your host and your guide, who will supervise your tenure here. I suppose you have many questions to ask me, as most guests initially do."

"Who are you?" I tentatively inquired. "Why am I here? What's going on?"

"I am Diogenes," the ghostly character revealed. "And *you* are here dear visitor, obviously because you're dead and your prodigious spirit desperately requires rest, rehabilitation, and requiem. Come with me inside your new lodging," the grayish apparition, dressed in ancient Greek garb, communicated.

"And if I refuse?" I defiantly challenged. "What will be the consequences? What will be my punishment?"

158

"You have no say in the matter, whatsoever," Diogenes grimly uttered. "You had surrendered your free will when your spirit escaped its confinement from inside your body. You have no choice as a dead entity other than to cooperate with my mandates. I can force you to perform any act that I want you to execute, so don't resist my standard commands!" my pallid-faced guide explained. "Insolence will not be tolerated. I repeat. You surrendered your free will when your spirit evacuated your body! Do you now comprehend that basic simple truth?"

My emotions were dominated by shock and awe. I remember thinking, '*You've* spent thirty-five years of your life teaching public-school kids' English grammar, vocabulary, writing, and literature, have finally reached retirement age, have begun a promising writing career and have sabotaged it all by suddenly becoming deceased on February 29th!'

My body reluctantly followed Diogenes away from the spooky ferry mooring, and then we meandered through the thick fog in the direction of a dilapidated structure that was situated on a high sand dune directly ahead. My restless spirit (or that element of it which still remained in my consciousness) demanded some plausible explanations from the hoary-looking guide dressed in a wretched-looking ancient mendicant's dull gray robe.

"I must've died in the automobile accident on the *Expressway!*" I gasped in horror. "Diogenes, did I die in an automobile accident? I just have to know *that* detail to alleviate my general nervousness!"

"What is an automobile?" the twenty-four-century old guide asked. "It really doesn't matter what that item is," he continued speaking like a verbal cadaver. "You're dead as a doormat and now charged to my professional custody, automobile or no automobile. Do you fathom my words? The ideas and objects of your former world, of *my* former world, no longer interest me. They're both irrelevant and obsolete here!"

We slowly paced forward in the direction of the ominous-looking *Hotel Delaware*, which was now visibly outlined in the very thick mist with a rickety-looking shingle hanging on one hinge indicating my whereabouts. I found my eerie-sounding escort's answer very incomprehensible (let alone reprehensible), but nevertheless, quite intriguing. "Diogenes," I boldly asked. "Are you the ancient Greek known to history as the *Cynic?*"

"You're quite a knowledgeable fellow, because not too many souls make that particular association," my spooky host articulated. "And yes, Stranger. You are correct in astutely making that connection. You must read books to be aware of that academic fact!"

"But how have you gotten from ancient civilization to the United States in the year 2004, and where did you learn to speak perfect English?" I stammered.

"Please, Sir. One annoying question at a time," my new guardian insisted with a stern grimace featured upon his ghostly, macabre-looking pale face. "I really don't know or care how I've arrived at *your* distant country. I can only tell you that once every three hundred and eighty-four years, I'm moved and re-stationed by the unpredictable *Powers That Be* to a new drab and monotonous assignment in an odd new land. And finally," Diogenes proceeded with his fascinating monologue, "I've learned and conquered your language from conversing with other guests that have stayed or are staying at the *Hotel Delaware*. Does that answer satisfy your rather simplistic, primitive curiosity?"

"Well, somewhat!" I marveled and replied. "I had read about you in a college philosophy class," I nervously stated. "And you were notorious for diligently walking the streets with a lantern looking for the face of an honest man. Is that legend actually true? Is that why you're still carrying your lantern?"

"You're most perceptive and appear to be highly educated," my alert guide observed and reluctantly complimented. "Yes, it is true, but historical truths are meaningless now, both to you and to me. The only significant fact that really matters is that we're both dead and that *you* must reside by Heaven's decree at the very serene *Hotel Delaware*. That is why the ferryboat delivered you to these obscure premises in that rather intense fog. Every time the mist settles I know I'll be hearing the ship's horns," the old withered specter lethargically related, "and then that ominous blast is my signal to come out from the hotel and cordially escort our latest guest inside. After that task is done my next responsibility is to make my most recent ward as comfortable as possible."

As my famous deceased mentor and I paced up thirteen flimsy steps, and gradually arrived at the *Hotel Delaware's* main entrance, the creaky door with un-oiled hinges slowly opened and Diogenes led me inside the musty building, which immediately reminded me of a dingy and despicable murky funeral parlor. Cobwebs, broken windows, bleak-looking dirty chandeliers and layers of dust everywhere suggested that the ramshackle hotel for death-transients was truly a ruinous unkempt *deathtrap.*

"Diogenes, is it true what I've read in encyclopedias that you believed that wealth and honor are of little value because those pursuits do not help men lead just and moral lives?" I instinctively asked my laconic host. "I recollect that principle as being the cornerstone to your philosophy."

"All of those seemingly important old ideas are quite immaterial and irrelevant now," Diogenes glumly answered. "Virtue, honor, wealth and morality are no longer essential elements of behavior. If I were you," Diogenes imperatively cautioned, "I would ask fewer questions and then pay strict attention and learn the fundamental elements of *your* new environment. Just remember Sir, you're now dead, and nothing else really matters. Please leave the myriad minuscule problems of the world to the living."

"But didn't you once visit and meet *Alexander the Great,* and he insisted on granting you any wish you wanted," I almost hysterically ranted, "and then you absurdly replied, 'Please move out of my sunlight,' and then *Alexander the Great…*"

"Silence, Fool!" Diogenes angrily exclaimed as he held his spectral lantern up, fully exposing his hideous skeletal face. "Any more outbursts from you will surely result in dire consequences for your captured soul. Heed my simple basic commands Stranger, or else you'll certainly be doomed to a far worse eternal fate than mere death! I trust now that I've concisely communicated that stark cause-effect relationship to you."

'*I'm* very much like Diogenes, an avowed cynic and a devout skeptic,' I rationally thought. 'Perhaps that is why I'm assigned here and *he* is here, too. The poor Greek scholar has been commanded to teach *me* what I need to know and what years of doubt could not make me realize,' I conjectured.

My heart felt tempted to mentally ask (for *we* were transmitting thoughts and words through a fantastic telepathy and not by using our mouths and voice-boxes) my distinguished escort if he had ever heard of an Athenian named Socrates, but since I didn't desire to antagonize the melancholy, morose apparition, and subsequently suffer his wrath, I refrained from making the inquiry. My mind fathomed that presently *he* had absolute dominion over my weak (and maybe absent) will.

Diogenes led me through the foyer of the shabby antiquated edifice to a gloomy dusty poorly lit lobby and we passed empty chairs with torn upholstery and several sofas neglected by time and quite apparently in dire need of repair. At the *Hotel Delaware's* front desk my escort solemnly asked me to sign both my real name "John Wiessner" and my pen name "Jay Dubya" in the ledger, which I cooperatively complied while coincidentally and obediently enacting his baneful command.

"How did you know my real name and how did you know I had a pen name?" I requested knowing. "You must be omniscient," I mentally transmitted.

"Knowledge in this afterlife is transparent and not opaque as it is in *our* former world," Diogenes telepathically related. "And it is not exclusively confined to a person's form or body. I simply read your vulnerable mind as if I was reading an elementary book or a tablet. It's quite easy once you learn the knack!"

"Well," I commented in sheer amazement, "what about heaven and hell and purgatory and what about everybody else that's dead and *Jesus* and..."

"Look!" my upset teacher said in an admonishing tone of voice, "the information you're requesting is not available or known on *this* lowly death level. Once you leave this holding area and move on into the greater transcendent after-world," Diogenes carefully enunciated, "then those typical questions that presently riddle your limited comprehension might be satisfactorily answered at the next higher phantom station. Now, do you fully evaluate your lowly status on the eternal ladder?"

"But if I died when my car had veered into the woods," I mentally rebutted, "how could I have lived to put air into my front tire several more times before arriving at the ferry terminal?" I desperately argued. "And Diogenes, if my car was wrecked-up, and if I was dead on impact, how did I manage to drive it all the way to Cape May to take the ferry across the bay to this horrible *Hotel Delaware?"*

"It probably takes about an Earth hour for true death to finally set in," Diogenes theorized and objectively communicated, "and you were still mentally carrying out your trip to the ferry during that delicate hour of transition from your former life to this one. So spiritually, mentally and emotionally," the ancient pessimistic sage cleverly observed and concluded, "you had completed that part of

162

your trip even though your body had perished in the accident you had previously so vividly described."

"Who else is registered here as a guest?" I inquisitively asked. "How many rooms does this place have for occupancy? It looks pre-Victorian in architecture!"

"Please, Sir. One appropriate question at a time," Diogenes aggressively chastised. "You have all eternity to learn and decipher what you feel you need to know. You'll soon discover that the *Hotel Delaware* has thirteen guest rooms. And I don't know if that mediocre number is symbolic of anything or not."

I glanced outside a window, and the only thing I could discern in the dense fog was the aforementioned unhinged black shutter hanging-down from the wooden outside wall. The object quite evidently needed several serious heavy coats of paint. "Oh," I thought and communicated. "That numerical symbolism makes a lot of sense, having thirteen rooms. Delaware was the first state, and there were thirteen original colonies that had united in the war of independence against England. One room for each colony is a wonderful coincidence! Wouldn't you agree, Diogenes?"

I learned from my orientation guide that the other spirit guests residing at the hotel were distinguished personages Benjamin Franklin, George Washington, Thomas Jefferson, Edgar Allan Poe, Abraham Lincoln, Ulysses S. Grant, Mark Twain, Henry Ford, Albert Einstein, Franklin D. Roosevelt, George Herman "Babe" Ruth, and Marilyn Monroe.

"But those people are all famous?" I challenged my honorable guide. "What's the meaning of all this? Where do I fit in, a common public school English teacher?"

"You mean they all *were* famous," Diogenes cunningly corrected and clarified.

"But tell me, why am I here with all of these deceased celebrities, inventors and presidents if I'm just an unfortunate ordinary dead person?" I demanded knowing. "Honestly, I certainly lack their accomplishments and their credentials!"

"Maybe you'll become famous after your death just like Herman Melville or William Shakespeare," my ancient Greek ghost page speculated and mentally conveyed. "My senses perceive that you had always wanted to communicate with the dead. Now here's your big chance."

I learned several bizarre things from Diogenes. When Babe Ruth had registered as a guest Christopher Columbus had simultaneously checked out and had been moved to another higher plateau in the afterlife. And when Marilyn Monroe's shade was accepted as an official resident, Henry Hudson's apparition was allowed to move on to loftier post mortem pursuits.

"At the rate of new guests and old ones coming and going," I commented to the stone-faced and generally apathetic Diogenes, "I won't get out of this lackluster *death trap* for another two hundred years judging by how long George Washington has been a prisoner, er, I mean a visitor here."

"That logical assessment seems about right," my ghastly-looking skeptical companion agreed. "But you must remember," Diogenes ruefully clarified, "time as you knew it is meaningless at this place. There is little difference between a minute, a day, a century and a millennium at this splendid and unique hotel. Time here can either expand or it can contract. As that fellow Einstein in Room 1955 once told me, everything including time is relative!" my host mentally related with a very weak-but-irritating smile vaguely reflecting from his countenance.

"Oh," I mentally answered, "now that explanation of yours makes perfectly good sense. When one person moves in, the lucky spirit that has been here the longest is finally eligible to move out. It's sort of like a predictable rotating lottery of sorts!"

"Right you are, Sir," Diogenes aptly concurred with my brilliant deduction. "When you moved in, Ben Franklin, according to the established rotation, must step onto the ferry and be taken to the next higher station, wherever that is!"

Just then the ferry horns blasted three times, suggesting that Ben Franklin was obediently ambling up the ramp and happily departing the dismal, dreary grounds and sinister vicinity of the *Hotel Delaware* to embark to some new destination in the extremely bewildering, indefinable death realm.

"But why have I been summoned to this morbid death holding station if I'm not famous?" I stubbornly asked my pale pathetic transparent partner. "I think I really don't deserve to be here! The accomplishments of your other guests certainly eclipse and dwarf mine!"

"Maybe you'll finally have become famous when it's time for your departure on yonder ferry," my gruesome-looking ghoulish host imaginatively suggested. "Don't short-change yourself, even after you're certifiably dead!"

"I would rather have led a full normal life as a nobody than to sacrifice twenty-five golden years of retirement for fame after my ill-fated automobile accident!" I strenuously objected. "Life is unfair and now I know that death is, too!"

My mind (or what was left of it) was in a complete quandary. I asked to be led to my assigned room, which was the only one situated on the hotel's second floor, ironically Number 2004. Then, a certain parallel relationship connected inside my confused, befuddled and disoriented mind. The hotel's room numbers corresponded with the exact year each person had perished. I had died in 2004 and I knew from biographical accounts I had read that Dr. Albert Einstein had died in the year 1955.

"Thank you for showing me my living quarters, or should I say my death quarters!" I mentally said to normally reticent Diogenes. "Are you the only employee here?"

"Why yes," the now guide-turned-butler cerebrally transmitted, still holding his trademark dimly lit lantern. "You'd better keep that exquisite sense of humor of yours," the notorious cynic smartly advised, "because it's guaranteed to raise everyone's *spirits* around here! Ha, ha, ha," he shockingly cackled like an obsessed maniac.

"Why do we have to enter and exit via doors if we're spirits?" I seriously asked. "Why don't we just filter through the walls like ghost vapors?"

"We could, but that would be impolite and too annoying to our other prominent guests," Diogenes reprimanded. "It obviously would infringe on their privacy. You wouldn't want that ferry to *barge* into your room, would you? Ha, ha, ha," the ancient Greek wildly cackled. "So, George W., Abe L. or Marilyn M. wouldn't enjoy *you* interrupting *their* privacy or their meditation by *your* intrusively whisking your way through the outer wall, would they? I doubt it!" the now-spirited ghost convincingly argued.

I asked Diogenes to provide me with an abundant supply of pens and writing paper, and to accommodate my requests the specter later rummaged through closets and through desk drawers and eventually located the prescribed requested items. I thanked my new acquaintance; prudently sat at the dusty desk, and assiduously began re-writing my manuscript that I had recently sent to my supportive Annapolis publisher. And after meticulously completing that project, which I thoroughly believed far surpassed the original version in quality, I commenced authoring the first of four prodigious novel-length manuscripts that I had felt inspired to write. 'I have two-hundred-years to write at my leisure,' I intrepidly surmised, 'and this is one labor of love that I feel compelled to perform. I must organize my novels and novellas as carefully as possible and make each page of superior quality. I'll be my own ghostwriter!'

Diogenes had told me that I could export (without penalty) one package into the "physical world", so I was elated when I was able to fill a storage chest with eight thick manuscripts, novels, and novella collections. The old chest, loaded to capacity, was then addressed and sent to my publisher in Annapolis, who would be shocked to receive the unanticipated documents authored by a dead writer, and surprisingly delivered via conventional parcel post. The details of exactly how this *novel* transaction was done or negotiated had never been disclosed to me, but I had placed implicit faith and trust in the integrity of the sad-faced Diogenes, who incidentally had expertly and expeditiously handled that special favor for me.

It has been a very strange existence for me in this morbid-but-placid afterlife, having no need for either eating or drinking. The desire for biological satisfaction (or for its accompanying pleasures) was totally absent from the *two-dimensional* death world to which I was confined, but I was happy to note that mental pleasure could still be experienced after I had finished the task of writing those assorted "perfect manuscripts."

Feeling exceptionally lonely, I finally summoned sufficient courage to exit my drab and uninspiring room and visit the eldest guest spirit at the *Hotel Delaware,* so I politely knocked on the door of Room 1799. George Washington graciously answered my knocks and the tall pale specter asked me to enter and review post-colonial history events for him.

"It's indeed a distinct honor to meet my country's first President," I anxiously began, "and you look identical to your famous portrait that appears on the one-dollar-bill."

"Sir," the eminent Founding Father and renowned military general said with his mind, "Confidentially, I've never visited anyone else in this confounded hotel. I was afraid that there might be some sort of supernatural reprisal associated with me leaving my humble quarters. Apparently, Sir," white-wigged George Washington continued, "you

166

possess great daring to act independently without knowledge of rules and death customs, or without fear of dire consequence."

Then, George Washington's specter stated that I too must be a famous person to be confined to the obscure sanctuary of the creepy *Hotel Delaware,* even though I was totally unaware of my fame or reputation by virtue of my untimely and premature departure from mortal existence.

I thanked the venerable American for his unsolicited praise and encouragement and then I learned that all of the books in General Washington's room had been printed *before* 1800. The poor fellow thirsted for knowledge about America after his unfortunate death on December 14, 1799.

"Tell me, Sir," the tall powder-wigged giant of history mentally said. "Has the *Constitution* and the nation adequately survived the past several hundred years?"

I cogently explained to President Washington all that had transpired from his colonial and *Revolutionary War* era up to the year 2004, including the sensational changes associated with the *Industrial Revolution,* the *Civil War,* the invention of the train and the automobile, the *Great Depression,* the two world wars, and the atomic and computer ages. I also divulged that the *Constitution* had been *amended* many times, and we further discussed those particular modifications in great length.

"Do you mean to tell me that you own a device you call a car that can go up to sixty-miles-per-hour in just six seconds, and you have a special gauge you call a speedometer that registers one-hundred-and-forty-miles-an-hour?" Washington marveled and mentally conveyed. "I guess the stagecoach and the horse and wagon are quite obsolete. These commentaries of yours are quite astounding! Oh, I get it!" Washington exclaimed. "The word automobile means that a coach could move all by itself without any horse pulling it! Quite in-genius terminology, if I may add!"

"Well, not exactly," I respectfully clarified. "People still go to race tracks and bet on horse races. A big one each May is called the *Kentucky Derby.* "

George Washington was fascinated by all that I told him, for we must have exchanged uninterrupted conversation, for at least a full Earth month, without the need of sleep, food, or drink. I never thought I could be so vociferous as I had been in *his* inimitable company. And when Washington discovered from our lengthy discourse that there were now fifty states instead of thirteen, his pale face produced a proud broad smile.

President Washington became rather disconsolate upon hearing about the notion of "separation of church and state" and how "the establishment clause" had been "misinterpreted" by a sequence of "unfortunate" *Supreme Court* decisions. "National morality cannot last in exclusion of religious principles," our first chief executive lamented and expressed. "And your public schools should not devoid of teaching morality based on religious principles, either," G.W. mentally elaborated. "Your institutions of learning are therefore producing a vile generation of bratty dolts who might have knowledge in subject matter, but who lack discipline, resolve- and wisdom that come from the practice of simple basic religious morality. The first *Ten Amendments* to the *Constitution* should be predicated upon the *Ten Commandments* handed down to Moses and embodied in the *Bible,"* George Washington adamantly insisted and emphasized.

I humbly informed my perceptive listener about abortion rights, about homosexual marriage and about criminal and animal rights. He nearly blew a fuse arguing, "It's a travesty to believe that such ungodly things have been resulting from the misguided interpretation of a Godly-inspired document such as the sacred *United States Constitution.* And when you tell me that God has been taken out of your public schools," Washington continued in an emotional state that bordered rage, "then I believe that I had fought the entire *Revolutionary War* in vain. Our nation is doomed to decay from within. Civil rights will ultimately destroy individual morality, which will produce the decadence that will weaken and then eventually erode away the foundational values of *our* great nation. There is no doubt in my mind that *that* catastrophic end will be inevitable!"

On the optimistic side, the first President was elated to know that the country had survived over two centuries of critical challenges since his death in 1799. The great statesman and military strategist found hope in the prospect that a national crisis similar to the *Civil War* or the *Great Depression* might once again shake the country out of apathy after the year 2004. George Washington's spirit explicitly indicated to me that there possibly would emerge a noble crusade to return to the great moral roots and the powerful American traditions strongly embodied in the *Declaration of Independence* and in the *Bill of Rights*. He referred to this phenomenon as "the Phoenix resurrection."

Upon leaving the General's "solitary confinement sanctuary," George Washington's ghost thanked me for my informative visit while regretting that I had conveyed some "distasteful news" about future events and changes in the "established moral codes" that have been over the years erroneously affected by judicial and legislative adaptations in the "legal codes".

I left George Washington's shoddy, modest accommodations at the singular *Hotel Delaware* and returned to my own morgue-like second-floor room. It again occurred to me that since I had died in the year 2004, I had the only *death quarters* on the second tier. Then, an interesting thought flashed through my transparent brain. When additional renowned people would die, more second-floor rooms would have to be added on to the ancient hotel so that the new restless spirits could peacefully dwell until they were allowed to ascend to the next dreadful echelon in the afterlife. 'Or perhaps there are many other death holding stations similar to this *Hotel Delaware* to allow for the other decedents,' I hypothesized.

I stayed dormant in my room for an unspecified interval of time, which to my comprehension remained quite anonymous and mysterious because there were no clocks or wristwatches or views of the sun and the moon from anywhere inside the dreary deplorable hotel. Then I attempted to prepare the outline to a new manuscript but ideas and words eluded me, so I temporarily abandoned that ambitious enterprise.

My mind decided that I would pay a visit to another extraordinary personage trapped in the archaic weather-worn domicile, so I elected to interact with a particular idol of mine from nineteenth century American literature. I had to choose between Edgar Allan Poe and Mark Twain. I chose the former, hoping to have an opportunity to speak with Samuel Langhorne Clemens at a future date (even though calendars and dates did not exist anywhere inside the very weird and mystical hotel).

My knuckles rapped on the door of Room 1849, and my brain mused that Edgar Allan Poe would assume that I was an itinerant raven determined to annoy and pester him, all relaxed and pensive in *his* tranquil solitude.

"Hello," I hesitantly greeted the literary master. "May I come in to chat for a while?"

"Certainly," Poe cooperatively-but-cheerlessly replied. "You look harmless, although I must laugh at the strange apparel ornamenting your body. I presume you are from a future age? You appear too casual to be dead. Is that how you were buried? Has formality been abandoned entirely?"

"No, Sir, er I mean, I don't think I was ever buried and have no knowledge of being buried," I stammered. "This is what I was wearing when I died."

"Well then," my illustrious academic erudite host persisted, "are you from *my* future?"

"Yes, Sir," I keenly answered the much-revered genius. "You happen to be a favorite author of mine and I immensely enjoyed teaching my students many of your excellent stories," I sincerely elaborated. "I was a school teacher during most of my life," I clarified, "and your tales of horror and your classic adventure stories were among the best I ever read or analyzed. I especially liked teaching my students your tales 'The Cask of Amontillado' and 'The Fall of the House of Usher'."

Poe was quite flattered by my complimentary remarks and asked me to sit down even though I no longer possessed a body that required rest from its weight or from its exertion. I respectfully honored my literary benefactor's request out of force of habit and out of reverence for past human courtesy customs.

"Well kind Sir," E.A. began. "You must know about my dear Virginia?"

"Your wife Virginia died of tuberculosis in 1847, so in all due deference," I acknowledged, "you know more about her last moments on Earth than I do since you had passed away in 1849."

"I apologize, kind Sir," Edgar Allan Poe mentally transmitted while momentarily exhibiting a rare smile. "But I originally meant the state of Virginia where I grew up and whose memory I have always held dearly inside my miserable heart."

And after I educated Edgar Allan that there were now forty-nine states in the Union besides his precious Virginia, the cheeks on the pale ghost's countenance almost turned from ashen to pink. He had accurately speculated that a bloody forthcoming *Civil War* was imminent after 1849, but a tear seemed to form in his right eye when I explained the tragedy and the widespread suffering in both the American North and the Dixie South. Many painful wounds had to be healed after the devastating conflict between the *Union* and the

170

Confederacy. "A period of *Reconstruction* had to be initiated," I very patiently revealed and explained. My listener was just as glad as George Washington had been about the acquisition of additional states to the *Union.*

I immediately identified with the dead man's unique sense of patriotism and with his skeptical outlook on death and its eternal idleness. Much to my surprise, Edgar Allan Poe was amazed that he would become a famous giant in American literature after his untimely death in 1849. The master of the macabre had been found lying outside a Baltimore voting place on October 3 of that year, and he had died in a city hospital four days later without ever regaining consciousness.

"Do you mean to say that my work is read in virtually every high school and college English class in the country?" Poe incredulously mentally asked and marveled. "I knew I would die in poverty and disgrace," he bluntly continued with remorse and disenchantment, "but I never reckoned I would achieve national and international acclaim. You, Sir, pardon my aggressive nomenclature," E.A. paused to measure my reaction, "are a most welcomed time courier. In you I see much of me, and I mean this with sincerity when I say that it is most grievously calamitous that you too are deceased and doomed to incarceration in this especially decrepit hotel. Have you attained notoriety during your lifetime?"

"No," I bluntly lamented, "and I really don't know why I've been assigned to and incarcerated here inside the *Hotel Delaware* with such a distinguished group of literary, famous and historical souls occupying the other rooms."

"Perhaps you too will be visited by a messenger rapping on your door several hundred years from now and told of your great contributions to civilization," Poe theorized and suggested. "Then, *you* will know the pure pristine genuine delight I'm presently feeling at learning that my life's work has achieved honor and prestige in the literary community, a community that vehemently abhorred me and my endeavors and one that I absolutely despised and loathed during my brief tenure on the all-too-mundane Earth."

Then, I had the pleasure of discussing with the master most of his outstanding literary gems including "The Cask of Amontillado," "Murders in the Rue Morgue," "The Fall of the House of Usher," "The Tell-Tale Heart," "The Black Cat," "The Pit and the Pendulum" and the "Masque of the Red Death." I was *literally* held spellbound and was thoroughly captivated by Poe's vivid animated descriptions and by his graphic explanations in regard to what critics consider his classic works.

In "The Purloined Letter," I curiously stated, "you had essentially invented the entire theory and methodology of the detective story," I praised the great short story author. "And thousands of writers since your time have imitated the superior model that you've so effectively pioneered. I believe," I respectfully continued, "that you Sir, and I sincerely mean this, have been perhaps the greatest influence on the course of American literature over the past two centuries."

"I always believed that the ideal critic should be objective while slightly leaning toward the negative side," Poe declared while alluding to his own literary reputation at being a premiere reviewer of essays and short stories. "So that's why I get along so well with Diogenes," the famous author humorously added. "But above all else, an author must possess originality, courage of heart and the grammatical skill to efficiently convey *his* intended message to his readers. Otherwise," the disconsolate and totally bored fellow decided, "the author is not an author at all but merely a very ambitious *writer* aspiring to great accomplishments but doomed to failure or in the final analysis, be destined to produce volumes of mediocrity."

I had fathomed and found much merit in Edgar Allan Poe's enlightening commentaries, and I only wished, at that moment, that I could return to my human form and pursue my literary aspirations with the superb knowledge I had absorbed during our most intriguing dialogue. When neither of us had anything additional to relate or to discuss, I bid the prolific genius (possessing a burgeoning vocabulary) "adieu", and next shuffled down the dank dim corridor and then climbed up the rickety wooden steps, ascending back to my non-inspirational room.

My consciousness was gratified by the keen insights that the eminent editorial authority had to share with one of *his* less-talented admirers. Poe's final words remained in my mind and after the comprehensive interview, my energized brain tended to review them incessantly. "Always remember, kind Sir," the literary master had imperatively transmitted. "A combination of truth, soul, passion, beauty, and creativity is what elevates literature to a higher shelf than the one occupied by traditional newspaper journalism and by ridiculously written political propaganda."

172

Throughout my humble life, I, like Edgar Allan Poe, tended to be reclusive, shy and moody. I never really liked gossip, small talk or was fascinated by glib and garrulous people. 'An introverted nature was also an introspective advantage that both Poe and I cherished and exercised during *our* separate writing sessions,' I realized. "We both like to be alone to ponder and to explore our inner souls and to investigate the deepest secrets lying within our secluded hearts,' I then understood. 'We both quietly loathed obnoxious and ultra-gregarious people.'

And soon, a much more enlightening theory entered my troubled mind. I was in one way or another much like all of the inhabitants of the deteriorating un-maintained *Hotel Delaware*. I was diplomatic and gentlemanly like Washington, introverted, and emotionally tormented like Poe, and inventive, with an *Alpha* (aggressive and determined) personality like Thomas Alva Edison, whom I had selected to be my next hotel resident to interview.

I had by then willfully accepted my possible two-hundred-year confinement in the gloomy *Hotel Delaware* in a rather stoical manner, and frankly, I finally became cognizant of another interesting facet of the complex bizarre puzzle. I was also very much like Diogenes, priding myself on being a skeptic and a cynic about most everything and most anything.

I confidently descended the decrepit staircase to the ground-level corridor and floated (without walking a single step) down to Room 1931 where Thomas Alva Edison's spirit was quietly kept to ruminate. The man's *shade* was a little hard of hearing but after I had introduced myself in a loud clear voice, Edison welcomed me into his disheveled room that had so many cobwebs that it reminded me of a monstrous cocoon. That graphic notion immediately made me contemplate that *we* were indeed trapped in some sort of indefinable chrysalis, waiting to be released into a new existence just as an ugly caterpillar transforms into a beautiful butterfly inside a second *natural* womb.

"I must say I admire your very evident audacity," Edison's ghost remarked as it eagerly greeted me at *his* door. "You demonstrate the daring of an old friend of mine, Henry Ford," the genius generously praised. "Make yourself comfortable if that's at all possible in this bizarre rudimentary plateau in the afterlife."

"Why, Henry Ford!" I exclaimed in a very un-ghostly-like manner. "He's staying in this same hotel in Room 1947. I remember his name and room number from the registry ledger that's kept down in the main lobby."

"Why, I'll be giraffe's grandfather!" Thomas A. Edison bellowed in an uncharacteristic and excessive display of emotion. "I've been staying here at this repugnant run-down hotel right down the hall from one of my favorite contemporaries, and have been completely ignorant of that fact until *you* came along and informed me. I'll have to garner-up enough gumption to mimic your fine example and pay the old coot a belated surprise visit!"

Edison was very anxious to know what had transpired in the world after 1931, and upon hearing about *Bose* sound systems, computer floppy and compact disks, video cassettes, color television, cell phones and the *Internet*, the great inventor, who possessed over a thousand United States' patents, heartily and exuberantly laughed out loud.

"You know," the incomparable inventor Thomas Edison responded, "I only wish that I could've lived to see in full operation all that you've so admirably described. I'm so glad and proud that my years of research and experimentation had led to the discovery of these phenomenal creations that you've so wonderfully related," the ingenious fellow mentally said and savored. "Your good news has brought joy to my heart and peace to my restless soul!"

"Yes," I matter-of-factly added. "And Sir, there are high schools, towns and townships named after you all over the United States," I congratulated, "and believe it or not you're still affectionately referred to as the *Wizard of Menlo Park.* And your famous statement 'A genius is one tenth inspiration and nine tenths perspiration' is widely quoted all the time all over the modern world," I sincerely complimented.

"Allow me to modify that if I may," Edison insisted. "It ought to be 'A genius is one-third inspiration, one-third perspiration and one-third desperation!" the great contributor to science and technology aptly joked. "If only I could return to my laboratory in Menlo Park for just one earthly minute! That would be a terrific moment I would definitely cherish for all eternity!"

Thomas Alva Edison and I conversed for the longest time, and reviewed just about everything from stereo radios to space satellite communications. Throughout our extended dialogue, the wrinkle-faced man was again a human dynamo exhibiting a great *spirit* and a youthful enthusiasm for all subjects our imaginations touched upon.

174

And when the accomplished inventor heard that his New Jersey research laboratory had been proclaimed a treasured national monument by President Dwight D. Eisenhower in 1956, Edison's sunken eyes seemed to illuminate and his mental articulation became most jubilant.

"You are indeed a Godsend," the creative guru triumphantly declared in appreciation of the intellectual stimulation our conference had provided. "I'm deeply indebted to you for verifying that my life's work has been worthwhile. I now feel that I had laid the foundations for the discovery of more intricate and sophisticated appliances and devices that'll most certainly be beneficial to mankind," the gray-faced spirit gleefully announced. "You have definitely *made my century!"*

Edison and I must have talked for at least several more Earth months without any trace of exhaustion evident in the rhetoric of either of us. Finally, after informing my prestigious host all about the capabilities of the *Hubble Space Telescope* and all about exploratory interplanetary probes to Mars and Jupiter, I left the highly esteemed inventor's company and returned to the quiet sanctuary of my shadowy second floor room.

Several more months must have elapsed before I decided to exit my "dying quarters", slowly amble down to the dark and dreary lobby and initiate a conversation with the sometimes' talkative-but-moody sage Diogenes.

"Well, Diogenes," I cunningly began. "I have had the pleasure of meeting the ghosts of George Washington, Edgar Allan Poe and Thomas Edison. Now I can't wait to mingle with Thomas Jefferson, Abraham Lincoln, Mark Twain, Ulysses S. Grant, Albert Einstein, Henry Ford and Marilyn Monroe, if I accurately recall all of the other hotel's spectral guests."

"Kind Sir," Diogenes answered. "Please examine the new names listed in the register. I believe almost two centuries have expired in the outside world since your arrival, and now I suspect that *you* are now the senior resident of the *Hotel Delaware*."

I gazed-down at the ledger situated on the dusty registration desk and noticed that all of the honorable names I had just enumerated were gone from the list. Instead, were unfamiliar appellations such as Sir Hiram Applebee, Salvatore Giovanni, Mildred Carson, Thomas Attanasi, Roseann Celia, Gerald Gares, Arthur Orsi, and William Burns.

"Who are these people?" I uttered in sheer protest. "I never heard of any of them! They must all be pedestrian commoners!"

"They are inventors, presidents, and entertainers that have become famous during *your* relaxing two-century stay at the *Hotel Delaware!"* Diogenes academically lectured quite nonchalantly. "However, they will certainly recognize your name since your glorious fame has certainly preceded theirs!"

"Do you mean it's already time for me to be transferred to a more enlightening holding area somewhere else in the afterlife?" I sadly asked my aged and withered friend. "I thought I heard the ferry's foghorns several times but I was so engrossed in meditating in my room that I never looked out the window into the dense mist or stepped downstairs to investigate its arrival," I reported to Diogenes in a melancholy tone of voice.

Just then the ferry's whistle blasted three times, and I instinctively knew that a new hotel occupant was about to come ashore. Diogenes left me standing in the dingy lobby, and several minutes later, the scary-looking apparition reappeared alongside a middle-age spirit still attempting to decipher and define his new gloomy surroundings.

"Hello," I said to the new *Hotel Delaware* guest standing next to me in the dark and dreary lobby. "My name is John Wiessner, and I'm glad to meet you!"

"John Wiessner!" the fellow gasped in astonishment. "You mean John Wiessner, alias Jay Dubya! Why you're my favorite author! I've read all of your short stories, *Hammonton Gazette* opinion columns, all of your novellas and all of your novels. This is indeed the highlight of my death experience!"

"And who might you be?" I curiously inquired. "Certainly, you must be famous to be invited as a welcomed guest at this temporary holding platform."

"My name is Jason Parsons," the dead fellow's ghost mentally stated. "And I perfected and then invented the *Babel Universal Communicator* in 2154. That's indeed my biggest accomplishment."

"What does it do?" I insisted on knowing. "Does it communicate with other planets in the *Milky Way?"*

"The Babel Universal Communicator is a hand-held computer device that enables people of different languages to communicate the brain pulses of their thought patterns in *their* language into the words and sentences of a person speaking another language, no matter what

it is," Jason Parsons eagerly explained. "A voice simulator I had developed and patented translates the words through a powerful micro-speaker into the second language so that two people of different nationalities or cultures could easily hold an intelligent extensive conversation upon first contact."

"Wow!" I exclaimed with great admiration. "Babel then refers to the *Biblical Tower of Babel* where everyone in the Babylon area suddenly spoke different languages. Jason Parsons, I'm very glad to make your acquaintance," I genuinely expressed, "and don't worry about a thing. Your stay at the *Hotel Delaware* will be both rewarding and soon completed before you know it, if you know how to use your time constructively and wisely. Now tell me, how did you happen to die?"

"I think my envious wife poisoned me when she found-out I was having an affair with a beautiful and voluptuous *Hollywood* movie star," Jason Parsons disclosed. "But I'm not sure if jealousy was her real motive or whether she simply wanted to inherit my fortune because she was having extra-curricular affairs with the gardener and also with the chauffeur. At any rate," Jason finished with a degree of anguish and distress. "I'm damned dead now and I don't give a Marley's or a Great Caesar's Ghost about it. I just feel extremely betrayed, that's all."

"Women led to *your* demise," Diogenes concluded and insisted as the cynic held *his* dimly lit lantern up to Jason Parsons' honest-looking face. "Both the woman that you desired and the woman that you had, namely your spouse, have each contributed to your eternal fate!"

Then, I heard the ferry horn blast three additional times, signaling its intent of disembarking from its mooring, and venturing-out into the thick *Delaware Bay* fog en route to the second level of enlightenment and emotional growth in the peculiar-but-fascinating vertical death tier hierarchy.

"Maybe now I'll find-out about heaven, hell, and Jesus and everything else," I mentioned to Diogenes and to Jason Parsons. "I'm now fully prepared to deal with the attendant duties and responsibilities of the next level of spiritual growth, whatever those specific details might entail!"

Diogenes adroitly escorted me to the *Hotel Delaware's* lobby door. I warmly shook his cold, numb hand; stepped out of the macabre dilapidated structure; descended the thirteen rickety steps, and hastened through the dense fog to the awaiting ferry. I enthusiastically ascended the entrance ramp with all the vigor that a veteran ghost could muster. I had no apprehension about, or fear of, my next surreal destination.

My mind then understood that I was mentally equipped and emotionally mature to sufficiently deal with the elements that would confront me on death's enigmatic second stage of existence. I intuitively also now fully understand that Diogenes had successfully shipped the wooden chest of manuscripts into the past via some wonderful alien method of postal time compression. The following revelation is now quite lucid in my mind. I now thoroughly comprehend and appreciate a third significant truth, a germane inspiration that currently is quite obvious in its essence. Quite remarkably, I had indeed become Jay Dubya's anonymous *ghostwriter* during my most memorable two-century hiatus at the singular *Hotel Delaware*.

I'm presently placing *this manuscript* describing my death experiences in an empty five-gallon plastic spring water bottle that I've fortunately found inside a remote storage compartment on the deserted ferry. And after inserting the cork tightly into the bottle's neck, I'll carefully toss the container overboard, hoping that some lucky mortal will someday discover the trove, and have a brief glimpse of the mystical spirit world awaiting him or her.

"The Rip Van Winkle Club"

William R. Stuyvesant unhappily lived with his domineering wife Gertrude in a magnificent Tarrytown, New York manor house situated on a palisade overlooking the majestic *Hudson River*. William often confidentially compared Gertrude (to male associates) to Dame Van Winkle, Rip Van Winkle's shrew of a wife who lambasted, browbeat and belittled the poor lethargic farmer every day from dawn until midnight. That is where the comparison between Gertrude Stuyvesant and Dame Van Winkle ends. William R. Stuyvesant was filthy rich and neither he nor Gertrude had to work another day in their lives to maintain their expensive tastes, selfish hobbies and extravagant lifestyles.

William Stuyvesant, just like legendary Rip Van Winkle, claimed that Peter Stuyvesant, an early Dutch governor of New Netherland (later New Amsterdam, and now New York) was one of his paternal ancestors. William had inherited a considerable fortune from his father, a shrewd shopping center and real estate developer in the New York City metropolitan area. The fortunate beneficiary was lucky enough to parlay most of his inheritance in the stock market's high technology "bull rally" in the 1990s into a fantastic financial bonanza. But William's prosperity, his mansion and the spectacular view of the *Hudson River* constituted meager consolation when equated with Gertrude Stuyvesant's petulant hostile disposition. William believed that he was on the brink of a nervous breakdown.

"Gertrude is much-too-demanding. She's never happy until she's made me feel inferior by nagging, embarrassing and berating me day and night, oftentimes in front of others," William divulged to Harry Jenkins, one of his business partners over the telephone. "And while she's been spending time out in Los Angeles shopping like there's no tomorrow on *Rodeo Drive*, I've taken the liberty of purchasing a nice home up above Hudson on the river. It's a little more than an hour's drive from Tarrytown Harry, and I plan to use my new dwelling as a retreat for myself and some new friends I intend to make."

"Oh really," William's partner and business consultant doubtfully said. "And how do you intend to acquire these new friends? Make sure you don't get involved with riffraff and swindlers! They're a dime a dozen nowadays. You might be putting your reputation in jeopardy so my advice is to be careful!" Harry Jenkins warned.

"Don't worry!" William R. Stuyvesant assured his apprehensive business contact. "Harry, I'll think of something to sift out the dirt from the gold."

William Stuyvesant was quite familiar with the stellar works of author Washington Irving and had often visited the literary giant's unique mansion *Sunnyside* located just below Tarrytown on the *Hudson's* eastern bank. The remarkable home, positioned just south of the *Tappan Zee Bridge* has been converted into a museum, and is now open to the general public. Along with being an authority on Washington Irving's (1783-1859) mansion as well as on *his* biography, the multimillionaire also memorized virtually every passage in the author's works *The Alhambra, Knickerbocker's History of New York,* and finally, *The Sketch Book,* which contained Irving's most popular tales, *The Legend of Sleepy Hollow* and *Rip Van Winkle.*

"You really love the *Catskill Mountains,* don't you, Bill?" the building/construction partner asked Stuyvesant over the phone. "My wife and I go up there all the time and stay at several plush resorts that we frequent. The *Catskills* are a great getaway in either summer or winter. We used to faithfully go to Grossingers, and now we occasionally vacation at Villa Roma."

"I sure do love the *Catskills*," Stuyvesant quickly acknowledged and agreed. "And next to Ichabod Crane, Rip Van Winkle, has to be my favorite Washington Irving character. I think it all started when I read as a young boy about Rip leaving his village with his faithful dog Wolf to escape the tirades of wicked Dame Van Winkle. The poor henpecked fellow ascended mighty *Thunder Mountain (Mt. Dunderberg)* to seek peaceful sanctuary from his scornful wife."

"Is that why you've bought that place up above Hudson on the river?" the voice on the other end of the telephone line asked. "Do you compare in your mind Gertrude Stuyvesant with Dame Van Winkle?" Harry Jenkins mildly interrogated. "You better not let Gertrude find *that* little secret out. She'll have you wallowing in bankruptcy in no time."

"Yes, Harry, as a matter of fact I believe I did buy that property for that particular reason," Will Stuyvesant readily admitted. "Gertrude's temper tantrums are probably even worse than any that old Rip had to contend with from *his* overbearing Dame Van Winkle. I hope to find refuge and asylum from my matrimonial misery, and I want to bond and commiserate with other wealthy men that have

180

egomaniac-type wives out to fleece their husbands of their hard-earned fortunes. Say, Harry," William paused and then continued. "Do you know what term Washington Irving coined for public consumption?"

"No, I haven't the slightest idea! What?" Harry's voice politely asked.

"The almighty dollar! Ha, ha, ha!" William Stuyvesant loudly laughed over the phone. "Those other rich fellows are guaranteed to empathize with my plight, because they'll be in the exact same predicament as I am: rich, despondent, abused, and perpetually badgered!"

"Okay, Willy, good luck," Harry Jenkins offered. "Let me know how your social experiment works out with your new friends. Gotta' go!" Click.

'Poor Rip Van Winkle had the right idea,' William pensively thought while rubbing his chin. 'Even though *he* was poor, the *poor* fool needed to escape constant verbal abuse. I can send Gertrude to California and around the world, and despite my great fortune,' Stuyvesant imagined, 'the witch of a woman still perpetually berates and haunts me over the telephone. I definitely need isolation from her relentless antagonism. Yesterday, the witch called me from Palm Springs and was shopping up a storm on Palm Canyon Drive. Tomorrow, she'll be ten-miles south in Palm Desert, and hitting all of the ritzy stores on El Paseo!'

Then, William R. Stuyvesant's mind was struck by a sudden inspiration. 'That's what I'll do,' the mogul instantly decided. 'I'll run a conspicuous ad in the business sections of *The New York Times* and *The Wall Street Journal*. I just want to see what kind of tangible results my lure will yield.'

The unhappy tycoon sat at his computer desk, went to his Microsoft Windows program, and composed the following quarter of a page advertisement:

ATTENTION

Eligibility for admission to the prestigious *Rip Van Winkle Club* is now open. Candidates must be of Dutch heritage, must have a domineering, demanding and out-of-control wife, and must also show proof of annual net income of over a half million dollars. Benefits include male bonding and many lucrative business investment opportunities. All interested parties should submit documentation (*IRS* annual tax statement and a bona fide copy of birth certificate) to:

William R. Stuyvesant
P. O. Box 1783
Tarrytown, New York 10591

A full week passed without any meaningful responses to William Stuyvesant's unusual solicitation for qualified men to join the newly formed *Rip Van Winkle Club.* After ten days had elapsed from the publication of the *New York Times* and *Wall Street Journal* ads, the disappointed real estate developer thought that his "different idea" to form a social club of disparate and desperate wealthy male Dutch socialites had been both frivolous and futile. 'Perhaps I was a little too optimistic and naïve?' the multimillionaire thought.

But on the thirteenth day, applications began arriving at P.O. Box 1783, Tarrytown, New York, 10591. Twenty-four interested men sent in letters of introduction along with duplicate annual tax returns to validate minimum $500,000.00 net income, along with presenting accompanying copies of birth certificates to confirm authentic Dutch ancestry and heritage.

William was elated by the favorable response to his announcement. The lonely capitalist immediately hired the services of a reputable private detective agency to investigate into the backgrounds and careers of all two-dozen applicants. After finding fault with some of the male applicants for either being a mere joint partner in the half million-dollar net income specification, or for having only one parent of pure Dutch ancestry, the final list had diminished down to the following twelve lucky individuals:

Arnold Tromp	Stockbroker, Company Vice President
Hans Duncan	Appliance and TV Chain Store Owner
Charles Andersen	Insurance Adjuster, Business Owner
Salvatore Von Velardi	Corporate Executive, Import-Export Firm
Andrew Kondrack	Builder/Contractor
Peter Van Brocklin	Law Firm Senior Partner
Jack Zeeman	Dentist, Investor
James Erickson	Author of Bestsellers, College Professor

Jesse Frank	Medical Doctor
Richard DeVries	Newspaper Publisher
Anthony Bosche	Accountant for *Fortune 500* Companies
Sam Vander Waals	Owner: Three Automobile Dealerships

'What an excellent list of fine distinguished entrepreneurial Dutch businessmen!' William thought and relished as he evaluated his final roster of names that had qualified for the newly amalgamated *Rip Van Winkle Club*. 'It's a wonderful cross-section of American free enterprise where honorable men of Dutch ancestry will exchange stock tips and share business investment opportunities while commiserating with one another the common bond of being continually badgered by bossy and dominant wives,' Stuyvesant thought and smiled. 'Gertrude's jet won't be flying home from *L.A.* until Sunday night. I'll have just enough time to schedule a cordial *Rip Van Winkle Club* get-together at my place for next Saturday afternoon. Then, after *we* get acquainted, we'll have a small motorcade up to Hudson on the river, and I'll show my kindred friends the newly renovated *RVW* club lodge, which will be available to any troubled member whenever *his* obnoxious wife starts to officially agitate and aggravate him.'

At six p.m. on Saturday, the newly selected members of the *Rip Van Winkle Club* assembled at the Tarrytown palisades castle of William R. Stuyvesant. It was an interesting mix of unique personalities, but everyone shared one common denominator: *his* wife was a shrew who would incessantly browbeat her successful husband into "chopped liver."

"Will, are you sure thirteen is a lucky number?" joked Andrew Kondrack, the real estate developer's new acquaintance. "I always had a weird phobia about the number thirteen! Not that I'm basically superstitious, or anything."

"Thirteen sure *is* lucky, Andy," William answered after closely studying the building contractor's name tag. "Just remember, Mr. Andrew Kondrack, how lucky the original thirteen colonies were to the birth of the United States of America. Thirteen might actually be the luckiest number in the universe for all we know!"

Everyone overhearing their genial host's remark laughed lustily after its utterance. Instant camaraderie abounded, and soon the phenomenon known as "male bonding" set in as the thirteen new *Rip Van Winkle Club* friends having common Dutch genealogies, incomes and interests discussed random subjects like polo, golf, tennis, business, world travel, but most importantly, their despicable leeching wives.

"My old lady, Helen, possibly makes Dame Van Winkle look like a novitiate nun," Richard DeVries, the flamboyant and effervescent newspaper mogul indicated to William and to Andrew Kondrack. "She's enough of a spitfire to make the Devil wish he was a blessed celibate saint! Helen's tongue must weigh more than three pounds, no exaggeration!"

"My spouse is so abominably nasty that our neighbor's three Doberman pinscher attack dogs are super afraid of her!" an eavesdropping Hans Duncan added to the conviviality. "She makes *mean* seem like *kind!* Once during *Halloween* trick or treat night, my wife scared two adults dressed like Dracula and Frankenstein right out of our neighborhood, and that's no hyperbole, either!"

"Will," Salvatore Von Velardi butted in as things quieted-down around the semi-circular bar, "when are we victims heading up to the *Catskills?* I need a little mountaintop rest and relaxation right this minute, so I hope we don't accidentally wind-up in the *Adirondacks.* I can't wait to see your glorious lodge up above Hudson! And judging by the elegance of *this* splendid mansion, Will, I'll bet your little hideaway is pretty damned spectacular."

"After the third round of drinks have been imbibed," Will Stuyvesant promised his new wealthy friends, "we'll then all be on the same attitude adjustment wavelength and ready to begin *our* much-needed northern expedition. I'll lead the caravan with my sports utility vehicle," the host cheerfully volunteered and pontificated. "And I've noticed that three of you men have 4-Wheel-Drive *SUVs,* too. Use your four-wheel drive shift when we leave the paved road and have to climb up some steep terrain to arrive at my rustic sanctuary, or should I say *our* rustic sanctuary," Stuyvesant corrected himself. "It's thoroughly removed from all semblances of the hectic big city concrete jungle civilization!"

The now-liberated men all boisterously cheered William R. Stuyvesant's exaggerated bravado, and after the third round of mixed drinks had been swiftly gulped-down by the jolly millionaires (assembled around the mansion's custom-made mahogany bar), the entourage was ready to embark on the first unprecedented weekend adventure of the newly formed *Rip Van Winkle Club.*

Quite soon the contingent of amiable half-intoxicated men left William's palatial residence and clambered into their respective vehicles. Four *SUVs* formed an impromptu mini-vacation caravan and William R. Stuyvesant led the jovial members in a military-type convoy north on *Highway 9,* which parallels the noble and serene *Hudson River.*

The small *SUV* fleet soon zoomed by *Sleepy Hollow High School* on the right-hand-side and shortly later down the busy road the autos' passed by Ossining, the infamous home of *Sing-Sing State Prison.* Buildings belonging to *West Point Military Academy* were soon seen on the opposite shore of the stately river, and as the cavalcade of *SUVs* meandered around rocky embankments northward past downtown Poughkeepsie, the highway inclines then became steeper and the picturesque landscape more rugged. All of the natural beauty brought out the "pioneering instinct" of the men sitting in William Stuyvesant's vehicle.

"Ah, communion with nature!" Will said to Jack Zeeman, his loquacious and very grateful front seat passenger. "*Henry David Thoreau* would certainly enjoy this impressive mountain excursion we're now conducting. Too bad the loner was a poor guy and wouldn't be ineligible for membership into our club if that *Walden Pond* fellow were still alive."

"Yes, I'm sure *he* would *Thoreauly* be thrilled by it!" Jack Zeeman imaginatively returned. "But I'm sure we'll certainly enjoy some Transcendentalism without old Henry's presence."

"Then, Jack, you prefer this *Catskills'* outing to listening to your tempestuous wife ranting and raving all the time?" Will deliberately inquired to get a reaction out of Zeeman. "We'll have to have a contest to see whose wife is more vicious! But I must admit that yours sounds hard to beat."

"The Rip Van Winkle Club sure beats Martha chewing me out about returning home late from night *Yankees* baseball games," Jack Zeeman merrily replied. "Martha's *barbs* are more painful than barbed wire!"

Backseat riders Charles Andersen and Jesse Frank found Jack Zeeman's marital impressions extremely hilarious, as the pair boisterously laughed in response to the all-too-true declaration by the henpecked dentist "riding shotgun" up front with Will Stuyvesant.

"Maybe your wife scolds you because she's an avid *Mets'* fan!" Jesse Frank amusingly suggested to Jack Zeeman. "There might be some hidden baseball vindictiveness there! Maybe Jack, Martha owns stock in the *Mets'* franchise without you even knowing about it. Ha, ha, ha!"

"Or maybe Martha is hard of hearing," offered Charlie Andersen, "because I know for a fact that people with severe hearing problems tend to yell when speaking to others, so that they can then hear themselves talking! And that's no joking either! I'm bet Jack that your ferocious wife Martha has some sort of wicked hearing disability. Ha, ha, ha!"

"I don't think so!" the blithe-spirited Jack Zeeman chortled from the front seat. "If George Washington's Martha was anything like Martha Zeeman is, then the great *Revolutionary War* General would have become a *Tory* and jumped over to the *British* side just to get away from his wife's flagrant diatribe. Old George would've been a turncoat for the redcoats!"

"If that's the case," William laughed as he rounded a sharp curve in the road, "then Benedict Arnold must've had an overbearing savage wife very similar to your Martha!" Stuyvesant gleefully exclaimed to Jack Zeeman. Wild cackling and guffawing coming from the back seat resulted from Stuyvesant's sarcastic but acutely humorous comment.

The short procession of *SUVs* proceeded with *their* small expedition up *Route 9* and at late twilight passed through Hyde Park, rapidly buzzing by the historic and picturesque home of the revered Franklin Delano Roosevelt, the mansion/museum now converted into a popular national shrine. After driving past the magnificent Hudson River *Vanderbilt Mansion,* situated on the left, the four-vehicle caravan continued on its itinerary heading north, the drivers' next destination being Rhinebeck, a town rich in tradition dating back to the early colonial era.

"I understand that good old George Washington once slept at the *Rhinebeck Inn,"* William informed his still giddy and amused passengers, "and it's really a pretty neat place to spend the night, even with *your* opinionated wife Jack! Maybe Gorge Washington's Martha is still in there," William joked to Jack Zeeman, much to everyone's delight.

"If Washington had slept at all these places that claim he had slumbered in their beds," Charles Andersen cynically volleyed from the rear, "then Washington would've slept his way right through the entire *Revolutionary War* just like poor exploited Rip Van Winkle had done."

"I guess that the signers of the *Declaration of Independence* put their money on Washington to be our nation's top general because they figured he'd be a real *sleeper!*" Jesse Frank obnoxiously hollered and punned from the backseat.

"You three guys are really a lot of fun!" William admitted as he stopped for a red traffic signal. 'I'm glad you all decided to get away from your nasty marital mates and get together for leisurely weekends up at my place in the *Catskills.* So far, you fellas' have been a real pleasure to be with," Stuyvesant commended his jolly passengers. "We all need to unwind from our daily stressful schedules and also need to evade our savage wives' negative bullying and intimidation."

Finally, the four vehicles followed *Route 9* into the somnolent town of Hudson, where the highway converted into Fairview Avenue, which the caravan stayed on until the appearance of Rod and Gun Road on the left. After several miles of asphalt surface, William held his hand out of the opened driver-side window, signaling to the three trailing *SUVs* to enter four-wheel drive and then take a stone and gravel road up to *his* secluded mountain retreat lording over the dignified placid *Hudson River.*

"You know," William said to his alert and jovial companions in a philosophical tone of voice, "I can just picture poor Rip Van Winkle ascending these steep precipices on a cloudy fall day with his hunting dog Wolf just to achieve some much-needed requiem from Dame Van Winkle's relentless tyranny. We all know poor Rip Van Winkle's burden all-too-well from local folklore! In fact, Washington Irving aptly described Rip's unenviable plight as 'petticoat tyranny'! Ha, ha, ha!"

"Make sure our first toast at the lodge is dedicated to the fond memory of Rip Van Winkle," Jack Zeeman recommended to his merry colleagues. "All in favor say 'aye'!"

"Aye!" his three merry cohorts bellowed in raucous-but-sincere unanimity.

* * * * * * * * * * * *

The good-natured men spent the night engaged in serious entertainment and whimsical amusement. They played cards, chess, checkers and dominoes. The revelers drank expensive whiskeys, imported beer and vintage wines. After eating a late catered supper featuring fried chicken, baked ham and basted turkey, the new fraternity members of the *Rip Van Winkle Club* reminisced about past steamy romances and about exotic tropical vacations in Hawaii, the Caribbean, and along the French Riviera. Will was elated that the members were all compatible, sharing and building a new-found camaraderie.

Next, the club members conversed about the simple joys identified with the biological processes known as eating and drinking, and finally the topic of conversation centered upon the very unfortunate marital predicament of the newly organized club's special namesake, Rip Van Winkle.

"Rip drank the delicious Holland gin obtained from an enchanted barrel at Henry Hudson's wild mountain party," Will nostalgically recollected (and reminded his new-found friends) from the Washington Irving legend, "and the powerful substance put our favorite reveler to sleep for twenty long years. That's not such a bad sentence when you're married to an overbearing shrew like Dame Van Winkle, who sounds almost as treacherous as Jack Zeeman's toxic wife Martha."

"That twenty-year sleep was more of a blessing than a curse," Andrew Kondrack steadfastly maintained. "Old Rip didn't have to confront or listen to his belligerent wife's ugly outbursts for two whole decades."

"Yes, most definitely a truism," Peter Van Brocklin chimed in, "but poor Rip lost twenty valuable years off his life where he could've enjoyed many satisfying draughts of ale at Nicholas Vedder's tavern. The impoverished Dutch farmer returned to his village twenty years later not recognizing a single inhabitant in the entire place."

"I really feel badly for the exploited gent, even if he was only a fictitious character," Anthony Bosche amiably qualified and contributed to the discussion. "First of all, we all sleep eight hours a day, so that means we really only consciously live around fifty years instead of the customary seventy-five-year average that biology textbooks and encyclopedias inaccurately state. One third of our lives is spent snoring in bed!"

"I see where you're getting at, Tony," interrupted William R. Stuyvesant. "Rip Van Winkle was callously cheated another twenty years by Henry Hudson's cruel sleeping spell, so in effect, Rip was an old man at only thirty years of age. What a lousy bummer no matter how one studies it!"

After cleaning-up the extensive waste the sumptuous feast had generated, the euphoric men strolled out to the four *SUVs* and removed their suitcases to lug into spacious "the RVW Lodge". Soon, the sportive gentlemen all retired to their assigned quarters, satisfied and content, waiting for a morning of adventure following a restful night's slumber.

The next morning, dark clouds shrouded the distant mountain peaks, making that particular extension of the great *Appalachian* chain appear clad in a dull blue and purple-hued haze. Peter Van Brocklin, Salvatore Von Velardi and Andrew Kondrack were early risers that could have taught the area Hudson roosters a lesson or two in "dawn punctuality". The three new acquaintances were casually standing on the back patio deck of William R. Stuyvesant's "backwoods retreat" and were admiring the scenic tranquility of the passive *Hudson River* down in the valley, while contemplating and discussing the awesome *Catskill Mountains*. William R. Stuyvesant exited the expansive converted ranch-home-to-lodge overlooking the *Hudson* and soon joined his rejuvenated guests. The sightseers were carrying three pair of binoculars with a fourth very expensive pair being strapped around Will's neck.

"Here, use these peepers to survey the pristine beauty that surrounds us!" Will suggested as he handed his high-tech' high-powered binoculars to the three men casually stationed on the wooden platform deck. The four spectators took turns peering into the new ultra-modern magnifiers and with their elbows casually resting on a sturdy black wrought iron railing, the men gazed out at the wondrous environmental splendors all around them. Suddenly something highly irregular had been spotted.

"Hey guys," Andrew Kondrack observed and said in a mellow-but-serious tone of voice. "There seems to be some kind of ancient ship anchored out near that rock formation down there to our right. Can you guys see it?"

All four pair of binoculars instantly focused on Andrew Kondrack's rather curious sighting. William R. Stuyvesant, a student of Dutch antiquity, immediately recognized the identity of the object in question.

"Well, I'll be a chimpanzee's first cousin!" Will emphatically marveled and exclaimed. "That ship down there in the river is a replica of *Henry Hudson's* prized vessel, the *Half Moon.* Has anyone read any recent newspaper articles about a model of the *Half Moon* visiting this area of New York north of Hudson? That's what that ship has to be, a magnificent replica!"

None of the men recollected reading any such journalism, so Will anxiously suggested that the *Rip Van Winkle Club* membership hop into the four *SUVs* and take a narrow side trail down the scenic mountainside to further investigate the strange ship anchored near the *Hudson's* shore.

The men inside the house were summoned from their shaving in front of vanity mirrors, from the breakfast table and from their beds, and in a matter of five hectic minutes, all thirteen adventurous souls scrambled outside the lodge and hopped into the vehicles. Will led the way in his silver *Ford Expedition* down the steep sloping trail to the vicinity where the mysterious ship had dropped anchor in the historic river.

Upon reaching a plateau overlooking the "facsimile *Half Moon,*" the four *SUVs* halted one after the other in military parade fashion and the thirteen intrigued occupants got out in a hurry to satisfy their heightened curiosity about the handsome ship of yore and its crew. Much to their astonishment, three little men, each no more than four and a half foot tall, were climbing up an embankment and slowly approaching the men's location from below.

Each of the tiny grizzled-bearded men was dressed in the antique Dutch fashion that was emblematic of late seventeenth century haberdashery. Their extraordinary attire was comprised of cloth' jerkins, and below the short coats the cute but sour-faced fellows wore several pairs of baggy breeches that were handsomely ornamented with rows of buttons lined down each side. Each diminutive "midget Dutchman" (as Will Stuyvesant had labeled them) had been toting on *his* shoulder a small barrel, more of a cask than a barrel, and each fellow appeared quite encumbered by *his* object's weight. The little gents seemed preoccupied with their strenuous labor, and were unperturbed by the sudden appearance and confrontation of the thirteen tall men recently arrived from the Rip Van Winkle Lodge.

"Hey, little guys," Will Stuyvesant affably greeted. "Let us help you carry your barrels up the mountain. We're just brimming with energy."

"This must be some kind of re-enactment of the *Rip Van Winkle* tale," Salvatore Von Velardi conjectured and articulated to all within hearing distance. "But if this experience is true and not a mass hallucination, then these tiny men will eventually lead us to Henry Hudson and his *Half Moon* crew."

Just then, a loud rumble of thunder rolled through the distant mountains, and the noise was succeeded by additional low growling peals to the northwest.

"Legend says that that's Henry Hudson and his crew of little men playing a friendly game of ninepins up in the *Catskills,*" Peter Van Brocklin related to anyone and everyone willing to listen. "If I'm not mistaken, these little men will take us to *their* leader just like they had done with Rip Van Winkle."

The thirteen visitors assisted the three wee individuals with *their* indigenous labor, thus alleviating much of *their* struggle and toil. About five hundred feet up a narrow rocky footpath, the head small Dutchman dressed in ancient garb solemnly uttered to a solid rock façade, "In Henry Hudson's great name, open a shortcut to *our* destination's game."

Amazingly, the dense rock façade slowly swung open as if it was a lightweight door on hinges. A long dark tunnel was immediately exposed and soon the sixteen human forms took turns lugging the three liquor casks further into the dark hollow, which extended a thousand feet or so into the base of the mountain ridge.

A dull light was visible at the tunnel's other end, and upon exiting the dark cavity, the sixteen trekkers instantly perceived a beautiful ravine with rolling mounds and lush green grassy meadows. Luxurious sunshine radiated down on the splendid dell, and at least fifty other little men dressed in the same-style sixteenth century ancient Dutch costumes were idly standing around and engaging in small talk. But oddly, each tiny gent had a very melancholy expression on his face.

"Why are they all so sad looking?" Andrew Kondrack whispered to Will Stuyvesant after the two millionaires lowered their heavy cask onto a wooden platform, which had been tacitly designated by one of the austere-looking diminutive fellows. "To use one of Jack London's favorite words, they all look 'lugubrious'."

"According to legend," Will speculated and whispered, "these little men are immortal. They are unchanging in age as time advances onward. Because they're all immortal," Will Stuyvesant continued his incredible explanation. "They're bored with their mortal existence and quite unhappy having to live forever. They've seen everything once too often and are not at all enamored with the monotony of life's repetitious events."

"And check out those other mischievous little imps partying over there," Jack Zeeman indicated to his companions with his right hand. "They're playing a game of bowling on the green and simulating the sound of thunder echoing through the mountains when the ball strikes the pins."

"Ninepins, not bowling," Will aptly corrected. "That game we're watching is often referred to as duckpins!"

Henry Hudson dispatched one of his chief wee English-speaking crew-members to the area of the thirteen spellbound twenty-first century Americans, and after a polite introduction, Heinrick addressed his former helpers.

"Thank you for assisting us in transporting the Holland gin to our big party," Heinrick began his impromptu speech. "As you gentlemen might know, every twenty-years the crew of the *Half Moon* returns to the *Hudson River Valley* to review and celebrate our past explorations and expeditions. It's quite a treat for us despite our customary sad-looking countenances."

"Have you ever heard of a fellow named Rip Van Winkle?" Jack Zeeman nervously asked Heinrick.

"That's confidential information I'm not at liberty to discuss," Heinrick diplomatically answered.

"Well then, how come there're three barrels of Holland gin and not just one?" Will politely asked the peculiar-looking neurotic-sounding little fellow. "Are you intending to have a bigger party than usual this afternoon?"

"Well kind, Sir," Heinrick defensively replied. "I strongly suggest that you listen attentively. The gin from each of the barrels will produce a different effect. One barrel's contents will have no effect on the drinker of its gin, one of the barrels will age the drinker twenty years, and a chug from the third random barrel will make the lucky drinker twenty years younger."

"Wow!" Hans Duncan (the wealthy appliance distributor) amply exclaimed. "It's sort of like a casino gamble on the wheel game with

192

numbers one to three rotating around," Hans accurately interpreted. "If I choose correctly and can tack twenty-years onto my life, and simultaneously become two decades younger in the meantime," Hans hypothesized and declared. "Then, it's worth the gamble to be able to outlive my nasty wife."

"And even if *you* choose to drink from the wrong cask," Charlie Andersen guessed and explained, "then *you* still might choose the barrel that'll have no effect at all and still enjoy a cool refreshing mug of Holland gin. That's now reduced to a fifty-fifty chance."

"But fellas'," Will Stuyvesant cautioned his new-found comrades. "If someone selects the wrong barrel out of the three, then that person will be doomed to losing twenty years off his already pathetic life and will wake up an old man ready for the cemetery. Is that gambol worth the gamble?"

"Do you mean to say that *you* actually believe all this idiotic nonsense?" Arnold Tromp criticized. "This is the most preposterous hoax I've ever witnessed. It *is* in my fairly astute estimation and educated opinion that this farce is absolutely beyond a shadow of a doubt a silly college fraternity-type initiation prank of the greatest magnitude!"

"Then, *you* Sir wouldn't hesitate to prove *me* wrong by taking the first sample," Heinrick offered Arnold Tromp as the gallery of fifty little men in attendance laughed exceedingly at their foreman's intelligent challenge to *his* dubious guest. "Would you care to sample a sip, Mr. Arnold Tromp?"

"Well, I'll have to think about it and reconsider my options," Arnold Tromp uneasily conceded. "This is indeed a most difficult choice we're being pressured into making. Hey! How did *you* know my name?"

Again, the fifty or so little dwarfs roared out in laughter as the sound of a small rolling ball smashed against a triangular formation of duckpins on the ravine's lush green.

"I'll bet a cool thousand-dollars with any of you that this decision Henry Hudson is presenting us with is for real," William R. Stuyvesant boldly offered the other twelve astonished members of the *Rip Van Winkle Club*. "Who's got the guts to put *his* money where his mouth is?"

All of the twelve other "party crashers" presumed and believed that the entire scenario was a "clever theatrical trick" that had been brilliantly contrived, paid for, sponsored and orchestrated by their illustrious host, William R. Stuyvesant of Tarrytown, New York. Salvatore Von Velardi was the first bold fellow to wager a thousand dollars, believing that Will would graciously reimburse him after the completion of "the chicanery". The other eleven meanderers all gave *their* pledge that they would pay William R. Stuyvesant a thousand dollars each should "the deception" indeed turn out to be a "functioning aberration."

William was nominated to choose first, so Stuyvesant drank a cup of Holland gin from barrel number three. Arnold Tromp, Salvatore Von Velardi, Peter Van Brocklin, James Erickson, Jesse Frank and Sam Vander Waals all were given empty mugs that were quickly filled, and the "guinea pigs" eagerly quaffed-down their draughts drawn from barrel number two.

The remaining six thoroughly entertained wealthy gentlemen all lustily drank-down Holland gin from the cask labeled in plain English, "Number One".

Will Stuyvesant began feeling dizzy; first losing his balance with wobbly knees, and then acting irrational with planets, stars and galaxies wildly spinning-around inside his head. The intoxicated multimillionaire staggered and tottered about, clumsily and awkwardly gyrating from side to side, as if he were a defective spinning top. The organizer of the *Rip Van Winkle Club's Catskill Mountain* excursion trudged-off, walking between and around several jagged crags, gradually disappearing over the horizon as the dizzy trekker cautiously attempted descending the rugged ridge, while still under the influence of the very potent Holland gin.

Will Stuyvesant's twelve skeptical and traitorous apostles also staggered around like a bevy of soused alcoholics, desperately searching for a soft spot on the velvet-green-grass to take much-needed naps. Each man's fate was determined by the numbered cask from which *he* had selected a draught to drink.

Hans Duncan, Charles Andersen, Andrew Kondrack, Jack Zeeman, Richard DeVries, and Anthony Boshe all unfortunately drank the Holland gin from barrel "Number One". Each man was destined to sleep in the mystical *Catskill Mountains* for twenty-years and thusly, validating himself as a true disciple of the inimitable Rip Van Winkle, and also demonstrating that *he* was a dedicated member of the *Rip Van Winkle Club.* Upon waking up, Richard DeVries, the youngest of the first cask group, would be age seventy-one in the year 2022, and Andrew Kondrack, the eldest among the ill-fated half dozen imbibers, would be ninety-two upon awakening from his unanticipated slumber two decades later.

As for the visitors that partook of the second cask, Arnold Tromp, Salvatore Von Velardi, Peter Van Brocklin, James Erickson, Jesse Frank and Sam Vander Waals, all were miraculously rejuvenated with twenty-years fantastically shaved off their ages. However, the sly and clever dwarf' Heinrick had not disclosed to the vain and gullible men that they would be assigned as cabin boys to perform myriad duties and drudgery-assignments on the good ship *Half Moon*. And regrettably, the six hapless victims of youth revisited were all now permanently destined to have futures laden with misery as servants of the no-nonsense taskmaster Henry Hudson and his disconsolate and temperamental crew of fickle little seventeenth century Dutch men.

As for William R. Stuyvesant, the foundering founder of the notorious *Rip Van Winkle Club,* his fate was not a benign one, either. The multimillionaire awoke (without aging) just before dawn on Sunday morning and found himself' lying on soggy turf between a termite-infested, hollowed-out, fallen oak tree, and a clump of mountain sticker bushes and accompanying briers.

William immediately recollected his misadventure the day before with the irascible little ghostly Dutchmen in the very outlandish *Catskill Mountain* amphitheater-like ravine. The victim felt arthritis in his wrists and elbows and rheumatism in his back's lumbar area. Will's initial instinct was to feel for a long, shaggy gray beard', which would be evidence that he had been betrayed by Henry Hudson and *his* naughty crew and that *he* had indeed slept for twenty years just like his legendary mentor, Rip Van Winkle. Stuyvesant was glad to note that no lengthy grizzled beard had grown from his face, and the befuddled and puzzled man was never so happy to feel his whiskers' bristles.

'I wonder what happened to the others?' William meditated as he feebly rose to his feet and then brushed some skittering insects and loose dirt from his light-blue denim jeans and from his navy-blue sweatshirt. 'I hope I can find my way out of this forsaken place and back to my *SUV*. Thank God I had only slept for one night!'

The addled fellow's head was still groggy from the potent alcohol he had consumed the prior morning, so Will' prudently shuffled down the ridge and soon recognized the verdant ravine where the games of ninepins had been played. 'This is also where I had made the mistake of taking the first sample of Holland gin from the third cask,' he regretted with a degree of guilt. 'This is like a nightmare revisited.'

Being distracted by his own self-preservation thoughts, William accidentally stumbled over a log, fell onto the ground, and then tumbled forward several-hundred-feet down a slope to the footpath, that led to the dark tunnel shortcut that channeled through the base of the mountain. 'I think I know where I'm at now!' the drunken man remembered.

After Stuyvesant had rolled down to the base of the ravine, much to his consternation the tunnel exit was not observable, so Will recalled the rhyming language uttered by diminutive Heinrick at the long, hollow dank rock corridor's other end. "In Henry Hudson's great name, open a shortcut to *my* destination's game!" Stuyvesant shouted with his hands cupped over his mouth, his voice echoing throughout the ravine and resounding through the surrounding mountain precipices.

The rock façade slowly creaked open like a squeaky door with rusty hinges, revealing the same fabulous tunnel shortcut that the three dwarfs had led the loyal members of the *Rip Van Winkle Club* through the morning before. 'This tunnel is like a magical umbilical cord, connecting the material world with a bizarre fantasy world,' Will's dazed mind thought and concluded. 'Now, all I have to do is walk the thousand-feet, get inside my *SUV,* and drive back to civilization. I almost want to see and hear Gertrude again!' the disoriented explorer insanely imagined.

The secret tunnel was just as damp and dreary, as it had been the day before, and upon entering the outside world dimmed by a dark cloudy overcast sky on the opposite end, the rock façade soon mechanically squealed shut, much to Will Stuyvesant's awe and bewilderment. Then, the solid rock door banged against the mountain base with a thud, quite effectively concealing its secret access to the secluded magical ravine.

Still stunned and mildly confused from his weird ordeal, William Stuyvesant cautiously descended the final three-hundred-feet down a ridge, the route leading to the aforementioned mountain trail where the four all-terrain vehicles had been neatly parked in a row the morning before. 'I must take it slow, for if I plunge down this last incline from this height,' Will assessed, 'then I'll risk breaking an arm, a leg or both. If I survive this arcane misadventure, no one's

196

ever going to believe my sensational tale! And all four SUVs are still parked down there!'

With careful diligence, the man's aching legs finally carried his weary body down the remaining part of the ridge closest to his trusty four-wheel drive vehicle. The sky was still partially dark with the new day's sun ready to perform its daily resurrection on the black and pink eastern horizon.

Arriving at his *Ford Expedition,* Will frantically fumbled in his jeans' pockets for his keys, but then the disoriented fellow remembered that in his rush to make contact with Heinrick and *his* two dwarfish associates, Stuyvesant had inadvertently left the starting device in the *SUV's* ignition. 'Thank God it's still there,' Will thought as he opened the driver-side door and gingerly entered his beloved vehicle. 'Now to get out of here!'

The reliable *Expedition's* motor whined and then started, and next Will methodically backed the vehicle up, and swiftly turned the *SUV* around, with his hood pointed in the direction of downtown Hudson. 'I should report the whole insane incident to the police,' Stuyvesant logically considered. 'But the cops would never believe me in a million years and accuse me of being delusional. The only thing I have going for me is my credibility and my track record of being a multimillionaire, along with the fact that twelve highly successful businessmen will soon be reported missing to the authorities. I feel that I'm responsible for all of these extraordinary things happening!'

William had an inclination to turn on the specially installed *Bose* radio system to listen to the news, but before the driver could honor his next impulse, the man's eyes instantly beheld a dark foreboding spectral image remaining stationary three-hundred-feet ahead. An ominous frightening figure, sitting atop an enormous black horse, stood directly in *his* path.

'Oh my God!' Will's mind immediately recognized and feared. 'It's the fabled *Headless Horseman of Sleepy Hollow!"* What utter craziness! How could a fictitious character from one eerie legend suddenly enter into the enactment of another? How horrendous! This torture is too surreal to be real! Not even Gertrude would wish such a cursed punishment on me!'

Will sat petrified like a contemporary Ichabod Crane in the front driver's seat of his dependable *Ford Expedition,* believing that *he* could outrace the formidable, ruthless *Headless Horseman* once *he* could safely make it to a paved highway. The driver slowly inched forward, waiting for the right opportunity to gun the silver *SUV* onto a side gravel and stone winding road, which paralleled the majestic *Hudson River*.

Showing marvelous timing and dexterity, Stuyvesant, out of his dire need for self-preservation, quickly rotated the steering wheel to the right, and soon his vehicle was speeding-down the mountain ridge trail with the jet-black horse and its tenacious executioner closing the gap between William and the rider's speedy stallion. Stuyvesant had never before been so alarmed, so desperate, so endangered and so panic-stricken in all his life.

Will's reliable speedometer registered fifty-miles an hour as the terrified man maneuvered around precarious curves and up and down treacherous terrain that would not ordinarily accommodate such high speed, but much to *his* trepidation, the well-conditioned horse remained close behind. Fortunately, a mile stretch of straightaway was dead ahead for Will, so Stuyvesant again mashed his foot down on the accelerator, with the dependable *SUV* rapidly attaining a speed of eighty-miles-per-hour. Still amazingly, the fleet galloping black steed was easily able to keep pace with the great instant velocity achieved by the silver *Ford Expedition*.

'This is impossible!' Will fearfully thought. 'Not even a gazelle or a cheetah could run this fast! This horrible anomaly is contrary to reason! It goes against both nature and science!'

The fantastic, wildly snorting black steed, with its determined headless rider in the saddle, then incredibly pulled alongside the terrified *SUV* driver. A totally hysterical and delirious Will Stuyvesant took a brief glimpse at the shocking apparition, which suddenly removed a handgun from a concealed pocket inside its ghostly apparel, and then aimed and fired the lethal weapon at the *SUV's* front wheel.

The bullets from the devastating blasts punctured the *Expedition's* left front tire. Will Stuyvesant abruptly lost control of the speeding all-terrain vehicle. The SUV swerved to the right, and then skidded off of the already dangerous stone and gravel road; careened down a ridge of smooth weather-worn rocks, and then violently plummeted into the formerly tranquil *Hudson River*. Both William Reynolds Stuyvesant's life and the short-lived *Rip Van Winkle Club* had been fatefully and simultaneously erased from the face of the Earth.

Much to the shock of Hudson River Valley aristocrats, after Will Stuyvesant's corpse had been recovered from the cold river, his

198

lengthy obituary appeared three days later in various New York City and Tarrytown newspapers. Accolades abounded in the various print media articles. William Reynolds Stuyvesant was described and praised as a "generous community-minded philanthropist" who will be deeply missed by his affectionate wife, Gertrude Stuyvesant, who tearfully eulogized her husband during his somber church funeral service. And then, completely out of character, the normally stoic woman later incessantly cried at her husband's solemn burial.

"Stairway to Heaven"

I had suddenly died in my home's master bedroom's bathroom while I had been staring into the vanity mirror after finishing shaving. A sudden pain spread from my left arm to my chest and the last thing I remembered as a human being was collapsing upon the brown-tiled floor. There is no doubt in my mind that my body had ceased functioning and that my awareness had slowly exited my form and then transferred into a strange energy-spirit state. I don't remember any spectacular catharsis when my soul had been ejected from its human shell.

Next, I was somehow cognizant of hovering over my lifeless corpse and a moment later my senses were aware of my wife's delirious screams as she frightfully bent over to touch my neck feeling for a pulse. 'So much for her being a veteran R.N.,' my still intact consciousness sarcastically thought. 'She does really love me after all!'

To my fallible knowledge, I never traveled through any dark tunnel to any ethereal bright light destination. I believe *that* scenario is what some minds fearfully manufacture when brain cells are rapidly deteriorating and nerve endings are desperately transmitting the wrong information because of severe oxygen deficiency. So, I firmly believe that after the spirit evacuates the body at the moment of the heart's cessation, the actual process of dying has just begun, for every cell in the human form must then soon die off one by one after breathing has permanently stopped. But still, conscience, mind and spirit survive the momentarily painful ordeal quite satisfactorily outside *the host* that had once sheltered *those* entities. I steadfastly maintain that death can be best described as a combination spiritual/biological process that has occurred.

The next event I remember was that my weightless atom-less spirit vertically floated through the ceiling and then right through the house's roof as if both physical objects were porous intangible imaginary masses. At that moment, I felt as if I had been a scintilla of light penetrating through two transparent thermo-glass window panes. I recollect drifting around fifty feet above the ground and my *new* keener senses detected a crowd of curious neighbors dashing out of their homes. Soon an ambulance with red flashing lights entered and screeched to a halt atop my former dwelling's driveway.

As a scene of mayhem developed both in and around my Hammonton, New Jersey ranch-home, my ghostly consciousness began gliding slowly downward in the direction of a gray limousine parked at the curb across the street from my residence. I passed through the density of a tall tulip tree, like water rushing through a teabag. While my *intelligent spirit* was descending, the limousine driver, a facsimile of the Grim Reaper (wearing a dull brown robe), opened the back door.

My soul easily entered the vehicle, and my three-hundred-and-sixty-degree consciousness was acutely aware that all participants and eyewitnesses involved in the pandemonium in front of my Valley Avenue home were totally oblivious to my ghostly departure. However, many spectators grieved, sobbed, and gasped when *they* observed two strong paramedics carrying my listless form out of the house on a Hammonton Rescue Squad stretcher. All attempts at reviving my body with special electric shock equipment inside the ambulance had failed.

My awareness felt no grief, remorse, shock, pain, or anxiety from my sudden death. My mind remained calm, curious and alert as the gray limousine gradually moved forward and passed right through four people standing on Valley Avenue without them one bit knowledgeable about the 'spiritual hearse' or the phenomenon that was occurring.

"I suppose the afterlife is not governed by the laws of physics," my *spiritual intelligence* said to the macabre driver, who passively ignored my attempt at initiating a telepathic conversation. All the Grim Reaper duplicate did was stare menacing at me in the rear-view mirror. My chauffeur's face featured giant voids in the hollowed-out bony cavities where its eyeballs should have been. A hood covered the forehead part of the driver's skull above his grotesque-looking skinless face. The chauffeur's super-white teeth appeared twice as large as the average human's would be. I remember how futile and stupid it seemed contemplating escape from my alien captivity.

I dared not speak to my eerie escort again, but instead, my cognizance used my *intelligent spirit* to scrutinize the passing environment I remember perceiving while somehow looking-out of dark-tinted windows, without possessing any functioning human eyes. 'I must remain rational and try to make some sense out of this new world I've entered,' I nervously thought. 'After all, everyone is going to eventually die, and go through the whole same experience,

202

too.' I did find some comfort in making that conjecture, even though I had believed that the process of dying was quite singular to the individual that was doing the perishing. 'Death seems to be much more morbid and harrowing to the survivors of the dearly departed than it actually does to the deceased,' I concluded while prematurely evaluating the nature of my own recent demise.

As my reticent driver's non-palpable gray luxury sedan zoomed down the White Horse Pike, my perceptive spiritual intelligence suddenly made a rather stark observation. All of the automobiles on the highway in my new dimension were limousines, and the vehicles were of three colors: black, gray, and white in their order of frequency. Instantly, my astute mind-spirit concluded that the black ones were on their way to hell, the gray ones heading to purgatory and the few white ones en route to heaven.

Then, I became a little more sober about my fascinating excursion, because I was certain that my destination was going to be purgatory. 'It's logical that the bulk of people are heading for hell, a small percentage to purgatory, and only a select few to heaven,' my mind-spirit surmised. 'I could've and should've led a better life,' I shallowly lamented without any evidence of heavy guilt, remorse or regret. It was more as if I was being disappointed rather than being angry with myself, and my soul was now resigned to accepting whatever fate awaited me without objection, or without endeavoring to rationalize fanciful excuses in defense of my past actions and misdeeds. I felt as if my entire free will had been sacrificed and surrendered.

My foreboding chauffeur stopped at the traffic signal at Fairview Avenue and the White Horse Pike. I remember thinking that he really didn't have to stop, so the driver must have halted for a specific purpose designed to enlighten me about some aspect of the afterlife. A black 'hearse/sedan was visible approaching on Fairview directly behind us, and as *our* limo' turned left on green, I noticed the black hearse turn right in the general direction of Woodlawn Avenue, apparently heading to Valley to make a pick-up at my former home. 'Fools,' I mentally criticized *their* human enterprise. 'That's only my limp body lying in the ambulance over on Valley Avenue. I'm now in this immaterial non-visible gray limousine, you' hapless, money-hungry incompetent morticians!'

I then saw the facsimile Grim Reaper driver nastily stare at me in the rear-view mirror, and my spirit became quite uneasy, when I realized that *he* could read my innermost thoughts that, in the conundrum-like dimension I had entered were now public knowledge (at least to him), and were no longer secret notions exclusive to myself.

'We're coming to Old Forks Road, and there's the new Hammonton High School up on the left abounding with vibrant adolescent life,' I genuinely thought. Soon, the gray limousine made a left-hand turn into Oak Grove Cemetery, and the unearthly vehicle first stopped at a recently dug grave with *my name* inscribed on the granite headstone. 'I'm now glad I had the foresight to buy grave plots and an en*graved* headstone,' my awareness concluded. 'But I'm sitting without any sensation of sitting in this sleek gray vehicle, and only an expensive bronze casket (as specified in my will) containing my embalmed remains will be deposited into that lurid, one-fathom-deep hollow.'

Then, I realized that time-warping was a unique characteristic of the afterlife I had entered, since I had just died what seemed moments before, and I now recognized that my grave-site had already been excavated, and a vault had been snugly placed inside. I stared at the vault's gilded golden lid as the gray limousine next moved slowly forward on the cemetery's narrow, leave-strewn, asphalt lane. I recalled I had died in early autumn, October 15th to be exact. 'One always knows the month he or she is born, but the individual seldom if ever considers which month he or she will die,' I philosophically pondered.

As the Grim Reaper (or his replica) drove me around the various twisting roads of all-too-familiar Oak Grove Cemetery, I soon realized that at age sixty, I knew more people that had already died than individuals who were still alive. But I still could not accept the notion that *I* had made any dramatic transition at all and had *crossed over* to anywhere except to Oak Grove Cemetery as a translucent passenger, now dressed as a two-dimensional ghost in a now white-shaded black suit and tie, I would be buried in.

My eerie-looking escort stopped at a particular grave-site, and then an ominous newsreel flashed onto the video screen located above the limo's back seat. Mark DiMeo was a good friend of my son, Steve. Mark had been killed in a tragic automobile accident. The teenager's parents had also been killed in an automobile accident twelve years earlier while crossing *Route 30* in a jeep. The young man had to be raised and mentored by his grandfather, and I would

204

often take Mark home after school events, or when the young man had visited my abode on Valley Avenue. I say *my* abode? How absurd of me! When a person dies, he or she has absolutely nothing: no home, no money, no possessions, no capital gains' assets, and certainly no material comforts. The richest man in the world isn't worth a mere brown penny once he succumbs to death.

The gray-shaded limousine driver very deliberately maneuvered the vehicle down and around a tree-lined oval lane and halted at the headstone of a former business associate. Our partnership had not been an amiable one, and I had outsmarted Jack Merlino in our one-sided business settlement. Merlino had bought me out and then went bankrupt ten years later. The sequence of events did not have to be reminisced, because the incidents involving Jack and me had all been captured on tape and then mercilessly shown to me on the back seat video screen. But being cleverer than Jack Merlino now all seemed quite irrelevant and meaningless.

Apparently, the visual representations on the television screen were not being presented in chronological order. A vision of me taking a final college exam' flashed upon the unique video monitor. I had needed an A on the difficult final to pass the "Educational Psychology" course and graduate, mostly because I had squandered valuable time being absent from class, relaxing in the student lounge, playing poker and pinochle. A fraternity brother had stealthily and illicitly acquired the professor's final exam', and he and I spent two entire nights figuring-out the seemingly enigmatic answers to the instructor's stolen "objective questions". I easily aced the final by cheating, but now I was specifically being supernaturally reminded of my unethical transgression that had somehow been mysteriously captured on some inexplicable, arcane videotape.

Then, it finally occurred to me that this uncanny itinerary through the cemetery was really a brief review of the good and the bad that I had contributed to civilization during my short lackluster tenure upon the Earth. An unsettling feeling drenched my spirit as the apparition of a female suddenly appeared sitting next to me. The woman's stone-cold face was horribly ashen, and as she turned her head to stare at me, her distinct image was that of Persephone, daughter of Zeus. I recalled from a myth I had read in college that the goddess had been abducted to the Greek underworld to be the companion of its heartless ruler/tyrant, Hades.

Persephone's grim and ghastly facial features then transformed into the countenance of Connie Morgan, a beauty queen I had dated in college, but then I had cruelly dumped her in favor of my present wife. I did not feel any guilt about my past un-meritorious deed. 'My comprehension of our college relationship is rational, objective and coldly analytical, just as my judgment by the *Powers That Be* will probably be conducted,' I all-too-hastily hypothesized, instinctively accepting the uncertain fate that awaited me.

Connie Morgan's image then magically transformed back into Persephone's face and form, which gradually crystallized, vaporized and soon vanished into thin air. 'My entire past has been systematically recorded on tape, to be used against me on Judgment Day,' I logically concluded.

The next cemetery stop was at my younger brother's grave-site. My grandmother had left me an inheritance and I neglected to share it with Tony, who had a not-so-easy life struggling to make ends meet. Then scenes of me' enjoying myself at Atlantic City casinos, going on expensive Caribbean vacations and cruises with my wife and children, and next buying new house furniture with stock market earnings, all appeared in my brief visual biography. I rationally concluded that every good and bad behavior of my preempted life had been systematically recorded and documented by invisible camera crews using indiscernible equipment. 'If excessive pride and hubris were convicting criteria for eternal condemnation, then I'm definitely a prime candidate for such a deserving sentence,' I uncomfortably generalized.

'But these are only venial-type sins I've been witnessing!' my consciousness rationalized. 'Certainly, any type of after-world justice would have to weigh all of the good against all of the bad,' my spiritual existence determined and justified. 'And undoubtedly, I have performed much more of the former in my earthly existence than the latter. These are *not* serious mortal sins I'm observing here!' my uncomfortable *spirit-intelligence* mentally editorialized.

The hideous-looking driver moved ahead and passed by the grave-sites of my father, mother, and my maternal grandparents. I was surprised that the limousine operator did not stop to haunt my mind with videotaped episodes of the insolence and defiance I had exhibited toward any of my dearly departed ancestors during my wild, rebellious adolescence.

Then, the gray limo' stopped at a Catholic priest's (who had willed to be buried with his family) tombstone. I recollected the name Father Thomas Randazzo, who had officiated at marrying my wife and me' in St. Joseph's Church on Third Street. Upon the now-familiar video screen appeared the image of my wife and three young sons, sitting in a church pew without their father during a Sunday service. I quickly understood how futile and flimsy my argument had been, that I hadn't been shown on the video screen any mortal sins I had committed. 'My six-decade life was not without deviation from expected behavior. In many respects, a model father I was not,' I too late recollected and decided.

Another tableau appeared on the monitor and depicted me indulging in food and drink at a local restaurant. Gluttony had been practiced by myself' on numerous occasions, and according to inflexible church teachings, *that* bad habit was not exactly a stellar virtue. Now, I immensely missed food and drink, and I no longer have a body that requires biological sustenance. 'Physical pleasures and sensations now have to be sacrificed to allow for spiritual growth to occur,' I reckoned.

Ever since graduating high school, I believed that sin had merely been an invention of religion designed to instill in worshipers a promise of eternal reward that functioned as a cultural mechanism, capitalizing on making churchgoers dread the possibility of eternal damnation. I had always thought that organized religion exploited one's hopes and fears to make individuals conform to certain austere and rigid codes of deportment. Now, I was being graphically confronted with the strong chance that I had been erroneous in my assumptions, and that the church's prescribed teachings (that I had liberally violated) had been infallibly right.

My mind was preoccupied pondering the nature and the structure of the overall afterlife that my spiritual intelligence had been gauging. 'Humans live in a parallel dimension, an alternate illusion to the fantastic actual mysterious reality I have entered. This *is* the real world that the material world wrongfully thinks is an illusion,' I theorized. 'And the real world is truly the fantasy experience, and the after-world venue is really the actuality of existence.'

My back-seat limousine imagining was interrupted by my awareness that *my* gray 'hearse/sedan was finally leaving Oak Grove Cemetery. In the distance, I observed a westbound funeral procession heading toward Oak Grove from downtown Hammonton, and then it dawned on my powerless soul that the automobiles in line were filled with family and friends assembled to pay their final respects to *me*. 'I always thought that there would be more than just twenty-two cars,' my restless spirit protested as I counted the automobiles entering the graveyard. 'I suppose I wasn't as influential on others as I had wrongly imagined!'

Apparently, time in the after-world had the ability to expand and contract, for it had seemed like only fifteen earthly minutes or so since I had suffered a fatal cardiac arrest to the moment when my mortal remains were about to be buried in Oak Grove Cemetery. Obviously, my corpse had been taken to the mortuary, been embalmed, had a viewing and a funeral mass while my underdeveloped soul was being given preliminary exposure to phase one of the afterlife. This knowledge led me to suspect *too late* that the body and its attendant pleasures were but irrelevant distractions in both corporal life and to temporal death. I finally realized *too late* that one's soul, one's spirit, and one's conscience were the only important factors in all human activities.

My morbid gray limousine turned west (left) on the *White Horse Pike*, just as *my* slow-moving funeral procession entered the main gate into the century-old cemetery. The grim chauffeur's creepy mouth seemed to sullenly smile in *his* rear-view mirror reflection, but I imagined that the ridicule was simply a manifestation that my addled mind had conjured.

The Grim Reaper's duplicate sped without detection through a police radar trap in Chesilhurst. My escort zipped through a traffic light in Atco, while simultaneously filtering through a bus, two cars, a dump truck, and a tractor-trailer that had been stopped at the congested intersection. The limo' then passed through the towns of Berlin and Clementon, with the speedometer registering a hundred-and-ten. Under ordinary conditions, I would have been petrified and panic-stricken at the dangerous speed but since I was already deceased, my faculties had evolved beyond normal fear, and I no longer was awed by anyone human or anything that had been produced by humans. My ride was all rather surreal, but in retrospect, quite humdrum, because all along, I knew I was already dead.

The gray limousine then turned right onto Linden Avenue, beyond Clementon, and I was just meditating about how much fun I had had as a teenager at Clementon Lake Amusement Park when my frightening-looking skeleton operator abruptly pulled into the

Lindenwold High-Speed Line's huge parking lot. The regular train service conveniently connected southern New Jersey to Philadelphia, and it carries over forty-thousand-commuters daily to the *City of Brotherly Love,* and then in the late afternoon transports them back home to suburban towns situated east of the *Delaware River.*

The robotic-like wretched chauffeur stopped the limo' in front of the main terminal entrance, and as I curiously glanced around, I noticed that the entire parking lot was filled with other nondescript empty gray limousines, rather than the usual standard array of domestic and foreign cars and trucks.

Two celestial-looking gentlemen converged on *my* vehicle, and the taller specter opened the back door. I obediently stepped out, and then after the door was slammed shut, remarkably without any accompanying thud, the Grim Reaper casually stepped on the gas pedal, evidently dispatched to journey and pick-up his next assigned, unfortunate, trans-migratory spiritual passenger.

'Hello!' my consciousness greeted, for I no longer possessed a functional tongue, throat or voice box.

'Welcome to a higher echelon!' the first figure returned in a weird sort of mental telepathy being exhibited. 'I'm Gabe, and my companion's name is Mike.'

Immediately, I felt inclined to query whether my new after-world acquaintances were the archangels Gabriel and Michael, but I did not have the audacity to pursue that particular presumption upon initial introduction. I did not perceive any fluffy white wings on their shoulders, any flowing radiant gowns around their forms, or any dazzling halos around their dual transparent heads. So, I did not wish to appear facetious or foolish during that initial encounter, even though the two immortal beings ostensibly knew exactly what I had been thinking and evaluating.

I glanced-up at the sky and perceived that it was overcast, and *that* impression instantly suggested to me a general mediocre dull atmosphere that appropriately corresponded to the thousand or so stationary, empty, gray limousines in the giant parking lot, and my casual observation reinforced the notion that *they* had been symbolizing purgatory. When my spirit endeavored to initiate a mental exchange of ideas, I quickly fathomed that Gabe and Mike could understand me completely, but I could not comprehend or decipher their inter-angelic communications. The phenomenon was analogous to high-pitched sound frequencies dogs could hear and identify, which happen to be out of the limited range of human auditory perception.

'Is this still the Lindenwold Station?' I mentally transmitted. 'I used to ride the High-Speed Line from this terminal into Philly' to take my wife shopping downtown; attend plays at the *Walnut Street Theatre,* or to visit *Thomas Jefferson University Hospital* for physical checkups.' The mere thought of my devoted wife made a trace of sentimentality surface from my *subconscious spirit,* which I suddenly fathomed was an important extension of (or a substitution for) my *subconscious mind* in the afterlife.

'You no longer have a free will to do whatever your hedonistic mind pleases or desires,' Gabe mentally informed. 'And your undernourished soul must now undergo massive cleansing and purging until you're ready to be reborn and live a better life than the uninspired lame one you've just left.'

'Do you mean that I haven't been resurrected?' I mildly balked. 'Now *you* are telling me I have to be reincarnated after I am somehow sanctified by penance and anguish. Don't you have any good news to report?'

'We don't like that obscene word reincarnation!' Mike corrected. 'Be careful of your nomenclature! Let's just use the terminology *regenerated.* It's much more accurate, discreet, and appropriate. There are entirely too many esoteric facts that an un-evolved dolt such as yourself must master. I advise you to learn to pay attention and to ignore your own limited mental impulses!'

After mentally trading several additional curious comments, I finally understood that this first phase of the afterlife was comparable to what humans do to *refuse* like paper, plastic, and metal cans; the used debris is recycled. That creative supposition was significantly consistent with what was happening to me, and to all other passengers, arriving in gray limousines under very dull and gloomy cloudy skies. *We* were in the sorting-out phase of being recycled before being washed and treated, but much to my bewilderment, the applicable and acceptable vernacular was being 'regenerated', and not 'reincarnated.'

'Well, then,' I cautiously persisted in my mental inquiry. 'Where is God the Father, Jesus, and the Holy Ghost? Will I get to meet Them'?' I innocuously and presumptuously desired to know.

'You ask too many impertinent questions for a lowly neophyte,' Mike mentally reprimanded. 'But if you really want to know, you're not evolved enough to have *that* kind of special audience. Don't try running when you haven't yet conquered the art of crawling! Sorry, but I had to relate the advanced concept to you in mental language you could readily grasp.'

'Are we going to board the next train?' I rambunctiously asked. 'I've never been an advocate or a practitioner of *mass* transportation. Are we going to a Catholic Church or to a religious tribunal?' I awkwardly mentally joked.

'You must learn to temper your curiosity, your impudent sense of humor, along with your rash opinions,' Gabe admonished with grim features showing on his angelic face. 'If you keep your soul open and receive knowledge and wisdom, rather than sending-out wild flurries of cynical questions, then you'll finally comprehend the abstract nature of your new environment. That kind of discipline must be fully realized by you before you can ever evolve to a higher rank,' Gabe telepathically elucidated. 'Don't expect *us* to volunteer information on demand. You'll soon be on your own, and have to journey through the emotionally grueling ordeal of final atonement all by yourself.'

The two enigmatic angels then grabbed me by the arms. The three of us effortlessly floated across the parking lot above the myriad gray limos' to the High-Speed Line's eastern terminal entrance ramp. I looked-up above the concrete platform's pavilion and read the strange designation: "HA" where the noticed, lettered appellation "Lindenwold Station" should normally have appeared on the overhanging shingle.

'What *on Earth* does HA indicate?' I mentally asked Gabe, who in truth seemed rather bored and annoyed with my perpetual inane inquiries.

'Why you really aren't too imaginative now, are you!' the winged escort thought-transmitted. 'HA is an abbreviation, or more specifically an acronym for Heart Attack Station. All New Jersey humans that have died of heart attacks, and who must be purged of past misdemeanors and indiscretions, must ingress to the next stage of their eternal existence from *this* particular platform.'

'Let's get on board or else *our* supervisors will warrant more menial jobs for us to complete,' Mike mentally declared to Gabe. 'I don't want to be demoted from management to labor! Not with all of my accumulated on-the-job experience!'

'There's just as much stupid bureaucracy in the afterlife as there is in real life,' I thought to myself, forgetting that my mind was being eavesdropped upon. 'I hope there isn't any work, or any prying government, or any abominable *IRS* to contend with!'

'I warned you to keep your grandiose, pin-headed opinions to yourself!' Gabe chastised. 'Try to impress us that you're more than the imbecile you boastfully appear to be!'

The three of us stepped into the nearest car, and within what must have been thirty earth-seconds, the doors closed and the train rapidly advanced on its rails in the direction of what used to be Philadelphia. I surveyed my surroundings, and quickly discovered that I had been the only heart attack victim to get onto the death train at the former Lindenwold Station terminal.

'This' is a pretty inefficient system,' I critically evaluated, again neglecting to remember that my private thoughts were now public. 'This entire train is operating just to transport one passenger to some obscure destination. This confounded world is even worse than the one I had just escaped!'

'You'll never adequately comprehend your new dimension until you abandon your propensity for fabricating ludicrous and inconsequential impressions!' Mike mentally chided. 'I strongly advise you, try respectfully learning your new environment, rather than merely engaging in all of this boring childish critiquing!'

Three-miles down the track the train jerked to a stop in front of what used to be the Ashland Station, which now bore the identification 'C,' meaning 'Cancer Station'. Four unfortunate doomed passengers were escorted onto the train by well-dressed supernatural beings that coincidentally looked like mass-produced carbon copies of Mike and Gabe.

'Well, I think the authorities oughta' have a crab up there on the sign to symbolize Cancer,' I mused, while forgetting that my two companions and the eight new archangels could easily intercept and interpret my caustic ruminations. 'Perhaps the next heavenly station will be Libra or Aquarius.'

'Show more compassion and sensitivity, you blundering ingrate-egomaniac!' one of the new angels who looked similar to Gabe mentally rebuked. 'No wonder why you have to be regenerated, you repulsive, self-centered, conceited cretin!' the very intimidating form pontificated.

It didn't take me long to ascertain that each new station had as its name a new disease or a particular cause of death. Those passengers that boarded with their angels at the next 'SD' platform (formerly Woodcrest Station) had suffered from strokes and had perished from drowning, Haddonfield was now renamed 'DMD' (The Drugs and Murder Death Station), and what was previously Collingswood now had the ominous title 'AND' (Accidents and Natural Disasters Station).

I glanced around the half-full car and counted a total of twenty-nine newcomers, escorted by fifty-eight very competent-but-bored angel guides. The next stop on the unorthodox train route was ordinarily Ferry Avenue Station. I wondered if the stop's name would remain the same with boating accident and ship sinking victims entering through the train's ominous portals. Mike again criticized me for being too arrogant and too immersed into my own thoughts rather than empathizing with the new admissions to 'the Purgatory Local'.

The new Ferry Avenue pick-up destination had the appellation 'GDW' (General Diseases and War Station). A horde of misery-faced victims and their divine escorts patiently waited on the cement platform, and when the doors opened, at least a hundred ghoulish-looking new riders were promptly escorted aboard.

'Why don't *they* simply pass through the doors rather than just stupidly standing there and be waiting for the portals to open?' I skeptically thought. I noticed infants that had died from birth defects being pushed in baby carriages by somber-faced guardian angels, and many of the deceased appeared to have been terminated by chronic neurological maladies such as multiple sclerosis and Lou Gehrig's Disease. The specters of six fatally wounded soldiers also entered, accompanied by *their* twelve nonchalant and apathetic angel hosts.

'Why must death come to innocent babies and patriotic warriors?' I considered. 'It all seems so wicked and unfair!'

'Your reckless words border on heresy,' Gabe very deliberately transmitted and pointed-out. 'And if you persist in continuing your abusive absurd remarks, you'll soon discover that you're only extending your stay on this perpetual elevated train ride.'

'It all seems like random arbitrary selection,' I imagined and inadvertently communicated. 'It's like we were all put into a worldwide lottery, and each unlucky recipient happened to wind-up a victimized duck in a giant shooting gallery. I wonder who's been taking the rifle shots that are eliminating each of us from our happy, earthly status?'

'You definitely are going to be made an example out of!' Mike mentally predicted and accused. 'Moral justice in *this* dimension is much more decisive and conclusive than political justice was in your former world. There are no appeals' courts in this afterlife you've entered after the sand in your *life-glass* had expired. You'll soon discover the profound significance of my statement. Now stop being so *damned* opinionated!'

I must confess that I always had a proclivity for being frivolous during crucial situations. For example, I had a tendency to always want to crack a joke at a funeral, or at a viewing, and had to exercise self-discipline not to do so, my spirit recalled. 'At least half of the people on the General Diseases and War platform must've succumbed to debilitating *terminal illnesses.*' Then. Gabe adroitly intercepted my most recent ludicrous brainstorm.

'If you persist in attempting to be an obnoxious comedian,' my ethereal companion's flawless superior mind conveyed, 'then Mike and I will be required by forces greater than ourselves to put you on a southbound *black* train at the next station. And believe me! You don't want to go there! Lucifer Prince of Darkness absolutely and positively loves tormenting and torturing pretentious morons such as you happen to be'.'

'I'm sorry,' my suddenly guilty consciousness automatically apologized. 'It was just my sanguine disposition surfacing from my subconscious mind, er, I mean from my subconscious spirit,' I mentally answered. 'I know I tend to be facetious and sometimes playfully sarcastic, but in this new dynamic mental environment, I must admit, I'm definitely at a disadvantage.'

'Control yourself! Harness your frivolous impulses, you' pathetic excuse for a human being,' Mike critically cautioned. 'And just absorb everything that your spiritual eyes witness. Otherwise, your actions will not only have severe consequences. They'll also be the genesis of diabolical results you'll long regret.'

Gabe informed me that he had to attend to another assignment and was scheduled to get off the phantom train at the next designated station. I did not possess sufficient courage to ask the specter to describe his next mission, so my two-dimensional form sat solemnly in my seat and contemplated the general morbidity of the other deceased and melancholy purgatory-bound passengers. The speeding train entered the familiar tunnel just before what used to be the Camden City Hall exit, and before Gabe departed my company, he handed me a gray pen to be utilized soon in 'your next major post mortem enterprise.'

I politely bade 'farewell' to my radiant, angelic chum, who then casually sauntered onto the former Camden City Hall platform, which now bore the reference 'ND' (Natural Death Station). Depressing apparitions with wrinkled elderly faces cluttered the subterranean platform, and many of the new arrivals crowded aboard the thirteen unlucky cars that constituted the 'Purgatory Express', as I had now preposterously labeled it. I imagined that the phantom express could hold over a million ghosts if it had to, since all of us lacked anatomies or forms to occupy real physical space, and *we* could have easily been stacked on top of one another like sheets of construction composition board, or otherwise simply frugally crammed inside.

'Does this underground tunnel we're now in represent some sort of a birth canal in reverse?' I mentally asked Mike. 'Am I reentering the womb, so to speak, er, I mean so to think!'

'You are undoubtedly and indisputably, a completely annoying dunce!' my all-too-perturbed escort reproached. 'It isn't like *that* at all. It's more like when light travels from air into water. It sort of gets warped or bent, going from one predictable medium into another. That's exactly what's happening to you right now. You're going from one medium to the other.'

'What happened to what used to be the Broadway Station in Camden?' my curious spirit inquired to my austere host.

'Oh now, you must be referring to the Limbo Station,' my illustrious guide matter-of-factly replied. 'LS is temporarily out of commission, because it's under repair and having drastic renovations being done to accommodate all of the horrible abortions being performed and all of the unfortunate still-borns being delivered back on Earth. Just look at all of the unnecessary work you daft former humans are causing the already-overtaxed eternal staff!'

The high-speed train surfaced from its subterranean cavity, and next crossed what used to be the *Ben Franklin Bridge* into what used to be center-city Philadelphia, but now the connection had the designation *Crossing Over Bridge.* I looked at the traffic on the span's seven lanes and readily determined that it consisted exclusively of white, black, and gray limousines, conducting novice ghosts to their more permanent destinations. A second more-deliberate analysis determined that there were only a few white limousines traveling on the mile-long span, suggesting that Heaven was indeed under-populated.

The first underground Pennsylvania train stop, which should have been Philadelphia's Eighth and Market Street platform, was now listed as 'CN' (Celebrity Notoriety Station). Transparent images of deceased rock and roll singers, movie stars, and political and historical figures were standing around, and idly conversing on the concrete walkway. I observed Elvis Presley interacting with John Lennon; John Wayne exchanging thoughts with Marilyn Monroe; Franklin Delano Roosevelt mentally mingling with Harry S. Truman and Dwight D. Eisenhower, and Edward G. Robinson sharing ideas with Abraham Lincoln and J. Edgar Hoover. Many other famous specters were visible on the dismal platform including Daniel Boone, Charlie Chaplin, Thomas Edison, and Edgar Allan Poe, but I had insufficient time to recognize the identities of all the distinguished phantasms.

'I have to get off at the next stop,' Mike imperatively stated. 'Here's a small gray notepad that you can write some of your impressions upon. I'll allow one written communication with a past acquaintance, so that you can then successfully forget about your former world and concentrate on being processed into your new *medium*. Do you have any final relevant questions? This is your last opportunity to ask them!'

'Er yes,' my spirit telepathically stammered. 'How do I mail this document after I have authored it?'

'Oh, pardon me for the silly oversight,' Mike courteously responded. 'I'm usually much more thorough and dependable. I suppose I'm suffering from chronic mental fatigue! Use the gray pen Gabe had given you, and jot-down your thoughts and reactions inside the gray notebook. Here's an official gray envelope. Address it to whomever you wish, and then drop the correspondence into the gray *Inter-Dimensional Mailbox* you'll occasionally see at selected underground train platforms.'

'But I won't have enough time to write-down all I want to describe!' my adamant spirit hastily communicated in a frustrated mood. 'Are you deliberately trying to aggravate me?'

'On second thought, seal and drop the envelope into the postal box's slot at the next station when the subway train again gets there,

216

sometime in your eternal future,' my guide suavely and convincingly advised. 'You must remember that you have all the time in the world to randomly scribble-down your notes in this book, so you don't have to foolishly rush. Practice good penmanship if you wish. Notice that adequate postage has already been attached to the standard gray mailing envelope.'

I was sage enough not to doubt the angel's veracity. 'My only alternative is to trust *his* instructions,' I logically decided. Then, the train slowed to another subterranean halt.

Mike exited the perfectly noiseless and quiet carriage at the vacant 'SH' (Stairway to Heaven) platform. I attempted to rise from my seat to take an instant shortcut to paradise, but some supernatural force field prevented me from accomplishing my selfish pursuit. I again tried standing-up. I experienced a sensation akin to a sleep paralysis I had once undergone while my mind was emerging from a strange dream. I could not move a muscle, feeling as if I was being subjected to a potent enchantment that completely enslaved my will and easily manipulated my spirit. 'Oh well,' I surmised. 'I have the entire future to be introspective and objective. I'll take my time in organizing this important narrative.'

The eternal high-speed train pulled-out from the rather fascinating, brightly lit', empty Stairway to Heaven Station, which in my prior life was known as 10th and Locust. The next stop of the High-Speed Line Express, which ordinarily was the last one, was 15th and Locust. I again tried to rise from my seat, but was thwarted by that same indomitable spiritual force's resistance. I glanced-around the filled-to-capacity train and confirmed that all of the other more compliant passengers were assiduously writing down notes into *their* small gray tablets. I figured it was time for me to abandon my intractable disposition and finally conform to Gabe and Mike's expectations, so I very obediently imitated my fellow passengers' appropriate example.

I then peered-out onto the platform from the window above my seat and read the name of the last station, which was peculiarly labeled 'FJ' (First Judgment Station). Standing on the platform were twelve individuals wearing long gray robes with accompanying gray-haired wigs that were positioned above their ashen-colored foreheads. The dozen jurors were all dead persons that I had wronged when the individuals and I were living our independent lives back in Hammonton, New Jersey.

I objectively speculated that the twelve Solons would be judging my candidacy for probation from my dull, uninspiring, subterranean purgatory. I theorized that if I eventually passed *their* verdict, I would be assimilated into Heaven's lowest denomination, once I had finished filling the small notepad and mailing it whenever the train were to again stop at a platform that had a convenient *Inter-Dimensional Mailbox*. Then, I assumed, my contributions and transgressions would finally be re-judged by a Superior Intelligence on *Judgment Day*.

'My arrogance and my defiance must be discarded in favor of humility and modesty,' I sincerely vowed. 'I'll eventually escape this wicked underground punishment, and hopefully qualify to ascend the *Stairway to Heaven* and be able to finally appreciate and 'see the light.' That is now my utmost aspiration in this mystical-but-monotonous underworld train afterlife. I feel like a groping lost charlatan in quest of admission to a tedious, incomprehensible world belonging to sage wizards.

'I will not send this manuscript to my wife,' I judiciously decided. 'I'll mail the package from an *Inter-Dimensional Mailbox* to Marilyn Jenkins, my editor and publisher at cyberread.com. She'll know precisely what to do with this vague glimpse of eternity, so that in the future, others may benefit from its content.'

"The Unique Juke Box"

Friday, July 4th had arrived in Hammonton, New Jersey and Eddie Palmer had dutifully taken his wife and three children down to Bellevue Avenue to watch the annual patriotic parade. As the small contingent of *VFW* survivors slowly marched by the Central Avenue viewing area, Eddie had a very selfish thought parade across *his* mind while standing next to the town's historic "Reagan Rock". 'Tomorrow, Kim is taking Jenna, Tommy, and Joey to vacation for a whole week at Long Beach Island,' Palmer contemplated. 'Then, I can use *my* vacation time to paint my newly constructed recreation room; to cultivate the tall weeds out in the vegetable garden; to mow the lawn, and to pick up my new juke box.'

Eddie was a '50s fanatic, such an addicted '50s fanatic who never fully evolved out of that glorious, memorable decade. Palmer still wore long greasy hair, had Elvis' sideburns, and on weekends, sported a black motorcycle jacket along with blue denim jeans, when he wasn't selling new and used automobiles for a local car dealership up on the White Horse Pike. Eddie Palmer took great pride in being the vice-president of the Hammonton Classic Car Club, himself owning a bright red 1958 Chevy convertible with an impressive Continental wheel attached to and extending from the back.

The following Wednesday, Eddie gave his closest friend Jack Nelson a call. "Say, Jack," Eddie prefaced from his often-used cell phone. "I need a big favor from you tomorrow morning. Do ya' think you can help me out?"

"Are ya' gonna' finally replace that faulty distributor in your '58 Chevy?" Jack Nelson curiously asked. "I'm a jewelry store owner, and I'm not too talented as a greased monkey!"

"No, Jack. I'm plannin' on havin' Anthony and Louie over at A.T. Auto Clinic on the Pike do that specialized maintenance for me," Eddie revealed. "It's a tough job, and I only want expert mechanics workin' on the project. But I need ya' to perform a much more challengin' duty with me."

"Well then, Eddie, what did ya' have in mind?" Jack instinctively inquired. "I could be available on Thursday morning. Like you, I'll take a day off from the office for mental health reasons. *Christmas* time is really my busy season in the retail jewelry business."

"Great!" Palmer instantly responded. "I need ya' to accompany me over to Bristol, Pennsylvania. I traded in my old Seeburg juke box and have upgraded to a colorful, rainbow Wurlitzer. It's a real beauty, Jack! I'm gonna' use my pickup, and I've arranged to borrow a dolly from Richie over at Chester's Hardware. We'll use boards as a tailgate ramp to get the heavy juke off the truck and into my den," Eddie anxiously informed. "Two men can easily handle the job. But Jack, we have to be exceptionally careful. I don't want to damage that baby! It's a priceless relic!"

"What was wrong with the old Seeburg?" Jack Nelson automatically questioned his excited pal. "That thing was also a collector's item. I would have bought it from you if I had known that baby was on the market!"

"Jack, you oughta' see this out-of-this-world Wurlitzer," Eddie eagerly answered. "It's been re-conditioned and is just like brand-new. I reluctantly traded in the Seeburg and got a premium price for it. Only problem was that the Wurlitzer came equipped with 33 rpm records, and I preferred to have '45s specially installed."

"Well, Eddie, do we have to transport the Seeburg up over to Bristol?" Palmer's pal asked. "You said you had traded the Seeburg in for the Wurlitzer, didn't you?"

"No," Eddie tersely replied. "The Liberto Juke Box Company had already picked the Seeburg up last week."

"Then, why can't they simply deliver the new Wurlitzer just like they picked up the used Seeburg?" Jack reflexively wondered and inquired.

"Because the company won't be able to deliver it until after *Labor Day,* but I want to have that beauty in my possession right now!" the '50s fanatic disclosed. "Jack, now do you understand all of the pertinent circumstances?"

"And you're getting '45s inserted to replace the bigger records?" Jack wanted to know. "I would have preferred '45s, too! Is that what you're tellin' me?"

"Exactly, Jack!" Eddie confirmed. "The Wurlitzer I purchased had to be sent-out all the way to Connecticut to be completely refurbished to allow for *that* particular custom-change. The freight bill alone to ship it back and forth from and to Bristol has been rather astronomical."

"Why didn't ya' just have it shipped from Connecticut directly to your home rather than back to Bristol?" Jack Nelson interrupted.

"That maneuver would have saved you money and saved *us* both plenty of time and labor!"

"Because the Liberto Juke Box Company over in Bristol wanted to check over all systems to make sure the Connecticut modifications had been satisfactorily performed," Palmer explained to his best buddy. "I've paid a pretty penny for the Wurlitzer, despite the Seeburg trade-in, and I need to know that it is in perfect condition before it ever reaches Hammonton."

"How much did this investment cost you?" Jack inquisitively probed. "I'll bet more than the average diamond wedding ring!" the gem expert remarked and giggled.

"More than the week-long vacation house Kim had rented at Long Beach Island," Eddie informed his friend. "Eight-thousand-bucks after the trade-in. The only way Kim has allowed me to purchase the Wurlitzer was for me to compromise and spend an equal amount of money on the family for *our* annual big vacation. That's how I've pulled the incredible juke box acquisition off!"

"My wife would divorce me in a New York second if I did a similar impractical thing like acquiring an exotic juke box for my own selfish happiness. Say Eddie, what time do ya' want me at your place?" Jack enviously asked.

"Be here at nine tomorrow morning," Palmer indicated. "And thanks, Jack. I really appreciate your loyal assistance. I'll buy you lunch sometime next week."

"Any time, Eddie," Jack Nelson replied with a mild chuckle. "I have to give you an A in courage and an A+ in shrewdness! Why not make it breakfast tomorrow morning, and lunch sometime next week? Bye now!" Click.

Eddie Palmer diligently finished his personal domestic responsibilities in the yard by Wednesday night. He enjoyed two cold beers that evening and watched a *Phillies* baseball game on television. Then, Palmer took his standard long hot shower; called Jack to remind him of *his* "Bristol commitment", and hopped into his lonely bed and eventually fell asleep. The dreamer was forgetting about his wife and kids vacationing on Long Beach Island while exclusively imagining his special, about-to-be acquired, refurbished Wurlitzer juke box.

At nine a.m. sharp, Jack Nelson appeared at the front door of 345 Liberty Street, just as he had promised his good friend. "I parked my *Mazda* in your cluttered back yard," Nelson disgustedly related to his disorganized pal. "Ya' never know about mindless vandalism with kids being the way they are nowadays. It's a whole different ballgame since the time *we* were growing up."

"You're perfectly correct in taking that precaution," Eddie commiserated. "Either teenagers will steal your car for joyriding, or they wanna' sell it to chop shops to get money to buy drugs. Occasionally," Eddie went on complaining, "punk, rebellious kids even take delight in atrociously demolishing a random vehicle with sledgehammers for their own destructive gratification. There are more punk juvenile delinquents around in 2003 than there ever were back in the late '50s when we were growin' up. Teenage defiance has certainly taken on an entirely new dimension."

"You're absolutely right on target!" Eddie's amenable companion concurred. "Insolent kids today rule the roost at home. Many of 'em boss their wimpy, doting parents around, smoke marijuana instead of cigarettes, don't respect adult authority, and don't give a hoot about their future," Jack pontificated. "The dimwits only live for today, and that's their entire motley existence!"

"And the young thugs all look like urban ghetto hip-hop wannabes'," Eddie elaborated. "The boys nowadays wear earrings and have five pounds of metal punctured onto their faces. They're like young jungle cannibals practicin' body mutilation, wearin' baggy pants that make 'em look like rag-pickers, and talkin' jive inner city nonsense rather than plain formal English. They're an absolute disgrace! What's this world comin' to Jack?"

"It's not comin' to anything," Eddie's alert listener mused and then declared. "The world just keeps circling around the sun each year, and eventually winds-up precisely where it had started out from!" Nelson joked.

"Well, regardless of astronomy," Jack's trapped-in-the-'50s pal commented. "Forget about teenage drugs and AIDS. Those problems were non-existent back in the nifty fifties. Let's change the subject. We're on our way to Bristol to get my mint-condition Wurlitzer, and right now, that's all that really matters with me. We'll stop at the Red Barn on *Route 206* for a nourishing breakfast. Then, it's off to the Liberto Juke Box Company on Mill Street."

"Sounds acceptable and almost plausible to me," Jack affably admitted. "I can taste those delicious blueberry pancakes, hot coffee, home fries, and eggs-over-light right this very second. Evelyn's a terrific cook over at the Red Barn. I wish my wife knew a few of *her* kitchen secrets."

The men enjoyed their sumptuous breakfasts at the popular and cozy Red Barn "kitchen restaurant". Eddie felt compelled to clarify several salient points to his loyal comrade. "The restored Wurlitzer comes re-done with flashing lights inside the rainbow circumference. And besides Jack," the avid '50s memorabilia collector said. "I had an option to get a hundred modern CDs in the Wurlitzer, but I chose to have 100 classic-song '45s, instead. Oldies sound better on vinyl, especially Little Richard, Fats Domino, Elvis, Chuck Berry, and Jerry Lee Lewis. The Wurlitzer will capture the original music without any artificially added studio track overdubs."

"I wish I were you," Jack enviously stated. "Helen won't even let me buy a new engine for my black '53 Mercury coupe. She says I gotta' save every extra penny for our kids' college educations," Nelson lamented. "To what remote solar system has all the world's justice disappeared? It's like I'm trapped in an endless economic nightmare! Whatever happened to smart kids getting scholarships?"

"How was the breakfast' guys?" Evelyn asked as the Red Barn owner scurried to the men's table. "I prepared the eggs special for you two connoisseurs."

"Just great!" Eddie exclaimed. "Jack's accompanying me over to Bristol to pick up a beautiful Wurlitzer juke box. When playing, the object pulsates like a flashing spectrum!"

"Terrific!" Evelyn sincerely answered. "Next time you have one of your famous '50s parties, be sure to invite me. I'd rather be there than be square! Sorry guys, but I gotta' scoot. I'm short a waitress this morning."

Eddie paid the bill, left a hefty tip, and then he and Jack departed the Red Barn establishment, hopped into Palmer's shiny black pickup having "Dealer" tags, and soon pulled out onto *Route 206.* Twenty-three miles up the two-lane state highway Palmer took *County Road 541* at the Slumberland Motel to bypass Mt. Holly, and twenty minutes later, the truck was crossing the Delaware River into Pennsylvania over the ancient but well-preserved *Burlington-Bristol Bridge.* After a mile on *Route 413,* Eddie made a right turn onto Pond Street, which soon led to Mill. Three blocks east down Bristol's one-way main street was the aforementioned Liberto Juke Box Company.

"Isn't this Wurlitzer a work of art?" Dave Liberto pointed-out to his ecstatic New Jersey customer. "It's one of the best I've ever labored on. It's a collector's dream come true!"

"Are you certain all systems have been checked out?" Eddie questioned the confident proprietor, while showing an excessive amount of obvious concern. "This item is putting a definite crimp on my family budget, and my squawky wife will be looking for even the most minor flaw."

"It's been checked over three times by my competent staff," the juke box merchant informed. "I assure you that everything is functioning perfectly. Did you bring along the quilt to wrap it up in so that it can be safely transported back to Jersey without any highway dust or bugs smacking into it?" the businessman asked. "The elements can be brutal at times to an exposed jukebox's many seams and crevices. Even an errant mosquito or moth could mess-up the coin slot, or tarnish a noticeable piece of the exterior."

"Yes," Eddie astutely stated. "I'll get it right now so that your shipping department can wrap the quilt up around the Wurlitzer and tie it with rope or twine. I trust that your 'competent men' will carefully load the apparatus onto my black pickup."

"Certainly," Mr. Liberto guaranteed. "And your final payment is three-thousand-dollars!"

Eddie Palmer eagerly signed the check and handed it over to Jean Liberto, David's crackerjack accountant/wife. Ten minutes later, the juke box enthusiast inspected his wrapped-up precious cargo, hoisted the tailgate, and drove his Ford pickup with Jack Nelson riding "shotgun" back toward Hammonton. The forty-mile return drive seemed three times as long as the trip to Bristol had for the enthralled '50s collector. The purchaser's anticipation at utilizing his new acquisition was quite emotionally overwhelming. "Well, Jack; looks like we're gonna' make it back to Hammonton just in the nick of time. Check out the bleak-looking sky!"

"Those black storm clouds to the west look rather ominous," the other cab occupant observed and stated. "We have to get this baby moved into your den before there's a wicked downpour. I hope we don't get drenched!"

"I hear thunder rumbling and see lightning flashing over to the west near Berlin," Eddie said. "It's a good thing we'll be on Liberty Street in about five-minutes once we pass the *Route 30* light."

The men wasted little time in strapping the quilted Wurlitzer onto the borrowed dolly, and then together gradually wheeling the horizontal cart down the tailgate boards serving as a convenient ramp. In five minutes, the prized juke box had been gently deposited inside Eddie's '50s-themed den. After using wire cutters to sever the twine, the quilt was gently unraveled, removed, folded, and placed in Palmer's cluttered cellar. Eddie wasted little time and immediately plugged in the renovated juke to ascertain if the electrical system was in good order.

"Eddie, it's goin' to pour in a minute, and I wanta' rush home and make sure all my windows are shut!" Jack pleaded. "I'll have to request a *rain-check* on fully appreciating the Wurlitzer, no silly pun intended!"

"Thanks for your capable assistance," Eddie answered. "Stop over tomorrow morning after the storm's passed, and I'll demonstrate this rare machine to you. My '50s den is now finally complete with its most treasured decoration!"

"Great, Eddie! Lots of luck with it!" the same street neighbor hurriedly agreed. "See ya' manana!"

After Jack Nelson quickly exited the ranch home to dash to his *Mazda,* Eddie Palmer delighted for several moments simply enjoying the mere touch of his magnificent juke box. 'This is a major upgrade from the old Seeburg!' the owner thought while completely ignoring the savage storm that was approaching the usually somnolent South Jersey' community. 'I'm very tempted to play an oldies song!' the nostalgic fellow mused as the man admired his latest possession and then studied the tunes that had been listed on the extensive menu. "Hey, here's 'Stormy Weather'!"

A lightning bolt crackled and collided with a nearby telephone pole, temporarily knocking-out all of the electric in the house. 'I'd better unplug the juke box and wait for the storm to pass,' Eddie prudently realized. 'It's not worth the risk to try and play this thing during a thunder and lightning display. I'll have to exhibit some patience and hold my horses for a couple of hours. This thing might be just as vulnerable to torrential rain electric storms as the sensitive modem in my computer tower is.'

Three minutes later, the house's power came back on, but true to his commitment, Palmer waited until after supper to operate his superb mechanism. He even watched the *Weather Channel* to determine that all showers had reduced to a passive level in the

Hammonton vicinity. When the '50s fan was certain that all atmospheric inclemency had passed, the proud man entered his recently painted '50s den and read the song titles listed inside the Wurlitzer. 'Now that the storm threat has sufficiently subsided, I can examine and experiment with my new fabulous toy,' Eddie reckoned. 'I can't wait to hear the quality of the speakers.' The blithe owner inserted the plug back into the wall socket, and after the rainbow lights illuminated, the juke purchaser then again analyzed the menu's song selections with keen attention.

'I guess it's now safe to give it a try!' Eddie reassured himself. 'I already changed all of the house's blinking clock readouts back to their appropriate times. Now, I gotta' find-out if the tempest did any damage to my new treasure.'

The Wurlitzer's menu contained an eclectic array of colorful '50s and early '60s oldies renditions ranging from Bill Haley's 1955 sensational hit single "Rock Around the Clock" to the Supremes 1964 Motown smash chartbuster "Baby Love". 'What song do I want to hear first?' the enamored fellow wondered. 'Hey, here's 'The Bristol Stomp' by the Dovells. I remember that vibrant song from back in '61. Jack and I had just been in Bristol, and that's precisely where the song originated.'

But soon, Eddie saw another item on the prodigious menu that made him change his mind. 'Here's 'At the Hop' by Danny and the Juniors. I remember that big hit from 1958 when I was still a young high school stud. I'll simply press buttons A-9 and listen to a rock and roll classic.'

Eddie's nervous fingers pushed 'A-9', and then the '50s authority watched the jukebox's selector locate the designated disk. After the machine's arm gracefully dropped the selected '45 onto the rotary, the needle arm lowered and began scraping against the spinning record. Palmer then closed his eyes and imagined his glorious youth. The opening notes and upbeat tempo of 'At the Hop's' first bar began. Eddie Palmer opened his lids and was astounded to find himself' situated in time and space at a familiar nostalgic 1958 record hop.

As the amazed middle-aged man glanced around, his eyes witnessed to his right three girls giggling like crazy. "Oh my God!" Eddie gasped. And then, Palmer became aware of *his* public exhibition of awkwardness and covered his mouth in awe. 'It's my old high school sweetheart Barbara Smidillo and her two girlfriends,

Judy Sacco and Gabrielle Attanasi. And they're all wearing poodle skirts. They're all laughing and making fun of my strange clothes!'

Eddie looked-down at his designer sneakers, yellow tank top shirt, and blue denim summer Bermudas and immediately felt mortified. 'I feel like a fish out of water!' Palmer embarrassingly thought.

"Say, Mister, where did you ever get those crazy threads and those boss bony knees?" Barbara Smidillo asked the elderly gentleman, whom she never for one second recognized because of the very apparent vast age differential. "And I think your knobby knees are so cute!" the high school cheerleader added with mild ridicule. "I'll bet you were handsome when you were a teenager!"

"Look, girls. I don't know exactly what has happened," Palmer tried explaining while sucking up his rotund beer belly, "but this record hop seems so very familiar. And 'At the Hop' is still my favorite oldies song."

"What do you mean by *oldies?*" high school prom queen Judy Sacco questioned the hop newcomer. "The song's brand new!"

"And how come an old geezer like you is crashin' a teen record hop?" head talent-show singer Gabrielle Attanasi demanded knowing. "Don't you have any friends your own age?"

"Hey old-timer, let's cut a rug!" Barbara Smidillo insisted as she grabbed Palmer's already trembling right palm. "Judy and Gabrielle, you two can join in and share my new man if ya' want to!"

The three attractive girls took turns jitterbugging with the thoroughly confused new arrival. When Barbara tapped Gabrielle on the shoulder signaling that she wished to again dance with the totally baffled Eddie Palmer, her jealous boyfriend David Noto accosted the Danny and the Juniors' fan and the antagonist instantly exhibited *his* ever-mounting animosity.

"Look, Mister. Barbie's my chick and I resent you foolin' around and makin' time with her!" David Noto emphatically stated. "Just for that, I'm gonna' give ya' a beatin' you're never gonna' forget, old man, or no old man!"

The "At the Hop" tune ended precisely at the moment when Eddie Palmer was the unfortunate recipient of an on-target powerful right cross originating from the angered high school linebacker. The next thing Eddie knew, his right hand was holding his throbbing jaw while lying on his den's tan carpet, next to the magical Wurlitzer.

'That young guy's fist must have been made of iron!' Eddie concluded as the recipient wiped a trace of crimson from the right corner of his mouth. 'Luckily, no teeth are broken! How would I have ever explained what had happened to Kim when she gets back from Long Beach Island with the kids? This amazing juke box can have very serious consequences!' Palmer realistically assessed. 'I better become more deliberate in how I intend to use it! I'm gonna' have to experiment and determine if what I had just experienced was a one-time fluke!'

Despite the apparent blood drops on his left hand and his aching swollen lip, the '50s devotee's mind still was a degree skeptical of the Wurlitzer's remarkable powers. It required a full hour of rest on the couch and a glassful of *Southern Comfort* on the rocks for the '50s collector to fully regain his composure, courage, and his sanity.

'I was back in 1958 for a little longer than two-minutes,' Eddie deductively determined. 'That's about how long the song 'At the Hop' is. I'll bet I stayed in the past the exact length of time as the song allowed. I gotta' test my theory on another less hazardous number. Let's see here!' Palmer speculated as the experimenter studied the jukebox's extensive menu. 'Here's 'Alley-Oop!' by the Hollywood Argyles. I really like the Dante and the Evergreens version better, but I just have to learn exactly how this marvelous machine works. Perhaps the electrical storm and the power outage had something to do with the time warp I had just experienced. At any rate, I'm not closing my eyes this time. I wanna' see everything that's happenin!'

Eddie pressed down 'B-7' with his left and right index fingers. The Wurlitzer's selector arm found the programmed disk, and soon "Alley-Oop!" by the Hollywood Argyles began resonating from the jukebox's powerful internal sound system. 'This is a song about a comical cartoon-character caveman!' Palmer recollected as all of the room's furniture began eddying around. A dense blur filled the enchanted den, and before Palmer could synchronize his senses to accurately perceive reality, the time traveler heard a distinct grunting noise. Turning to his left in what appeared to be a prehistoric tropical setting, Palmer recognized the approach of a muscular, short hairy Neanderthal Man carrying a heavy club. The antagonized caveman was loudly snorting and grumbling in what sounded like very primitive gibberish.

Eddie bent-down and stepped backwards to avoid detection, but his left foot accidentally crushed a fallen twig that had been situated on the ground. The discernible crunch made the caveman's eyebrows slant downwards as *he* perceived the existence of some possible enemy hiding in his midst. The very real anachronism cautiously approached the rock behind which Palmer had been hiding.

The man from the future bolted from his stationary position and took-off down a narrow jungle trail. Soon, the hungry and incensed prehistoric hunter was actively pursuing Eddie Palmer. 'I hope he's not cannibalistic!' as the worried runner dashed forward.

A vicious saber-toothed tiger was startled by the intense jungle chase and aggressively fled in the opposite direction to evade the unpredictable screaming human and the equally-bizarre growling humanoid giving pursuit.

The last refrains of the novelty number "Alley-Oop!" permeated the jungle atmosphere, as Eddie Palmer was wildly sprinting for his life. 'Thirty-seconds until the song's last note!' Eddie estimated as he sped with all his might past lush green bushes, speeding down the winding trail. 'I hope this ancient lunatic doesn't pass through some weird time portal, and then manages to crazily chase me around my den and all over my house!'

The 1960 music finally stopped, and Palmer suddenly emerged out of his smoke-filled, hazy time vacuum, and found himself' stupidly scurrying in circles around his comfortable den furniture set. The frightened '50s collector stopped in his tracks, took ten deep breaths, and wiped-away what seemed like a half-pound of sweat that had accumulated upon his brow.

'I can't believe it!' Eddie concluded as he plopped-down on his green cloth recliner and then critically doubted his own veracity. 'I can't keep this phenomenon a secret any longer. I'm gonna' give Jack a call, so that he can come over and share some of this ongoing, inexplicable adventure. I have to see if the extraordinary device will work the same with two people.'

"Jack, I finally got my Wurlitzer workin' and I'd like to invite ya' over to see it goin'!" Eddie conveyed over the kitchen's landline phone. "What time can ya' come over!"

"How about after supper at around eight!" Nelson suggested. "Helen plans to stay home and do some *Internet* surfing, and the kids will be almost ready for bed. I'll tell my skeptical wife that you need me to help fix a loose part in your new juke box. Little white lies come in handy sometimes.”

“Okay, Jack. But please be prompt and punctual!” Eddie genuinely requested. “You’re gonna’ have the absolute time of your life, buddy! I assure it!”

“Just have a couple of delicious, thirst-quenching cold beers and some tasty pretzels ready,” Jack healthily laughed. “That’s about all the excitement that my fragile weak heart can sustain! I’m no young pup anymore!”

Jack Nelson arrived at Eddie’s place at the specified time. After some light conversation about forthcoming joint Caribbean vacations, classic car shows, and the improbable prospect of the *Phillies* making it to the *World Series,* the host shifted the focus of discussion to the reason for Jack’s requested visitation. Palmer drew his guest’s attention to the wonderful Wurlitzer juke box.

“This dandy has a most excellent sound system,” shrewdly began Palmer. “And it has several remarkable features that no other brand or model possesses.”

“Like what?” cynically responded Jack as the Liberty Street neighbor looked for a convenient place to put his empty brown beer bottle. “I didn’t come over here and leave my nagging wife and demanding children just for a tiny bit of sentimental fun!” the visitor facetiously continued with a wry smile. “This better be something special or I’ll have to protest by writing my congressman!” The visitor then crunched his teeth down on a salty hard pretzel.

“This listening experience is literally out of this world!” Eddie Palmer promised his friend and comrade of forty-years. “Just relax, enjoy your freedom, and appreciate the speaker differentiation after I select a fast-paced song.”

“What are ya’ goin’ to play?” Jack phlegmatically asked. “I can’t believe that this juke box sounds better than my four-speaker stereo sound system I bought myself’ last *Christmas!* I’ll wager there’s no comparison!”

“Here's a blast from the past! I’m gonna’ select ‘Boogie Woogie Bugle Boy of Company C!” Eddie decided and relayed to his companion. “I really like the rhythm and the tempo!”

“Say, wait a darn minute!” Jack strenuously objected. “That’s a 1940s *World War II* tune. I think either the Fontane Sisters or the McGuire Sisters recorded it! I thought you specialized in early fifties and sixties pre-acid rock and roll!”

230

"Normally, I do," Palmer honestly admitted, "but Bette Midler recorded a more modern version of 'Boogie Woogie Bugle Boy' in 1973. For some obscure reason," Eddie related, "that song is mixed up on this oldies' juke's listings with '50s and early '60s numbers. Bette Midler's interpretation has tremendous sound and voice modulations. It's a classic presentation with a great instrumental background."

"Okay, maestro," Jack reacted with a forced grin, before taking another swig from his new beer bottle. "Let's hear what's so dynamic about your new Wurlitzer."

"Jack, I recommend that you put your second beer bottle down on the table, and completely swallow your pretzel, so that you can get the machine's full effect," Eddie seriously directed. Palmer then very dramatically pressed down keys 'E-5', and after the selector placed the disk on the rotating wheel and the needle subsequently descended, a visual whirlwind suddenly encompassed the den, and soon quickly enveloped the two eyewitnesses.

"Hey, what's goin' on?" loudly yelled Jack. "This must be some psychological illusion! What's with all the visual effects? Are we in some sort of time travel movie? Does *that thing* come with a disco?"

"Just about!" Palmer affirmed. "If my assumption is accurate, we're on our way to 1973. If we're lucky, we'll get Bette Midler's autograph!"

As soon as the incomparable voice of Bette Midler sang the initial words to "Boogie Woogie Bugle Boy", the cyclonic, atmospheric surroundings diminished, and then soon vanished into thin air. The two time-itinerants were standing in a restricted area in front of a large auditorium's stage, and people sitting behind the new arrivals were shouting for the pair to locate seats and to stop blocking *their* view. The music was so fantastic and so loud that it drowned-out the many vociferous complaints originating from irate people sitting in the audience's first row.

"This is some sort of trick or hallucination! It's gotta' be a mirage or something!" Jack screamed into his companion's ear. "Don't try and tell me that your juke box sent us on this fantasy time excursion, and that we're really livin' right this minute in 1973!"

"Just savor the great song's lyrics!" Eddie Palmer replied. "I'll try and tell you everything when we get back to my house! It's all way beyond being remarkable! I suppose it's more like a supernatural miracle, than anything else!"

"When will that be?" inquired the still-awed Jack Nelson. "How long does this incredible spell last!"

"It's about maxed-out right about now!" Eddie alertly noted as he detected three burly security guards heading down a side aisle in *their* direction. "We'd better scamper the heck out of range, or else we'll soon be clobbered and then physically abused and mauled."

The two men bolted across the theater in front of and beneath an oblivious Bette Midler, who was preoccupied wailing away on the high stage with her popular song rendition. The fleeing men scurried up the opposite aisle as four additional theater guards and ushers joined the hunt and gave pursuit. The entire chase scene represented only a mild distraction to a portion of the enthusiastic and boisterous hand-clapping audience.

The two frenetic escapees skittered-out of the theater's swinging back doors and ventured into a mezzanine sales counter section. The duo next sprinted and tripped down fourteen steps, and then fled down a richly carpeted corridor until they quickly exited the premises through heavy leather-padded doors onto New York's Fifth Avenue.

"Please tell me what's goin' on?" bewildered Jack Nelson hollered as the two time voyagers scampered south in the direction of *Times Square*. "Are you some kind of space alien or something?"

"I can't believe that the music can not only change our time into another decade, but it also can transform the city we're bein' sent to!" Eddie yelled as his throat struggled to inhale more oxygen.

"What in the world are you babbling?" Jack Nelson criticized and panted with total astonishment. "You're makin' me a candidate for the loony bin!"

"Only about thirty more seconds to the song!" Palmer declared. "Then, we'll be back in Hammonton in 2003, and I'll be happy to give you all the pertinent details! Say, Jack. You run better than my refrigerator does!"

* * * * * * * * * * * *

After the rotating whirlwind finally decreased to a cessation, Eddie Palmer took ten deep breaths and then conscientiously educated his amazed, spellbound, dizzy listener of the unique jukebox's special characteristics and abilities. Jack Nelson sat on the soft couch, totally flabbergasted and quite mentally disheveled.

"You mean to say that your juke box has the power to transport us to the time and place of the recorded song!" Nelson marveled after polishing off another cold beer. "Are you sure your name isn't Rod Serling, that '50s *Twilight Zone* announcer I still watch on the *Sci-Fi Cable Channel?*"

But after the juke box owner told his friend about Alley-Oop and about David Noto giving him a swollen lip at the high school *sock* hop, Jack Nelson again lapsed into his dubious state of mind. "Did I hear you say that a caveman and a saber-toothed tiger were chasing you through a jungle in around 100,000 BC?" Eddie's close chum incredulously asked. "And that your high school nemesis punched you in the chops for flirting with luscious Barbara Smidillo! Where's the nearest insane asylum? I think we both require professional help! Say Eddie. That Mrs. Barbara Noto is still a very lovely woman!"

"I can't state for sure what the year was," Eddie clarified. "But I can claim that the experience and the ultimate pursuit were real for the duration of the song. I actually met and interacted with a fictional prehistoric figure named Alley Oop!" Eddie reminded his baffled neighbor. "The saber-toothed tiger became frightened and took off into the jungle. But only the Wurlitzer knows the exact answer to *our* most recent quandary!"

"This juke box makes weird seem like normal!" Jack rationally maintained. "And your lip is still swollen with a blood clot on it, even though your honest account defies all regular logic. I guess *that* fact could be construed as proof. And yet," Jack conceded, "Bette Midler seemed as real as the pounding headache I'm now feeling. Eddie, that 1973 concert was both real and surreal at the same time. I'll tell ya' what. Let's have another time transition to see if your crazy hypothesis is really bona fide."

Eddie advised that Jack examine the Wurlitzer's array of songs, and then select another oldie tune in order to verify Palmer's rationalization. Nelson rubbed his bearded chin and next verbalized some of the selections, reading each one aloud. "I sorta' like 'Peggy Sue' by Buddy Holly and the Crickets. And then there's 'Rockin' Robin' by Bobby Day. And here's 'Little Darlin' by the Diamonds."

"Those three numbers are from '57 and '58, the Golden Age of rock and roll," the '50s expert confirmed. "I like all three. And Jack, here to the left is 'Come Go with Me' by the Dell-Vikings. That's one of my all-time favorites. And to the right we have 'The Great

Pretender.' That golden oldie' Platters' tune happens to describe each of us perfectly!"

"Here's one of my favorite' '60s picks!" Jack gleefully exclaimed. "It's 'California Girls' by the Beach Boys. That choice seems pretty safe and tranquil. How could we go wrong lookin' at beautiful young ladies in bikinis for two-and-a-half-minutes or so? Let's get the show on the road!"

"I think you've convinced me on that one," Eddie happily agreed. "Kim and Helen don't look half as good in bikinis now as the wives had back in the mid-sixties when that song was the rage."

Without initiating any further exchange of dialogue, Eddie Palmer emphatically pressed ruby red keys marked 'D-3'. The standard and expected cyclonic effect transpired when the juke's needle touched the disk, which incidentally was turning at the precise rate of forty-five rounds per minute. The den then gradually dimmed, and in an instant, the voyaging music lovers were standing in their blue denim Bermuda cutoffs on a hot California beach, crowded with gorgeous buxom girls scantily clad in two-pieced bikini bathing suits.

"Jack!" Eddie merrily yelled. "There must be at least ten-thousand fabulous dolls with great bellybuttons on this crowded beach, and we're the only two guys. I'm gonna' play California girls on the juke box until the record decays and finally disintegrates."

"And look!" the stunned companion yelled back. "Six luscious young ladies are coming-up to introduce themselves to us. This has gotta' be the most magical moment of my life!"

"They're probably wonderin' where the loud Beach Boys' music is comin' from without us havin' any powerful radio," Eddie speculated and then related.

The six comely young ladies began touching the two men's arms and chests, and the receivers of the overzealous caresses began to worry about the females' very amorous intentions. And then, a dozen other affectionate, tanned chicks paced-over the hot sand to duplicate what the six knockout girls were doing. The California time-visitors began getting intensely nervous at being conspicuously situated at the center of the male fantasy universe. The duo's wildest dream soon transformed into a bizarre nightmare, laden with a vast contingent of beautiful, aggressive promiscuous young women.

"Let's make a run for it!" Eddie loudly insisted. "We'll never be able to satisfy all of these lusting ladies in a thousand years. An excess of anything including sex can be detrimental to our health! Neither of us has enough hormones for this outrageous challenge!"

The pair of neurotic time journeyers desperately ran down the California' beach, zigzagging between exotic females lying on assorted beach towels and blankets. Other thin and trim fair damsels observed and heard the men's distress, and soon took-up the chase from other locations, and the frantic time-travelers had no alternative other than to leap into the surf and begin frenetically splashing their way out into the Pacific.

The highly motivated girls followed the panicky men's awkward example. Many of the female aggressors were stellar swimmers, and were shortening the distance between them and the extremely frightened males, whose arms were now churning through the choppy waves like swirling windmill blades. A score of hysterical, curvaceous girls happened to be riding surfboards, and were deftly using incoming waves as an additional method of also harassing the delirious male swimmers.

Fortunately, the song "California Girls" terminated, and Eddie and Jack instantly discovered themselves in a frenzy, rotating their arms and flipping their legs on Palmer's tan den rug. The new arrivals abruptly stopped their unnecessary behavior and stared disbelievingly into each other's eyes.

The embarrassed twosome then got to their knees and finally managed to stand upright. The fact that the neighbors were both soaking wet from head to toe supported the notion that their encounter with the over-stimulated California females was definitely not a mere figment of their imaginations. Eddie advanced to the ranch home's bathroom and obtained two towels for Jack and him to dry off.

"I never realized that such romantic pleasure could turn into a life-threatening situation," Jack concluded and remarked. "Those young horny girls would've torn us to shreds if the dolls had a little more opportunity to do so. I'm sure glad Helen has gone through menopause."

"Let's discuss what to do next over another cold brew," Eddie intelligently suggested to his exhausted chum. "I still have two more bottles in the 'fridge. I'm really thoroughly fascinated with the Wurlitzer's astounding ability. I want to have one more time-trip tonight. Are you game, Jack?"

"Well, sort of," Nelson hesitantly replied in a very evident puzzled tone of voice. "I still can't figure-out how an electrical storm could change your ordinary juke box into a musical time machine. It all defies accepted scientific laws, you know!"

"That's what makes it so damned interesting!" Eddie bellowed with a lusty laugh. "It's an exceptional device, indeed, as long as it doesn't get us killed. It's certainly adventurous to say the least. I mean, it really proves that the hunted generally experiences more thrills through fear than the hunter does, all throughout the violence of the chase. My new extraordinary juke box really gets rid of the boring aspects of everyday life, that's for certain."

"Sometimes, I think you need the services of a good psychiatrist that specializes in exorcisms," Jack joked in an effort to camouflage his own haunting consternation. "You could even convince the Pope to switch religions and become a Muslim! You certainly have that strange knack! Let's drink to the female libido!" The two fatigued men then returned to the '50s den.

"Hey, this song listed here has gotta' be an awesome choice!" Palmer triumphantly uttered to his still very bewildered friend. "Love Me Tender," Eddie reverently read. "I always wanted to see Elvis performing in person. If we're lucky, we'll get up close to the stage, just like we had done with Bette Midler."

"I think you don't have enough limbs on your tree," Jack vehemently protested. "I mean, you almost got us apprehended by security guards in 1973, and then you virtually had us pulverized by swarming females in skimpy bathing suits in 1965. I just don't know what danger will happen next!"

"That's the fun of it all, Jack!" Eddie effectively argued. "I'm fascinated by the unknown! And now tell me, how detrimental can 'Love Me Tender' really be?" Palmer questioned.

"But just the song title is written in on the menu without any artist being provided," Nelson countered. "I'm mighty suspicious of *that* detail! Maybe it'll be sung by the Devil in hell, for all we know!"

"No one else has ever sung 'Love Me Tender' as a #1 smash hit' single except Elvis Presley," the '50s whiz persuasively volleyed. "And besides Jack, you once told me that Elvis was the greatest singer ever!"

"Okay, I'll concede that fact," Jack reluctantly acknowledged. "Let's go back to the '50s and see Elvis on stage somewhere in the world, before I sober-up and change my mind."

236

The intrigued juke box owner anxiously pressed 'F-2' for "Love Me Tender", and when the dependable selector located the appropriate disk, the room again became a hazy cyclone of whirling furniture and lamps. When the needle lowered to the spinning '45, an open field scenario crystallized all around the two human anachronisms, time traveling into the past from the year 2003. Soldiers in gray uniforms were firing cannons to Eddie and Jack's left, while army men clad in blue were blasting cannonballs from cannons to their right.

"Holy smokes, Eddie!" the almost-petrified Jack Nelson shrieked. "We're in the middle of the *Civil War!* I'm not stickin' around to figure-out exactly what battle we're involved in!"

"We just have to survive for two-minutes!" Eddie nervously answered. "Love Me Tender" is a very short song. I hope the Wurlitzer's needle doesn't get stuck!"

"There's a dense-woods on the other side of that ravine," Nelson informed his colleague as *he* pointed to the right. "Let's make a dash for it! It's our best chance to escape doom!" Jack yelled as a blast exploded to their right, and a lone sturdy elm tree next to their position instantly snapped in two.

The pair zipped along as fast as their legs would carry them towards the ravine and woods that Jack Nelson had perceptively identified under intense and extreme pressure. The two-hundred-yard-exodus was augmented by gunshots and screaming coming from the hoarse throats of determined military personnel on either side of *their* valiant hustle.

"You might know plenty of details about the 1950s, but you don't know squat about American history!" Jack puffed as the two bolted across the open field.

"What's that supposed to mean?" Eddie defensively asked. "How could I ever have known we would wind-up on *this* wicked battlefield? And Elvis isn't singing the lyrics to 'Love Me Tender'! Listen, it's an instrumental version playing, instead!"

"The song 'Love Me Tender' is really a re-doing of a tune popular during the *Civil War* era called 'Aura Lee'," Jack gasped and shared. "The notes and melody are identical," Nelson shouted as the companion desperately ran parallel to Eddie. "And 'Aura Lee' was then changed to 'Love Me Tender' in the '50s, and the new lyrics were written especially for Elvis!" Palmer's companion yelled, huffing and puffing all the way.

"Now you tell me!" Eddie Palmer panted just before the runner tripped and tumbled to the ground. Jack assisted Eddie to his feet, and as the horrified pair was about to continue their incredible race to the woods, a loud blast exploded nearby. Both men collapsed in agony to the dusty ground.

* * * * * * * * * * * *

Jack Nelson found himself lying wounded in a pool of blood on the tan rug in Eddie Palmer's den. He had the presence of mind to exhaustively dial *911* on the table touch-phone before lapsing into unconsciousness. A Hammonton Rescue Squad ambulance was immediately dispatched to the Liberty Street residence. The local police broke-open the door, and Eddie's closest friend was given first aid, and soon swiftly transported to Kessler Memorial Hospital.

Jack Nelson had suffered multiple broken bones in his arms and legs, along with first and second degree burns on all his appendages. Although seriously injured and afflicted with amnesia, Nelson's vital signs remained strong, and the survivor is expected to live and was listed in "Critical Condition". The victim, however, does fade in and out of consciousness and does not remember anything pertinent from the past, ranging from his own name to that of his closest friend.

As for Eddie Palmer, the time-traveler has mysteriously disappeared from the face of the modern-day Earth. The Hammonton Police are investigating a possible "house robbery attempt and aggravated assault case", but local detectives are completely baffled by the existence of only "weak circumstantial evidence", and perplexed by the lack of a motive for the suspected dual crimes.

Kim Palmer returned from Long Beach Island with her three children in a state of shock, and the aggrieved wife sadly conveyed to area newspaper reporters and to the assembled television media, "I will not play my husband's new Wurlitzer juke box until Eddie finally returns back home. I sincerely request that the abductors who had kidnapped my husband from our home, and who had hospitalized Jack Nelson, will have the decency to release Eddie."

The New Jersey Crime Fighters Chapter has offered a fifty-thousand-dollar reward for information leading to the capture of Eddie Palmer's kidnappers and Jack Nelson's assailants. So far, there have been no takers.

"June 30, 1956"

Samuel James Parsons led a happy life living with wife Linda and children Bobby and Carolyn on 228 Francisca Avenue, just off the Pacific Coastal Highway, Redondo Beach, California. The medical supplies salesman had earned a company promotion to District Sales Manager, beginning February 1st, 1956. Bobby was a fifth-grader playing *Little League Baseball,* and Carolyn was a studious fourth-grade' honor student. Linda Louise Parsons was pregnant and expecting a third child in early October, and Sam's neighbor, Craig Armstrong and he often went fishing out in the Pacific in Craig's small motorboat. But on the afternoon of Friday, February 10, 1956, Samuel Parson's entire life quickly transformed from dull and predictable to extremely bizarre.

'Life is good!' Sam thought as he was returning home from work on West Imperial Highway in his green and cream '55 Chevy Bel Air coupe. 'Linda and I live just four blocks from the ocean; I'm scheduled for another big pay raise in September, and our third child is due in October. Craig's gonna' soon get a bigger fishing boat, so we'll be able to go out as far as Santa Catalina Island on future Pacific excursions! I'm living the American Dream!'

Samuel James Parsons reverie was rudely interrupted at the busy Imperial Highway and Hawthorne Boulevard intersection. A drunk driver in a red and white '55 Ford Crown Victoria ran the Hawthorne Boulevard red light and smashed directly into Parson's right front fender. The '55 Bel Air flipped over twice from the jolting impact.

Paramedics found Sam unconscious and rushed the injured man in an ambulance to the California Medical Center, where the "accident victim" remained in intensive care for four days. After Parson's broken right wrist had been set in a cast, the accident victim was finally released from the hospital on Tuesday, February 21st, and loyal Craig Armstrong visited the very lucky medical sales manager's home the following evening.

"Those drunk drivers should all lose their licenses for five-years and spend at least six-months in jail," Armstrong began in criticism of the negligent motorist who had nearly killed *his* best friend. "That wrist will soon mend and we'll be goin' out into the Pacific and reeling in some real whoppers! Say, Sam. Sarah tells me Linda's due in October. What are ya' hopin' for, a boy or a girl?"

"It's going to be *our* second girl, and Linda's goin' to name her Jill," Sam answered quite matter-of-factly. "The baby's goin' to be healthy and will someday graduate with honors from the *University of Michigan.*"

"You gotta' be kidding!" Craig indulgently laughed. "What's wrong with *UCLA* or *Southern Cal'?*" How could you possibly know those things?"

"I can't explain it, but I just know them!" Sam adamantly insisted. "I think the automobile collision must've affected my brain. I now sometimes have visions that belong in the future. But Jill's goin' to come into the world on Wednesday, October 3rd. And that's no silly educated guess, either!"

"Maybe you need to see a brain doctor or something," Armstrong honestly suggested. "You might have some tissue that needs to be re-attached inside your head."

"No, Craig. X-rays show that there has been no brain damage," the slightly injured man maintained. "I only have to heal this broken right wrist, and also, a half-dozen lacerations in delicate places, and then I'll be a hundred-percent again. And these annoying skin cuts actually hurt more than the broken wrist does."

"Okay, Sam; if that's what the doctors told you," Craig diplomatically replied. "Say, where's Linda right now? Doin' some last-minute grocery shopping, or getting a new hairdo at the corner beauty parlor?"

"She's using *our* rented car to pick up Bobby over at his friend's house, and also busy transporting Carolyn over to the school play practice," Sam remembered and reported. "My daughter's the co-star in a *St. Patrick's Day* show her teacher's directing. The big production is slated for about four weeks from now."

"When will you be getting your green and cream Chevy back?" Craig innocently inquired. "That neat coupe model is gonna' be regarded as a classic car someday."

"It's been totaled!" Sam disgustingly exclaimed. "I'll have to wait and see what sum the insurance adjuster gives me, and then buy a new practical means of transportation. One thing's for damned sure, Craig. My next vehicle's not going to be a red and white Ford Crown Victoria!"

"Whatever you say," the jovial neighbor agreed. "And now that it's all over with, I must tell you that you're a fortunate pup, escaping that terrible accident with minimal injuries."

"It's really pretty ironic, isn't it?" Sam responded with a rhetorical question. "I'm a hospital supplies district manager, and I wind-up in the California Medical Center, requiring the services of products I just happen to distribute! What a weird coincidence! It just doesn't get any stranger!"

"Yes, it does!" Craig challenged. "You thinking that you know the sex of the baby Linda will be having next October!"

"On Wednesday, October 3rd!" Sam clarified and reiterated. "Jill will be born at exactly 5:15 a.m. See you' tomorrow, Craig! And stay out of hospitals. too! See ya', good buddy!"

On Wednesday afternoon, March 21st, the auto parts distributor received a call from the almost fully recuperated medical supplies district manager. "Craig, how about you and Sarah goin' out to the movies with Linda and me tonight. We got my talkative nosy mother-in-law on babysittin' patrol this evening."

"No thanks, Sam," the normally jolly neighbor replied. "Sarah wants to stay home and view the *Academy Awards* on TV. She says the suspense is better than that of any of the melodramatic soap operas my wife habitually watches."

"Why waste your time on something that is so predictable?" "Swami Parsons" questioned his close acquaintance. "*Marty* is goin' to get the outstanding movie award, and its star, Earnest Borgnine, is goin' to win the Best Actor Oscar."

"I think *East of Eden* is goin' to get the Best Picture Award and James Dean is gonna' get the Best Actor for his role in *Rebel without a Cause,*" Armstrong maintained.

"You're all wrong, Craig; wrong as usual," Sam jokingly objected. "Close, but still wrong."

"What do ya' mean?" Armstrong mildly protested. "I do have a brain, ya' know!"

"James Dean was in *East of Eden,* but Jo Van Fleet is goin' to get the Best Supporting Actress Oscar for her part in *that* fantastic film," Sam stubbornly persisted. "And Anna Magnani will earn the Best Actress golden statue for her role in *Rose Tattoo!* What a terrific performance!"

"You're crazy! Gone off your long pier into the deep end!" Craig accused. "How can you be so confident about future things nobody really knows about! Are you psychic or something?"

"Well, yes, I guess I am," Parsons modestly answered. "I just have a peculiar gut instinct that I can't rightly explain about a lot of upcoming future events."

"Maybe the car accident has rearranged your cerebral activity and made you psychic, while coincidentally destroyin' some major brain cells," Sam's humorous neighbor whimsically theorized and expressed. "I happen to think and believe Natalie Wood is gonna' get the Best Actress Award."

"Not a chance! She's too young to win it," Sam answered with absolute certainty. "And Jack Lemmons is gonna' surprise everyone by getting the Best Supporting Actor presentation for his stellar performance in *Mr. Roberts.*"

"If you're right, I'll let you pilot my new boat with your one good arm out to *Santa Catalina Island* on its first fishing expedition!" Craig promised. "I'm getting it tomorrow!"

"The neat song 'Santa Catalina, 26 Miles Out to Sea' by the Four Preps will be coming out two-years from now on March 3rd, 1958," Sam informed his confused listener over the phone.

"I think you need to go back into the hospital!" Craig jested. "But this time it oughta' be inside a mental institution. Say, how was Carolyn in the *St. Patrick's Day* play?"

"Now my daughter's the one that really deserves an Oscar," Parsons joked. "Se ya' tomorrow, Craig!" Click.

The following afternoon, Sam visited his loyal neighbor, who was totally stunned by the accuracy of Parsons's Academy Awards predictions. "I don't know how ya' did it, but all five of your crystal ball prognostications came true. Do you have any other future news to report?" Craig asked his amazing friend. "With you around, I'll never have to buy another newspaper as long as I live."

"I'll tell you all about it if you take me out to Santa Catalina on your new *yacht,*" Sam jested.

"Okay, but I'm a guy that keeps his promises," Craig verbally volleyed. "You're gonna be the first captain on my new yacht's maiden voyage, broken right wrist and all."

Craig drove his fishing buddy out to the local marina's parking lot in *his* new blue and white '56 Pontiac sedan. Soon, the men hopped into Armstrong's "new nautical toy", and Parsons proudly took over the helm.

"Well, good buddy," Craig said as "Sam the man" steered Armstrong's new outboard out of the Redondo Beach Marina in the direction of Santa Catalina. "Only twenty-six miles and we'll' finally get to *our* heavenly destination. Now, tell me the truth," the curious man continued. "What's gonna' happen in the form of major news that the reporters haven't learned yet?"

"National or international news?" Parsons defensively qualified. "Please be more specific and discriminate better when you ask me random questions."

"National issues would be just fine!" Armstrong apprehensively answered his psychic neighbor.

"Well, a series of catastrophic tornadoes will pound the Midwest April 2nd and 3rd," Sam indicated with a degree of body animation. "And unfortunately, forty-five people will be killed, and over fifteen-million-dollars in property damage will occur in the states of Mississippi, Wisconsin, Kansas, Tennessee, Michigan, Oklahoma, and Arkansas. I tried calling the weather bureau and warn them, but the guy on the other end called me a 'crackpot' and hung-up before I could finish telling the jerk the remainder of the vital information! This psychic ability I possess does have its credibility problems with the rest of our species!"

"And what other important news is about to happen?" Craig inquired. "I always say that no news is good news! That mantra is my favorite credo."

"Yes, Craig, now I remember. On Sunday, April 8th six Parris Island Marine recruits will unfortunately drown while on a platoon disciplinary march," Sam matter-of-factly related. "A drill instructor named Sergeant Matthew C. McKeon will be convicted later this year for causing the unnecessary tragedy. McKeon will be found to be drunk while on duty and guilty of negligent homicide," Sam predicted. "He'll be disgraced and demoted to the rank of private," Parson's elaborated, "and he'll also spend three-months rotting away in the brig'!"

"April's too far ahead to even think or worry about. I have trouble just making it through March. Any good news to balance-out the bad?" Craig incredulously asked his enigmatic friend. "I mean, what's gonna' happen soon in the ever-competitive sports world? Now the *NCAA Basketball Championship* game is scheduled for tomorrow, Friday March 23rd. What team do ya' think is gonna' emerge victorious?"

"I'm not an avid college basketball fan," Sam humbly apologized, "but I'm quite positive that *San Francisco* is gonna' beat *Iowa* to win the big tournament, and the score is gonna' be 83-71! Yes, that's what my mental vibrations are tellin' me! 83-71!"

"If you get the score exactly correct," the auto parts distributor chuckled, "you can be my sports adviser forever, that is, as long as your forecasts are on target!"

"No problem, Craig!" Sam amiably agreed. "You don't even have to waste your time watching the game on TV. I guarantee that the outcome's a lead-pipe-cinch!"

San Francisco, starring Bill Russell, did capture the college basketball crown, and the final score was exactly what Sam Parsons had amazingly augured. Craig decided he would start making sports bets on Sam's uncanny knack of perceiving future events. When Parsons stated that the *Philadelphia Warriors* would defeat the *Fort Wayne Pistons* for the *NBA* championship, four games to one on April 7, Armstrong contacted a local bookie without his best friend's knowledge and soon thereafter, collected three times *his* original wager. And when the medical supplies district manager foretold that on Tuesday, April 10th the *Montreal Canadiens* would vanquish the *Detroit Red Wings* four games to one for the coveted *NHL Stanley Cup* trophy, Craig contacted his bookie and got a thirty-five-dollar return on his ten-dollar investment.

"Well, Sam," Craig addressed with admiration as Parsons again steered with one arm Armstrong's new outboard out of the Redondo Beach Marina in the direction of scenic Santa Catalina. "Only twenty-six miles and we'll finally get to *our* heavenly destination. Now, tell me," the curious man continued his inquiry. "There aren't any important sports events until the big 60th *Boston Marathon* on April 19th. What's gonna' happen there?"

"Somebody named Antti Viskari from Finland is gonna' win the marathon with a record time of two hours, fourteen minutes, and fourteen seconds," the temporary boat captain revealed. "You can bet your house on it!"

"How do you spell *that* name?" Armstrong asked as the fellow rapidly searched and soon found a pencil and memo' pad in a side compartment of his new blue and white, twenty-foot-long motorboat. "Spell it out Sam."

"A-n-t-t-i V-i-s-k-a-r-i!" the pilot returned. "He's definitely from Finland!"

"Sounds like the guy has wings instead of *finn!*" Craig laughed. "And ya' say his time is gonna' be two hours, fourteen minutes and fourteen seconds?"

"That's right!" the navigator answered in a distinct melancholy and apathetic voice. "Say, Craig. I should've called the forty-five people that had died in the Midwest tornadoes on the telephone. I knew their names and numbers but never even once picked up the phone. I feel really guilty about it, now!"

"It was an Act of God!" Armstrong sympathized. "And neither you nor I can do anything to change God's will! And besides that, those forty-five people would call you a quack, and then give you a tin ear to match your hard plaster-right-wrist."

"Thanks for the phony encouragement," the boat guider readily acknowledged. "But I shoulda' also called and notified the six Marine recruits that needlessly drowned at Parris Island. What a horrible, preventable tragedy!"

"The recruits and their bosses would've accused you of being a nuisance or a weirdo, and would've then angrily hung-up on you, too!" Parsons' supportive fishing companion insistently argued. "Now, just get your mind focused on catching some striped sea bass. Remember this is a fishing trip and not a guilt trip!"

"Our luck's gonna' be weak today. We're just goin' to reel in a couple of small sand sharks and toss them back into the blue Pacific," Sam predicted. "Knowin' what's goin' to happen next takes all the fun out of life! The present can become pretty boring if you know all about it beforehand."

"I can't be too skeptical of reality!" Craig promptly responded. "Who'd ever think that a guy from Finland is gonna' be triumphant in the *Boston Marathon?* And one more thing pal, and this is really important."

"What's that?" Sam facetiously asked while knowing exactly what was on his buddy's puzzled mind.

"Yesterday, I listened to the radio all day long and never once heard that tune 'Twenty-Six Miles Out to Sea' by the Four Preps! You said it was due out March 3rd."

"You'd better get the wax unclogged from your ears!" Parsons genially criticized his forgetful fishing partner. "The Santa Catalina Island song will first hit the music charts on March 3, 1958. We're still living in April, 1956!"

Antti Viskari did win the April 19th *Boston Marathon,* and Craig Armstrong had converted his hundred-dollar bet into a handsome two thousand bucks. 'My bookie is getting mighty suspicious of my good luck streak,' Armstrong realized the next morning while shaving in the master bathroom. 'I'm gonna' switch to another guy that my store manager, Jim Reynolds, has recommended. I can't wait for the 82nd *Kentucky Derby* on Saturday, May 5th. Sam says Needles is gonna' win in two minutes and three and two-fifths seconds with Dave Erb aboard as the jockey. I've parlayed the two thousand bananas I won on the Bean Town marathon, and if I hit again on the *Derby,* my return will be ten-grand. Sam better be right on this one!'

Craig did hit the horse-race jackpot, winning his ten-thousand-dollar *Kentucky Derby* bonanza. He kept his winnings a secret from his "honest gifted neighbor", and hoped that Sam wouldn't shortly receive a second blow to the cranium that might return him back to normalcy. A delighted Mr. Armstrong called his chum on the phone about Needles and jockey Dave Erb taking the Churchill Downs Winners Circle photo-shoot.

"Sam, you were right on the money with Needles coming in first in the Derby!" Craig characteristically praised. "Is Needles gonna' win the *Triple Crown?*"

"No sir, Craig," Parsons calmly-but-emphatically answered. "The May 19th 81st *Preakness Stakes* will be won by Fabius in one minute, fifty-eight and two-fifths seconds with Bill Hartack as the jockey. And then," Sam quite naturally proceeded, "Needles with Dave Erb again in the saddle will come back and take the big *Belmont Stakes* on Saturday, June 16th with a great time of two minutes, twenty-nine and four-fifths seconds."

"I have a terrific idea," Craig declared. "Why don't we both quit our monotonous jobs and go into the entertainment industry. Sam, you could be a mentalist or magician, or someone famous like that, and I'll tour the country as your grateful manager. I'll even introduce you on stage."

"Thanks, but no thanks," the humble neighbor said over the phone. "I'm basically very shy and have a dreadful phobia about appearing or speaking in front of large audiences. Performing in show business is not exactly my cup of tea! I prefer demonstrating my mental magic in private and exclusively to my closest friend. See ya' later, good neighbor!" Click.

Craig Armstrong was really acquiring the gambling fever, especially with the odds drastically tilted in *his* favor. 'I can't go back to the local bookies because they're beginnin' to gossip about my good luck skein,' the wannabe' 'entertainment manager' thought. 'I'll have to fly or drive out to Vegas where the big betting action is. Even when I win thirty-thousand, that's gonna' be just small potatoes to those big operators practicin' their fine art on *The Strip*."

Craig accumulated a stupendous sum for his *Kentucky Derby*, *Preakness,* and *Belmont Stakes* winners and never disclosed his new-found prosperity to his shy good neighbor. And after Sam predicted that Patrick Francis Flaherty from Chicago was destined to win the 40th *Indianapolis 500 Auto Race* in three hours, fifty-three minutes and fifty-nine seconds at an average speed of one hundred twenty-eight and a half miles an hour, Armstrong anxiously caught quick back and forth commercial airplane shuttles from Los Angeles to Las Vegas, and then back to L.A. His colossal winnings came to over fifty-thousand-dollars, and "a buzz" was rapidly circulating up and down Fremont Street and around the flashy illuminated Vegas strip casinos about the lucky guy from L.A.

Early Sunday morning, June 3rd a rather euphoric Craig Armstrong visited Sam's place for coffee and doughnuts. "Say, Sam. Linda and the kids still in bed?"

"No, she's getting Bobby and Carolyn ready for church," the introverted mentalist-turned-clairvoyant answered. "Here; have a doughnut. They're only a day old."

"Thanks a lot," the visitor gratefully accepted. "I'm only gonna' stay for about ten-minutes. I got plenty of yard work to catch up on, and Sarah is in one of those erratic, tyrannical woman moods, if ya' know what I mean. She's ready to start chewin' nails and then spittin' sharp metal chunks in my face if I don't get motivated and begin mowin' the lawn."

"Did you have anything particular or special in mind you wanted to discuss?" Sam perceptively queried. "Usually, you sleep late on Sunday mornings."

Craig wanted to share some of his secret gambling profits with his astounding neighbor, and the businessman finally figured-out a way *he* could do it. Armstrong proposed that Sam and he, and their wives take a week-long vacation starting Saturday, July 7th in Atlantic City. "The treat will be on me!" Craig offered. "And you've often confided that you'd like to stroll the world-famous boardwalk. I'll arrange all of the details with my travel agent."

"You must be unaware of one important date and fact," Sam responded before taking another sip of black coffee. "Your second cousin, Jerry Gares, is getting married on Saturday, July 7th up in San Francisco. Sarah is gonna' insist that you both attend the ceremony and reception, so you'd better cancel any plans you have for Atlantic City. You're gonna' be spending most of your vacation time up in Frisco'. Don't forget to visit *Alcatraz!*"

"But Sarah and I haven't received any invitation to any wedding yet?" the prospective guest exclaimed. "And how do you know that my wife's second cousin's name is Jerry Gares? I've never mentioned *that* nutcase to you before, anywhere!"

"The printer had a delay in running off the invitations," Sam rationally explained. "You'll be receiving the wedding notification in tomorrow's mail."

"Okay, but I want to establish a rain check vacation date with you and Linda sometime in the early fall," Craig regretfully uttered. "Perhaps the four of us can do a four-day Las Vegas pleasure junket instead of Atlantic City. And speaking of *Alcatraz,*" sometimes I think I'm living there with Sarah as the warden!"

The postman did deliver the fancy wedding invitation to the Armstrong's mailbox, and that evening, the gambling addict opened the elaborate envelope and silently read the notice, feeling great disappointment. 'Well, there goes the fabulous Jersey shore trip,' the unlucky recipient of the San Francisco bad news lamented. 'I suppose Atlantic City boardwalk thrills will have to be postponed until next summer.'

On Sunday afternoon, June 10th Sam accompanied Craig on what had become their weekly fishing pilgrimage to Santa Catalina. "I'll be doin' about twenty knots, so we'll be at the island in a little more than an hour," Craig Armstrong told a temporarily aloof Sam Parsons. "This new boat really has some acceleration when I open it full throttle. Say Sam," the weekend mariner articulated. "How about providin' some juicy futuristic news. My imagination is starvin' for some extraordinary ideas to consider."

The boat passenger was passively gnawing away on a peanut butter and strawberry jam sandwich that Linda had considerately prepared in a brown paper bag, and after swallowing a tasty well-chewed mouthful, the "nautical guru" then expressed several sensational prophecies to his very alert fishing mate. "On July 10th the *National League* is goin' to win the 23rd annual *All-Star Game,* 7 to 3," Sam almost lethargically uttered.

"That's too bad!" Craig replied as the boat navigator made a mental note of the yearly baseball contest. "I've always been an *American League* fan, and I love the *Red Sox* and Ted Williams. Did you know that I was born and raised in Boston?"

"Why yes!" Sam Parsons automatically answered. "I've been cognizant of that rather remote fact ever since I came out of unconsciousness after the auto' accident."

"And while we're on the subject of baseball," Craig resumed as the blue and white motorboat exited San Pedro Channel and entered the dark blue Pacific heading southwest. "What about the *Fall Classic.* Who's gonna' win the *World Series?"*

The up-to-then listless *ESP* practitioner paused momentarily and closely examined the cast on his fractured right wrist to dramatically enhance his careful response. The passsenger drank two ounces of orange juice from a bottle with his good left hand and then said, "The *Yankees* are gonna' beat the *Dodgers* four games to three. On Monday October 8th Don Larsen will pitch a fantastic no-hitter, and the *Yanks* will win that game, two to nothing. That exceptional accomplishment will represent the first no hitter ever in *World Series* history."

"Don Larsen!" Craig bellowed with an attendant laugh. "He's the worst pitcher on the entire *Yankee* staff. You gotta' be wrong and have your wires crossed on that one!"

"Well, you oughta' be glad an *American League* team is gonna' win the *Series,"* the mentalist concluded and nonchalantly stated. "But Craig, you're gonna' have to become a *National League* fan because the *Dodgers* are gonna' move from Brooklyn to L.A. in 1959, and the *New York Giants* are gonna' come out west to San Francisco a short time later."

Craig Armstrong's stimulated mind was in a quandary, trying to assess and record the series of startling revelations. Sam's neighbor asked his incredible friend about what was going to transpire in the rough and tumble political arena. 'They take political election bets in Las Vegas, too!' he greedily contemplated.

"On November 6th Dwight David Eisenhower will be re-elected to a second term winning over Democrat Adlai Stevenson, 475 electoral votes to 74," Sam Parsons incidentally communicated. "Eisenhower will get 35,387,015 popular votes to Stevenson's 25,875,408. And on *Election Day,* the Democrats will gain one seat in the Senate, giving them a 49-47 majority over the Republicans. And also, the Dems' will also gain an additional seat in the *House,* affording them a 233 to 200 advantage."

"Eisenhower's okay, but I don't trust his running mate, that Nixon guy!" the boat navigator opined.

"Richard M. Nixon is going to be the *President of the United States* and later involved in an immense scandal that'll be called *Watergate!"* Sam nonchalantly disclosed.

"I hope I'm dead and buried when that happens!" Armstrong verbally rendered. "I don't like that guy's small beady eyes and his broad sneaky smile! Say Sam, are ya' feelin' all right? You look a little despondent and green in the face!"

The listener hesitated for a moment to further garner his sensitive thoughts. Then, Parsons asked his friend "the Skipper" for help in undertaking a most dangerous enterprise. Craig Armstrong was spellbound as he listened with his mouth agape to his companion's remarkable tale. Soon, the good-natured fellow responded to his friend's inordinate request for assistance. "Look, Sam. I trust your integrity and your honesty more than anyone else's!" Armstrong supportively verbalized. "I'm with you on this project a hundred percent as long as no one gets hurt or killed, especially me!"

Sam's fertile mind had had a terrible psychic manifestation that his second cousin, a brilliant electronics engineer, was going to perish in a tragic airplane disaster. Parsons had visited his relative living in nearby Hawthorne, explained the situation, and was thanked for his speculative concern. However, the endangered cousin placed little credence in the predictor's warning saying, "You should've been an *Old Testament* prophet preaching the end of the world. You *were* named after the prophet Samuel in the *Bible,* you know!" the psychic's fated cousin recalled and chuckled.

"Exactly how and where will this airline calamity occur?" Craig asked as the blue and white boat reached the eastern tip of Santa Catalina. Parsons quickly recovered from having his almost-hypnotic daydreaming interrupted.

"Over the *Grand Canyon* on the morning of June 30th!" Sam informed his most-trusted friend. "My cousin will be aboard a *TWA Super-Constellation,* and the other plane involved in the midair collision will be a *United DC-7.* The irony is that both planes will be

250

taking off about the same time from *Los Angeles International Airport,* and then flying east at different altitudes of 21,000 and 19,000 feet."

"Then, how are they gonna' smash into each other?" Craig queried as he momentarily became distracted and forgot about steering the boat. "That's quite an altitude gap, even by large airplane standards, about a half-a-mile!"

"From what my psychic impressions currently suggest," Sam very deliberately expressed, "the *TWA Super-Constellation* will be assigned to 19,000 feet and the *DC-7* to 21,000. The *TWA* captain will request a clearance to ascend to a higher altitude to avoid turbulence while the *DC-7* cockpit crew was probably showing its passengers a glimpse of the *Painted Desert,* and then planned to view the *Grand Canyon.*"

The boat Skipper next made a sage observation and deduction. "Then, the *TWA* crew probably knew about the *DC-7* being in the vicinity, but the *United Airlines* plane was unaware of the *Super-Constellation* penetrating into its air space!" Craig declared.

"That conclusion is correct," Sam confirmed. "Both four-propeller planes will leave the air traffic control that's maintained by the *Los Angeles International Airport* tower. They're each basically on their own, thinking that they have been separated from one another by sufficient time and space."

"But how are we gonna' survive if we're both riding on one of the ill-fated planes?" Craig finally asked. "Isn't this putting both of us in jeopardy if the fatal air accident is inevitable? I think *that* that one little overlooked matter should be of paramount importance to the both of us!"

"Craig, *we'll* be passengers on the *United DC-7,* so that my cousin won't recognize me because he'll be on the *TWA Super-Constellation,*" Sam methodically explained. "We'll enter the cockpit and draw pistols to make the *United* pilot change course and avoid the midair collision. I'll use my mental powers and make sure the odds for survival are in *our* favor."

"Why are you so fond of this special cousin, the electronics engineer?" Craig curiously inquired. "Is he actually worth us risking *our* lives for?"

"The guy's an absolute genius," the boat passenger related. "If he lives, he'll meet a guy named Bill Gates, and then go into something that will in the future be called the computer industry. They'll both become multi-billionaires, and you and me will have cake executive positions in the massive corporation."

"Keep talking!" the boat captain urged. "This wild story is getting mighty interesting!"

Sam hastily described the future computer industry, and told his companion all about desktops, laptops, hand-held devices, and the *Internet*. Suddenly, Craig Armstrong stopped the boat; shut off the motor; dropped anchor, and sat mesmerized, listening to his friend's intriguing exposition.

"How we gonna' board the *DC-7* and get by airport security and ticket takers?" Craig asked. "It seems that too many things have to go perfectly right for your plan to succeed."

"I have a friend working in security at the airport who owes me a big favor," Sam conveyed to his captivated but slightly dubious listener. "We'll be able to slip onto the *DC-7* from the tarmac. The plane will only have sixty people aboard, including the three-crew-members and *us*. There will be seats available in the back, and since we're not riding in a train, no conductor is gonna' come-down the aisle and check for tickets."

"How many people will be on the *TWA Super-Constellation?*" Craig wanted to know.

"A total of seventy!" Parsons excitedly exclaimed as the future-teller saw that he was convincing Craig to go along with his bold strategy. "Just think. We'll be revered heroes in every big city newspaper if we can successfully save a hundred and twenty-eight innocent lives!"

"Okay, Sam. But can you just tell me how we're gonna' get into the cockpit to give directions to the flight crew!" Craig demanded. "That point needs some clarification."

"That's easy!" Parsons enunciated with a grim expression upon his almost pallid face. "Listen carefully! Here's how it's all gonna' be done!"

Early Saturday morning, June 30th, 1956, Sam ambled over to Craig's kitchen door and then the two "Good Samaritans" walked to a popular Redondo Beach coffee and doughnut shop and had a brief breakfast. The dual adventurers next ambled three blocks and caught a northbound bus that would drop the pair off near the bustling *Los Angeles International Airport*. Sam and Craig met-up with Jake Ryan as scheduled in a terminal Men's Room. Ryan then inconspicuously led the two through an unmanned door reserved for transcontinental airliner crew-members and onto the tarmac where the daring duo casually boarded the *DC-7* ten minutes before the regular passengers had been allowed admission through the airline's assigned loading gate.

"That exercise was a breeze!" Sam confidently commented to his fidgety accomplice from his *DC-7* seat. "Let's pretend to be reading these newspapers I've brought along until we're finally rolling down the runway."

Everything went according to plan. The other passengers entered and occupied their assigned seats listed on their ticket stubs. The stewardesses were so preoccupied with their myriad loading responsibilities that the airline employees failed to recognize that two well-dressed stowaways in business suits were on board, sitting quietly in rear unsold seats. Soon, the *United DC-7* was taxiing to the end of the runway, and in another five minutes, the enormous four-propeller plane was zipping off the ground and heading into the clear blue sky.

The "Un-Fasten Seat Belt" signs began blinking fifteen-minutes after takeoff, and the two plotters heeded the flashing instructions. The *United* flight had already circled over the Pacific and then headed inland toward the California and Arizona deserts. Soon, the Los Angeles metropolitan area below gave way to towns and farms, and then to vast arid wasteland. Sam had little time to initiate the next phase of his grandiose scheme.

"Stewardess, could you tell the captain that his favorite cousins Tom Wells and this fellow, Ray Cross, are surprise passengers on this flight?" Sam requested. "I know he'll be happy to see Ray and me!"

"Certainly, Mr. Wells," the accommodating and alert attendant agreed. "I'll do that right now!"

"Next, we'll be flying over the *Painted Desert,* and then keep your eyes open for a spectacular view of the *Grand Canyon,*" the public-relations-minded captain stated over the airliner's intercom.

Five minutes later, the pretty brunette stewardess gingerly stepped down the aisle and approached the two illegal, anonymous passengers. "The captain says he'll be glad to show you gentlemen the plane's sophisticated instrument panel," she cordially informed. "Please follow me to the front cabin entry door."

After Sam and Craig entered the cockpit, Armstrong slammed the portal shut. The captain turned his head and said, "Hello….say, you're not Tom and Ray!" as the pilot noticed the pair of drawn handguns pointed directly at *him* and his exasperated copilot.

"This is not a hijacking or a holdup!" Sam apologetically yelled with a pistol in his shaking left hand. "There's gonna' be a fatal midair collision with a *TWA Super-Constellation* over the *Grand Canyon,* so we've got no time to explain how I know this! Just please steer the plane south to avoid going over the canyon and then we'll surrender our weapons and do whatever you tell us. Captain, we mean you no harm and only want to avert a major disaster!"

The very rattled captain gestured to the *DC-7's* nervous copilot to cooperate and to follow the intruders' strange commands. A minute later, a loud shout was emitted from the already-disturbed copilot's lips. "Watch out, captain! An unidentified aircraft is closing in on us from the right at an altitude of twenty-one thousand. It's not a *Super-Constellation!* My God! It's circular! It's one of those *UFOs!*"

The captain quickly rotated the steering control to the left, and the interplanetary near-air collision was skillfully averted. "What was that thing doing? Sightseeing over the *Grand Canyon?*" the pilot angrily squawked. "Anyway, we're now fully out of *Los Angeles International's* air control. We're on our own!"

"Maybe the saucer was on a secret government reconnaissance mission," Sam speculated and then uttered. "Oh my God, captain! We've changed course and are heading north again! Quick captain! Turn this airplane south right this minute! Turn it south, or we're all doomed to die!'

"Captain," the panicky copilot shouted. "We're in a dense cloud cover, and oh my God. I think I see the gleam from another large plane heading right....."

The midair collision between the *TWA Super-Constellation* and the *United DC-7* occurred directly over the *Grand Canyon.* All one-hundred-and-thirty-people aboard the two prop' liners died. Swiss mountain climbers were flown in from Europe to attempt recovering the victims' bodies, but many were never found.

Jake Ryan never mentioned a word about his collaboration with Sam Parsons and Craig Armstrong being smuggled aboard the *DC-7* out of fear of losing *his* airport position, and also, then worrying about going to prison for being a participant in a major manslaughter case involving a possible failed hijacking. According to Los Angeles police reports, Parsons and Armstrong were officially placed on the area "Missing Persons' List".

Addendum Note: The author's wife's second cousin Thomas Sulipuzio had been a passenger on the ill-fated *United DC-7.* Tom was thirty-years-old at the time of the accident, and was a brilliant electronics engineer working out of Philadelphia for the *Rheem Corporation.* Ironically, my wife's cousin died in the mid-air catastrophe. Oddly enough, his purpose in traveling from Philadelphia to Los Angeles was to present plans to corporate and government officials for developing a "Collision Avoidance System" to prevent mid-air commercial plane disasters.

The great air calamity shocked and alarmed the American public. As a result of the horrible air tragedy of June 30, 1956, the government laid the groundwork for what eventually materialized into the *Federal Aviation Administration,* which now in our "jet age" is responsible for monitoring air traffic control on all flights flying from coast to coast.

"Immoral Immortality"

— The four *Rowan University* professors were returning south to Glassboro from a teacher union seminar given at the *College of New Jersey* in Trenton. While traveling south on *Route 73* near the town of Berlin, Henry Chapman, a U.S. History and Political Science instructor, suggested that he and his colleagues should stop for an early supper.

"Good idea, Hank," Lester Schaffer agreed. "My stomach's growling as if there's a bear inside. I'm so hungry I could eat a moose. Well, a chocolate mousse, anyway," the zany Mathematics Professor declared.

"You're the driver, Hank," Vince Olivo, a distinguished-looking Grammar and Writing authority chimed-in from the back seat. "I'll have to venture anywhere your discretion takes us."

"The Pallas Diner is two-miles up ahead at the Berlin Circle," suggested Anotal Suez, a widely acclaimed *Rowan* Music Professor sitting next to Dr. Olivo. "It's got a decent reputation for steaks and seafood at affordable prices, along with a variety of other terrific dishes on its menu."

"How come it's not called the Palace Diner instead of Pallas Diner?" Les Schaffer reflexively asked. "Is that some sort of discrepancy?"

"Because the owner is a Greek and named his establishment after Pallas Athene, goddess and protector of Athens, way back in the glory days of antiquity," Anotal confidently explained. "The Parthenon up on the Acropolis was constructed during the Golden Age of ancient Greece. The architecture's inspiration was the impeccable goddess Pallas Athene."

"How do you know so much minutia outside the realm of music?" Hank Chapman asked his acquaintance. "I have trouble remembering the generals at Bull Run, Gettysburg, Vicksburg, and Antietam. And the south won at the first battle of Bull Run because the northern army was *as slow as Manassas,"* the effervescent history professor jested while deftly implementing a rather clever play-on-words.

"I'll have to remember that one the next time I pour some molasses on my pancakes," Vince Olivo indulgently laughed. "Hank, your foolish sense of levity is sometimes wittingly senseless!"

"Say Anotal, I'm with Hank about you," Les Schaffer humorously interrupted. "You seem to know a lot of academic trivia outside your field of knowledge for a fellow that was named after an important strategic canal! Could you expand on how you know so much data that isn't related to music?"

"Oh, I do plenty of reading in my spare time," Dr. Suez readily replied. "I'm an expert on virtually everything and an authority on almost anything that's purely academic. I am especially well-versed in medicine, poetry, and in astronomy, particularly our nearest star the sun, which has always fascinated me," Anotal immodestly added.

"Hey, Hank. There's Pallas Diner halfway around the circle!" Les Schaffer indicated from the front seat passenger side. "It's time to feed our faces!"

The driver pulled into the restaurant's recently resurfaced parking lot. Professor Chapman stopped his aqua Honda sedan between two parallel lines, and the four men got out of the reliable vehicle. The honorable gentlemen ascended the classy diner's marble steps and Les Schaffer opened the glass door leading into the foyer. A beautiful marble statue guarded the eating establishment's front entrance.

"Wow, a magnificent statue of Venus!" Hank Chapman exclaimed. "She's a real beauty, even in this crazy day and age we're living in."

"That's an amateur representation of Aphrodite and not Venus!" Anotal immediately corrected. "Aphrodite was the sacred goddess of beauty in Greek mythology, and her counterpart, Venus, was the Roman substitution for the love deity in *that* culture's religious tradition."

"Well then, Anotal, who is that marble figure standing over there in the other corner of the vestibule?" Dr. Hank Chapman rather innocently asked.

"That's certainly a mold-cast model of Athene, but in Roman mythology, her counterpart would be Minerva," Dr. Suez lectured without the aid of a lectern. "Unfortunately, today the Roman names are much more popular than the original Greek identities."

"Suez, my friend, you probably don't realize it," Vince Olivo courteously stated, "but you speak of these defunct deities as if they're your close acquaintances. If you can get me a date with either Aphrodite or Athene, and not their dusty skeletons, or their marble statues, I'd be much obliged!" the confirmed bachelor said with a broad smile.

258

A pretty brunette hostess showed the four new arrivals to an empty booth, and after studying the menu and ordering "a late lunch", the professors began discussing the boring seminar on retirement investment options and health care benefits, which the group had recently attended. Soon, however, the conversation switched to political science, Hank Chapman's forte.

"Tell me, Anotal," the gadfly history researcher implored. "What would Socrates and Plato have to say about boring union seminars and about white marble statues of scantily clad Greek goddesses adorning diner foyers? I understand that both critics despised bureaucracy and female nudity, too!"

"Socrates and Plato were both stupid imbeciles who didn't have a clue about the topic of excellence; about feminine beauty, or about true wisdom," Anotal emphatically professed. "Mediocrity was *their* societal watchword, even when Plato and his mentor Socrates challenged the shallow hypocrisy of the sophists."

"Anotal, you speak of Socrates and Plato as if the sages were both your personal adversaries," Lester Schaffer marveled and questioned. "How could you condemn their great contributions to *Western Civilization?* Are you speaking from envy or jealousy? Why do you have so much contempt for those classical philosophers? Have you no respect for the dead?"

"Those two clowns were absolute idiots!" Professor Anotal Suez stubbornly maintained. "I have read Plato's *Republic* numerous times, and also have diligently studied the moronic Platonic Dialogues, where Plato attempts to celebrate his contemporary Socrates as a heroic benefactor of general philosophy. Plato's poor writings and Socrates' foolish speeches are all a bunch of rubbish, plain and simple!"

"How could you possibly make such an unwarranted assertion?" Vince Olivo aggressively challenged. "Surely, Anotal. You must be making light of the two eminent founders of certain academic disciplines. Anotal, are you acquainted with a certain scholar at our university named Daphne Agora?"

"The attractive Ancient History instructor with the conceited attitude?" Dr. Suez answered.

"Yes," Professor Olivo confirmed. "Daphne could defend Plato and Socrates to the hilt and make mincemeat out of your inane generalizations and criticisms."

"And I'll wager a hundred-dollars that you, Dr. Suez, couldn't even manage to get an ice cream parlor date with the gorgeous prudish woman," Les Schaffer chimed-in. "The two of you would hardly be compatible according to any zodiac combination matching I know of. And besides that, Daphne Agora might be a lesbian!"

"I'll also wager a cool hundred-dollars," Hank Chapman enthusiastically offered. "What about you Vince? Want to make some easy money?"

The English Rhetoric Professor contemplated the temptation and then vociferated, "I'll also gamble a hundred bucks. That's three hundred saying that Anotal couldn't get to first base with the very enchanting Dr. Daphne Agora."

"Okay, foolish gentlemen. I wholeheartedly accept your daunting proposal," Dr. Suez very seriously mentioned. "I'll effortlessly sweep the defiant woman right off her dainty feet with my intensified, magical charm."

"It's a deal!" Hank Chapman indulgently laughed. "It's such a fabulous consideration. Anotal Suez doomed to failure! How funny can it get? Ha, ha, ha!"

After the four fatigued men's dinners had been served, the conversation next focused on the nature of the universe, and then shifted to analogous historical events. Hank Chapman was responsible for generating most of the radical topic transitions.

"Speaking of ancient mythology," the history and political science professor prefaced his remarks. "The zodiac constellations are named after legendary heroes and various creatures from ancient civilizations. But science has replaced astrology as the fundamental basis for understanding the complex nature of our galaxy, along with the functioning of the universe itself'."

"To a certain extent," Anotal instantly disagreed. "For what the ancients lacked in knowledge, the scholars more than made up for in wisdom."

"I thought *you* had just insisted that Plato and Socrates were total jerks, and now you're defending the ancients as great benefactors to modern science and civilization!" Vince Olivo pointed-out to Dr. Suez. "I think your statements, Anotal, are both contradictory and ambivalent. Wouldn't you agree with my plausible assessment?"

"When I had alluded to the ancients," Anotal defensively responded, "I was referring to the ideals endorsed by ancient immortal Greek gods, and not referring to the vanities of immoral men. The Olympian gods epitomized the pursuit of perfection, whereas; *our decadent age* encourages the pursuit of happiness. That is the essential distinction between then and now. Poseidon, Hades, Zeus, Hermes and the rest of the Olympians all sought achievement, and explored glory in their own impeccable ways."

"But man's modern technology has given us computers, cable television, and fantastic automobiles," Les Schaffer effectively argued. "How could the Greek gods ever have contemplated such brilliant innovations? I submit that the Greeks fabricated their gods in man's image!"

"What you speak of Lester is emblematic of mere knowledge and has little connection with actual wisdom," Anotal maintained. "Mankind still has the blight of war; new grotesque diseases; animosity towards his neighbors, and every other negative thing that originally flew out of *Pandora's Box.* Little has changed over the past thirty-centuries in the area of human wisdom. All man has learned how to do is manipulate his environment through inventions and knowledge, while humans have neglected the advancement of what I call 'genuine behavioral progress'. Yes, my colleagues. That example is the essential difference between then and now!"

Hank, Les and Vince respected their eccentric colleague's very obvious mental capabilities and were in great awe of his wild outlandish comments. Several years before their present verbal exchanges, Anotal had warned his associates to avoid attending a North Jersey union conclave. The event had been scheduled to take place at *Paterson State University* on September 11th, 2001. The three skeptics had not heeded Dr. Suez's sage advice and were caught in massive traffic jams on the *Garden State Parkway* and on the *New Jersey Turnpike* all the way from Wayne to Glassboro.

And then once when Hank Chapman had called Dr. Suez "a soothsayer", the Glassboro professor had demanded that "the prophet" provide proof by auguring the outcomes of certain forthcoming sports events. Anotal had accurately predicted the participants, the scores, and the victors in the 2001 World Series, a full three-months ahead of time. The three suspicious professors discredited Anotal's exceptional ability and called the apparent uncanny, articulated phenomenon "incidental "bizarre coincidences", "demonstrable psychic voodoo", and "amazing and lucky clairvoyant predictions. Soon, dessert was served, and the rejuvenated diners rekindled their stimulating, intellectual discourse.

"I believe that the universe is made-up of integrated mathematical truths," Lester Schaffer attested. "Remember when Anotal claimed that something unexpected would occur on *9-11*, and then hit the identity of the 2001 *World Series'* champions right on the head? Well, it is my contention that everything happens as part of some inexplicable arithmetical formula. We only see bits and pieces of the colossal puzzle, but ignore all of the prominent factors in the complicated given equation."

"Please, Les, would you mind explaining yourself less vaguely without putting your wide foot inside your big fat mouth?" Hank Chapman requested. "You tend to be quite nebulous at times."

"Okay, Hank. *9-11* occurred on September 11th. 9 plus 1 plus 1 equals the number eleven. September 11th was the 254th day of 2001. 2 plus 5 plus 4 comes out to eleven," the mathematics instructor seriously disclosed. "New York City has eleven letters, and so does the words *The Pentagon*. New York was the eleventh state admitted to the new democracy. The *Twin Towers* were vertical parallel skyscrapers that stood side by side forming the number 11. Afghanistan is a word composed of eleven letters. Ninety-two passengers were aboard Flight 11. Nine plus two amounts to 11, and sixty-five victims were traveling on Flight 77. Six plus five is equivalent to eleven. Do you cynical gentlemen now see the merits of my universal mathematical hypothesis?"

"Yes, quite astounding when you consider all of the unique circumstances," Vincent Olivo concurred as the instructor performed a simple mathematical procedure on a Pallas Diner napkin. "And after September 11th, there were an additional 111 days left in the calendar year. I do believe you have something relevant and plausible there, Dr. Schaffer."

Professor Hank Chapman figured that he could contribute significant evidence from history to substantiate Lester Schaffer's remarkable arithmetical claim. "What about the Kennedy and Lincoln assassinations?" the notorious public speaker asked the other intrigued informal forum members.

"Well, Hank, what about the comparable items concerning the dual historical tragedies?" the mathematics guru questioned his social science associate. "What are the basic outstanding similarities?"

"Well, Lincoln was elected to Congress in 1846, and Kennedy exactly a hundred-years later in 1946," the social studies expert maintained. "Abraham Lincoln was elected President in 1860, and a

262

century later, John F. Kennedy was elected to the highest office in 1960. Both men were shot on Fridays, and both Presidents' wives lost a child while living in the *White House*. Lincoln had a secretary named Kennedy, and Kennedy had a secretary with the last name Lincoln. And Lincoln was shot inside the Ford Theatre in downtown Washington, and Kennedy was riding in an open Lincoln in Dallas when he was assassinated. As you know, Lincolns are made by the Ford Motor Company."

"Wow!" Vincent Olivo exclaimed. "And both Presidents were shot in the back of the head, while their grieving wives witnessed the abominable acts taking place. There evidently are many incredible coincidences!"

"And don't forget the vital mathematical aspects," Lester Schaffer insisted as the theorist attempted bringing the debate back to objectivity. "Both assassins had *three* names, John Wilkes Booth and Lee Harvey Oswald. And both Booth and Oswald were each killed before ever being convicted of political murder in an objective government trial."

"And don't forget other historical parallels," Professor Chapman reminded his attentive listeners. "Lincoln was shot in a theater and his assassin fled to a warehouse, and Kennedy was shot from a warehouse, and then Oswald cowardly sought shelter and escape in a theater. And in addition," the history authority excitedly elaborated, "Abraham Lincoln's successor was Andrew Johnson, born in 1808, and John Fitzgerald Kennedy's replacement was Lyndon Baines Johnson, who entered this very violent and confusing world in 1908. Say Anotal, you've been mighty quiet during this most compelling dialogue. What do you think about all of these incredible relative facts and mathematical statistics?"

"My intuition clearly dictates to my consciousness that there is extraordinary profound truth in Professor Schaffer's arithmetical theory," the sly maverick and sometimes aloof pedagogue concluded and enunciated.

"Give us some justification of your claim!" an adamant Les Schaffer demanded of inimitable Anotal Suez. "As a dedicated mathematician, I need to have valid and reliable quantitative proof!"

"Okay, Lester, if you insist," Anotal casually acceded. "Here's a bona fide hundred-dollar-bill. Go alone this evening to Bally's Casino and step up the aisle to the seventh roulette wheel on the left from the main boardwalk entrance. Do not play any rows or wager on black or red numbers. Instead, buy and put a one-hundred-dollar chip down on number nine, and then parlay your winnings onto number eleven. See what happens, and then report back to me."

"You gotta' be kiddin'!" Dr. Schaffer politely objected. "Why should I waste a silly trip to Atlantic City and squander your hard-earned money in a dumb spin of a roulette wheel. It just defies logic and reason. It goes drastically against the most extreme odds! Now, I do think you've absolutely fallen off your rickety rocker!"

"Could Lester have an objective Atlantic City eyewitness?" Vince Olivo pleaded. "I'll be glad to accompany him on this most peculiar gambling enterprise."

"Count me in, too!" Hank Chapman energetically volunteered. "I can't wait to prove you wrong, Anotal! You've really painted yourself into a precarious corner this time!"

"Why most certainly!" Professor Suez cooperatively acquiesced. "Three dumbfounded fools are much better than one. But remember gentlemen, after Hank drops me off at my place tonight, the three of you agnostics will have to travel with dispatch to Bally's Casino to conduct your field experiment in advanced celestial mathematics. Now, let's pay our bills and exit this majestic marble and tile eatery."

At 10:30 that night, Anotal Suez was watching a *History Channel* cable special about the battle of Thermopylae where three-hundred courageous Spartans, led by King Leonidas, admirably held-off a vital "hot springs" pass from the Persian Immortals, under the dominion of King Xerxes. 'They don't make warriors like those three hundred valiant Spartans anymore,' the *Rowan University* professor decided. 'I don't know why Ares didn't directly interfere with the outcome of that particular engagement. The outnumbered Spartans had a philosophy that if they didn't come home victorious carrying their shields, then the defeated soldiers had to be transported back to Sparta dead on their shields. How wonderfully noble and worthy of praise their fighting spirit was!'

Just as the Spartans were about to be showered by a plethora of Persian arrows on the television screen, Dr. Suez's telephone rang. The euphoric caller was none other than Professor Lester Schaffer.

"Calm down, Les, so that I can comprehend exactly what you're saying," Anotal recommended. "Now, please tell me in a rational manner precisely what has made you so utterly exhilarated."

"Anotal, everything at Bally's happened just as you had crazily prophesied," the math wizard began. "I played nine and won big, and

264

then parlayed the total on eleven. Everyone at the roulette wheel, including the croupier, thought that I was insane, even Vince and Hank," the caller panted. "And when the spinning ball landed squarely on number eleven, all of their mouths were agape. The pit boss came over with an astonished look on his face, wondering how I had performed the mathematical impossibility. And then, fifteen minutes later, the casino head honcho very reluctantly handed me a crisp, new check in the outrageous amount of $125,500.00."

"What are the odds of doing it once?" Dr. Suez patiently asked.

"At least thirty-five to one!" Les exclaimed. "But to achieve those formidable odds twice in a row on two different numbers is virtually astronomical in magnitude. I wish I had the entire event filmed on video. I would show it over and over again until the tape broke."

"And what are you going to do with your prodigious winnings?" Anotal calmly inquired. "Do you plan to donate the money to your favorite charity?"

"No, Sir! I've decided to split the proceeds four ways among you, Vince, Hank, and myself'. I could use a new car with my trade-in, and then have enough left to underwrite a Vegas vacation."

"Thanks for your kind and generous endowment!" the music professor matter-of-factly acknowledged. "But Les, I want you to know that I overcame even greater odds than you did tonight at Bally's."

"Well, Dr. Suez. Could you identify exactly what you are describing," Dr. Schaffer requested.

"Why certainly, Les. I recently gave Professor Daphne Agora a surprise call after researching and then locating her number in the faculty directory," the classical music connoisseur disclosed. "And guess what? Daphne has consented to going-out on a date with me, and she thinks I'm rather suave and intelligent."

"Well, congratulations my dear Anotal!" Lester boisterously boomed. "That *is* quite remarkable! Where are you taking her?" Schaffer wondered and asked. "She looks like she'd be a little too fussy and way too fastidious for my taste in women."

"To the Philadelphia Zoo," Dr. Suez succinctly replied. "Daphne told me that she loves animals, especially carnivores and reptiles."

"Well, dear friend, let me tell you that this has been a most festive and joyous evening for all of us," the caller concluded. "Thanks again for those terrific mysterious gambling tips. You ought to be a feature on Ripley's *Believe It or Not!* Goodnight now!" Click.

The following Saturday, Anotal pulled-up to Daphne Agora's Glassboro condominium in his sky-blue 1988 Dodge Aries. The music professor hopped-out, ambled up the straight flagstone walkway, and rang the appropriate doorbell. After being greeted by his lady date, Daphne locked her front door and the pair stepped to Anotal's vintage automobile. The driver gallantly opened the passenger-side door for his afternoon date to enter and gracefully sit down.

"Why do you drive such an old car, Professor Suez?" the querulous woman curtly chided. "Surely, you could afford either a 2004 Honda or Toyota."

"I'm fascinated by Greek culture and ancient myths," Anotal answered as the *Rowan University* professor turned the key and fired-up the ignition. "Ares was the god of war, and Aries as in *Dodge Aries,* is the zodiac constellation for The Ram. A-r-i-e-s was the closest that I could come to A-r-e-s, so I'm stubbornly keeping this old sluggish, dilapidated puddle-jumper until it can no longer mechanically function on the highway!"

"I think you're just fabricating all of those esoteric academic references because you're aware that I'm a professor of Ancient History, and now you're vainly trying to score some favor points with me. I'm wise to your unscrupulous, devious tactics, Anotal Suez, and quite frankly, I'm hardly impressed!"

"Okay, you win Daphne. I was just going to reveal that I am a good acquaintance of Ares, the god of war, but I now see that I can't deceive you in any way. Your reputation among the male faculty members is that you are tough as nails, and you're convincingly exhibiting that stellar persona right now. Are you an Aries?" the music prof' coyly asked as Dr, Suez turned left from *322* onto busy Delsea Drive.

"No, I'm a zodiac Gemini," the pretty-but-haughty educator facetiously answered.

"I see, your birthday is anywhere between May 20th and June 20th. I'm a Leo," Anotal lied.

"That means that you were born between July 22nd and August 22nd," Daphne stated, demonstrating her mastery of astrological time divisions. "Really, Dr. Suez. Perhaps you shouldn't endeavor dazzling me with your great acumen in legends and myths. Consider changing the subject to another one of your trite venues."

"Okay, Dr. Agora. Did you know that this highway is appropriately called Delsea Drive because it takes summer vacationers that come from Delaware right through Glassboro, down to the shore. It goes from Delaware into Glassboro and then down to the sea at Cape May, hence the word Delsea."

"I believe we should return to the topic of the ancient world," Daphne suggested, intentionally showing her familiar and haughty contrary side. "I find *that* discipline area much more interesting than hackneyed etymologies."

Anotal turned-up the tape player volume, which featured classical renditions of Wagner's "Ride of the Valkyries" and a powerful version of "Thus Spoke Zarathustra". Little Conversation ensued between the polarized pair until the Dodge Aries passed by the architectural splendor of the *Philadelphia Museum of Art,* situated on an elevation above the upper bank of the Schuylkill River.

The driver lowered the volume on the tape player and spoke to his rather apathetic passenger. "The art museum is my favorite building in all of Philadelphia," Anotal divulged. "Its majestic columns are designed and constructed in the tradition of the Athenian Parthenon, situated at the summit of the Acropolis. It's the most picturesque setting in all of Philly'!"

"I know, next you're going to tell me all about the vertical Ionic columns and how Greek the pillars look!" Daphne reactively predicted and criticized.

"You can't trap me, Professor Agora," Dr. Anotal Suez fired back. "I'm not one of your lackluster undergraduate students. Those stately columns are more akin to Doric pillars, like the ones on the Parthenon, than they are to the standard Ionic design. You must admit that the columns are more Doric than they are either Ionic, or Corinthian!"

"Tell me more trivia about the art museum," Daphne implored in a semi-demanding tone of voice. "You seem to know as much about ancient architecture as I do, and I'm a highly qualified Ancient History professor."

"The art museum was founded in 1876, but the newer structure we just passed was erected in 1926 to 1928," the driver stated as Professor Suez skillfully wove his vehicle in and out of heavy Philadelphia highway traffic. "The most wonderful part of the architectural masterpiece is the sculptures of the Greek gods and goddesses portrayed on the north side. Phidias himself would be green with envy just observing and admiring them. The museum is quite comparable in exterior design to an ancient Greek temple."

"Very captivating, indeed!" Daphne concurred and exclaimed. "And are the appealing sides made of yellow-shaded marble? I never heard of pure yellow marble."

"No; the museum's façade is composed of dolomite that had been delivered all the way from Minnesota," Anotal elucidated. "The total appearance makes the edifice one of the most spectacular architectural wonders in the modern world. It's a tremendous tribute to the nobility and resplendence of the omnipotent Olympian gods."

"Perhaps we should've toured the inspiring art museum instead of visiting the Philadelphia Zoo," Daphne reconsidered. "Your research into the history of the building far supersedes my general knowledge of it. You're beginning to affect my curious psyche, Anotal Suez. Not every man can establish a fluid channel of communication with me. Congratulations for being temporarily successful."

Soon, the driver steered the sky-blue Dodge off the crowded *Schuylkill Expressway* down the Girard Avenue exit ramp, until he came to 34th Street, the location of the world renowned Philadelphia Zoo. After parking his vintage vehicle, Anotal escorted his finicky date to the ticket booth pavilion, purchased two admissions, and then the couple entered the asphalt promenade that spiraled between the various, sturdily-constructed animal exhibits.

"I simply love it here because the creatures are displayed in simulated natural habitats," Daphne snobbishly opined. "That sort of presentation shows virtual authenticity. The zoo takes all precautions for duplicating natural environments, ranging from tropical jungles to adverse arid deserts. There's almost as much art shown *here* as there is at the art museum."

"Quite brilliantly put, dear Daphne!" Anotal rather impetuously praised. "Now, what species do you prefer seeing first? Mammals, Reptiles, or Amphibians."

"I think that Mammals would be a very good choice," the sophisticated lady professor declared. "Since *we* are mammals, let's now investigate mammals."

"Well then," Anotal answered. "Would you like to see Ungulates, Primates, or Carnivores?"

"What are Ungulates?" Daphne asked in a baffled tone of voice.

"They're hoofed animals like zebras, gazelles, and horses," her date explained. "Even a rhinoceros is classified as an Ungulate, even though it looks more like a Pachyderm."

"I think carnivores would be my first desire," the very discriminating female replied. "I'm fascinated with tigers, leopards, panthers, lions and bears, as long as I can observe the creatures from a safe area."

The couple was gradually gaining compatibility as Daphne began admiring Anotal's extensive warehouse of infallible facts on just about anything and everything. The pair eagerly toured the Carnivora House, the Bird House, the Primate-Tree-Serve, the Amphibian House, and the Pachyderm House. After buying some tasty refreshments from a zoo fast-food concession, Daphne preferred viewing the Reptile House next.

"Right after we wolf-down our hot dogs and wash -down our *Cokes,*" her date promised. "Then, we'll check-out some lizards and snakes." Soon, the couple entered the portals of the aforementioned Reptile House.

Walking midway through the magnificent setting, the two touring professors heard shouting and screaming down the aisle, the clamor originating from the other end of the congested chamber. An enormous python had managed to exit its confinement and was harassing and intimidating several frenzied tourists, who were erratically scurrying and evacuating the Reptile House in all imaginable directions.

Without wasting a precious second, Anotal leaped onto the huge reptile's back, and with an exertion of massive strength, the rescuer intensely squeezed the scaly creature's neck with great dexterity. The snake hissed and twisted, attempting to coil its body around its antagonist, and then strongly constrict its attacker. But in a matter of thirty seconds, Anotal had not only strangled the monster to death, but had also snapped its neck with the great force exerted by *his* clenched fists and powerful fingers. Everyone who had witnessed the incredible demonstration gasped at the savagery of it all, and then warmly applauded the triumphant "beast killer". A confused zoo attendant came-over to investigate the cause of the incident.

"Sir, you possibly had just saved someone from being severely crippled or killed," the uniformed zookeeper appreciatively praised. "The zoo and its staff are deeply indebted to you!"

"Even though the python is regarded as an endangered species," a higher-ranking zoo employee added, "under the circumstances, you, sir, have bravely acted in self-defense to protect yourself and other visitors. The zoo will not press any charges against you, Mr…"

"Mr. Suez," the reptile conqueror sternly answered. "Anotal Suez. I used to wrestle ferocious anacondas down in Venezuela, so this python was really no match for me. And I know a certain trick I often used to kill the gargantuan snakes from my experiences along the Orinoco. I've also tamed similar beasts in Brazil while on an expedition along the muddy Amazon. I suppose it was just an example of fortuitous serendipity that I just happened to be present in this specific place at this particular time."

"Well obviously, Mr. Suez," the second very impressed employee uttered, "the Philadelphia Zoo is obliged to thank you for your intrepid response under what I can only describe as extreme duress. Thank you so very much."

The next morning, the muscular music professor received a phone call from Hank Chapman. "Hey Anotal, what's this I hear from Daphne Agora that you single-handedly strangled and mangled a giant python that was terrorizing innocent tourists at the Philadelphia Zoo? Is this true?"

"That's a gross hyperbole!" Dr. Suez modestly answered. "It wasn't that big of a snake or that big of a deal. Women always tend to exaggerate about things like that. They have a propensity for getting over-emotional. I didn't do anything sensational that you, Les, or Vince wouldn't have done under similar circumstances."

"Okay, then, you've overwhelmingly convinced me," the history instructor conceded. "Now Les, Vince, and I want to take you out Saturday afternoon to dinner, so that we can officially recognize your valuable insights pertaining to certain gambling hunches. What's your preference?"

"How about either the reputable Oceanos Restaurant over in West Berlin, or the Adelphi over in Woodbury, across from the Deptford Mall. My car will be in the shop at *Midas Mufflers* getting a new exhaust system, so one of you savants will have the responsibility of getting us safely to either place, and then back to Glassboro. What's your choice between my two suggestions?"

"I think the Adelphi would be par excellence," Professor Chapman automatically articulated. "That saves me a bumpy ride in your archaic Dodge Aries. I hope you're getting new shocks put into that old decrepit chariot of yours."

"No, just a brand-new Midas exhaust system," Dr Suez admitted. "And pick me up around two in the afternoon on Saturday. I'm working on a very intricate musical composition I plan to get published, and want to get it completed sometime Saturday night. And then, Sunday afternoon, I have an important dinner date with Daphne Agora."

"Okay, we'll pick you up at two on Saturday and dine at the Adelphi according to your wish," Hank confirmed. "See you then. Got any more sure-shot gambling tips?"

"No Hank, not right now. I don't want to jinx either you or me with your continued good fortune. Just be content with your substantial bonanza, and be happy with your current good health. Hubris and greed often lead to self-destruction. So long for now, Hank." Click.

On Saturday afternoon, the four opinionated professors were enjoying delicious meals at the popular Adelphi Restaurant Bar and Grille. The music professor was trying his best to act nonchalant about his amazing intervention into what could have potentially evolved into a tragic zoo development.

"Sometimes, life is like taking a small ship sailing between Scylla and Charybdis," the eccentric music mentor observed and stated. "An individual sometimes finds himself vacillating between danger and jeopardy, and must make an unenviable choice. I had only acted in instinct at the Philadelphia Zoo. It was simply a situational reaction that required little or no thought or preparation," the enigmatic music professor editorialized. "A deer or a squirrel would have run away from the hissing python, but humans have evolved beyond the elementary *cause and effect* thought patterns that dominate animal behavior. *We* can reverse *that* action into becoming *effected by a cause*. I didn't run away. I basically was intellectually stimulated to *effectively* and rationally respond to an impending emergency."

After the dining party had thoroughly discussed Anotal's phenomenal heroics at the popular Philadelphia Zoo, the conversation assumed a more erudite, philosophical twist when it turned to the topic of immortality.

"Speaking of animals," Vince Olivo transitioned. "I've read in *National Geographic* where animals live anywhere from ten-to-fifty-years. I'm sure glad I'm a human and get to stay around for a few more decades than an alligator or a crocodile, that is, if I have a normal longevity."

"A common dog lives an average of thirteen years," Les Schaffer contributed. "And I read where certain types of condors get to fly around in the sky for fifty-two years. Those seem to be in the same number-range as Vince had identified."

"Well, now fellas'," erudite Anotal Suez promptly interrupted. "An elephant in the wild lives an average of sixty-years, and red and blue macaws enjoy sixty-four years of existence on this planet. But certain box turtles can live to be a hundred-and-twenty-five-years if not abused or mistreated."

"You must spend a good deal of your leisure time reading encyclopedias and a plethora of non-fiction books," Hank mildly balked. "And Anotal, how come you don't seem to age like the rest of us mere mortals? You've been on our faculty now for thirteen years, and you look just as vernal as when I had first met you. What's your secret?"

"Well, Professor Chapman," Dr. Suez coyly responded with a wry smile upon his countenance. "In addition to an occasional good lobster, I also consume small quantities of my favorite drink and food, nectar and ambrosia. That's what makes me virtually immortal!"

"You're developing a healthy virile sense of humor," Les Schaffer complimented his strange *Rowan University* faculty peer. "Anotal, you seem to have an illustrious cryptic answer for just about everything we ask."

"Perhaps our science department should study the box turtle and figure-out a way of increasing the human life span," Vince Olivo proposed. "The longevity secret might lie in the creature's genetic composition. Perhaps Owens over in biology could get a grant to study all of the various implications."

"I suggest that *you* stick to your students' sloppy and inferior English compositions," Anotal lightheartedly advised his English Department colleague. "You're much more competent in your own area of expertise than you are awkwardly cavorting around in the more demanding scientific realm."

"Now, Anotal. You had told us several weeks ago that Socrates and Plato were complete imbeciles," Hank Chapman remembered and declared. "If my memory serves me correctly, Aristotle was the genius that had classified animals into each phylum that zoologists and biologists' study today. Is Aristotle a doltish nincompoop, too?"

"Beyond the shadow of a doubt," Dr. Suez instantly replied, much to the amusement of his enthralled audience. "Aristotle knew as much about music as today's rap chanters, and about as much about medicine as that lame-brained fellow Hippocrates did. The only major thing Aristotle ever did was to teach young Alexander of Macedonia the art of greed, and how to go-out and savagely conquer the ancient world."

"You tend to be more than a trifle antagonistic and petulant this Saturday afternoon," Les Schaffer orally injected into the lively symposium. "What's wrong with rap singers?"

"Their obnoxious music isn't music at all!" Anotal barked back, quite perturbed. "It is dissonance, chaotic repetitious mind-controlling stupidity! Rap is like looking at a rainbow having only one color. The lyrics have little or no variety in musical scale. The words reflect no intellectual merit, and there are no instruments played except maybe a dull redundant drumbeat," the music instructor zealously maintained. "The rapper's voice is monotonous and does not ascend to any soprano or alto tonal modulations. The entire presentation is inadequate, inferior gibberish, absolute rubbish, lacking necessary depth and quality, yet young people are influenced to believe that the gross travesty known as rap is a viable form of musical expression. What a grotesque pity!"

"Waitress, we'd like to order dessert now!" Les Schaffer signaled and bellowed. "Now Anotal, I too share your acrimonious feelings about rap singers. But please tell us more about this esoteric nectar and ambrosia business," the mathematics pedagogue jovially insisted. "I'd like to be around to see another age of cultural enlightenment where college students will again be enchanted with geniuses like Verdi, Brahms, Beethoven, Bach, and Mozart."

* * * * * * * * * * * *

On Sunday afternoon, Anotal drove his repaired, sky-blue Dodge Aries to a Glassboro florist to purchase a dozen roses. Such extravagance was contrary to Suez's frugal nature, but Daphne Agora was no ordinary female specimen. While the floral shop clerk was organizing Anotal's order, the customer glanced at a commercial golden rendition of a Greek god speeding along his merry way with inordinate dispatch.

"That's the ancient god Mercury," the chatty shop attendant informed his amused sole patron. "He's the floral industry's rapid delivery symbol."

"It's really the Greek god Hermes," the astute music professor corrected. "Mercury is the Roman counterpart of the Greek deity Hermes. So, Hermes would be the most accurate nomenclature to use in describing him."

"Whatever you say," the accommodating cashier harmoniously compromised. "I'll have to remember *that* vital fact and politely admonish my boss the next time he uses the improper name."

Next, the usually passive music professor motored over to Daphne Agora's condominium to honor the dinner engagement he had proposed to the austere Ancient History professor. Anotal exited his light blue automobile, sauntered-up the familiar straight flagstone walkway, and rang the doorbell three times.

"Oh, what really beautiful red roses!" Daphne exuberantly exclaimed in utter surprise and totally out-of-character emotion. "I'll have to put them in a suitable vase. Thank you so much for your thoughtfulness!"

After the gorgeous flowers had been neatly arranged in a desirable vase, the music instructor and his attractive brunette companion left the well-decorated and warmly furnished condominium. Daphne locked the front door, and the pair strolled arm in arm to the escort's nondescript Dodge Aries.

"The sun's really bright this afternoon!" Daphne commented as the gorgeous woman entered the vintage automobile.

"The sun's not only the source of all earthly energy," her didactic date lectured, "but I assure you, Daphne, it is also the origin of all truth and inspiration on this diabolical Earth. If it weren't for our nearest star, only bacteria and other resilient, hardy microorganisms could exist on this rather despicable, mediocre globe."

"Your words are virtually poetic, even though your opinions being expressed are borderline sarcastic," Dr. Agora appreciatively lauded and simultaneously verbally assaulted. "You seem to be an authority on everything, including the sun. Quite frankly, I find you more dynamic and puzzling with each successive contact. Please elaborate on your sagacity about the sun."

After forty-five minutes of pleasant conviviality, Anotal steered his substandard automobile into the Radisson Hotel parking lot on *Route 73* in Mt. Laurel.

"This is the Wyndham Steak House that's inside the Radisson," the driver communicated to his receptive passenger. "It has the finest grilled lamb chops, salmon, rib eye steaks, surf and turf, and filet mignon around. Tonight, my dear Daphne, you'll be treated and entertained like a goddess."

"Your charm is beginning to erode my resistance," the lady professor admitted. "I'm already lightheaded without even imbibing any champagne."

After wining and dining for two solid hours, the music professor enticed his lady friend up to an elegant suite he had specially reserved at the Radisson. Another bottle of champagne was ordered, and subsequently delivered to the door. And soon, after an hour of reminiscing, conversation magically changed into romance. Then after making his conquest in seduction, Anotal Suez hopped-out of bed and anxiously began dressing.

"Where are you going, darling?" Daphne questioned, almost in a daze. "Let's snuggle up together again. This comfortable bed is so exotic and elegant!"

"I've accomplished my prime objective," Dr. Suez bluntly replied. "And now it's time for me to pursue other romantic challenges. You were a difficult quest and conquest, My Lady. But now, Daphne I must explore other rigorous relationships with the opposite gender."

"What do you mean!" a jilted Daphne Agora yelled as she pulled her satin covers up to conceal her healthy, exposed breasts. "Of all the unmitigated audacity!"

"Enough of your belligerent, condescending attitude!" Anotal screamed at the now almost-hysterical woman, cursing a slew of consecutive invectives from the king-size bed. "I told you I would treat you like a goddess, a promiscuous goddess at that, and so I have honored my pledge up to this point."

Then, the now-irate music professor peered into a mirror, and his business suit instantly sparkled and then glistened, and soon his black polished shoes disappeared. Next, the man miraculously transformed into the Greek god Apollo, wearing golden sandals and a sublime white gold-trimmed tunic.

"Now, let your mortal eyes behold who I really am, Daphne!" Apollo turned and boomed in a deep, mellow voice. "I am truly the enlightened god of art, music, medicine, and the sun!" the renowned chariot master loudly exclaimed to the horrified woman. 'She has not yet figured out that Anotal is my mother Latona's name spelled backwards, and that Suez is my father Zeus's designation reversed, also. And yes, Latona is the proper Roman name for the Greek appellation, Leto.'

And then, without any further utterance or gesticulation, Apollo pointed a finger at the still-astonished Daphne Agora, now lying petrified inside the huge luxurious bed. An aura crystallized around her, and much to the sophisticated lady's dissatisfaction, she was swiftly beamed outside the Radisson Hotel, where she miraculously reappeared as a laurel tree, situated on the main entrance lawn.

'Another laurel tree right here in somnolent Mt. Laurel, New Jersey!' Apollo mused as the Greek deity again admired his divine countenance in the room's gold-framed wall mirror. 'I had easily performed *that* deed, just like I had turned another Daphne into a laurel tree many centuries ago in mythology, or should I say *history?* At any rate, I also killed a savage python at Delphi before my sacred Oracle had been established there. I suppose that a reliable axiom of life is that either history or mythology, is destined to repeat itself!'

The handsome Greek god exited the Radisson's third floor-room, took the elevator down to the lobby, and soon was the subject of patrons' laughter and gossip as Apollo proudly stepped by the registration desk and paced out the hotel's electronic front doors.

Apollo conscientiously scrutinized his wristwatch that was in the shape of an ancient sundial; took a glimpse of the newly im*planted* laurel tree; looked-up to the clear heavens, and let out a rhythmic whistle. Soon, an immense white flying horse descended from the twilight sky and majestically landed upon the hotel's asphalt driveway, standing amidst a gathering of fifty or so bedazzled, gawking bystanders.

"Well, I guess it's time for me to assume another identity in another time and place!" Apollo dynamically related to the still-flabbergasted crowd of well-dressed, shocked gossipers. "It's indeed time for Phoebus Apollo to establish himself in another century and artfully entice another Daphne, and if the occasion arises, slaughter another python. Come Pegasus! Take me to Mt. Olympus, where I can freely replenish my dwindling supply of nectar and ambrosia! And you may take the scenic roundabout route if you wish."

276

The muscular, gleaming god then nonchalantly mounted the fabulous, obedient, white-winged stallion, who immediately raised its noble head and gently ascended-up into the dusky sky. The magnificent creature, and its eminent rider, triumphantly circled above the Mt. Laurel Radisson Hotel, and then wonderfully disappeared over the western horizon, heading in the direction of the setting sun.

"That'll Be the Day"

It had been a glorious spring break vacation for college seniors Jeff Moore and Fred Durham. The *Rutgers University* seniors had flown from *Philadelphia International Airport* west to Denver, and then boarded a second *United Air* flight out to Palm Springs to enjoy the luxurious Southern California desert sunshine. After renting a sporty car from *Avis,* Jeff drove down Tahquitz Canyon Way from the airport to Palm Canyon Drive, and then headed south on *Highway 111* from Palm Springs to Palm Desert.

"New Jersey sure doesn't look anything like this!" Fred Durham exclaimed from the passenger side of the rented white *Pontiac Grand AM.* "Check-out the red mountains surrounding this desert valley! Pretty magnificent, if I must say!"

"And there's gorgeous girls all over the place," Jeff Moore replied as the driver proceeded south on one-way Palm Canyon Drive. "And what a terrific coincidence, Fred! My sister and her husband are vacationing on a *Mediterranean* cruise, and we get to stay at their cozy Palm Desert pad. The directions are to take *111* south and then take Deep Canyon Road several blocks past Fred Waring Drive, and soon we'll find 105 Cachanilla Court, Palm Desert, 92260 inside a secluded gated community. I sure hope that the pass code entry numbers that my sister gave me to raise the gate are still working."

"You make it all sound too easy!" Fred typically criticized. "First, we have to pass through Cathedral City and Rancho Mirage, which happen to be towns geographically situated between Palm Springs and Palm Desert. Then, I'll read you the specific directions to your sister's place. But I gotta' admit, Jeff. This entire area is spectacular. I've never seen a cloudless dark-blue sky like that before! It's almost like we're traveling on another planet! And the air is fresh and clean too, virtually pollution-free!"

"It sure beats New Brunswick, New Jersey, that's for sure!" the preoccupied driver observed and opined. "The daytime temperatures here in the winter are in the seventies and the eighties. The only downside is that with the desert down here in the valley all around us, there's always more-brown showing than green."

"Who cares?" Fred Durham instinctively challenged his close pal, Jeff Moore. "I'll take dolls in two-piece bikinis over naked deciduous trees any day of the week! And it doesn't matter whether those gorgeous babes are doing spring break in South Padre Island, Texas, or in Palm Springs, California!"

The pair safely reached their ultimate destination and spent four wonderful days in the excellent Palm Desert and Palm Springs resort areas. On Monday, the college roommates strolled along El Paseo, the "Rodeo Drive" of Palm Desert; ate a sumptuous dinner at the Kaiser House, and that evening met several vivacious *UCLA* girls that were staying at the *Palm Mountain Resort,* located at the foot of the scenic *Santa Rosa Mountains* in Palm Springs. Jenn and Sharon were looking for some exciting male companionship, so the four hung-around together on Tuesday and Wednesday, and besides some intense partying, the couples managed to incorporate a few normal tourist activities into their schedules by taking the *29 Palms Highway* into the mountains, and visiting *Joshua Tree National Park,* the only place in the world that has the right combination of climate and elevation for Joshua trees to grow. And then, the following day, the foursome stayed in Palm Springs and that afternoon rode "The Tram" (which slowly rotated a full three-hundred-and-sixty-degrees) up through five separate ecological zones, as the famous "lift" ascended from the hot arid valley up into the chilly snow-clad mountains.

Wednesday afternoon was spent relaxing at the *Palm Mountain Resort* outdoor pool, and then after having supper at the Chop House, over on Palm Canyon Drive. The four carefree college souls trekked over to the Indian owned *Spa Casino* (between Indian Canyon Drive and Amado Road), where everyone tried their luck on the slot machines. On Thursday, Jeff and Fred had to unfortunately adhere to their schedule and drive through the deserts and mountains to Las Vegas, where they had booked two nights at the fabulous *New York, New York Hotel and Casino,* before having to fly back east from Las Vegas to resume their grueling *Rutgers* academic doldrums.

En route to Las Vegas, the young vacationers had been remarking how all houses and motels in the Palm Springs/Palm Desert area were "gated" to extend the idea of "privacy and security" to residents and visitors alike. Then, the conversation naturally switched to Jeff and Fred's most recent *UCLA* female companions. "Jenn and Sharon promised to write us when we get back to *Rutgers!"* Jeff reminded Fred as the Don Juan drove on *I-15* on the way to Vegas.

"That'll be the day!" Fred replied. "And I'm not referring to Buddy Holly's oldies hit record, either!"

"Here's some trivia for you Mr. Know-It-All!" Jeff chuckled. "Did you know that Buddy Holly came-up with the title of that song from words that John Wayne had said in the classic 1956 movie 'The Searchers'?"

"You don't say!" Fred acknowledged. "I'm a big Buddy Holly fan too, you know! It does make sense in that 'That'll Be the Day!' and 'Peggy Sue' both came out in '57. But right now, Jeff, my mind is still focused on Room 301 of the *Palm Mountain Resort,* 155 South Belardo, Palm Springs, California. That was some last night we had spent with those fabulous chicks!"

"The Beach Boys had it absolutely right when the group sang 'Wish They All Could Be California Girls'!" the driver declared with a broad smile expressed upon his face. "East Coast girls are hip, but golden sunny California dolls are definitely where it's at! I mean Fred, who really cares if we lost a hundred-bucks each at the totally magnificent *Spa Casino?"*

"You're absolutely right, Jeff!" Fred Durham amiably concurred while again faithfully riding "shotgun". "You know how I love to eat delicious food, and the Chop House, the Oasis Buffet at the *Spa Casino,* and that LGS Steakhouse on Palm Canyon Drive were really great restaurants."

"And what about the pretty neat mist vapors that were sprayed-out from restaurant canopies on sidewalk pedestrians walking along Palm Canyon Drive," Jeff Moore recollected and shared as the speedster accelerated past a tractor-trailer. "But in spite of the awe-inspiring Tram adventure, the incomparable *Joshua Tree National Park,* the loose atmosphere of El Paseo, and the sophisticated *Spa Casino,* Jenn and Sharon were without a doubt the highlights of our spring break vacation thus far! Let's see what Las Vegas has to offer! I hear it sure beats Atlantic City!"

"Only three more hours and we'll be meandering around on the Strip!" Fred confidently predicted. "And as they say and exaggerate on television commercials, anything can happen in Vegas! Say Jeff. How much did your sister and brother-in-law's Palm Desert house cost?" the *Grand Am* passenger curiously asked the driver.

Jeff Moore sanctimoniously explained that his sister and brother-in-law had gone west seven years earlier; had both gotten licensed in real estate, and that the couple was presently making an attractive living flipping houses. The 105 Cachanilla Court Palm Desert ranch home had cost them five-hundred-thousand-dollars, but it was now on the market for eight-hundred-grand. The New Jersey college travelers mutually decided that real estate was a most favorable and lucrative future career pursuit.

* * * * * * * * * * *

Thirty-miles outside Las Vega,s the young men's dialogue again had Buddy Holly as its central theme, with both Jeff Moore and Fred Durham attempting to impress each other with their mastery of picayune details pertaining to the '50s rock star sensation's musical biography.

"You know, Fred," Jeff bragged as the driver navigated the white *Grand AM* through some heavy *I-15* traffic. "Buddy Holly's real name was Charles Hardin Holly and he was from…"

"From Lubbock, Texas," the impatient passenger automatically answered. "And his last name on his birth certificate was spelled H-o-l-l-e-y and not H-o-l-l-y. And H-o-l-l-e-y is how it's spelled on his tombstone. Buddy's buried in…"

"In the City of Lubbock Cemetery," Jeff Moore academically finished his friend's trivial question. "My photographic mind recalls that Holly was born on September 7, 1936, and Buddy unfortunately died on…"

"On February 3, 1959 in a small plane crash just outside Clear Lake, Iowa, not far from Mason City," Fred Durham interrupted. "That winter evening, Buddy Holly had given a performance at the…."

"At the Surf Ballroom in Clear Lake," the driver insisted with egotistical certainty. "But the bus the singer was touring with had broken-down, and so he and the Big Bopper, also known as J.P. Richardson, along with Ritchie Valens. rented a four passenger…"

"A four passenger Beechcraft Bonanza while a terrible blizzard was in progress, in order to get to their next singing destination in Minnesota," the passenger knowledgeably contributed. "But then, the rest of the tragedy is all recorded rock and roll history. Say Jeff," Fred Durham elaborated, "did you know that the Big Bopper, who incidentally had only one major hit record 'Chantilly Lace' was really a former…"

"A former chubby disc jockey from Beaumont, Texas," "Jeff the Navigator" haughtily responded. "And regrettably, the catastrophic airplane crash happened at precisely 1:05 a.m. in a remote Iowa cornfield!"

The *I-15* travelers had reached a stalemate after each knew that Buddy Holly had competed in Hutchinson Junior High School talent shows; had broken the color barrier by being the first white act to perform before a jam-packed audience at Harlem's *Apollo Theater;* that the renowned performer had broken a '50s cultural taboo by marrying a pretty Puerto Rican girl named Maria Elena Santiago, and that the British rock group the Hollies had been named in tribute to the '50s singing legend.

"Let's change the subject back to Jenn and Sharon," Fred Durham suggested. "Although they never sang for Coral Records, which as you probably know was a subsidiary of Decca Records, and despite the fact that neither of the girls wears black-framed, horn-rimmed glasses, or ever professionally sang 'Maybe Baby' or 'Oh Boy!',", the passenger almost arrogantly commented, "That'll Be the Day if we ever see them again! Such is life, I suppose."

* * * * * * * * * * * *

Soon, the avid travelers finally reached Las Vegas late Thursday afternoon. And after unpacking their bags in Room 528, the duo wandered all over the public sectors of *New York, New York,* familiarizing themselves with all aspects and features of the spectacular casino/hotel. After eating a light supper at an "O. Henry-style Central Park Restaurant" having 1890s' décor and appearance, the twosome left the creatively-designed building to stroll the Vegas Strip, sauntering in and out of the five-thousand plus room *MGM;* the elegant *Mandalay Bay,* and the fascinating architectural wonder known as *Caesar's Palace*, where the pair then sat near a talking statue of the Roman god Bacchus. And after the god-of-wine's verbal presentation had terminated, the itinerant travelers discussed the glittery adult paradise that were visiting for the first time. Jeff had to spoil the wonderful "escape and escapade from reality" by reminding his now-apathetic excursion partner about some other relevant and practical elements of *their* young American lives.

"In a few days, we'll be back in lackluster New Jersey hitting the books and getting ready to graduate," Moore reminded Durham. "And then, it's functioning in the grueling dog-eat-dog real world, after finally obtaining our sheepskins and getting out of *Rutgers*."

283

"What an enormous bummer!" Fred evaluated and honestly stated. "Why don't you enroll in graduate school and prolong your adolescence as long as possible, just like I intend doing? Jeff, we can successfully delay unnecessary things like marriage, kids, and other annoying adult responsibilities by at least a few years! Then, you and I could become enthusiastic real estate agents, and eventually evolve into reputable property brokers."

"Every once in a blue moon, Fred, when you aren't being disingenuous, you show occasional symptoms of brilliance!" Jeff optimistically joked. "Stop imitating me and find your own sense of identity! And Fred, don't forget that we have to call the *United Airlines'* desk at *McCarron International Airport* tomorrow evening to confirm our Saturday morning flight back to 'Philly."

"Okay, but let's push the exhaustion envelope tonight and tomorrow," Fred Durham facetiously recommended. "We can always sleep on the five-hour flight back to Philly'. And who knows? Maybe one of us will hit a giant jackpot this evening, and we could then forget all about our dreaded admission into adulthood! Let's tour the *Mirage* and the *Venetian* and have a few drinks while we try our luck at the poker and roulette tables. Being twenty-one does have some distinct advantages, you know!"

At midnight, the fatigued and half-inebriated friends returned to *New York, New York* three-hundred-dollars richer, more than retrieving their losses from what the pair had "willfully donated to the *Spa Casino* back in Palm Springs, California". Finally, at three in the morning, the friends managed to return to Room 528 and get some much-needed sleep.

After waking-up at noon on Friday, Jeff and Fred purchased tour-bus tickets (with their "windfall gambling profits") and accompanied some other Vegas vacationers out to the incredible *Hoover Dam* on Lake Meade, where the tourists marveled at the landmark phenomenon built to govern and harness the power of the mighty *Colorado River*. Upon leaving the "colossal engineering wonder", the two adventurers climbed-back onto the tour bus for their pleasant trip back to the glitzy Vegas Strip. Soon, Jeff and Fred were again dining in their authentic-looking "O. Henry Central Park restaurant" and reviewing the sensational highlights of what amounted to their very educational day trip.

"Everybody should come out here and visit this area at least once in their lives," Jeff Moore remarked to Fred Durham before biting into a very delectable charcoal-broiled hamburger. "Atlantic City may have its famous boardwalk, but *New York, New York* even has a small Coney Island-type wooden promenade upstairs. And it's too bad we didn't even have time to try-out that rollicking roller coaster that goes around the first few floors of this magnificent building."

"Well, anyway, Good Buddy. We did get to stroll across the miniature *Brooklyn Bridge* in front of the hotel and take some digital pictures of the replica *Statue of Liberty* and the New York Harbor fire-boat outside," Fred replied.

"I want to hang around the casino floor until midnight," Jeff indicated.

"How come? Do you feel *that* lucky?" Fred asked.

"No, but while you were up in Room 528 using the facilities, I had bought several raffle tickets on that fabulous red and black '56 *Ford Crown Victoria* that's slowly revolving on that platform over there!" Jeff informed his now-amused chum. "Let's go over and inspect that beauty! It's definitely a blast from the past!"

The duo stepped-over to the "nostalgic piece of history" to thoroughly admire its' mint-condition excellence. The interior was in superb splendor, appearing as if the impeccable vintage automobile was brand-new.

"My father has photographs from the '50s when dad had lived in Levittown, Pennsylvania," Jeff Moore casually related to Fred Durham. "And my grandfather once owned a similar '56 *Ford*. Next to Buddy Holly's *Cadillac* convertible and the classic '57 *Chevy*, the '56 Crown Victoria has to be my favorite '50s car. If I win this baby at midnight," Jeff Moore wished and expressed, "and I know it's quite a long shot, Fred, we're gonna' call the *United* desk at *McCarron International Airport;* cancel our scheduled flight, and drive this honey cross country back to New Brunswick. As Aerosmith often sings, 'Dream On'!" the quixotic romantic laughed. "You might snicker, Fred, but I have a hunch that I'm in the running to win this splendid vintage automobile!" Jeff Moore confided.

At midnight, the winning raffle ticket was drawn and announced, and for several dramatic seconds, the flabbergasted New Jersey visitors had trouble catching their breaths and eventually shouting-out their gleeful triumphant yells. "It looks like we're driving this boss chariot back to New Jersey!" Jeff Moore jubilantly shouted to his still-astonished college roommate. "I told you we were going to cancel our flight reservations and drive this honey back East! Say

Fred, remind me to buy that Aerosmith *CD* when we finally get back to good old *Rutgers!*"

* * * * * * * * * * * *

Euphoria reigned supreme as the ecstatic pair traveled east in the newly acquired red and black 1956 *Ford Crown Victoria.* Jeff Moore and Fred Durham spent a full day sightseeing in Denver, and then stayed overnight in attractive *Ramada Inn* accommodations. After a comprehensive breakfast of bacon, eggs, and pancakes, the two were again heading east on *I-70,* and the driver was about to disclose to his relentlessly gabby passenger his personal desire to take *I-80* to Omaha, Nebraska.

"I think you should take *I-70* all the way east, instead," Fred firmly articulated. "*I-80* is too far north, and we still might be subject to an early spring snowstorm. I strongly suggest we take the safer southern route."

"Fred, I just have to honor my inspiration to drive through Clear Lake, Iowa in my handsome '56 *Crown Victoria,*" Jeff honestly revealed. "I gotta' see if the Surf Ballroom is still in existence in memory of the late-great Buddy Holly! Did you know, Fred, that Buddy went on the winter bus tour without the Crickets?"

"Yeah, and the group was supposed to get together again in Minnesota," Durham disgustedly answered. "But as rock and roll history has accurately documented, *that* reunion never happened as a result of the horrible airplane disaster of February 3, 1959, the day the music died, which is profoundly chronicled in Don McLean's unforgettable 'Bye, Bye Miss American Pie'. That's why you really want to take *I-80!*"

"You don't have to be a perceptive clairvoyant to read between the lines! Sometimes, you know me better than I know myself!" Jeff readily admitted.

"Okay, you're the boss!" Fred conceded. "I don't want to stand between you and your dream! If I had done that back in Vegas, then we could never be riding in your fantastic '56 dream machine!"

"Yes, and this baby's been modified with deluxe power steering and brakes, along with a twelve-speaker stereo system," Jeff Moore proudly elaborated. "We just got to be the envy of every car and truck driver that sees us. We'll spend the night in Sioux City, and then journey on to Clear Lake, Iowa first thing tomorrow morning.

And if we get distracted, who the heck cares? So what, if we miss a day or two of boring academic classes before we eventually get back on campus!"

"Well, I just gotta' commend you on your originality!" Fred facetiously volleyed back. "You do have a flair for the bizarre! Only another two hours or so, and we'll be on *I-80* on our way to Sioux City, Iowa. I hope we don't get into any serious litigation with any remaining Sioux (sue) Indians! And thank goodness this remarkable car came with temporary license plates!" Durham frivolously punned and jested.

After a good night's rest at a *Holiday Inn Express* on South Lakeport Street in Sioux City, the following afternoon, the red and black '56 Crown Victoria was exiting *Interstate-80* and soon onto *I-35* and heading north toward Mason City, Iowa. Both occupants felt a surge of energy rush through their veins when they were finally on *Route 18* and motoring west in the direction of Clear Lake. Much to their consternation, an early spring snowstorm had descended on the area, and the fellows were caught in what Jeff Moore aptly described as "the beginning of a savage blizzard".

"You'd better turn around," Fred Durham cautiously advised his traveling companion. "Put Clear Lake on hold! Go back to *I-35,* and we'll find some comfortable lodging to see this nasty storm pass through!"

"I'll get gas at that old-fashioned service station up ahead!" Jeff said with an element of disappointment evident in his tone of voice. "Then, we'll turn around and locate a convenient motel just off the Interstate. I should've listened to you in the first place when you were futilely trying to convince me to take *I-70* instead of *I-80*."

"It's too late now!" the wary passenger gloomily answered as his hardheaded partner pulled-up to the ancient-looking gas pump. "Say, Jeff! This station's closed!"

And then both young men incredulously stared-up at the overhead hanging sign. *"Esso!"* Fred exclaimed. *"Esso* changed its name to *Exxon* many moons ago!" And then, Durham read a sign hanging inside the closed station's dusty office: "Monday, February 2, 1959."

"That's impossible!" Jeff shouted in absolute amazement. "It's Wednesday, March 28, 2006! Are we trapped in some kind of dangerous time warp?"

"I've never been so baffled in all my life!" Fred Durham gasped.

"Let's drive into Clear Lake, find the Surf Ballroom, and discover the honest-to-God truth for ourselves!" the anxious driver replied. "If it's really fantastically Monday, February 2, 1959, then we have a chance of saving Buddy Holly from imminent disaster!"

* * * * * * * * * * *

Snowflakes kept coming-down heavily as Jeff Moore slowly drove the *Crown Victoria* into downtown Clear Lake, Iowa. All of the vehicles he and Fred Durham passed or encountered were vintage 1959 models or earlier. The driver managed to find an available space, and then carefully parked his prized automobile on a side street two blocks behind the famous Surf Ballroom.

"We aren't exactly equipped for this special mission weather-wise," the apprehensive driver cited. "But Fred, I suppose our fall lightweight jackets will have to serve our purpose in being here. It's a good thing '50s kids were very polite, and that security for the big concert will be minimal for us geniuses to figure-out and violate."

"It's almost eight-thirty right now, and with the windows opened a crack, we can hear the great music originating from several blocks away," Fred keenly perceived and declared. "But we'll only have a small window of opportunity to pull this caper off!"

"Let's hope that we can inconspicuously get into the auditorium from a backstage entrance!" Jeff anxiously said to his co-conspirator. "We'll sneak in, and then Fred, leave the rest to me. Remember; our goal is to prevent a major rock star from perishing."

Fred Durham was predictably quick to challenge his friend's very valid talking points. "But what about the Big Bopper and Ritchie Valens? If I recall the story, Dion was also supposed to be on that plane, but Buddy went in *his* place. Maybe if we only rescue Buddy, then Dion will die as his substitute."

"That's the lousy chance we'll have to take!" Jeff Moore replied, showing a degree of conviction mixed with apparent uncertainty. "Let's stop jabbering and start our strategic plan into action. Any police officers or security guards assigned to the show are probably stationed in the audience, or at the front doors, thinking that anyone trying to crash the concert would not be so bold as to enter from the backdoor. Remember, Fred," Jeff Moore strongly emphasized. "It's now 1959 and not 2006. And by all means, let me do all the talking until we get Buddy out of the building and safely into our custody."

288

As luck would have it, the two young men managed to sneak inside the Surf Ballroom from the unattended rear backstage door, when everyone in the auditorium was paying attention to the talented Buddy Holly singing his medley of stellar hit songs. Fifteen-minutes later, the accomplished performer had completed his grand finale curtain call, and upon exiting the stage, briefly spoke with several other back-stage entertainers involved in the program. Then, the famous singer stepped to the rear wall payphone to make a call, presumably to his pregnant wife.

"Buddy Holly, you'd better come with us!" Jeff sternly insisted. "I have a gun concealed in my jacket. If you dare try to get anybody's attention, you'll regret the consequences and never see Maria Elena again. But we promise you that you won't be harmed! Come quietly with us! It's extremely important! Here's my *Rolex* watch you can hold as collateral!"

After swiftly and surreptitiously exiting the building via the backdoor, and then walking two snow-laden sidewalk blocks to the red and black '56 *Crown Victoria,* the three men entered the car, with Buddy Holly obediently following directions and sitting in the front passenger side seat. Jeff Moore sat behind the wheel with Fred Durham (also claiming to have a pistol) sitting in the rear.

"Are you two guys professional kidnappers, or gangsters, or what?" the concerned hostage demanded knowing as the famous singer incredulously stared at the expensive *Rolex* watch. "Are you trying to extort ransom money out of me?"

"We're trying to save you from getting killed, Buddy!" Jeff Moore asserted as the driver fired-up the engine while almost simultaneously blasting the heater. "Just relax and listen to our phenomenal story, and then decide for yourself."

As Fred Durham exited the *Crown Victoria* to remove excess snow with his bare hands from the front, back, and side windows, Jeff Moore began his unbelievable dissertation to the now-intrigued '50s rock star. Five-minutes later, the almost frozen human snow scraper re-entered the '56 Ford to engage in divulging additional background information to the now-spellbound singer/hostage.

"You say that there's going to be a small plane crash later tonight, and that I'm going to die in it!" Buddy exclaimed. "How do you know that our bus broke-down; that Dion is sick, and that there's talk about me and two other entertainers flying to Minnesota?"

"It's all history!" Jeff maintained as the chauffeur activated the windshield wipers and then gingerly drove the automobile out of its side-street parking space. "Just listen to us babble for a few hours as we deliberately keep you out of harm's way! I guarantee you, Buddy, that you're not going to believe a single word that your ears are about to hear!"

The very curious listener heard a full-hour of discussion about the past, the present, and the future. Finally, when Jeff and Fred completed their confounding explanations, the still-bewildered front-seat passenger had several pertinent questions to ask.

"Well, what's the damned future like? Will I still be famous? What'll happen to my wife and son?" the awed captive wondered and inquired.

"Well, in the future there's going to be computers and cell phones, and *VCRs* and Apollo moon landings," Jeff inadequately explained as the garrulous speaker drove down Clear Lake's main street in the direction of what he believed was *I-35*. "And your faithful wife Maria Elena will grieve your death for many years. That's what we're trying right now to prevent from happening."

"But if you guys are from the year 2006 as you claim, then why are you driving around in a boss 1956 *Ford?*" Buddy interrogated in a skeptical tone of voice.

"One question at a time!" Fred sternly instructed from the back seat. "First, we'll drive around Clear Lake and tell you all about computers, *CDs,* and cell phones! Then, we'll tell you how we've miraculously obtained this *Crown Victoria!*"

The very interesting conversation continued for another full-hour, as the 2006' time travelers endeavored to convey and encapsulate nearly a half-century of human history and rock and roll music into sixty additional minutes of important dialogue. Soon, the slow-moving red and black vehicle was approaching the entrance ramp that Jeff Moore theorized was the way to *I-35*.

"Jeff, you can't go onto *I-35!*" Fred objected in the midst of myriad swirling and eddying outside snowflakes. "It's still 1959! The highway ramp hasn't been constructed yet!"

"The exit on the opposite side of the highway got us from 2006 into the year 1959, didn't it?" Moore persuasively argued.

"Are you trying to take me into *your* future?" Buddy Holly worried. "Are you guys for real? I think I'd rather stay and live in good old 1959 without this fancy watch! I don't want to live in 2006 before I really have to!"

"You're both right!" the driver promptly acknowledged. "I'll turn around at the first exit and take our distinguished guest back to Clear Lake, now that he's missed his airplane departure flight!"

And after uttering those particular amazing words, Jeffrey Moore stared to his right with his mouth agape, and then in the rear-view mirror observed a similar expression featured on Fred Durham's face. Buddy Holly had remarkably vanished from the front passenger side into thin air. A red *Nissan Maxima* and a tan *Acura* soon slowly passed the red and black *Crown Victoria* after it gradually made its March 28, 2006 entrance onto snow-covered *Interstate 35*. Jeff Moore promptly glanced-down, and much to his utter confusion, his treasured *Rolex* watch was functioning back upon his left wrist.

"Butterton Woods"

Dave Anderson owned a four-hundred-acre blueberry and peach farm, principally situated at and behind the intersection of Walker Road and *Route 30,* the White Horse Pike in Elm, New Jersey, just outside the Hammonton town border, and a little west of the Atlantic/Camden County Line. Dave and Jill Anderson's comfortable residence was a seventy-year-old white Dutch colonial home located at the junction of the busy highway and serene Walker Road. In the late 1970s, blueberries became the dominant fruit crop in Hammonton and vicinity, and like many other area growers, Anderson followed the money and began removing his Blake and Red Haven variety peach orchards and replacing them with fields of Duke and Blue Crop variety blueberries.

The original fifty-acre homestead had been "grubbed" in 1902 by Dave Anderson's grandfather, who like most enterprising British and Italian immigrant farmers, planted peach and apple trees, popular regional crops that were then sold locally. But soon after the invention of the automobile, and just prior to World War I, trucks began hauling fresh "Hammonton fruit" to Philadelphia, New York, and other metropolitan markets situated along the Eastern Seaboard. After Dave Anderson's grandfather died during the height of the Great Depression, his father (like many area bootlegging farmers) drove trucks during the wintertime, transporting "moonshine whiskey" from stills kept in woods and barns during the "very difficult and dangerous Prohibition Era", when extra money was needed simply to survive with adequate food on the kitchen table; enough revenue to pay property taxes, and needed cash to maintain cherished farm equipment. Many proud-but-desperate local farmers (out of economic necessity) capitalized on "the tough times of whiskey deprivation" that were (according to older citizens) caused by the 1920s women's suffrage and temperance movement.

David Henry Anderson's conscientious father profited from the annual "winter bootlegging bonanza", and during the Great Depression, managed to save sufficient funds to buy an additional seven-acre tract of land behind the original homestead from an English immigrant named John Butterton, who (along with *his* descendants) is presently buried in Oak Grove Cemetery on the White Horse Pike in Hammonton. Hence, the small section of forestland is commonly referred to as Butterton Woods, which Dave Anderson presently calls his "personal hunting preserve".

The end of Prohibition and American involvement in World War II gradually brought the USA out of the Great Depression, and Hammonton area farmers enjoyed a time of prosperity with the prices of quality summer peaches and fall apples skyrocketing. Dave's ambitious father was able to expand the family farming operation from one-hundred to four-hundred acres along Walker Road, and then extending his little empire across Union Road to the far end of the property, which was referred to as "Texas", because it was so distant from the original homestead tract. When Anderson's father died in 1974, Dave bought-out his younger brothers Thomas and Frank, and soon became the exclusive owner of the sprawling estate.

David's best friend was an amiable Hammonton High School English teacher named Jack Elder. The two men had been chums ever since ninth-grade, even though ironically, Dave had graduated from Edgewood High in Atco (Winslow Township, Camden County) and Jack from Hammonton High (Atlantic County). On their weekly "Boys Night Out", Dave and Jack would frequent the popular West End Grille on the south side of the railroad tracks in downtown Hammonton, and then habitually enjoy three games of competitive bowling at DiDonato Lanes and Cocktail Lounge on *Route 30* on the east side of town. A week after Thanksgiving, Jack Elder paid a friendly visit to his buddy Dave Anderson's home.

"Hi, Dave! Where's Jill?" Jack asked. "Is she at the grocery store or at the hairdresser?"

"No, she's first taken the kids to school, and then my wife drove to her sister Gloria's place over on Fairview Avenue," Dave informed his inquisitive visitor. "The girls are heading-out to Consumer's Square over in Mays Landing to do some heavy-duty clothes shopping and gossiping. I *swear* that Jill's wardrobe must rival Queen Elizabeth's, Jack. And I think I gotta' build three more closets onto my house!"

"It isn't healthy to swear Dave, especially in a court of law," Jack Elder facetiously joked to his farmer friend. "Aren't ya' gonna' ask where I've been? Or are you so self-indulgent that all you can think and talk about are yourself, your wife, your kids and your huge farm! I mean, start showing a more profound interest in others!"

"Okay, then Mr. Noun, could you educate me about what location you're coming from?" Dave Anderson replied to his public-school instructor pal with a broad grin on his face. "It's not the busy harvest season, so I have the rest of the fall and all winter to listen to your inane prattle."

"Well, I'm just returning from Dr. Joe's chiropractic office over in Atco," Elder said with a straight face. "And Dr. Matt gave me a great adjustment, along with much needed heat and powerful electric stim'. I always get and deserve the four-pad upper and lower back treatment, ya' know! So, ya' see Dave, I'm not playing hooky from school, and I have a legitimate medical excuse for being absent," the gregarious guest continued with his rambling drivel. "But the real reason I go to that clinic in Atco is because the place has a great Hydro-bed, featuring warm water vibrations. And also the clinic has a moving roller bed, or I should say a bed with moving rollers where the muscles, vertebrae, and joints in my back are thoroughly massaged for a full fifteen-minutes. Ya' gotta' come with me some time for a trial treatment," Jack insisted. "It's guaranteed to improve your much-to-be-desired posture, and modify your atrocious bowling game, too!"

"I'll consider your stellar invitation after you accompany me out to Butterton Woods on a little walking expedition," Anderson stated and requested. "Rabbit season will soon be over, and deer hunting starts December 1st. I wanna' check my recently constructed deer stand and make sure no greedy poachers are staking-out the woods with deer bait and plannin' to use my stand as an observation post and shooting platform," Dave Anderson convincingly communicated to Jack Elder. "And after we finish our little Butterton Woods' inspection, we'll head on over to Mary's Restaurant on *206* for a late morning breakfast, my treat of course!"

"Sounds pretty copacetic to me!" Jack Elder promptly replied. "Either Mary's or the Red Barn for breakfast. Either of the two *206* eateries will be just dandy! When a man's stomach is growling like mine is right now, pancakes, bacon, and eggs and strong coffee will taste just as great at either restaurant."

"I remember when *Route 30* used to be the major east-west thoroughfare around here," Dave told his best friend as the friends entered Anderson's red Ford 150 pickup. "But then, the State expanded *Route 322,* and soon the Black Horse Pike was taking traffic away from the White Horse, and giving this parallel highway serious competition with the Philadelphia and Pennsylvania people heading down to the Atlantic City Boardwalk and to the Jersey Shore. And then in 1964...."

"The Atlantic City Expressway had opened right between the White Horse Pike and the Black Horse Pike, and *that* high-speed toll road seriously hurt your family's retail farm market business," Jack finished Dave's all-too-predictable speech. "Dave, I've heard *that* monotonous, redundant sob story a thousand and one times, and quite frankly, it sounds worse than a broken record. Now, let's scoot over to Mary's before it's already suppertime, and we'll have to eat filet mignon instead of hotcakes and eggs! We'll swallow-down some buttermilk pancakes and then tour Butterton Woods to alleviate your paranoia! Ha, ha, ha!" Elder indulgently laughed. "You're a very successful multimillionaire Dave, and all of a sudden you're needlessly worried that your farm market isn't doing as well as it had done forty-years ago! Ha, ha, ha! You should've been an ancient barbarian, because sometimes' you really slay me! Ha, ha, ha!"

An hour later, after sharing and exchanging a few choice anecdotes with several patrons at Mary's Restaurant, and after enjoying delectable breakfasts, Dave Anderson drove his shiny new red Ford 150 (with Jack Elder riding shotgun) back to Walker Road, taking Union Road west from two-lane *Route 206*. The prominent, full-bellied farmer pulled-off the recently paved country road into a dirt lane that separated his main irrigation pond from "the landmark Butterton Woods". A thousand-feet down the dirt trail, the truck's operator gently applied the brakes.

"Okay, Jack. Let's hike five-hundred-feet into the woods and locate my new sacred tree stand," Dave Anderson directed. "If nothing's been tampered with, and if no deer bait is detectable on the ground, then I predict we'll take a quick cruise over to Atlantic City in my new Lexus. And thanks to my good nature, both lunch and your first hundred bucks of gambling money will be on me!"

"If it's *your* sacred tree stand, perhaps we should build a makeshift altar underneath and make it into a shrine! But I gotta' confess that your' buying me lunch is mighty generous of you, Dave!" Jack quipped with a wide smile accentuating his pearly white teeth. "You'll have to sell eight more crates of blueberries next summer than you did last season to make-up for the additional expenditure. But then again," Elder amiably vociferated, "I don't believe I have any other friends that would simply hand me a hundred bucks to casually blow away at the blackjack tables."

296

Two-hundred-paces into Butterton Woods, on-a-mission Dave Anderson was relieved to discover that his revered deer hunting platform was still securely nestled high up in the sturdy tall barren oak tree, without any sign of senseless vandalism. And the serious hunter was happy to notice that no deer-baiting apple or sweet potato pile had been surreptitiously dumped-off by a greedy, trespassing poacher. Being satisfied that nothing irregular had occurred since *his* last cursory inspection of the area three days before, Anderson was about to remark to Elder how delighted the property owner was about his favorable observations when his keen ears distinctly discerned juvenile-aged voices originating from his far left.

"Duck down!" Anderson softly ordered and then motioned to his less wary companion. "Jack, I think I hear intruders talking behind that clump of pine trees. Let's slink-over there and investigate who's trespassin'!"

One hundred additional feet into Butterton Woods' dense interior the men came across three boys dressed in 1970s winter apparel, lighting left-over caterpillar meshes that had been woven upon and still remained on a short, naked deciduous tree's lower limbs. The new arrivals skulked-down on their knees and intently eavesdropped on the teenagers' odd conversation.

"I told you guys I had a great idea playing hooky and comin' out here in these woods for a couple of smokes and a little mischief!" the first kid said. "Edgewood High's a real bummer, so I thought we'd come out here to the edge of these isolated woods and have a little amusement, ha, ha, ha."

"Great idea, Robbie!" the second kid commended. "It does beat goin' to chemistry class! But make sure you don't carelessly set these woods on fire! I don't wanna' have to spend time in juvenile court explainin' why we're avowed junior pyromaniacs with dreams of becomin' full-fledged arsonists. It might interfere with me watchin' my nighttime TV cartoon shows, ha, ha, ha!"

"Don't flip-out and hit the panic button, Charlie!" the third encroacher laughed. "The only thing ya' gotta' tell the judge is that we ran out of matches, and so did Yogi Bear and his close pal Smoky! This woods' ain't exactly Jellystone Park, ya' know! Ha, ha, ha! Hand me a cancer, stick, will ya'!"

"Shut-up, Steve, before I give ya' a deluxe knuckle sandwich! Your stupid bull runnin' from your filthy mouth is makin' me nervous!" Robbie reprimanded his punk associate/junior comedian.

"Now, just look what ya' two clowns made me do! This whole damned tree's caught on fire!"

"It's spreadin' too fast to put-out with all of the leaves and dry brush layin' around!" Charlie panicked and yelled. "Let's bug-out of here quick before the cops and the fire engines arrive. I'm not too good at honestly answerin' tough questions."

"Quick! Let's hustle back to my jalopy on Walker Road!" Robbie shouted at Charlie and Steve. "We'll drive up to the Pic-A-Lilli on *206,* have lunch, and pretend like nothing unusual ever happened! All we did was play hooky and drive through the Pine Barrens to have a bite to eat. And if the cops ever ask us anything, we just took a little nature walk over in Wharton State Forest near Atsion Lake."

The three delinquent youths bolted left, and then wildly dashed out of the burning woods. As the fire rapidly raged, its hunger soon consumed additional trees and bushes. Quickly, Anderson and Elder rose to their feet, hustled over to the roaring inferno, and began tossing dirt and sand onto the flames. But their heroic efforts were to no avail. Soon, firehouse sirens were heard originating from the west in Elm and from the east in Hammonton, so the frustrated men reluctantly abandoned the proliferating blaze and swiftly fled in the direction of the newly constructed tree stand and the nearby red Ford 150. Being reputable adult citizens, neither Anderson nor Elder wanted to be associated with the blaze-in-progress.

Stopping at the tree stand, an out-of-breath Dave Anderson had several extraordinary sentences to express to an equally exhausted Jack Elder. "Jack, I know this sounds like *Twilight Zone* science fiction stuff, but I know those three boys that started the woods on fire," the fatigued farmer revealed. "In fact, I vaguely remember one of them telling me the same story we had just witnessed back at the old Gem teen hangout on Central Avenue."

"I suppose that even the impossible is possible in this day and age," Elder gasped and panted. "Don't keep me in suspense, Dave! Who were the young culprits?"

"You won't believe the *time discrepancy,* but the kid that accidentally set the fire was Robbie Williams, who's now serving time in Camden Prison for wife-beating and for armed robbery," Anderson explained before inhaling three consecutive deep breaths. "And the second derelict thug was a constant troublemaker named Charlie Gallagher, who was always either suspended from school, or serving time in office detention. And the third obnoxious punk was a nasty, temperamental kid named Steve Preston who…"

"Who died in a motorcycle accident in 1990!" Jack remembered and indicated with his mouth agape and his eyebrows raised, forming two brown arches. "Hey, wait a cotton-pickin' minute! Holy cowhide, Dave! I also knew those three incorrigible juvenile delinquents! They were always in trouble, and the vice-principals didn't know what to do with them! But please tell me; how could we have observed the three juvenile delinquent punks setting the woods on fire back in 1978 when we're standing right here in 2007! And with Steve Preston being dead that means…"

"We've just experienced something like a mass hallucination!" Anderson suggested in an amazed tone of voice. "Next time you buy me a drink over at DiDonato Lanes, just make sure it's a ginger ale light. Now Jack, forget all about *our* paranormal experience! Let's exit the woods before the fire trucks arrive. I don't want to have to disclose to either Chief Donio or to Chief Sirolli how that crazy conflagration ever got started!"

"You're right about one thing, Dave!" Jack confirmed in a non-too-confident tone of voice. "For verification purposes, I distinctly remember reading in the *Hammonton News* back in 1978 that Butterton Woods had caught on fire, and that both the Hammonton and Elm fire departments had been dispatched to extinguish the flames. And we just saw a 1978 event transpire from our unique vantage point right here in 2007," Elder emphasized and ranted. "Now, I gotta' confess that I definitely believe in ghosts, in the Loch Ness Monster, and in UFOs!"

* * * * * * * * * * * *

The bewildered owner of Butterton Woods was quite certain about a particular cognizance, which Dave Anderson was hesitant of disclosing to his closest friend. "Jack, please don't laugh at me! I don't exactly know how to tell you this truth, but I'm now lost in my own damned woods. This is only a seven-acre stretch of woodlands that I'm quite familiar with and know as well as the back of my hand, yet it seems so vast like, well, like Robin Hood's Sherwood Forest," Dave guiltily divulged to Jack Elder. "I've without a doubt lost my bearings, and my normally dependable senses think we're walking in circles. But what's haunting my mind the most is the idea that

Butterton seems to be fifty-times its regular small dimensions. It's like a weird..."

"Time and spatial distortion, a peculiar time and space warp," the English teacher helped Anderson define *their* mutual dilemma. "Say Dave, be quiet and look over there!" Elder whispered while firmly grabbing his fellow trekker's arm and nodding his head to the right. "I don't know whatever happened to the firemen and their trucks, but I just caught a glimpse of a couple of men from a bygone era carrying primitive-looking shotguns. I don't want to get blasted being mistaken for a deer or a rabbit, so let's not confront these newly arrived trespassers in your woods."

The perplexed friends simultaneously crouched-down to further scrutinize the new-found interlopers. David Anderson was shocked to see *his* father Peter, being accompanied by *his* Uncle Joe, ambling through the woods with shotguns in their right hands and with three rabbits each strung together with thin hemp, the dead creatures dangling from *their* left shoulders. Immediately, Dave believed that the sight his eyes were beholding was a cruel mental aberration, because his father had died in 1974 at the age of seventy-one, and equally as astonishing, his Uncle Joe had passed away in 1968. But presently, the rabbit-stalking, deceased brothers appeared to be young hunters not a day over forty, both gentlemen appearing strong, ambitious, and vibrant. After the avid rabbit hunters had meandered out of sight on a narrow woods' path, Anderson, who was nearly traumatized from his most recent "psychic experience", summoned the courage to express his troubled mind to his companion.

"Jack, those men were my father and my uncle, but as you well know, both have been gone for many years," the shocked farmer sadly related. "Dad served in the Army from 1942-'45 and felt compelled doing so, after the terrible Pearl Harbor sneak attack. Uncle Joe ran the farm for those three-years until Pop proudly returned to the States. My father honorably served his country and fought at the Bulge, I believe, and also at Ardennes Forest," Anderson reviewed and described some family history. "He never liked discussing his heroism, but I know he was shot at numerous times by Nazi soldiers, and I know for a fact that many of his buddies were wounded or killed in action."

"This is some sort of convoluted anachronism," Jack Elder said, "and the amazing conundrum is..."

"Speak plain English!" almost-neurotic Dave Anderson sternly objected. "Stop being so disturbingly academic!"

"What I meant to say is that *we* don't belong in the last two times and places our eyes have witnessed," the English instructor clarified, using more conventional nomenclature. "And what our mortal pupils just perceived doesn't belong in *our* 2007 reality. I think there's some sort of crazy anomaly at play here, er, excuse me Dave," Jack promptly corrected himself. "I meant to say some sort of confusion, or distortion of historical time and of physical space. Everything appears to be bent or skewed, or both bent and skewed."

"Have you considered the wild prospect that if Steve Preston, my dad, and my uncle are all dead and buried, then quite possibly we could be dead, too?" Anderson suggested, feeling an element of hysteria settling into his mind. "I mean there's a distinct possibility that…"

"Nonsense, Dave!" Jack sharply interrupted his now thoroughly distraught friend. "We're still breathing, our hearts are still beating, and the other two kids besides Steve Preston we had seen starting the woods on fire are probably still alive in the year 2007. But maybe," Elder pondered and then slowly uttered, "and this bizarre theory may sound as an implausible stretch of the imagination, but maybe the world has ended since our entrance into Butterton Woods, and perhaps Heaven and Hell forgot to inform us of what had happened to our former reality."

* * * * * * * * * * * *

While still trying to decipher the time-space differentials associated with Butterton Woods, Dave Anderson and Jack Elder persisted in their mania, and after assiduously exploring the vicinity, the duo arrived at an unbeknownst clearing where their keen eyes spotted a pair of early American Indians, apparently holding an impromptu powwow. "Hide behind these two trees," Jack whispered and advised, momentarily taking awkward command. "I can't believe my pupils, Dave! This is absolutely mind-boggling! They're Lenni-Lenapes!"

"Lenny who?" the distraught Anderson stammered. "Sometimes you're speaking to me in an alien form of the English language, where I can't make heads or tails out of your odd jargon! Why would an Indian be called Lenny?"

"Lenni-Lenapes, an old Indian tribe that inhabited this area before the clans were driven west by white British settlers, or put on reservations," the erudite teacher explained in a low voice. "Remember Dave, Indians once populated the entire East Coast, long before there ever was a colony called New Jersey!"

"I get it now," Anderson finally comprehended. "Lenape High School over in Medford has an Indian for its mascot, and my farm market used to get corn from Indian Mills, which is north of Atsion Lake on *206*."

"That's right!" Elder verified in a low voice. "Indian Mills was at one time a reservation for the leftover Lenni-Lenapes. My whole point is that *that* Indian tribe hasn't been around these parts for over a century, and hasn't been wandering-around, hunting for food since the days of George Washington. But don't worry about being attacked, Dave!" Jack softly stated. "The Lenapes were reputed to be peaceful natives that often traded with early South Jersey pioneers. At least, that's what I've read in textbooks! I think your scalp is safe from being non-surgically removed."

"I only hope that some of our demented friends are playing an ugly joke on us, and masquerading around here in Butterton Woods trying to drive us insane," the property owner wished and shared with his all-too-knowledgeable pedagogue pal. "But those two feather-headed Indians patrolling the area with their bows and arrows, who are now walking away into that bracken, look too damned authentic to be wearing costumes and disguises."

"Look, over there!" Jack Elder whispered. "There's a break in the woods, and an open field on the other side with plenty of sunshine beaming-down from the sky. We're almost out of this rustic and very complicated maze; we're gonna' exit this queer contradiction that you had erroneously thought was a small seven-acre parcel of woods exclusively belonging to you."

When the fatigued-but-relieved itinerants eventually departed the weird, verdant flat labyrinth, commonly known as Butterton Woods, the trekkers found no evidence of any red Ford 150 truck, but much to their satisfaction, the woods again appeared (judging from its perimeter) to be its standard dimensions. But Walker Road was no longer paved, and the path was now a very narrow one-lane dirt trail, devoid of telephone poles, electric wires, blueberry fields, peach orchards, farm labor houses, and human activity.

"You know, Jack," Dave Anderson commented before taking two much-needed inhales of oxygen. "It looks like we aren't staggering around in the year 2007 anymore, that's for sure! We're a disoriented pair of time travelers, yes, two pathetic, lost aliens trapped in a different age and time. Look up ahead to what used to be the White Horse Pike!" Anderson implored Elder. "There's an old bearded man behind a horse drawn carriage, heading west toward Berlin, which in colonial times was called…"

"Long-a-Coming!" the scholarly but still-stunned high school teacher answered. "It looks like several passengers seated in the coach are being transported, if not to Berlin, I mean to Long-a-Coming, then to some other western destination, perhaps Camden or Philadelphia. I mean to say, Dave," Jack considered and stated. "Hammonton wasn't incorporated until the 1860s after the Civil War, which quite apparently hasn't even happened yet."

"Now, I get it Jack!" Dave Anderson hollered, exhibiting a degree of enthusiasm. "I see a definite pattern! We've been going backwards in time, ever since we entered Butterton Woods."

"Yes, a reverse chronological order!" Elder astutely recognized and verbalized. "It's all so logically illogical! Consider the three teenagers setting the woods on fire; your' father and uncle hunting rabbits, and then the Lenni-Lenape Indians looking for wild animals to shoot and kill with their bows and arrows," Jack recollected and shared. "This whole incredible scenario is too uncanny to fathom. But somehow, crazily, it all does make a strange sense when you actually think about it!"

The two bewildered amblers trudged ahead, their minds focused on the past, the present, and the future. The companions theorized that if they had somehow migrated from the twenty-first back into the eighteenth-century, then the duo would have to adapt accordingly to their new time/place environment. 'Was George Washington the President of the United States? Had the Revolutionary War occurred yet? If so, how many states are now in the Union? Was the War of 1812 going on?' Jack Elder mused. 'Have Edgar Allan Poe and Mark Twain been born yet?'

Certain intricate thoughts were also rattling around inside Dave Anderson's mind. 'I wonder what my wife and kids look like if I have a wife and kids? I might even have a new wife without having any children? Or I might be a colonial-era bachelor energetically trying to tame my immediate environment!' Anderson speculated. 'I wonder if I'm even married at all?' Both the man's curiosity and his random reverie were snapped upon again hearing Jack Elder's shaky baritone voice.

"Dave, there's a dilapidated house up ahead, and I gotta' believe it's yours," Elder articulated while having difficulty retaining his very active excitement. "There're several pig and chicken pens in the rear, and a few goats and cows inside a fenced-in pasture. And that old barn is probably used to house the family horse, if indeed you're wealthy enough to own one," Jack lectured without any lectern. "But it's certainly not a Dutch colonial house I see, even though we're apparently trapped in colonial times! I'm really baffled! This entire bizarre phenomenon is all still very incomprehensible to me!"

"My God!" the still-astounded David Henry Anderson bellowed. "My home-sweet-home isn't exactly made out of chocolate and strawberry shortcake! But Jack, we'll have to forget all about the year 2007, and learn how to live and survive in the distant past!"

"You know, Dave. Now I wish that you'd never brought me out to Butterton Woods to check on your highly coveted tree stand," Jack Elder regretted and complained. "But I'll tell you one thing worthy of hearing!"

"What's that?" Dave fearfully replied as the farmer stared at the ramshackle wooden dwelling and accompanying stone chimney, three-hundred-feet ahead.

"It's a lot better being alive in the year 1750 or 1800 than being dead in technologically advanced 2007," Jack Elder sermonized to Dave Anderson. "At least that's my personal opinion. Take it for what it's worth!"

"The Fabulous '50s"

Kirk Mason and Phil Lindsay had been close friends ever since their early teen years at the Hammonton Middle School. After graduating from Hammonton High in 2005, The New Jersey duo attended *Rowan University* in Glassboro, with Kirk Mason studying journalism, and Phil Lindsay aspiring to be an electrical engineer. Kirk was a Democrat/Presbyterian and Phil a Republican/Roman Catholic, but the one major bond that the Mimosa Dorm' roommates had in common was their dual infatuations with the long-gone Fabulous '50s era. Their second-floor dorm' room was loaded with '50s memorabilia, and Kirk had a fantastic 45 rpm record collection of '50s hits, and Phil owned reels of rare-and-vintage black and white video footage from such early television teen shows as *American Bandstand, Hullabaloo,* and *Your Hit Parade.* Mason often said, "We really major in '50s nostalgia with a minor in the best songs, television shows, and movies of the early 1960s." The Marilyn Monroe, John Wayne, and James Dean posters adorning their Mimosa Hall room walls adequately verified the pair's fascination with *that* legendary, and often glorified, past American decade.

"It's finally arriving on the calendar! Next week's spring break," Phil reminded Kirk while standing in line for coffee inside the massive *Rowan University Student Union* downstairs lounge. "And I'm really pumped-up about our upcoming trip out to Los Angeles. We might even get to see a Hollywood star or two in our travels! Or perhaps while in L.A., we could rent a car and take a side trip into the desert to Palm Springs to see the winter homes of the stars. And I've been intensely studying a map of *that* exotic resort area," Lindsay continued his extended oration, "and Fred Waring Drive in Palm Desert, and also Dinah Shore Drive and Bob Hope Drive located in nearby Rancho Mirage, all seem worthy of us visiting. That is," Phil proceeded with his lengthy litany, "that is if we get tired of touring *Disneyland* in Anaheim and looking at and admiring an empty *Dodger Stadium* in Chavez Ravine."

"Yeah, it sure beats the monotony and the drudgery of taking final exams' in mid-January, or even finals in early May," Kirk readily agreed. "And I can't wait to leave the cold winter weather behind and trade it all for a whole ten days, just to walk around in the warm California sun. Hey Phil!" Mason noted while sporting a genuine smile. "That catchy tune 'California Sun' was a 1964 hit performed by the Rivieras and manufactured by Riviera Records, not to mention that most excellent Beach Boys' 1965 classic masterpiece 'California Girls' produced by Capitol Records. And also while on the relevant subject of West Coast culture," Mason characteristically vociferated, "let's not forget the Mamas and the Papas 1966 smash 'California Dreamin' on the Dunhill label. Now Phil, right now I feel like singing 'California Here We Come,' but *that* weird tune was popular way before our generation, and it was played exclusively on the radio even before the advent of the Fabulous '50s! I think way back then all of the records were 33s and 78s."

"Well, Kirk," Phil Lindsay replied before paying for his coffee, "we've been saving our spare cash for two whole years now to fly out west and experience California, the birthplace of Jan and Dean and Beach Boys' surfing songs. And maybe if we hang around a few drugstores in the vicinity of Hollywood and Vine, some alert talent agent will discover us, and we'll wind-up at Paramount Pictures or Universal Studios," the young dreamer mused and laughed. "Or if that unlikely occurrence doesn't happen, and the scandal-oriented tabloids never find out about us and our talent," Lindsay satirically jested, "we could always buy some standard tour bus tickets and enviously gawk at the Beverly Hills mansions of the old movie stars. Unfortunately, we both have the dream and the drive, but not the required singing skill and good acting ability!"

The highly anticipated March date of departure finally arrived, and Jim Armstrong, a Mimosa Dorm' friend of the two avid '50s fans, drove Mason and Lindsay to the United Airlines Terminal at Philadelphia International Airport.

"Don't sign too many autographs out West!" Jim quipped as Kirk and Phil exited Armstrong's rusty *Ford Focus*. "And if you two college dreamers ever manage to become stars, I'll study about you in Dr. Adrian's astronomy class!"

"I'd tell you off Wise Guy if Phil and I didn't need a ride from the airport back to Glassboro after our return flight!" Kirk sarcastically-but-jokingly retorted. "Now Jim, don't forget where your gas pedal is before you get a traffic ticket for illegally stopping in this No-Parking Zone to discharge passengers. Can't you read the signs? This is a restricted area!"

Fifteen-minutes later, the westbound roommates had satisfactorily cleared their security checks, and then two hours afterwards, were boarding their United Airlines jumbo jet. And after a brief stop at O'Hare in Chicago several hours later, the enthusiastic pair was again airborne and swiftly heading toward the West Coast. Everything was progressing smoothly, "according to Hoyle", without an interruption or a hitch.

"We'll rent a car at the airport and then drive to the Best Western Sunset Plaza Hotel, which according to this map, is conveniently located in downtown L.A.," Kirk mentioned to his favorite companion while flying over Colorado. "I'm really glad we were able to book that place. And in the flight magazine I was just reading stated that Warner Brothers Studios of 3400 Riverside Drive, Burbank 91505, conducts comprehensive movie lot tours. Now Phil, contrary to my propensity for being disorganized," Mason jested, "I think we oughta' prioritize our destinations! Let's put *Dodger Stadium,* Beverly Hills, and *Disneyland* on hold. And as the inimitable Randy Newman often sang..."

"I Love L.A.!" Phil finished his euphoric pal's statement. "Oh yeah, Kirk! I can feel it already! Palm trees, warm climate, bagel joints, and Starbucks coffee palaces all over the place. Let's leave South Padre Island, Texas, and Panama City, Florida to the dull, uninspired college crowd! Southern California is where the real action is, without a doubt. I have a feeling that this is going to be a spring-break vacation to remember! And I know you're just as excited as I am about this trip."

* * * * * * * * * * * *

After renting a cheery-looking blue *Chevy Malibu* from *Budget,* Kirk cautiously drove through heavy downtown traffic to the Best Western Sunset Plaza. After checking into the well-maintained hotel, the two new guests promptly changed into their swimming trunks and sat poolside, drinking large *Pepsi Colas.* Contemplating their prospective Warner Brothers Studios tour, *that* particular venue highly anticipated dominated their conversation.

"I had inquired about some tour information at the main desk while you were preoccupied buying a newspaper over in the lobby gift shop," Kirk Mason said to the easily distracted Phil Lindsay, whose eyes were focused on two bikini-clad girls. "A bus to Warner Brothers departs just three blocks from here at 8:30 tomorrow morning. And who says I'm not a valid humanitarian?" Mason rhetorically asked. "I've already obtained two authentic tour tickets. I'm not gonna' tell you how much they cost, because *your* tour admission is a belated birthday present. Now Phil," Kirk stipulated with a wry grin expressed on his countenance upon him also noticing the two scantily clad dolls, "my birthday is in three days, and I fully expect you to reciprocate my generosity."

"I shall!" Philip Jackson Lindsay answered and promised, using extraordinarily proper English grammar. "I can't wait to inspect the various Warner movie sets and sound studios! I'll bet we'll recognize each one we visit. I hope they still have some stuff from *Rebel without a Cause.* James Dean and Natalie Wood were really tremendous in that outstanding flick! That's gotta' be my favorite film from the '50s!"

"Yeah, without a doubt!" Kirk Franklin Mason affirmed, showing mild disappointment as a pair of muscular studs arrived at poolside to casually converse with the dual knockout chicks. "But *American Graffiti* and *Grease* from the '70s, and *Eddie and the Cruisers* and *The Outsiders* from the '80s were really decent '50s era films, too. But you're absolutely right about one very important thing! *Rebel without a Cause* was a very realistic '50s movie that was *actually* filmed in the 1950s!"

"And let's not forget *Blackboard Jungle* and *The Blob!"* Phil academically added. "That science-fiction marvel, of course, I'm referring to *The Blob,* was Steve McQueen's first movie. It was mostly filmed in Downingtown, a small community just outside of Philly'. I could watch the really cool blob attack inside the town's movie-house over and over!"

"And *Blackboard Jungle's* familiar theme song was 'Rock Around the Clock' by Bill Haley and the Comets," Kirk knowledgeably added. "That band originated from Chester, Pennsylvania, and in the mid-50s Bill Haley often played gigs at Wildwood clubs and at other small bar venues up and down the Jersey shore! That wonderful breakthrough song was released in 1954, but only sold around thirty-thousand copies," the expert '50s music encyclopedia remarked. "But then after *Blackboard Jungle* hit the wide silver screen, a year later, in 1955, 'Rock Around the Clock' became the replacement national anthem for '50s teenagers. The new-beat record sold well over a million copies, and it instantly launched rock and roll music and teen rebellion into national prominence, much to the dismay of apprehensive politicians and

308

worried parents! I truthfully wish I could've lived during that wonderful time."

The following morning, Mason and Lindsay strolled the three city blocks to board the red and white bus to Warner Brothers Studios. Twelve other tourists, hungry for a taste of Hollywood, had also purchased tickets at their respective hotels. The designated bus soon rumbled its way towards Burbank, while tour guide Mrs. Joan Cameron narrated and described various points of interest along the route. When the half-full vehicle finally reached its destination, everyone departed, and soon the anxious newcomers were instructed to wait at an assigned merchandise concession stand while Mrs. Cameron received specific directions about her group boarding smaller vans, to either tour certain set locations, or visit specific sound studios where famous movies had been shot. But being rambunctious college students, Kirk and Phil were very independent-minded and had their own sense of adventure, especially when their restless spirits felt challenged to clandestinely explore new environments.

"Let's wander down the street a bit and check-out a few things on our own," Kirk Mason softly suggested. "Mrs. Cameron will never notice that we're missing, and our little deviation from the group will only take about five-minutes or so. I've always loathed the idea of being one of the mindless masses! And besides, most of the others we're with are gabby senior citizens, relentlessly flashing their precious AARP cards around!"

"I hate the herd mentality just as much as you do," concurred Phil Lindsay. "The word 'Don't!' isn't in my vocabulary, and ever since I was a mere toddler, every time somebody in authority tells me 'Don't!', I can't resist the temptation to behave to the contrary. That's my general nature in a nutshell, and I haven't changed my stubborn disposition since kindergarten!"

The two audacious wanderers promptly trekked a block from their aged-and-retired tourist peers, none of whom noticed their departure because the other Warner Brothers' guests were busy exchanging anecdotes about the various sights that Mrs. Joan Cameron had pointed-out en route to the "Studios". The bold-hearted New Jersey duo soon approached a dark alley with a traffic sign giving the imposing warning: "Do Not Enter: Off Limits to the Public."

"I never liked grammar imperative sentences, even in middle school English class," Kirk commented after reading the posted language. "Call me a potential anarchist if you like, but I never savored being told what to do, or what not to do!"

"You're right about that and I share your defiant attitude!" Phil acceded, showing some recalcitrant gumption of his own. "I interpret the warning as an open invitation for us to dare venturing where threatening words forbid us from entering. Let's scoot down the shadowy alley pronto, before any loyal and alert Warner Brothers' security guards detect our presence."

At the end of the narrow, shaded lane was the very conspicuous entrance to Lucky's Night Club, a '50s restaurant with an art deco exterior and glitzy interior design, featuring neon beer brand signs, and also wall sketches of famous '50s stage, TV, music, and movie icons. The establishment's bar, which had been constructed with traditional concave and convex square glass tiles, was not well illuminated, and an abundance of dense smoke filled the shadowy room's air. Kirk and Phil slowly sauntered through the clusters of chatting patrons and were amazed at the very familiar identities of those customers congregated there.

"This must be some sort of masquerade; a weird costume party that we've accidentally intruded upon," Kirk perceived and uttered to his equally stunned associate. "Look over there! If I'm not mistaken, the two bartenders look like carbon-copy facsimiles of Jackie Gleason and Jimmy Durante."

"Oh my God!" Phil exclaimed, slapping his face to confirm his own perception of a convoluted reality. "Look all around us at the clientele standing and sitting around the circular bar. There are comedians Red Skelton and Phil Silvers to our left, and over to our right, we have Milton Berle conversing with Ernie Kovacs. And further to our left is Danny Kaye having a dialogue with Groucho Marx! God Kirk!" Lindsay gasped and then coughed. "The heavy cigar smoke in here is as thick as soup!"

"And just look at the famous patrons sitting at the various tables!" Kirk whispered after curiously turning-around to survey the rest of his surroundings. "There's Charlton Heston, Dinah Shore, Johnny Carson, and Lucille Ball at that first table, and Faye Emerson, Elvis Presley, Arthur Godfrey, and Arlene Francis seated and chatting at that second one. And over there to the left we have..."

"The McGuire Sisters at the table underneath the colorful Tiffany lamp, eating suppe. with Lawrence Welk. And that's Janet Leigh, Stuart Granger, Mickey Mantle, and Walt Disney sitting adjacent to

310

the three singing sisters, who incidentally are speaking and not singing! And oh yes. I recognize Burt Lancaster, Kirk Douglas, Frank Sinatra, and Ted Mack parked at that corner table to the rear. And over there we have…"

"Marilyn Monroe, Vincent Price, Red Buttons, Captain Kangaroo, and Pinky Lee!" marveled and exhaled Kirk Mason. "Phil, I honestly don't know whether this is an enchanted dream or a horrendous nightmare! I gotta' pinch myself to make sure everything my eyes are currently witnessing is real!"

Jimmy Durante approached the alarmed twosome and announced in a deep bass voice, "Good night, Mrs. Calabash, wherever you are! Ha, ha, ha!" much to the delight and humor of the congregated and already-amused bar regulars. "What'll it' be boys? Scotch and soda? *Southern Comfort* Manhattans? Screwdrivers? Martinis? Whiskey sours?"

"Just give me a….ah yes, a frosty bottle of *Budweiser!*" Kirk answered before accidentally saying *Coor's Light*, which according to his memory, probably didn't exist back in the '50s.

"I'll have the same!" chimed-in Phil Lindsay. "Yeah, a cold bottle of *Budweiser* sounds good to me!"

"You guys make my job entirely too easy!" the big nosed, deep voiced drink server facetiously complained. "How are you two young handsome fellas' ever goin' to get dates to your college mixers when ya' don't even order mixed drinks! Ha, ha, ha!"

Everyone standing and seated around Lucky's Bar boisterously laughed in response to Jimmy Durante's lackluster play-on-words. While the congenial bartender opened an ice chest to acquire the two ordered brown bottles of *Budweiser,* Kirk softly said to his good friend, "This whole place is givin' me the creeps! It's a good thing I saw that *Budweiser* neon sign on the side wall over there, or else I might've out of force of habit ordered a *Coor's Light* or a *Michelob Light!* I could've had a lot of explaining to do to these human illusions, or these apparitions, or these impersonators, or whatever else *they* happen to be!"

"Then, who knows what might've happened next?" Phil Lindsay neurotically replied, shaking his head in disbelief at the incredible anachronism prevalent all-around Mason and himself. "Here comes Jackie Gleason steppin' over to jolly us! Let's try and figure-out what this crazy zombie scenario is all about!"

"Hey guys!" Jackie amiably greeted his new customers. "One of these days, one of these days, pow! Right in the kisser!" the chunky comedian un-loquaciously screamed, making a clenched fist and then winding-up and delivering a wild pretend punch to an imaginary face. All of the famous, surreal personages who were gathered around the bar, again broke-out into a howling roar, the overall clamor echoing off of all of the extraordinary nightclub's walls. And then Jackie Gleason raised his huge elbows, along with his chubby left leg, and elicited another burst of laughter by loudly yelling, "And away we go!"

"Here's your two cold bottles of *Budweiser!*" Jimmy Durante politely stated. "Drink to your hearts' content, even though the brew is goin' directly down to your stomachs! Ha, ha, ha!" Everyone (except Mason and Lindsay) crowded inside Lucky's Night Club broke-out in another display of wild hysteria. The two strangers were on the verge of experiencing mutual panic attacks.

"Hey, what do you two greenhorns think of the new four cent stamps' that were just issued!" Jackie Gleason asked, feigning a serious tone of voice. "Most people think that the increase in postage is way too expensive!"

"Well, I guess inflation is happening all across the nation," Kirk nervously answered. "And the government needs the extra revenue to pay its bills. But the real danger is that inflation could lead to an economic recession! And the country doesn't need to revisit 1929, now does it?"

"How do you like the way the *Korean War* went?" Jimmy Durante seriously asked Phil above the din of the crowd. "And give me your honest opinion. Do ya' think that Eisenhower is a better President than Truman was?"

"I believe that they were both very good chief executives," Lindsay diplomatically replied, before wiping some accumulated sweat beads from his brow. "But I was taught as a youngster that it isn't polite to discuss religion or politics with strangers, or with talkative bartenders in public."

"Okay, then Wise Guy. Who do ya' like winning the upcoming World Series, the Milwaukee Braves or the Yankees?" Jackie Gleason asked Phil. "I'm an American League guy, and I got my money on the Bronx Bombers!"

"Definitely the Braves!" the *Rowan University* student with the photographic memory replied. "They're gonna' get especially lucky in this year's Series, just you wait and see."

And after Jackie Gleason and Jimmy Durante turned their backs to privately confer on a confidential matter, Phil impatiently said to Kirk, "These obnoxious celebrities think it's the fall of 1957. The Milwaukee Braves beat the New York Yankees in the World Series, four games to three," the '50s sports' guru said. "And something's really bothering me, Kirk. These notorious people gathered in this oddball bar and restaurant are mostly…"

"All dead!" Kirk realized and expressed with horror. "All deader than door-nails, as Charles Dickens once said, er, I mean wrote!" Mason paraphrased.

Then, corpulent Jackie Gleason again wandered-over to their vicinity, faced Kirk and Phil, and ominously said with his hands on his hips, "Tell me, Creeps! What do ya' have to say about that Sputnik satellite the lousy Russians just launched into space? I hate to admit it, but those raunchy Communists have a better education system than we do. Just like the newspapers say, we need more math' and science in the public-school curriculums, yes, we do!"

"It's only a temporary advantage that the Soviets are enjoying," Kirk almost apologetically replied, using his knowledge of modern world history as his basis for answering. "Have faith in America. The United States will eventually catch-up and then easily surpass the narrow-minded Russians."

Everyone assembled at the crowded bar and inside the tavern had suddenly become quiet, and the smoky chamber was as silent as the moon, just when Kirk Mason had convincingly given his sage and historically accurate commentary. Dinah Shore unexpectedly came traipsing over to the weird bar and then sang out loud, "See the USA, in your Chevrolet!" And not to be outdone, Betty Furness showed-up next to pretty Dinah Shore, put her hand over the blonde-hair singer's mouth, and yelled out, "You can be sure if it's *Westinghouse!*"

"Buy those two young geniuses drinks on me!" Red Skelton bellowed, referring to Mason and Lindsay, while holding his martini high into the air. "Those nutcase lads are okay in my book! Give the talkative fools anything the dumb morons want!"

"Yes, buy them each another drink on me, too!" Milton Berle boomed. "I'm in an uncommonly generous mood! I'll even pay for two drinks each!"

Soon, Phil Silvers, Red Buttons, Pinky Lee, Danny Kaye, and Ernie Kovacs were all demanding that each entertainer should also buy drinks for Kirk and Phil, and even previously unnoticed patrons Bob Hope, Judy Garland, Steve Allen, and Jack Paar were insisting on treating the two young visitors to potent alcoholic beverages.

"We'd better get the heck outa' here before we're so inebriated that we can't stand up!" wisely recommended Kirk Mason. "These wacko TV, radio, and movie stars are gonna' kill us by means of intoxication. Let's pretend we gotta' hit the latrine and then scamper out of here like two frightened jackrabbits, while our vital motor skills are still functioning!"

"Tonight, we're going to have a really big show!" a previously undetected Ed Sullivan loudly shouted into Kirk's ear. "Next week, we're going to have Elvis Presley as our special guest singer! Now let's show our appreciation by having a good round of applause for these two young men, who have bravely stepped-up to the bar from our viewing audience!"

"My sentiments exactly!" Phil Lindsay very passionately verified to the now-aghast Mason. "This crazy asylum scene is somewhere between atrocious and abominable! Let's drastically run for our lives while we still have lives to keep!"

Without demonstrating any more procrastination, the startled friends simultaneously turned and then bolted like frightened antelopes through the '50s celebrity crowd, quickly exiting the premises via the front door, which mysteriously doubled as a portal into an Old West town's frontier studio setting.

Both Mason and Lindsay were confounded, finding themselves standing in front of a livery barn with the Laredo Sheriff's Office and a stereotypical saloon, featuring swinging-wooden-doors. The saloon was located directly across the dirt and gravel street from the Livery. A grim-faced John Wayne was seated upon a well-groomed chestnut horse, organizing a posse to pursue the villainous Dalton Gang, who had just pilfered a stash of cash from the all-too-vulnerable Laredo Bank. Suddenly, the motion-picture hero recognized the presence of the two new arrivals.

"Hey, you two Strangers over there!" the eminent actor yelled at Mason and Lindsay. "Yeah, I mean you two cactus heads! Go into the Livery and tell Old Hank ya' need two fresh steeds to complement my posse. Then, join-up with me, and I'll officially deputize ya' both to help bring law and order to this uncivilized

314

town!" John Wayne vehemently ordered. "Now, get goin' before I have a hankerin' to throw ya' two weird-lookin' dudes into the hoosegow for defyin' my authority and rest assured *Pilgrims,* it'll be my unique pleasure to then toss away the rusty key!"

Mason and Lindsay's eyes keenly surveyed their immediate environment, and the perceptive intruders easily identified other members of the assembled posse as Hopalong Cassidy (William Boyd), Roy Rogers, Gene Autry, the Lone Ranger (Clayton Moore), Tonto (Jay Silverheels), Cochise (Michael Ansara), Marshal Matt Dillon (James Arness), the Cisco Kid (Duncan Rinaldo), Pancho (Leo Carillo), Paladin (Richard Boone), Bret Maverick (James Garner), Bat Masterson (Gene Barry), the Rifleman (Chuck Connors), Wild Bill Hickok (Guy Madison), and last but not least, raspy-voiced Jingles (Andy Devine).

The Lone Ranger approached Mason and Lindsay and inquired in a stern-but-honest tone of voice, "Have either of you greenhorns seen the new Broadway play *A Visit to a Small Planet?* It's based on the book having the same title, written by Gore Vidal, I believe? I can't wait to go to New York and see it!"

"Er no, but I've heard about it!" Mason stammered and then paused. "But I didn't know that flying saucers and space aliens were popular in the Old West!"

"This isn't the Old West!" interrupted Paladin. "Don't you two encroachers get it? This is only a silly movie set, constructed to look like the Old West!"

"I presume you've both seen the science fiction movie *War of the Worlds.* But what about *The Music Man?"* masked Clayton Moore persisted. "It's a terrific musical! Meredith Wilson had authored it. And it's gonna' open in two months at the Majestic Theater in New York. I've read in the newspapers that the stage show's gonna' star Robert Preston and Barbara Cook. I can't wait to attend that baby! I hear the songs are spectacular!"

Before either Mason or Lindsay could formulate a logical reply, Richard Boone felt obligated to present himself as a misplaced motion picture critic. "I predict that *The Music Man* will be such a Broadway success that there's gonna' be a Cinemascope film made of it, being produced within the next two years," Paladin seriously prognosticated. "And I augur that the upcoming movie will be just as profitable as last year's Academy Award winner *Around the World in*

Eighty Days, even though I can't stand David Niven and think he's an absolute pompous snob!"

Sheriff John Wayne then angrily shouted from atop his chestnut, "Hey you weird-looking two buffoons over there! I already told you varmints to get your rear ends over to see Old Hank right this second, or else you'll both have so much heavy buckshot up your butts that you'll never again be able to get the lead out!"

Being overwhelmed with intense anxiety, Kirk and Phil scurried down the western town's only dirt street until the road surface finally turned to asphalt. The fatigued pair ceased their scampering just before encountering Dean Martin talking with two voluptuous buxom Janes, Jane Russell and Jayne Mansfield.

Glancing to their right, Mason and Lindsay hastily read the heading over a nearby building's entrance: District 5 Police Headquarters. Seeking protection from their "insane *Psycho* surroundings," the addled visitors to Warner Brothers Studios innocently stepped inside the edifice to escape the general lunacy that seemed to have enveloped them outside. Seated behind cluttered desks inside the musty police department office were *Dragnet's* Sergeant Joe Friday (Jack Webb) and Detective Frank Smith (Ben Alexander), Peter Gunn (Craig Stevens), Eliot Ness (Robert Stack), and in the far-right corner stood Efrem Zimbalist, Jr. and Ed "Kookie" Byrnes, popular actors from the '50s hit TV series, *77 Sunset Strip.*

"I want the facts and only the facts!" Sergeant Friday sanctimoniously demanded. "Now then, what do you two pathetic clowns think of Vice President Richard M. Nixon's recent activities? He seems like an honest and decent guy to me, but I've heard some confidential reports that the fool is a conniving weasel that can't be trusted!" Jack Webb snarled. "We're coordinating our efforts with the FBI, and together, we're collecting a portfolio of evidential information on the unstable, insecure Republican politician. I'm determined to pin some rap on Nixon, if it's the last thing I do!"

"There might be some truth in *that* allegation about Nixon being a sinister person," Kirk boldly declared and then gulped. "His clandestine activities might actually be investigated in the future. Your Vice President might, in the end, turn-out to be an unscrupulous, scurrilous character!"

"Say, isn't he *your* Vice President, too?" maintained Jack Webb's investigative partner. "Nixon can't be all that bad!" Detective Frank

Smith argued. "After all, the newspaper polls show that he and Eisenhower will surely be re-elected to second terms. I disagree with what Joe says. Richard M. Nixon is all right in my book. And my ugly wife and my pretty girlfriend both think that his dog Checkers is pretty swell, too!"

"Have it your way," conceded Phil Lindsay. "Every dam has its water gate!"

"What's *that* idiotic comment supposed to mean?" yelled the formerly reticent Peter Gunn. "Tell that *dam* stuff to Herbert Hoover's ghost, ha, ha, ha!"

"You two punks out lookin' for Frank Nitty or Al Capone?" Eliot Ness asked. "What about John Dillinger? Are you two guys private investigators? Say, you two strangely dressed knuckleheads aren't involved with bootlegging activities and the flourishing illicit speakeasy trade, are ya'?"

"Er no," Mason defensively answered. "We're like water to a tea bag, just passing through!"

"Oh, regular Wise Guys!" Efrem Zimbalist, Jr. concluded and expressed. "Your last name is probably Mr. Lipton! And I suppose that you think that the average factory worker is worth more than $2.08 per hour. You two bozos are probably liberal spending, war-mongering Democrats, huh?" the enraged detective weirdly accused, gesticulating wildly with his hands.

"What do you' dumbbells think of the recent racial violence in Little Rock, Arkansas?" Sergeant Joe Friday toughly interrogated his two itinerant visitors. "Eisenhower just sent a thousand U.S. Army paratroopers into Little Rock to enforce the integration of Central High School. What a national fiasco!"

"That's cool as a ghoul in a swimming pool, and the folks there are sayin' there's a fungus among us!" jive-talked the previously reticent Ed "Kookie" Byrnes. "Tell your mama, tell your pa', we're gonna' send ya' back to Arkansas, ha, ha, ha! Hey, Big Daddies. Can either of you two cool cats lend me your comb!"

Hawaii Five-O's Jack Lord appeared in the foyer doorway and announced in a threatening tone of voice, "I don't even have to say 'Book 'em Danno' because I'm here and could perform *that* needed duty all by myself!! Let's get the cuffs out, and slap the derbies on these two obnoxious imbeciles!"

Thinking that it was then time to immediately evacuate the arcane police headquarters, Kirk and Phil spontaneously became dashing young men as the pair scooted in unison to the precinct's front door. Soon, the terrorized escapees were hustling up the asphalt street and sprinting right past Art Carnie (dressed as Norton), affably chatting with Audrey Meadows and June Allison. The exhausted duo then ceased their bustle and observed an overhead marquee, its singular ledger reading: "Enter: Live Studio Audience Television Show Now In Progress."

Four burly, overzealous stagehands quickly opened a door, grabbed Mason and Lindsay by their arms, and physically dragged them in the direction of the live program's Master of Ceremonies, Ralph Edwards. "Okay, ladies and gentlemen. It's now time for us to meet our principal guests for today's very important show. May I proudly present to our studio and national television audiences our two honored guests from New Jersey. Yes, Kirk Mason and Philip Lindsay, this is your life!"

The befuddled, on-stage honorees were both staggered and surprised. "Have a seat, gentlemen, and welcome to our program where you'll both be receiving ample public recognition. As you know," Ralph Edwards read from nearby raised Idiot Cards, "our last honoree was Marilyn Elaine Van Derbur from Colorado, our reigning Miss America, who was recently crowned in Atlantic City. Marilyn was our main biography before her debut on 'This Is Your Life!' Before *her* recognition was non-other than U.S. Surgeon General Leroy E. Burney. Have you two gentlemen gotten over your surprise, and are you now ready to have your secret lives revealed to all of America?"

Not wanting any undesirable '50s notoriety, Mason, followed by Lindsay, stood-up from their chairs and alertly fled the theater's stage, much to the anger and chagrin of Ralph Edwards. In seconds, the duo was speeding by the muscular stage hands, and soon Kirk and Phil were again positioned outside the studio upon the asphalt street, their sweating bodies darting by crooner Dean Martin, still conversing with Jane Russell and Jayne Mansfield. A moment later, the dazed and flustered *Rowan University* students stopped on the city set's pavement to catch their breaths.

"I don't wanna' have my whole life exposed on national TV to a lot of gossiping people we don't know," Kirk confessed to his equally distressed traveling mate. "Maybe even our parents will be watching as teenagers, never even realizing that we're their kids! I

318

just had to get out of that place before my privacy rights, along with my shrinking sanity, were violated."

"Who says that '50s television wasn't intimidating, intrusive, and threatening?" Phil Lindsay sympathetically agreed, fearing the unknown unintended consequences that might have occurred should the two had remained on the stage with bossy Ralph Edwards. "I can't resist the dire hope of getting out of this queer dimension, the sooner the better! *Rowan University* and Mimosa Dorm' never looked so good!"

The discomfited friends meandered up the ancient in-need-of-repair sidewalk, weaving their way through knots of famous and not-so-famous people, and heading in the direction of Lucky's Night Club. Something significant then popped into Kirk Mason's head, who shared a pertinent observation with his staunch companion.

"Say, Phil. We just walked from the police station to the TV studio, and now we're incidentally back in the vicinity of Lucky's Night Club," the '50s memorabilia buff stated. "But we never passed through ..."

"Laredo!" Phil Lindsay exclaimed. "The whole old Wild West town with John Wayne in charge of law enforcement has somehow mysteriously disappeared. It's now completely absent from the space it had formerly occupied! To be even more specific, Kirk, the space the town had occupied is missing, too!"

And then to add to Mason and Lindsay's overall consternation, Jackie Gleason, wearing a dirty white apron, exited Lucky's Night Club and aggressively accosted the pair. "Sorry, Gentlemen," the obese comedian sarcastically began. "But it's my distinct pleasure to inform you that you'll both have to spend the rest of your lives as set extras, working here on location until you die. After *that* inevitable event happens to you two Dolts," Gleason stressed with a contrived smile, "then you two nosy punk trespassers can become behind-the-scenes members of our synonymous '50s Movie and TV Guild."

Not wanting to believe the veracity of Jackie Gleason's depiction of *their* present reality, Kirk Franklin Mason and Philip Jackson Lindsay again sought escape and requiem from their enormously incredible "imaginary dilemma". The very frightened California dreamers fled down the dark alley and darted towards the Warner Brothers Studios' main tourist area. Suddenly, both young men violently collided with a Plexi-glass partition separating their very captivating '50s world from the 2008 tourist scenario quite observable to them on the other side.

"Get us out! Get us out!" Kirk futilely screamed while thrusting and futilely banging his fists. "We're trapped! We're trapped! Get us the hell out of here!"

"It's no use!" Phil yelled to his paranoid companion. "The listless people on the outside can't hear or see us, but we can hear and see them! Kirk, we're destined to become life-long masochists! How torturous can life be?"

"Dunderheads, pound-away to your hearts' content!" an out-of-breath Jackie Gleason yelled and then snickered. "That solid transparent barrier is both soundproof and sight-proof from the outside! Ha, ha, ha!"

"Now people," Mrs. Joan Cameron lectured to her phlegmatic and tired tour bus passengers. "Where can those two defiant young men have gone? Their names are Kirk Mason and Philip Lindsay," the peeved woman in the red uniform revealed to her obedient senior citizen listeners as she again studied the list of names in her hands. "They've already missed three really great studio tours! If they don't show-up in two minutes, we'll have to board our bus and return to center city L.A. without them."

"Does this sort of thing happen often?" a concerned elderly tour bus lady asked.

"Much more often lately!" Mrs. Joan Cameron answered in utter disgust. "If only people would learn to follow simple directions, it would make my job and my life so much easier!"

"The Music Portal"

Up until four months ago, I had regarded my very ordinary life as being a dismal failure. My mediocre occupation, ever since I was fresh out of high school, has been that of a dissatisfied shoe salesman at Brock Shoes Outlet in Berlin, New Jersey. For thirty-one miserable years, I would loyally commute each working day from my French Street home in nearby Hammonton, a flourishing agricultural community located twelve-miles east of Berlin that is conveniently situated midway between vacation destination Atlantic City and bustling Philadelphia, Pennsylvania. The distance being thirty-miles in either direction from my house to the East Coast gambling Mecca and to Benjamin Franklin's City of Brotherly Love.

The principal factor that I do remember about my former employment was that I absolutely loathed being a common shoe salesman, feigning cheerfulness daily, having to look at some very ugly feet over the course of the last three-plus decades, and unfortunately, having to smell some horrible stenches emanating from the toes of people who apparently neglected taking frequent baths and showers. Many shoe customers showed little regard for the psychological needs of a disgruntled oxfords, loafers and sandals' salesman, who never seemed to have the desired exact size or the precise color on the Brock Shoes Outlet's stockroom shelves.

And my family life (or lack thereof) also had immensely contributed to my chronic emotionally depressed condition. My materialistic wife Virginia had left me seven-years-ago for a more prosperous man, a prominent Hammonton blueberry farmer owning (through inheritance) a highly lucrative five-hundred-acre plantation on Middle Road. And to add to my quandary, my three children have disowned me, preferring to side with their now rich mother who continuously and generously dotes on them. My former wife helps the avaricious siblings with their high-cost college tuitions, with their monthly car payments, and with their often-solicited recreation money.

Yes, all was utter despair in my lackluster financial existence, with my only real joy being the bad habit of blowing most of my spare money in various Atlantic City casinos. In time, *that* wretched addictive activity had become almost an uncontrollable obsession. Bally's Casino, Harrah's Hotel, the Showboat, Caesar's World, the

Trump Taj Mahal, the Trump Marina, the Trump Plaza, Resorts International, the Borgata, the Claridge, and the Hilton all provided my need for greed with basic gambling venue/entertainment while simultaneously confirming to my fragile psyche that I was a born loser, and was surely destined to die as one.

But then last July 16th, 2008 (on a Wednesday if my undependable memory serves me correctly), I had attended the annual carnival feast of Our Lady of Mt. Carmel at the fairgrounds on Third Street, across from St. Joseph Catholic Church. Although I'm not the most congenial or convivial person in the world, I've always been a religious fellow, and somewhat superstitious too, if I may mention *that* ancillary fact.

After attending the morning Mass that commemorates the annual festival, I sanctimoniously lit a candle next to the Hammonton church's altar and tabernacle. Then, after stepping outside the building, I faithfully pinned a hundred-dollar bill on the statue of Our Lady of Mt. Carmel in the traditional Italian noon street procession that immediately followed the sacred church observances.

Later that afternoon, I indulged in swallowing-down two pepper and sausage sandwiches at the Assumption Concession Stand that had been erected inside the St. Joseph Church asphalt parking lot to accommodate hungry feast-day patrons. Everything occurring on that particular July 16th seemed normal, copacetic and consistent with my overall nondescript life.

Exactly one week later, on Wednesday, July 23rd, the all-too-familiar brown UPS delivery truck pulled into my French Street driveway at 5:30 p.m. After exchanging a few casual pleasantries with the likeable driver, I carried my compact package into the house. The delivery was a small carton weighing about two-to-three pounds. My curious eyes keenly noticed that the item's shipping address had been mysteriously labeled "Freiburg, Germany".

'This must be some mistake or error, or perhaps it's even a weird practical joke being played on me,' I initially considered. 'I don't know anybody that lives in Germany, let alone residing in a remote place like Freiburg. The town sounds pretty rural. True, my cleaning lady is from Germany, and the janitor over at the elementary school is too, but outside of those two vague acquaintances,' I presumed and speculated, 'I have no other connections or associations with *that* particular European country.'

Before opening the unexpected brown-wrapped package, I rechecked the mailing address to ascertain that the always- reliable UPS man had made an accurate drop-off. Feeling satisfied that my assiduous inspection of the item's exterior had been complete, I ventured over to my den's book shelf and pulled-out *Encyclopedia G*. After leafing through the thick book's pages, my intensive research eventually located the "Population Distribution" map of Germany. After admiring impressive color photographs of the Rhine River Valley and of the architectural wonder known as Hohenzollen Castle, my cursory 'information investigation' discovered that Freiburg, Germany was located in the vicinity of the Bavarian Black Forest.

After completing my basic research, I eagerly tore-away the package's outer brown paper covering, and then meticulously opened the small carton, making certain not to damage the contents inside. Much to my curious surprise and wonder, a small computer-like instrument, comparable to a Blackberry hand-held device, had been neatly tucked inside. The device had been enveloped in wrinkled-up German language newspaper pages. With my fascination running wild, my eyes closely examined and then really scrutinized the very intriguing object of interest, its purpose at that specific moment representing an enigma to me.

'Let's see,' I pensively analyzed, attempting to objectively keep my volatile emotions in harness. 'I must not allow my heart to interfere with my mind's goal. Here's a folded-up instructions' leaflet,' I astutely observed, 'and wow, by coincidence, it's written in English, too! I don't even have to consult the German-to-English dictionary on the *Internet* to render an interpretation. All there is on the facing of this intriguing device is one 'On' and one 'Off' switch, along with a standard liquid display readout at the top!'

Then, I carefully read the directions to the remarkable "Music Portal Product", and all along, my mind was unusually captivated with its new-found interest. The extraordinary mechanism instantly manifested itself as a potential source of personal wonder.

> "Use this very special communicator only in a dire emergency where your life might be in danger or in jeopardy. There are twelve relevant songs programmed into this very sensitive instrument, the purpose of each tune you'll be able to accurately

323

hypothesize after your first usage of the 'Music Portal'."

Then, I read a more vivid description.

"The first ten songs will pertain to your ability to deal with unsavory people that might be endangering your physical well-being, while the final two musical arrangements will be pertinent to your much-needed growth as an individual, helping you achieve mortal self-actualization, and therefore affecting *you* to ultimately finding a genuine reason for directly participating in the efficacious development of your psychological/spiritual self-fulfillment."

I next finished comprehending the remaining instructions.

"It is strongly advised that you implement and use this wonderful gift wisely. Simply plug the accompanying earphones into the device, and when threatened, use the first ten tunes to eliminate your immediate problem. And then upon developing the necessary courage to overcome your ten prospective adversities, responsibly activate the final two songs at your own volition, and during the transition, courageously commence discovering the essence of your purpose-driven life."

Your sympathetic Freiburg friends

My re-energized thought processes contemplated the intricate invention's possible significance in relation to my monotonous, dejected life. I truly wanted to avoid any possible discrepancies concerning the successful operation of the Music Portal, while my fertile imagination considered what would actually happen upon my intentional activation of the 'very handsome-looking foreign made computer.' My captivated mind still being somewhat befuddled, I very deliberately thrice re-read the very explicit directions on how to effectively optimize my ownership of the newly-acquired electronic tool. It didn't take me too long to perceptively figure-out the fascinating magical power associated with the exceptional miniature apparatus, that had by good fortune, been obtained via standard UPS delivery.

On Monday morning, July 21st I had to honor a scheduled 10:00 a.m. doctor's appointment at *Thomas Jefferson University Hospital*, Philadelphia. I drove my blue *Nissan Altima* from Hammonton to the Lindenwold High Speed Line Terminal just west of Berlin, purchased my round-trip ticket from the lady cashier, and soon boarded the nine o'clock train into Philly'.

My scheduled appointment (and routine medical checkup) went smoothly, and I was very happy with my heart doctor's favorable report. I exited the brick-façade 1600 Walnut Street Building, very warily strolled the several blocks east, and then ambled south to the Port Authority Subway Station at 10th and Locust. Without any warning, four young city punks wielding switchblade knives accosted me at the base of the otherwise empty subterranean station's steps.

Startled as I was, luckily, I was holding the Music Portal Device in my right hand while wearing the accompanying attached earphones. Instinctively, I entered my survival/self-preservation behavioral mode. I forcefully pressed the "On" button, and my auditory senses heard the 1974 ABBA hit "Waterloo" being played through my devices' earphones. Instantly, the four unsavory city thugs disappeared into oblivion, the fantastic event occurring as if they had never occupied that particular time and space. It was then and there that I superficially grasped the specific functionality of the most incredible Music Portal Device.

'I wonder if those four villainous creeps are actually right now at the Battle of Waterloo with Wellington's, or with Napoleon's troops; or perhaps instead, they've been marvelously conveyed to a 1970s ABBA concert,' I conjectured and assessed. 'In my opinion, those future criminals need all of the history lessons they can get. Could it be that the Music Portal is indeed some phenomenal kind of sophisticated geography and time travel piece of equipment? Whatever the circumstances,' I thought with relief, as my eastbound train approached the underground station platform, 'I'm really glad to have the amazing thing in my possession!' And after I boarded the subway train, I reckoned, 'And I was never really a big ABBA and disco fan, always preferring to listen to classic rock and roll back in the flashy bell-bottom jeans, Strobe lights, and polyester clothes'

'70s era!' I mused and then chuckled as tunnel lights flickered on and off, and metallic wheels screeched around a bend outside the train car.

After finally getting off the partially-filled High Speed Line train at Lindenwold, I slowly trekked a good distance to my trusty car, which was parked around a quarter of a mile away in the far corner of the massive lot. As I grabbed for the front door handle of my *Altima,* an armed robber (that was hiding behind an adjacent vehicle) suddenly appeared and demanded that I hand over my wallet. Being inspired after my former musical success in the Locust Street Subway Station, my right thumb adroitly hit the contraption's contact button, and instantaneously, the shocked and petrified lowlife instantly vanished into thin air. Simultaneously, my ears discerned the familiar rhythm and beat of Jan and Dean's catchy 1964 car song, "The Little Old Lady from Pasadena".

'Could it be that the wicked, nasty-tempered robber has been inexplicably transported to distant Pasadena, California?' I asked myself. 'If so, I hope he stays there and gets to see the next *Rose Bowl Game!* And if he's meandering around Pasadena right this second, is he in the year 1964, or is he still in 2008? Oh well,' I concluded and shrugged my shoulders. 'That scar-faced scoundrel would be better off taking-up home burglaries instead of attempting bold-faced armed parking lot robbery as a chosen profession. In retrospect,' my captivated mind reviewed, 'it's pretty hard for *him* to get teleported to a remote Golden State destination when nobody's there inside the place to operate a facsimile Music Portal mechanism to send *him* back here to Lindenwold! Maybe the relocated idiot will get to visit and tour 'Surf City' too, while he's fully enjoying his unanticipated surprise West Coast jaunt!'

On Saturday morning, I did my usual grocery shopping at the nearby Wal-Mart and ShopRite stores, and then after unpacking and putting away my new food products in the refrigerator, inside the freezer, and into various respective cupboards, I changed out of my blue denim jeans, donned my jogging outfit, and drove my *Nissan* down the White Horse Pike to somnolent Oak Grove Cemetery. I had once checked the mileage on my car's odometer, and if I traverse the entire graveyard's asphalt surface twice, my diligent labor would result in a very beneficial cardio-vascular-friendly three-mile hike. Of course, my *Altima* was parked in its regular shaded location beneath a canopy of three tall oak trees, and I felt especially secure walking around inside the old cemetery, carrying my Music Portal while performing my habitual weekend exercise routine.

As I was circling the caretaker's maintenance building, situated in the center of the cemetery, six motorcycle villains drove their gleaming machines inside the graveyard to pay their respects to a recently deceased gang member. Seeing me innocently pacing in their direction, the tough-looking bikers all perceived me as being an easy target, first for blatant intimidation, and second for committing larceny. The Harleys speedily rumbled up to me, the riders thinking that I was unprepared to defend myself against their aggressive demands and against their spontaneously planned molestation. But I was fully ready to deal with any of their antagonism and prospective havoc.

"Okay, let's make this little encounter short and sweet!" the very arrogant head honcho belligerently declared in a gruff tone of voice. "Now Pal, just hand over your wallet, and I'll gladly confiscate all your cash. Don't worry, though!" the disgusting black-hearted maniac clarified. "We ain't all that bad! You'll get to keep your credit cards, your driver's license, and all of your other personal ID! It's a lot better to be a live victim than a dead hero, that's what the hell I always say! Ha, ha, ha!"

The five other formidable-looking bikers all indulgently laughed at their leader's threatening comments, and then mockingly applauded my apparent situational futility. Before any additional harassment could ensue from any of their lips, I nonchalantly touched the "On" button, and without any sign of hesitation or delay, the Music Portal played the melody and lyrics to the 1959 hit tune "Kansas City" by Wilbert Harrison. And before I could even begin to say *'Dick Clark's American Bandstand,'* the six nefarious derelicts that had been ridiculing me were miraculously erased from my presence, either swiftly being sent on their way to Kansas City, Missouri, or to Kansas City, Kansas.

'I hope those desperate degenerates have enough dough to buy themselves some delicious Black Angus steaks,' I amused myself with a reflexive smile. 'Maybe they'll somehow be converted into bunkhouse cowboys working for a living on a sprawling dude ranch. I think that the flat-lands of the American Midwest would be a welcome change in scenery for those societal parasites, when compared to the all-too-predictable South Jersey pine barren forest landscape that *they* no doubt have constantly abused in the past! Oh well, what could possibly happen next?'

The first Sunday in August, I was driving south to Vineland to have a delicious lunch at Esposito's Maplewood III Restaurant, because I really think *that* establishment has the best tomato sauce and Italian pasta anywhere in South Jersey. After paying my moderate bill and leaving a generous tip, I sauntered out of the popular eatery and then hopped into my car, which much to my annoyance, failed to start. Upon opening the hood to diagnose the cause of the electrical problem, I recognized (much to my frustration) that the automobile's battery had been stolen. I angrily got out my cell phone and anxiously began dialing "Local Information" to obtain the name of the nearest road service that would dispatch a mechanic out to Delsea Drive to replace the vital missing part.

Suddenly, three really mean-looking Mexicans emerged out of nowhere, violently opened my car door, and then signaled for me to exit my vehicle. I ceased my cell phone dialing and gestured to the triumvirate of wise guys that I was going to obediently follow their command.

I gingerly lifted-up my Music Portal from the passenger-side front bucket seat and slowly inserted the corresponding earphones into their appropriate auditory positions. My index finger methodically made contact with the "On" button, and before I could blink an eyelid, or even fabricate a wink, the three dumbfounded desperados vaporized into the separate spaces that they had been occupying, their astonishing disappearances all occurring in unison with the very identifiable sound of Marty Robbins' 1960 number "El Paso" being wonderfully discernible to my ears.

'Oh well,' I reflected and mentally weighed with a huge sigh of relief. 'The song selection could've been 'Tijuana Taxi' by Herb Alpert and the Tijuana Brass, or maybe even Ritchie Valens' terrific version of 'La Bamba', or perhaps even the good old-fashioned favorite 'The Mexican Hat Dance!' Those three missing-in-action Hispanic jerks were probably the same dastardly rogues that had stolen my car battery! Now they're probably already trying to get to the *Rio Grande* to come back to New Jersey and get even with little old *me,* their chief antagonist!'

I finally got my blue *Altima* operational again late that Sunday afternoon. On Tuesday after work at the shoe store, I checked my refrigerator and noticed that I was completely out of beer. The *Phillies* were playing an important baseball game on television that evening, so I decided to drive over to Canal's Discount Liquor Store on Broadway and *Route 30* and conveniently purchase a cold six-pack of *Coor's Light*.

A desperate-looking fellow quickly entered the crowded store while I was checking out my beverage acquisition at the main cash register. The on-a-mission psycho' immediately pulled-out a handgun and boldly announced that a major holdup was in progress. Naturally, I inserted the designated earphones and quite matter-of-factly, hit the Music Portal's "On" button.

My ears promptly heard Elton John singing his 1975 smash hit "Philadelphia Freedom", and I assumed that the *Quaker City* was the audacious petty thief's appointed destination. 'The *Philadelphia Freedoms* were once a pro' tennis squad back in the long-gone 1970s and Elton John had written and dedicated the upbeat tune to one of his closest friends, team captain Billie Jean King!' my non-photographic memory recollected. Then, my very active mind conjured-up some additional spontaneous reactions.

'I hope that the criminal nutcase winds-up inside the 10th and Locust Street subway station and gets mugged by equally diabolical street hoods from the 'hood!' I creatively conceived and joked. 'One thing's for darned sure. Metropolitan crime is gradually trickling out of the urban areas and insidiously infecting the suburbs! If it weren't for this tremendous Music Portal Device,' I realized, 'I'd already be dead at least five times over!'

When I finally returned to my modest French Street residence, my rowdy immature neighbors were haughtily entertaining some of their very boisterous piney hunter friends at a "disturbing the peace" backyard picnic. The raucous, intoxicated rednecks apparently were quite disenchanted with my audacity because I had called the police to break-up several other clamorous next-door warm weather parties, one on *Memorial Day,* and the other on the 4th *of July*. I was busy putting my lawnmower inside my outdoor utility building when all twenty-four inebriated revelers (that had been attending the loud backyard barbecue) trespassed onto my property and then insolently began badgering me with a barrage of rather disparaging insults.

"Look!" I diplomatically answered. "My ears are very sensitive! I don't like excessive noise, and I don't relish the shooting-off of loud fireworks. Let's all have some moderate behavior here! Why don't you' kind folks just learn to be a little more civil and respect other peoples' rights! Then we could get along like good neighbors, and not have this type of unnecessary cultural conflict all the time!"

"You're now goin' to get the worst damned beatin' of your life!" my nasty, hostile, bellicose, under-the-influence, twenty-two-year-old neighbor/nemesis predicted. "Now I'm challengin' you in front of all of these witnesses here to act like a man, so let's see how tough ya' really are when your very survival is at stake!" the incensed psychopath yelled as he angrily clenched his raised fists. The other defiant barbarians (assembled on my back lawn) shouted a bevy of brazen cheers and jeers in response to the offensive knucklehead's sarcastic rhetoric.

Without wasting a second of precious time, I suavely activated the invaluable Music Portal, and my ears eagerly listened to Glen Campbell singing his 1969 hit "The Wichita Lineman". The twenty-four baneful delinquents magically dissolved into thin air with not a trace or a vestige of anyone or anything (in their possession) remaining behind.

'Those drunken Jersey hillbillies frequently terrorize the Wharton Tract woods up on *Route 206,* and the ruffians hang-out at the infamous Pic-A-Lilli Inn,' I remember thinking. 'The rogues all belong to a deer club that just uses hunting season as an excuse to get drunk, to cause a ruckus, and to commit perpetual gluttony. Maybe while they're trekking around out in Wichita, Kansas,' I mentally humored myself, 'perhaps those two dozen un-illustrious dregs will introduce themselves to the six obnoxious cemetery bikers that I had very conveniently teleported out to Kansas City while talented Wilbert Harrison was singing his mantra-like verses!'

At that psychologically rewarding moment of proud triumph, I must confess that I was feeling rather superhuman and omnipotent. It did dawn on my awareness that the wonderful Music Portal Device must contain some revolutionary proprietary technology that if "the science" ever became available to the general public, and then be universally used, the plethora of "magical music devices" would have everyone sending everyone else into different times and/or into different places, thus contributing to mass societal chaos and ultimately, possibly causing the end of civilization itself. 'Not everyone can be trusted with possessing such a powerful device!' I academically surmised. 'Evil people cannot have access to such a marvelous disciplinary thing! I mustn't share the secret of this wondrous Divine Providence with anyone!'

Two more notable incidents had occurred later in August. Being totally bored with my less-than-mediocre shoe salesman job, I had driven forty-miles from Hammonton up to *Six Flags Great Adventure* amusement park in Jackson on the fourth Saturday in August for some leisurely diversion, and to pursue a much-needed attitude adjustment. 'In terms of its structure, this Music Portal appears to be just another typical cell phone,' I remember thinking as I paid my hefty park admission fee. 'Whoever owns the patent to this electronic gizmo will certainly make an unbelievable fortune!'

Three drunken New Yorkers with heavy Brooklyn accents attempted to instigate a fight with me inside a crowded park men's room. Without uttering any derogatory expletives or counter accusations, I confidently hit the readily available 'transportation switch', and upon me hearing the introduction to Freddy "Boom-Boom" Cannon's 1962 top seller "Palisades Park", the trio of punks promptly vanished from my midst.

'Palisades Park was torn down many years ago,' I later recalled as I chewed on a hot dog near the Batman Roller Coaster Thrill Ride. 'So, if the three Gotham alcoholics were not time-travel-teleported back to 1962, then they're probably walking around Palisades Park, New Jersey right now in 2008, wondering what the heck had happened to them. The three tipsy bullies more-than-likely now think that they've somehow been the victims of a mass hallucination!'

On Sunday morning, I needed some relaxing diversion in my life, so I attached my twenty-four-foot-long boat trailer to my 1997 red Ford 150 truck, and towed the "Sea Daze" to a launching slip at a local Sweetwater marina. A forklift operator soon lowered and then deposited my boat into the *Mullica River*. An hour later, my small Sea Daze was anchored in shallow water, and I was quietly fishing in the vicinity of Crowley's Landing when three destructive wise-guy teenagers appeared on the riverbank and started cursing and throwing large stones at me. I nonchalantly activated my Music Portal, and my ears heard the refrains of the "Bristol Stomp", a lively 1961 classic rock and roll tune sung by the Dovells. 'Well,' I philosophically mused. 'Those three despicable adolescents are probably now wandering on the banks of the *Delaware* in Bristol, Pennsylvania instead of bothering the daylights out of me here on the *Mullica!*' I logically concluded. 'Serves the reprehensible hooligans right! Maybe their little excursion into Bucks County, Pennsylvania will teach the discourteous instigators some much-needed manners!'

The second Saturday in September, I felt an urge to drive thirty-miles east to Atlantic City, stroll the world-famous boardwalk, buy some tasty salt water taffy, smell the fresh ocean air, and blow five-hundred hard-earned dollars at Caesar's World Casino. I parked my blue *Altima* in a lot on Pacific Avenue, obtained the mandatory parking stub from a courteous attendant, and while peacefully walking towards the A.C. Boardwalk, I was accosted by a mugger who stopped me on Missouri Avenue to falsely ask directions to the *Steel Pier*.

Without thinking twice, Pattie Page's 1957 calming rendition of "Old Cape Cod" sent the annoying thug off to either Hyannisport or Provincetown on the famous Massachusetts peninsula. 'Maybe that vile fellow will be exposed to some New England culture, or more-than-likely, he'll be manhandled by police and arrested for trespassing onto the Kennedy Compound,' I imagined and laughed. Then, my devil-may-care disposition changed to a more solid, serious mode. 'The Music Portal's instructions indicated that I would have ten danger uses and then two additional personal growth uses,' I mulled-over in my mind. 'That gives me just one more opportunity to successfully dispose of harmful evil-minded individuals!'

Later that Saturday afternoon, my gambling habit was rewarded when I hit a three-thousand-dollar jackpot on a Caesar's World nickel slot machine. While mentally reveling my good fortune in a jovial mood, I drove from Atlantic City and stopped in at Tony's Bar on *Route 322*, the Black Horse Pike, to down some hard liquor shots and watch the featured go-go doll dance around a brass pole situated near the bar. The girl's boyfriend (who was also her pimp) tried soliciting me for a three-hundred-dollar hit, and feeling threatened by his obvious gruff demeanor, I sent the saucy fellow down to Southern hillbilly country when my ears heard the unique guitar riff to Lynyrd Skynyrd's 1974 smash hit "Sweet Home Alabama".

'Well,' I steadfastly evaluated. 'This last tenth episode has exhausted all of my Music Portal opportunities. October 6th is my birthday. I think I'll begin exploring my personal growth segment then. If my brain remembers the exact instructions,' I paused before I gulped-down a second shot of 100 Proof *Southern Comfort,* 'I only have two future chances to reach self-actualization. I wonder what side of Nirvana *that's* on? Oh well, instant karma or no instant karma, I think I'll order another jigger of whiskey, and then hit the road before the bartender and the go-go dancer finally notice that the pushy pimp is missing-in-action.'

The gorgeous go-go-dancer with Rockette-type legs approached me and asked if I had seen a "Tall, handsome, muscular, brown-eyed, young man with a dimple in the center of his chin!"

"I think he's away applying to the *University of Alabama!"* I cleverly answered the voluptuous, well-built, scantily-clad blonde. "Yes, I think he had mentioned something about being a freshman and drowning in the Crimson Tide!" I creatively jested.

The knockout, well-endowed doll just stared at me with her mouth agape, as if I was an unstable mental patient that had just escaped from the nearby Ancora State Hospital high-security psycho' ward.

* * * * * * * * * * * *

I had reserved a non-smoking room for October 6th at Caesar's World Casino/Hotel so that I could quietly and privately celebrate my birthday. Since I had earned a Harrah's Diamond Card, I often enjoyed the benefits of food and room comp' privileges at the corporation's four Atlantic City properties: Harrah's, the Showboat, Bally's Casino and Caesar's World.

Inside the confines of my seventh-floor-suite, I felt motivated to take the time to again closely examine the amazing Music Portal Device. And then feeling a sudden compulsion to further explore the dimensions of my own predicted "Self-actualization," I gathered my wits and courage and gently pressed the "On" button. Immediately, I heard the harmonious Olivia-Newton-John song "Xanadu", and my suddenly-disheveled mind found myself in a dazzling nightclub with several-hundred roller blade showoffs (along with equally skilled roller skaters) effortlessly whizzing by and all around me.

'Xanadu was definitely a weird movie about a romantic person's fondest dream of a romantic Utopia!' I recollected as adroit roller skaters rushed by my stationary roller rink presence in all different directions. Then, my overwhelmed brain found the wherewithal to recall a theory that I had once studied in a college psychology course. 'Maybe in order to reach my own special Utopia, I have to explore my twelfth and final song and see how I can ascend to the very top of Maslow's Law of Human Hierarchal Development! Yes,' I astutely decided. 'Now I'm beginning to understand this rather puzzling phenomenon! Self-actualization should exist on a higher plateau than fundamental biological needs, and *it* should also transcend emotional gratification, too! *Its* awesome fruition should be the perfect culmination of all mortal enterprise, with *its* manifestation represented in the full maturity of the human spirit, and in *my* case, *my* full emotional and mental maturity!'

After pressing the mechanism's "On" button for the twelfth time, my ears heard a familiar instrumental song which at first, my memory couldn't recall the melody's title. But in the meantime, my fantastic Music Portal Device had magically transported me to a beautiful mountainous pine forest environment. Then, my dizzy mind finally recognized the title of the rhythmic song, "A Walk in the Black Forest" by Horst Jankowski. 'Of course!' I jubilantly thought as I intensely gazed upon my stunning new-found surroundings. 'The houses on that hill over there, and the architecture of those buildings in the town down in the valley, are German in nature! I'll bet I've arrived near Freiburg!'

I hastened along a narrow dirt path until all out of breath, I reached a remote monastery retreat. I stubbornly rapped upon the large wooden door and was reluctantly greeted by a monk who spoke English with a thick accent. Father Sebastian escorted me inside the medieval-looking stone edifice, and after we were sitting in two hard wooden chairs that occupied a corner of his crudely furnished office, we discussed how I had been successfully "recruited" into the select ranks of "Music Portal assemblers".

"How will I be able to achieve self-actualization?" I inquisitively asked my laconic, pious sponsor. "I understand that *that's* the principal reason why I've been guided and conducted here."

"You'll have plenty of time for introspection while doing your required daily *Bible* reading," Father Sebastian aptly and curtly replied. "You'll become most inspired reading essentially assigned passages, especially those moral lessons organized throughout the New Testament. That daily regimen will indeed accelerate your moral growth!"

My cynical side soon surfaced and its ego-based ugliness momentarily dominated my cerebral activity. My skeptical "outside world thinking" was not synchronized to my new self-examination reality. 'Father Sebastian and his fellow priests are isolated up here on this remote mountain, and their narrow minds are trapped inside separate religious cartons!' I suspiciously conjectured. 'These holier-than-thou morons, or should I say these sanctimonious religious zealots, are quite ostensibly incapable of thinking outside the box!' I negatively and critically thought.

"You'll gradually learn self-discipline and after mastering that," Father Sebastian un-eloquently elaborated in an emotionless tone of voice, "you'll eventually rise above your propensity to vaguely communicate pessimistic ideas and also, at *that* juncture in time, you'll then finally conquer your affinity for being too liberally disingenuous!"

"Well then, Father, what will be my assigned responsibilities here at this remote monastery?"

"First of all, you'll only be allowed to speak in sentences of ten words or less when sitting with others on our staff during our three regular daily meals, which are generally the only times that trivial conversation is tolerated," the no-nonsense priest informed me. "And starting first thing tomorrow morning, you'll be learning how to make Swiss cuckoo clocks, and then you'll also be acquiring the art and science of beer brewing along with some preliminary exposure to botanical gardening; and after excelling in those rudimentary, mundane trades," the austere abbot continued his sermonizing, "we'll swiftly assign you, at *our* discretion, to help build sophisticated Music Portals that will be sent to psychologically depressed people all over this imperfect planet. But you'll be an expert at only one phase of the manufacturing process, and will never know how to fully assemble a functioning Music Portal entirely on your own skill; and if I may add, no schematic of the entire design will ever be shown to you. Now then," Sebastian sternly stressed. "I'm a very busy man. Do you have any more curious questions?"

"Yes, Father. Will I ever be permitted to leave this cold, drab, all-stone monastery? Am I trapped in here?"

"After seven-years of marvelous indentured labor, you'll be allowed to travel within a hundred-fifty-mile radius of this rather insular retreat," Sebastian objectively related to his new subordinate. "Once you prove your worth through self-discipline, and once you demonstrate an enviable work ethic, you'll be able to travel all around what is known as Baden-Wurttemberg, and if your enlightened *spirit* moves you, you'll eventually even be able to visit the Rhine River Valley and tour Hohenzollen Castle, which as you know Cinderella's *Disneyland* and *Disney World* castles were modeled after. You could even visit Munich and engage in an inspirational Octoberfest or two! But first, you must start at square one!"

Right after that initial mind-opening interview with Father Sebastian, my cerebrum realized one very salient concept. My mind and body had been transported in geographic space to Freiburg, Germany, but according to the hanging calendar in the abbot's office, the date was still October 6th, 2008. Based on my utterly illuminating experience here in this solitary-confinement-like enormous monastery, *that* sage 'date observation' simply means that all of the people that I had teleported (when I had felt threatened during the ten confrontations involving the Music Portal Device) probably also had been transported in space to new locations mentioned in the various song titles, but probably not dispatched into other times or into other distinct historical eras.

I'm finally becoming acclimated to (and actually now enjoying) the stringent agenda associated with my daily secluded, monastic way of life, the discipline of which I strongly believe has been helping me elevate my former inferior self-esteem and deficient confidence levels. I'm happy to report in this strange-but-factual humble autobiography that I'm learning some common German words and phrases, and now can almost fully interpret what the sagacious priests and my fellow resident craftsmen are saying in abbreviated sentences at meals and during morning Vespers. Most importantly, I've now become accustomed to rejecting the traditional lavish lifestyles that are greedily pursued in the baneful, outside materialistic world, egregiously practiced by mostly self-centered humans.

I've been industriously making the first phase Swiss cuckoo clocks, and conscientiously experimenting with basic beer brewing and botanical gardening for two glorious months now, and my ever-growing *spirit* is enthusiastically awaiting my eventual assignment and transfer to the highly prestigious Music Portal Assembly Workshop Wing. I truly wish to help other moral-but-depressed people all over the world, and give them hope for self-actualization by rescuing them through "music geographic transfers" when the recipients happen to discover themselves being in harm's way. That genesis phase of "melancholy re-location displacement," as I now fathom it, is the primary stage of "*Spiritual* Self-actualization".

In retrospect, as I author these final very realistic words, the package that I had anonymously received from Freiburg via UPS is now fully comprehensible, and now its ultimate implementation makes perfect sense. I can't wait to make my significant contribution to the moral stability of civilization by helping to manufacture new innovative and sensational "next generation Music Portals" at my designated workstation, and then, in the process, attain great satisfaction by having the finished products of my extensive labor delivered to deserving-but-despondent human beings all over this dangerous-but-wonderful world.

"Window of Opportunity"

The May Installation Meeting assigning new officers for the Hammonton, New Jersey Lions Club had just adjourned, and afterwords, two recently-appointed minor functionaries were discussing their basic roles with an elderly club member in the upstairs bar of Rocco's Town House on North Third Street. The all-too-garrulous District 16-C Governor had already departed the premises, and Liontamer Mitchell Spencer, Tailtwister Michael Giberson, and feeble Past President Julius Stetson were standing at the tavern's bar, casually engaged in a genial conversation over their after-meeting cocktails.

"It's good to see new blood coming into the club and accepting active roles," eighty-two-year-old Julius Stetson praised the local Lions Club's two new energized recruits. "I was a charter member of the club way back in 1963," Julius informed his respectful listeners before sipping his cold *Southern Comfort* on the rocks. "And we had only a dozen members when John F. Kennedy was the country's President, mostly businessmen owning stores and properties up on Route 30. One guy had a liquor store; another guy was a produce broker; a third had a gas station and auto' repair garage, and a fourth fella' owned a popular diner that stayed open until three in the morning," old Julius Stetson reminisced. "Those fun-loving guys are all dead now, and I'm the only original charter member left. At the time, the town's Kiwanis and Rotary clubs were the top civic organizations in Hammonton, and the fledgling Lions were like the town's orphan upstarts. After the Lillian-on-the-Lake eatery closed for business," Stetson related, "our tiny club had to meet in the small back room of the Hacienda Restaurant, while the hotshot and snobbish Kiwanis guys got priority and enjoyed their meals inside the big dining area."

"Hacienda Restaurant?" Mitchell Spencer politely interrupted Julius. "I've never heard of it!"

"Where have all the years gone? The stucco, Spanish-styled place used to be located at the intersection of *Route 30* and *Route 206* where the Rite-Aid Pharmacy is now situated," Lion Stetson nostalgically revealed. "The Hacienda was demolished back in the late 1970s, just a few years before either of you two whippersnappers were ever born, let alone conceived."

"Were you a conscientious Lion when you joined the club?" Liontamer Mitchell Spencer courteously inquired. "I presume you must've been. I mean, I've never heard of a vegetable vendor selling rotten tomatoes from his fruit and produce wagon! You had to be a true-blue Lion right from the outset in order to have been a dedicated member all these years."

"Like yourself, Mitchell, I started-out as the lowly Liontamer, taking care of the club's banner, gavel, gong, microphone, and table podium," Julius nonchalantly informed his avid audience of two. "Then I was promoted. The next year, I became the Tailtwister, the club sheriff levying fines on members that came late to a meeting, or who had forgotten to wear their club pin on their jacket lapel, or who had neglected to wear their membership badge, or who neglected to have their Lions International Card in their wallet. And if the member checked-out okay with those essential credentials in their possession," Julius bragged and prattled before imbibing a swig of sweet liquor, "I'd then fine them on the spot if the violators couldn't answer a simple question like 'Who founded Lions International in 1917?' or 'Who challenged the Lions to become Knights of the Blind at an early international convention'?"

"Melvin Jones was the founder of Lions International," Liontamer Mitchell Spencer proudly answered with an air of certainty evident in his voice. "And Helen Keller gave an important speech at the early convention you had mentioned and got the first wave of Lions interested in becoming champions for the blind and crusaders for the hearing impaired. She also encouraged the Lions to help the less fortunate in their communities. But unfortunately," Mitch Spencer continued his informal lecture, "presently the government is taking over the function of charity through welfare programs and redistribution of wealth, so I fear that the need for service clubs assisting the needy is rapidly diminishing all throughout the country."

"Okay, Wise Guy," old Julius Stetson amiably stated with a smile. "Who was the first president of Lions International?"

"Melvin Jones?" Mitchell tentatively answered. "Obviously, yes. I'm quite certain that it must've been Melvin Jones if *he* was the founder of Lions International!"

"No, Mitch. it was a man named Dr. W. P. Woods, so that'll be a dollar fine!" knowledgeable club historian Julius Stetson joked and amply laughed. "And as the District Governor had lectured tonight, our international headquarters is in Oak Brook, Illinois, just outside Chicago. But over the years, Lions International has grown to over 30,000 clubs in over 150 countries, and our international membership now totals nearly one-and-a-half-million members," Julius confidently reviewed. "In fact, Gentlemen. In many parts of the world like in India and Japan, for example, it's a distinct honor to become a philanthropic Lion."

"You must be pretty bored with all of the redundant routines and monotonous speeches after nearly a half-century of involvement?" high school English teacher Mitchell Spencer asked his sponsor and mentor. "I mean, Julius, how many times do you have to hear the same rhetoric about membership drives, the value of newspaper public relations, and the need for participation in club fundraisers?"

"Well, I gotta' admit," Julius replied and then paused to carefully select his next words. "Over the years, our charity fundraisers have switched around. In the beginning, we had a Turkey Shoot, and we also collected money donations out in front of a grocery store for White Cane Day. Then later on, we had a Bike-A-Thon and sponsored a Tri-Ath-A-Lon, mostly because four ambitious state troopers had joined the club and insisted on us having fundraisers that focused on physical fitness. Now, of course," Julius paused and elaborated, "we have the Gold Raffle Dinner where we give-away seventeen-thousand-dollars in cash and prizes. And as you two members know, we also loyally sell muffins, pies, strudel, and turnovers at the annual Blueberry Festival in late June. Those two events alone earn the club over twenty-thousand-bucks a year, and I predict that someday, both of you two greenhorns will be chairmen of those two highly-profitable fundraisers."

"Well, Lion Julius," Mike Giberson commented before swallowing-down the remainder of his cordial drink. "What in your whole recollection were the craziest things you can remember the local Lions doing back in the good old days?"

"Ha, ha, ha," aged Julius Stetson giggled and then smirked. "In the beginning, when there were only men in the club, we did some nifty things. It was sort of like a fraternity for adult males. Once we hired a stripper to entertain us in the back room of an out-of-town bar to honor the achievements of an outgoing president. Another time, twelve of us journeyed in a van down to Ocean City, Maryland, and we paid a surprise visit to an enterprising club member who owned several thriving summer boardwalk businesses own there," Stetson recalled with a wide grin. "The shocked fella' treated us all to a fantastic crab and spicy shrimp feast at Phillip's Restaurant. But the neatest occurrence that I can recall involved a new member who had transferred into the Hammonton Lions from a club up near Yonkers, New York. Yes, that zany new member precipitated something special."

"Tell me quick, what happened!" Tailtwister Mike Giberson insisted. "I have to soon get on the road and pick-up my son at the elementary school after his Tuesday night basketball practice. I don't want to keep his coach waiting as a babysitter."

"Well, this new member, his name was Henry Thomas, had three of his old friends drive down from Yonkers, New York, and lo and behold, the mischievous culprits stole our club bell. So, eighteen of us Hammonton rascals rented a gigantic RV and drove up to Yonkers to retrieve the bell, according to standard Lions' custom. The idea behind that kind of good-humored theft is designed and endorsed by all Lions' clubs to promote fellowship and subsequent visitations to other clubs in order to advance the cause of sharing a good time."

"Is that all?" Giberson asked in a disappointed tone of voice. "I was expecting something a little more dynamic! Did you guys ever retrieve your club bell?"

"You didn't allow me to finish my terrific story!" old Julius facetiously balked. "On the way up to Yonkers, I was driving the mammoth RV on the *New Jersey Turnpike*. Traffic was bumper-to-bumper early that evening. The other guys were pretty inebriated by that time when we had reached the vicinity of the Newark Airport, and I must confess, including myself. In the midst of the massive automobile congestion," Julius expounded on his tale, "I awkwardly tried changing lanes, and in the process, I partially ripped-off the RV's back bumper when a stubborn tractor-trailer driver wouldn't let me switch lanes. There wasn't any noticeable damage to *his* big rig, but the RV bumper was more than a trifle mangled."

"What happened next?" Tailtwister Giberson curiously asked. "Did you have to pay for the bumper repair? Did you have to buy a new one? Either way, it must've cost you a decent fortune!"

"You're too impetuous, and in my opinion, Mike, your spoiled kid and his impatient coach can wait for you an extra five-minutes at the school gym!" Julius chastised the recently installed club enforcement officer. "It was during the early '70s, yes, during the

Carter Administration, and there was gas rationing and long gas station lines everywhere," Lion Stetson recalled and shared. "Anyway Fellas', on the way back from Yonkers, we stopped near the north end of the Garden State Parkway to purchase gas. At the time, a fuel rationing crisis was rampant across the nation, and if your license plate ended in an even number, you could only buy gas on an even number day of the month. Well, it was an even number day, and we had an odd number ending to our RV's license plate, so the attendants refused to sell us fuel."

"How did you get home?" Liontamer Mitchell Spencer wanted to know. "This story is now becoming quite intriguing. How did you avoid being stranded a hundred-and-twenty-miles away from Hammonton in a gas-guzzling RV?"

"You're just as immaturely impulsive as Tailtwister Mike Giberson is!" Julius Stetson merrily chided Liontamer Mitch Spencer, before imbibing another tasty gulp of sweet *Southern Comfort*. "The four audacious state troopers in the club, all of them thoroughly groggy from gulping-down hard whiskey, well, they showed the suddenly alarmed attendants their State Police ID badges, and blatantly flashed guns from their shoulder holsters. The State Cops told the petrified gas station employees that *they* would be accused of harmfully obstructing justice since the damaged RV was on a secret drug raid mission, and consequently, the totally intimidated gas station guys immediately filled us up without any further controversy whatsoever."

"Ha, ha, ha! That was rich!" Tailtwister Michael Giberson commended the old-timer. "I wish I had been in the RV to see the frightened expressions on the gas station workers' faces! But how did you ever get the rear bumper fixed!"

"Well, now Boys, that's another fascinating tale that actually happened!" Julius Stetson merrily maintained. "When we eventually got back to Hammonton, the already drunk member who owned the large garage up on Route 30 got into the RV's driver seat, put the immense vehicle into reverse, and then violently slammed into the cinder-blocked side of his service station. Miraculously, the bumper was pressed back into its proper place without any notice of ever being in an accident, or ever being tampered with."

"That's really an incredibly-nifty narrative!" Mike Giberson congratulated old Julius. "Sorry Guys, but I gotta' split! Hope to see you both in two weeks at our next meeting."

After the newly appointed Tailtwister departed the sparsely populated Rocco's Town House bar area, Julius Stetson had a personal question to ask Liontamer Mitchell Spencer.

"Mitch, I'm a fairly good judge of human character, and I think you're a fine young man. I honestly believe that you remind me a lot of myself when I was financially struggling back in the midst of the 1950s recessions," Julius prefaced his odd and unexpected remarks. "I hear that you're thinking about dropping out of the Lions Club for money reasons. I know that you're an excellent high school English teacher, and I'm also aware that you make just an ordinary income."

"Well, quite frankly Mr. Stetson, unfortunately, I've accumulated considerable debts that I find myself drowning in," Mitch confided. "My divorce last year set me back big time; I have a tremendous mortgage on my home out on Second Road and I have to pay for my former wife's new condominium over on the bay in Brigantine. I have to pay her alimony, along with child support for our two kids now in her custody, by the judge's ruling. And finally, I have accumulated over forty-thousand-dollars in high interest credit card debt. My overwhelming total financial obligations are in the neighborhood of..."

"A half-million-dollars," sage Julius Stetson passively declared before finishing his second delicious whiskey. "Like I said, Mitch, I really like you and feel sorry for your unenviable plight. As you might know from town gossip, my wife is dead; I have no children of my own, and I absolutely despise my still-living avaricious niece and greedy nephew on my deceased wife's side. I'm eighty-two years old and have bad cases of colon and prostate cancer. Confidentially, the doctors at Jefferson Hospital over in Philly' say that I have only a month or so left," the old gentleman frankly divulged. "It's too late for me to incorporate you into my will. But should you happen to read my obituary in the local papers, I'm going to give you an extra back door key to my mansion over on Third Road. After my death, you must go to my residence immediately to avoid any complications with my money-hungry niece and nephew." The old man then reached into his pants pocket and exhibited a common key, finally surrendering its possession to the astounded, wide-eyed young Liontamer.

"What will this key lead to?" Mitch marveled and uttered, intensively scrutinizing the ordinary-looking object very closely.

"Specifically, what's it really for, other than to gain access to your home? Of what value is it to me?"

"Inside my cluttered master bedroom closet, you'll find a big wall safe concealed directly behind and above my shoe rack," Julius indicated without showing any emotion. "In the safe, I'm going to leave a half-million-dollars in cash for you to pay-off your massive debts, so that you can start your life all over again and avert the grievous mistakes that have brought you to the threshold of bankruptcy. You'll find that *that* same key will open both the back door and the master bedroom closet wall safe."

"I can't believe your unexpected generosity!" Mitchell Spencer exclaimed, getting the attention of several idle tavern patrons seated on the opposite side of the oval bar. "Thank you so very much! You're an absolute Godsend!"

"But please, listen carefully, and fully heed my words," benefactor Julius Stetson whispered to his jubilant, prospective beneficiary. "When I had been a flashy show business performer back in the late 1940s, I had amassed a fine reputation as a class-act magician. Inside my hall cedar closet, I've painstakingly had constructed what I call 'my Window of Opportunity', which will become *your* 'Window of Opportunity'. Open the stained-glass window leading to a hidden room, and I promise that you'll discover additional rare treasures awaiting you!"

All that totally-thrilled Mitchell Spencer could do was stand there at the bar with an astonished-but-grateful expression upon his florid countenance, all the while wildly imagining exactly what the mysterious 'Window of Opportunity' could actually be.

* * * * * * * * * * * *

Two weeks passed, and the English teacher faithfully carried the 'gift key' in his pocket to Hammonton High School every single workday. 'Julius said that I must go to his home as soon as I learn of his passing and use this back door key immediately so that I can remove the half-million cash from the closet wall safe, and then determine what's behind the mysterious 'Window of Opportunity' inside the cedar closet,' Mitchell kept reminding himself during seventh period while his advanced academic students were taking their *Hamlet* written examination.

That Tuesday evening, Lion Julius Stetson did not attend the bi-weekly club meeting, and it was reported that the aged member was home suffering from a mild spring sinus infection. And at the meeting, it was reported that the old gentleman seemed to be in good spirits when the distinguished elderly 'Past President' had called the club secretary and had informed the club executive of *his* legitimate excuse for being absent.

An additional two weeks passed, and another scheduled Lions Club meeting commenced at Rocco's Town House. After the customary Pledge of Allegiance, the opening prayer, and the traditional Lions' Toast, during *his* introductory remarks, the club president announced that revered Lion Julius Stetson had "suffered a devastating stroke" that afternoon and that the eighty-two-year-old-multimillionaire had been rushed by ambulance to Mainland Hospital in Pomona, the renowned state-of-the-art medical facility being seventeen-miles east of Hammonton.

'My cousin Helen Reynolds is a night nurse in the emergency room at Mainland Hospital,' Mitchell Spencer astutely and mentally associated. 'I'll quietly text message her during this boring meeting to learn more about Julius's condition. My cousin's very reliable. I'm sure that if Helen is not in surgery right now, she'll be able to give me an update on my benefactor's condition in the form of a prompt reply.'

Forty-five-minutes later, just before the standard meeting ending "fifty-fifty drawing", Mitchell received a return text message from nurse Helen Reynolds stating that Julius Stetson of Hammonton had died at 7:35 p.m. that evening, and that his next of kin were presently being notified, along with a prominent Hammonton undertaker.

'It's happened! God rest *his* soul! The initial suspense is now over!' Mitchell sadly evaluated with perspiration appearing on his forehead, just before he won the sum of thirty-dollars in the fifty-fifty drawing. "I'd like to give the money I've just won back to the club!" Spencer articulated as the seated members unanimously gave him an appreciative round of applause.

Then, an image of the prospective half-million-dollar 'cash bonanza' focused inside Spencer's actively racing mind, and the Liontamer's thoughts greedily contemplated the swift acquisition of his highly anticipated good fortune. 'I'll act calm and collected; pretend that nothing relevant has occurred, and then unobtrusively leave the meeting and evade the subsequent small talk and

346

chitchatting as soon as possible. Next, I'll waste no time being off to Julius's mansion to claim my spectacular windfall before his covetous niece and nephew, or the Hammonton Police can beat me there to check his home.'

Every operational phase at the Third Road mansion smoothly developed and transpired, just as Julius Stetson had accurately described to Mitchell Spencer only weeks prior to the old man's demise. The designated key easily opened the back door. After surreptitiously flicking on a flashlight to locate the master bedroom's closet, the eager interloper anxiously moved the vertical shoe rack, and the ecstatic searcher easily located the wide-spaced wall safe. The key insertion worked perfectly, and just as dependable Julius Stetson had predicted, the half-million-dollars in hundred-dollar-bills had been left inside the safe, stashed in a utilitarian white linen bag.

'Oh my God! My life has been rescued from disaster!' Mitchell Spencer euphorically reckoned. 'I'll never forget *your* compassion and your kindness! Thank you Julius! Thank you from the bottom of my heart! Now to find the Window of Opportunity in the hall cedar closet to retrieve my special bonus!'

* * * * * * * * * * * *

Mitchell Spencer hastily maneuvered his way down the straight, light blue-carpeted hallway, and soon his curiosity found the object of his quest. In the center of the long corridor, the highly-focused, intensely sweating house-explorer quickly located the door to the prized storage room. 'It's locked!' Mitchell instantly recognized and regretted. 'Ah, the magic key also opens this closet door, too! I believe that Julius had mentioned *that* isolated fact to me! I'll close the door behind me, turn on the overhead light, saving the batteries in my flashlight. Then, I'll carefully open that beautiful stained-glass window at the other end of this closet. I see that it features two heavenly angels blowing their celestial golden trumpets. I can't wait to discover my promised bonus reward!'

After cautiously accomplishing those rather facile, elementary tasks, the perspiring searcher was completely thrilled about admiring the singular and resplendent 'Window of Opportunity', and his totally engrossed mind never for one suspicious moment ever comprehended that his physical existence had been permanently locked inside the enormous rectangular cedar closet.

Firmly gripping and holding the linen bag containing the half-million-dollars, the obsessed young man gently lifted the bottom window frame, and much to his utter shock and horror, Mitchell Spencer's body was instantaneously sucked inside the aperture by a powerful, mystical supernatural force.

And before the frightened and petrified victim had a chance to either scream or shriek, the mystical Window of Opportunity quickly descended like a guillotine blade, and the device forcefully slammed shut. Incredibly, the magnificent pair of handsome angels that had splendidly decorated the inimitable, stained-glass portal momentarily transformed into malicious-looking, red-skinned demons. And then, the wicked window that had been so maliciously constructed inside the cedar closet's back wall abruptly disappeared into oblivion.

* * * * * * * * * * * *

A dimly lit dense fog shrouded and enveloped a cold and barren subterranean swampy moor. The vigilant and awesome Black Angel of Death patiently awaited the arrival of the en route, newly acquired transmigrating soul, for to the gargantuan immortal winged creature, time was not ephemeral, and its mundane passage had no boundaries or particular definition. Finally, the rejuvenated spirit and psyche personage of one wily Julius Stetson materialized on the hazy and nebulous moor. The space/time voyager's past personality now parasitically residing inside the physical appearance of its new host, one Mitchell Spencer.

"I must compliment you on a most propitious and effortless spiritual transfer!" the austere-looking Black Angel bluntly stated. "I must confess that your diabolical Window of Opportunity trick has again been skillfully employed. The deceased spirit and soul' of your targeted subject has been symmetrically aligned with and absorbed into your former eighty-two-year-old frail, lifeless body. And simultaneously, your former corrupt spirit, by virtue of *our* contract agreement, is now speeding on its way to Hell. Now Sir, alias Julius Stetson, your unscrupulous heart and mind, by virtue of your devious canard, have been meritoriously transplanted into Mitchell Spencer's vernal form, and you've successfully earned a new extension to your mortal existence. And as you're well-aware, you've coincidentally inherited and obtained a vibrant new, slightly-used soul to complement your new virile body. And just to think," the thwarted and outsmarted Black Angel uttered and summarized, "our friendly relationship all started around three-hundred-and-ninety-years ago in Florence, Italy during the time of..."

"During the time of Galileo and the despicable Inquisitions, when scientific thought was readily condemned by the unrelenting Catholic Church bureaucracy. Technological progress was deemed sheer heresy," the newly exchanged spirit of Julius Stetson answered the sinister Devil's Messenger.

The dead man's resurrected soul was now-residing inside Mitchell Spencer's strong, vernal anatomy. "That's when I felt compelled to sign my binding contract with *you!* But as is outlined in Paragraph One, *you* can only mortgage my soul when I fail to find a vulnerable substitute every six decades or so."

The Black Angel was somewhat perturbed that his subject had again evaded *his* relentless pursuit. "Wily Magician, I promise to apprehend your soul and escort it to Hell the first time you fail at performing your simple-yet-odious deception. Yes, but upon rehashing our odd history together, Sagacious Sir, I recollect that our second devilish encounter had occurred during..."

"During the Great Age of the Illuminati in Southern Germany; yes, Black Angel, in medieval Munich, and if I also recollect, a half-century later, our third assignation, like the second one, had similarly transpired in this very same gloomy moor. That specific third development had happened immediately after *my* dupe's death in Marseilles, France during that intellectual genius Voltaire's most-splendid Age of Enlightenment."

"Affirmative, but please don't forget one significant detail Masterful Wizard," the solemn-faced and lugubrious Black Angel articulated, showing a defeated, frowning expression evident on its formidable-looking visage. "You're no longer Julius Stetson, but technically, to the not-too-brilliant human world, you're now Mitchell Spencer, professional educator. Do you plan to continue your mediocre career as a high school English teacher?"

"Hell no, Black Angel! As Mitchell Spencer, I'll wisely use-up my remaining sick days, and then, I'll resign from the school district effective July 1st," the self-centered, four-century-old, re-formatted human being replied. "And of course, I still have in my possession my luxurious mansion, which naturally I had perceptively willed to myself (Mitchell Spencer) along with my five-million-dollars in my Merrill Lynch stock account, and also my five-hundred thousand dollars in cash now concealed inside *my* upstairs cedar closet. The glorious and reliable Window of Opportunity, which as you've already acknowledged, was really an exceptionally clever trap, because it was *my* very necessary Window of Opportunity that was exclusively designed for *me* alone to live another fifty or so years inside this naïve, gullible idiot, Mitchell Spencer's youthful body. Perhaps I shouldn't criticize my new self so severely!"

"That's precisely why my immediate superior and awesome Commander-in-Chief Lucifer positively covets *your* calculated cunning so much. Because Sir, your charming character is insanely disingenuous, and you indeed are a virtual expert at executing marvelously heinous schemes!" the Black Angel commended his illustrious and very lucky mortal acquaintance. "Tell me now, Triumphant One. Will you be attending the dupe's, or should I say *the unfortunate victim's* funeral? After all, as bizarre as it may sound or seem, you will be *your* own fortunate heir."

"Yes, under the circumstances, *that* benign social gesture would be the appropriate and ethical thing to do, since as you've just mentioned Angel Friend, I, Mitchell Spencer, have been delegated as *his* sole and exclusive beneficiary!" the re-generated medieval alchemist and potent accomplished sorcerer cleverly remarked. "And soon thereafter, Black Angel, I'll be moving to another unsuspecting community; that is, after I legally acquire and sell my inherited Hammonton mansion, ha, ha, ha! I think and believe that I'll try living in Italy again!"

"Well now," the contemplative Black Angel very respectfully addressed its human companion, who apparently was reveling in achieving *his* recently earned new lease on life. "You always accomplish your 'transmigration of soul tricking routine' within the required seventy-two-hour parameters. I suppose that our next incidental meeting will be in approximately another fifty-to-sixty Earth years, when *your* then decrepit spirit and debilitated psyche will again require replenishment, reincarnation, and transmigration into a new body," the Black Angel matter-of-factly declared.

"That is absolutely correct!" the rejuvenated, wily Alchemist wholeheartedly verified. "To be sure as reality!"

"Indeed, Dracula and his vampires have nothing noteworthy over you!" the enormous Black Angel stoically admitted. "Good luck in scamming another unwary young male, while you again gamble your already-damned soul. And I congratulate you for adroitly eluding your eternal fate! I feel obligated to inform you, Mitchell Spencer, that my supernatural senses confirm the reality that my Satanic Colleagues now have the former Julius Stetson's body and soul in their custody, while the former Mitchell Spencer's suspended pristine soul is presently on moral probation, comfortably residing inside *your* new, young, human form."

"So long, my four-century-long Satanic Friend!" the most fortunate, resourceful magician replied. "Truthfully, I think I need a change in venue from living in Hammonton, New Jersey. First, I intend to move down to South Padre Island, Texas and begin a new fresh existence. But this time I think I'll join either the Kiwanis or the Rotary Club down there near the Mexican Border. When I tire of Texas, I'll then migrate over to wonderful Italy. I presume we'll again rendezvous in this same ominous swampy moor a half Earth century or so from now!" the mortal soul enthusiastically commented. "Over the centuries, this Window of Opportunity bait idea has worked extremely well for me, and as is my standard practice, I won't deviate one iota from again successfully using it in the future! Fearsome Black Angel," the shrewd Alchemist declared, "my proven strategy might sound like an overused cliché, but the fact of the matter is, 'Nothing really succeeds like success'!"

"Soldier of Misfortune"

Dr. Angelo DeMarco had recently retired as the head psychiatrist at New Jersey's Ancora State Hospital in order to devote his full time to expanding his private practice, which was located inside a second-floor office suite at the southeast corner of 2nd Street and Bellevue Avenue, Hammonton, New Jersey. The psych' physician was perusing a letter received from Noreen Pearson, the wife of a twenty-five-year-old Army Corporal, and the distraught enlisted soldier had been complaining to his spouse of severe migraine headaches, of terrible repetitious nightmares, and also the afflicted young serviceman was often heard uttering "indiscernible gibberish" during his erratic nightly sleeps.

Dr. DeMarco considered the prospective case study of his latest accepted patient, Jack Pearson, to be quite novel and intriguing, because in her curious letter of introduction and referral request, Mrs. Noreen Pearson had thoroughly described her husband's insistence that he had been suffering from symptoms of a baffling multiple personality disorder caused by regenerative experiences of 'organized, chronological, military service reincarnation.'

The psychiatrist's receptionist/secretary politely escorted Mr. Jack Pearson into Dr. DeMarco's spacious office, where initial casual conversation gradually led to the standard doctor/patient interview. The mental health expert explicitly explained to Jack that all human beings were similar in that humans respond to general fundamental needs and drives, but each person's relationship to his or her behavior is expressed in an individual, unique, and specific way.

"Frankly Jack, there are basically two types of needs," Dr. DeMarco pontificated to Pearson. "Physical needs such as the need for food, shelter, and clothing to protect the body from the elements, and then there're also human psychological needs, such as the need for approval, acceptance, attention, self-esteem and last buy not least, the need for love and security. And then, of course Jack," the eminent psychiatrist sternly continued his monologue, "there are those strong basic drives that often motivate and compel people to act, such as the characteristic hunger, greed, and sex drives. Your unusual mental condition might very well be a combination of any two or more of the traditional needs and drives that comprise the

"

'typical human profile'. Now Jack, your very concerned wife Doreen stated in her letter that you believe that you're over two-hundred-and-fifty years old! Is her remarkable assertion true?"

"That's correct Dr.," the somewhat addled patient quite matter-of-factly answered. "But the stressful dreams that I've been having stay in my subconscious mind, and I'm frustrated because I can never fully recall any specific details of my involvement, anywhere from the beginning of my restless slumber to the end. All I can remember about my dreams, or should I say 'my nightmares', is that I'm predictably engaged in some kind of major war battle. But in each instance, the battles are with all kinds of different enemies of various nationalities. Now please tell me, does that odd portrayal make any sort of sense to you?"

"I believe that I see what you're attempting to explain!" Dr. Angelo DeMarco stated, pensively rubbing his clean-shaven chin. "Since my ten o'clock appointment has canceled because *that* patient has developed flu symptoms, I'll have up to two-hours to objectively observe your deportment under hypnosis. I'll be recording and evaluating your verbal responses to my oral prompts. Now Mr. Pearson, I find the notion that you honestly think that you're around two-and-a-half-centuries old very fascinating indeed! I think that your abnormal nightmare events represent a distinct challenge to my general knowledge of human behavior and development. Let me ask if you are now emotionally ready for me to delve into your psyche, your id, and your ego?"

"Yes, Dr. I've seen enough of this sort of stuff in the movies. I presume that I should first lie down on your leather couch over there," Jack indicated, pointing at the comfortable-looking piece of furniture with his index finger. "Honestly now, for my sake and for my wife's peace of mind, I hope that this experimental session turns out to be successful."

"If possible, Jack, when you respond to a particular question, please inform me of the exact setting of your mental manifestation; that is," the psychiatrist stipulated and then paused to perfectly enunciate his additional words, "provide me with the exact year of the incident you're describing. And also, if you could, tell me the geographic location where the battle that you're directly involved in is taking place. I trust, Mr. Pearson, that you'll be able to do that simple task without experiencing any harmful duress or emotional stress."

354

Jack then voluntarily assumed his horizontal position upon the soft black leather sofa, and in a matter of several suspenseful minutes, Dr. DeMarco had effectively hypnotized Pearson, using a watch dangling and oscillating from a gold fob chain. When the soldier/patient appeared to be fully relaxed, the all-too-confident mind doctor commenced with his formal interrogation, which a remote camera was capturing on film.

"Please remember Mr. Pearson, you still possess your free will and should only verbally respond to my well-intentioned suggestions and comments if you so desire. Now then, as a brave and loyal soldier of history, where are you located now, Jack, and what time period is it?"

"I'm somewhere in Massachusetts in June of 1775," Jack began his bizarre recollection. "Yes, I'm helping in the effort to fortify the Charlestown Peninsula. The British barges are currently ferrying opposing troops across the river, and my commander, Colonel William Prescott, has ordered me and the other soldiers to make a stand and defend Breed's Hill. We had held our ground twice, but now we've run out of gunpowder," the hypnotized subject expressed. "The redcoats are shooting at us, volley after volley. Boston and vicinity must not fall to the enemy! Oh my God!" Jack exclaimed. "I'm wounded; shot in the back while I was turned around and reloading my musket! My legs are paralyzed. The pain from my shoulders to my hips is excruciating! I'll never be able to escape the peninsula alive! I'm passing out! Everything's hazy all around me! I'm sure I'm dying! Goodbye cruel world!"

"All right Jack, you're safe and sound now, and you've miraculously fled the enemy. Your pathetic injuries have completely healed!" Dr. DeMarco declared as his eyes noticed that his patient's changed breathing was gradually becoming more normal and regular. "You've been safely evacuated out of the Battle of Bunker Hill, and you've triumphantly endured *that* important-but-pivotal conflict of the American Revolutionary War!" the mind doctor loquaciously communicated. "I now recommend that you take ten deep breaths, and then again tell me where you are and what activities are occurring in your immediate vicinity."

Jack had effectively calmed-down from his initial ordeal, and the stabilized patient very deliberately articulated that the new date was January 8th, 1815, and that Pearson, along with other assigned riflemen, were occupying an entrenchment while observing highly-trained units of British soldiers marching in neat rows directly into the pre-set American trap. General Andrew Jackson soon gave the command to "Fire!", and the ambushing American marksmen easily defeated the advancing, hostile-but-surprised foreign enemy. But during the termination of the rather fierce engagement, a blast from a distant cannon sent Jack Pearson hurtling through the air, his fragile body being violently crushed upon impacting a sturdy tree trunk.

"I am an avid student of history and evidently, you had just participated in the Battle of New Orleans during the War of 1812," Dr. DeMarco immediately recognized and related. "But don't worry one iota, Jack; you've apparently endured and survived your ordeal with flying colors! If my memory of history serves me correctly, the battle was unnecessary because a peace treaty had already been signed at Ghent, Belgium, several weeks before the violent conflict had happened. But because of the lack of speedy communications across the Atlantic Ocean," the highly-skilled consultant elucidated, "neither the British commander, General Edward Parkenham, nor your own dauntless General Andrew Jackson were ever aware of the cease fire being in effect! You're doing quite excellent, Jack!" Dr. DeMarco praised. "Where are you now?"

"It's February 23, 1836, although in truth, I haven't looked at a calendar or an almanac for several months," the amazing military patient prefaced. "There's this popular belief of 'Manifest Destiny' going all around America, and presently, Texas Territory is under Mexican dominion. I'm standing on a rampart, so to speak, defending a Spanish mission, the Alamo, so I suppose that Davy Crockett, Jim Bowie, and me are all 'on-a-mission' to fight to the death using our muskets as clubs. That is, after our ammunition supplies have been used up. Oh, how agonizing!" Jack Pearson anguished with conviction from his trance-like state. "A Mexican bayonet has just entered my chest and I'm bleeding to death while lying helplessly on the ground. My spirit is about to exit my body. Oh Lord, please save me! Forgive me for my numerous sins and grant me life everlasting! Lord have mercy on me!"

'My patient's entire narrative is positively incredible!' Dr. DeMarco marveled and contemplated. 'This very special man, at least according to this subject's extraordinary testimony, is an actual true-blue American patriot! And he's candidly and persuasively presented his recollection of virtually almost dying three consecutive times in precise chronological order, originating with the

356

Revolutionary War, followed by the War of 1812, and now Jack's vividly describing his heroic actions during the quest for Texas independence at the Alamo in 1836. If I recall from my knowledge of U.S. history, the battle was a major episode in the prelude to the Mexican-American War where General Sam Houston eventually vanquished Santa Anna at San Jacinto,' Dr. DeMarco's keen mind imagined. 'But how could Jack Pearson possibly be inventing such phenomenal fiction while being totally submissive and obediently compliant under professional hypnosis?'

Dr. Angelo DeMarco then hypothesized that according to the patient's exceptional 'already-established time line', Jack would naturally next declare his personal association with the Civil War. The man's unique narrative was unlike any commentaries that the psychiatrist had ever before heard in *his* noteworthy thirty-five-year professional career. To the astounded interviewer, Jack Pearson was like an addiction, and Dr. Angelo DeMarco wanted more of his subject's strange attestations.

"What's your next war adventure?" the captivated questioner courteously and suavely interrogated. "Verify for me, Jack. Are you fighting for the North or for the South?"

"Definitely for the Union Blue!" Jack emphatically confirmed. "It's September, 1862, I believe, somewhere in Maryland at a creek called Antietam near the town of Sharpsburg. My commander, General McClellan, has vigilantly pursued the Grays there, but then backup Confederates have unexpectedly showed-up coming from the direction of Harpers Ferry, West Virginia. During the wild and bloody confrontation, I've just been mortally wounded and am rapidly losing consciousness. I've got enemy shrapnel in my arms, stomach, and legs!"

"Well, Jack, I have good news to relate. You've magically managed to survive the bitter Antietam altercation unscathed," consoled and comforted the veteran interviewer. "And you're fortunate to have come out of that formidable war zone still alive and able to speak! Your escape to safety is borderline miraculous. Over twelve-thousand brave Union soldiers had perished in the wild siege," Dr. DeMarco, amateur historian, expounded in a soothing tone of voice. "All because General Robert E. Lee wanted to record his first victory on land that had been controlled by the North. But in the final analysis," the mind-doctor indicated to his new patient, "Lee had to admit being out-manned, and subsequently, the

Confederate General reluctantly retreated his exhausted army from Maryland back into Virginia."

The professional examiner was not especially skeptical of his new client's veracity, but the mental health expert suspected that Corporal Jack Pearson might just have been suffering from delusional imaginings, with certain ideas being spontaneously generated from *his* most creative subconscious mind. Dr. DeMarco accurately anticipated that his subject's next graphic depiction would entail *his* supporting role in the Spanish-American War that had begun in 1898 with the sinking of the battleship Maine in Havana Harbor, occurring during Republican President William McKinley's Administration. The excited psychiatrist then expertly transitioned Jack into *his* new dangerous scenario.

"I had fought with Colonel Teddy Roosevelt's Rough Riders at the Battle of San Juan Hill, but fortunately for us, only mostly enemy Spanish soldiers were killed during the brief encounter," Jack uttered and disclosed in a more relaxed oral delivery. "But because of poor sanitary conditions and camping-out in a mosquito-infested tropical environment, I did almost die in Cuba, but not from any destructive cannon blast or gunfire. I had somehow contracted a repugnant case of Yellow Fever, and then somehow avoided passing-away on August 1st, 1898, exactly one month after Colonel Roosevelt and his rambunctious Rough Riders had basically run rough-shod over their intimidated Spanish adversaries."

"And if I may suggest your next wartime engagement, I suppose that twenty or so years later, you were part of General John J. Pershing's advancing American Expeditionary Force in France," the knowledgeable history buff/psychiatrist asked his immobile, mesmerized patient. "I've avidly read in various encyclopedias where over two-million American soldiers had valiantly fought in France during the famous 'Lafayette We Are Here!' campaign. Did you ever sing the famous song *Over There?*"

"Yes, I did sing that inspiring George M. Cohan marching song in the rural sectors of France in 1918," Jack rather lethargically confirmed. "I had gotten separated from my platoon after the left side of our trench had been demolished by a direct mortar hit. Bloodthirsty and aggressive German soldiers surrounded me near the Siegfried Line, and I was immediately captured and tortured somewhere inside a dense forest without ever having a chance to raise my hands and formally surrender."

358

"Well, in the 1930s there was the Great Depression scourge, along with Prohibition in America, and then there was the infamous rise of Adolph Hitler and his Nazi regime in Germany in the mid and late '30s," Dr. DeMarco recalled and commented. "And after the Japanese squadron planes attacked Pearl Harbor, the United States responded to the belligerent assault by joining the Allies to fight the Germans, who were aligned with the Italians under Mussolini and also with the Japanese imperialists' fearsome military juggernaut. And don't forget, Jack, the Jewish Holocaust, too, where over six million innocent people perished for no apparent reason at all, except for probably being Hitler's personal scapegoat!"

"World War II was an abomination, an absolutely atrocious ugly conflict waged against brutal and ruthless German fascists," Jack Pearson uttered in a monotone voice from his trance-like state. "My Army unit was advancing north inside Italy, and we were about to fight for control of Rome and then move on towards Florence in Tuscany. We were hunkered-down, occupying a building in the town of Cassino, situated about midway between Naples and Rome," the perplexed man lying prone on the black leather sofa orally reviewed. "The Allies' planes then bombed the monastery at the top of Monte Cassino, thinking that it had been housing German and Italian troops. But then, an errant shell landed squarely on top of the building I was in, and I instantly was injured in my face and hands from what might be today described as 'friendly fire'!"

"Well, Jack, after World War II, the U.S. troops returned home. And there was a tremendous industrial renaissance throughout the entire land with suburban communities and shopping centers popping-up outside and around every major urban metropolitan area," Dr. DeMarco lectured to his now quietly-resting patient. "The short-lived peace was interrupted, however, with the initiation of the Korean War between the North Korea Communists and the United States. Was that particular war in your experiential repertoire?"

"No, Sir. I don't recall any Korean War," the placid patient maintained. "Instead, I remember the year being 1968. I was savagely wounded by a Viet Cong surprise sneak attack outside a coastal city called Hue. Apparently, my platoon had wandered too close to an underground enemy tunnel hatch entrance, and before I knew it," Pearson stammered and then regained his subconscious confidence, "three of my companions and I were viciously attacked, and two of my buddies died, being cruelly maimed by several tossed hand grenades that landed near their American targets."

"And by virtue of deductive logic, because of a time sequence war pattern you've experienced over the last two-and-a-half centuries, I reckon that you had to also be a participant if not a casualty in the 2003 Iraq War?" Dr. DeMarco speculated and conveyed. "Were you also a victim in that modern-era conflict?"

"Yes, Sir. I did eventually die after receiving a bullet to my throat. I had passed-away inside a temporary Kuwait military tent hospital, after the sudden firefight I had been describing flared-up near the Iraqi border," pallid-faced Corporal Pearson divulged. "All together, I have accomplished dying, or nearly dying, nine times in nine separate American Wars. But each time, I had other last names than Pearson; names like Adams, Jensen, Douglas, Johnson, Burns and McFarland, but in each instance, my first name was always 'Jack'. I trust that my stated observations have managed to clarify certain important psychological concepts for you!"

Having to learn and ascertain another salient relevant fact, inquisitive Dr. DeMarco momentarily hesitated, his keen mind grappling with another question while his eyes gazed upon and studied inimitable Corporal Pearson. The patient was dressed in civilian attire, still lying flat upon the black leather couch.

"Jack, in my professional opinion, I find your unconventional multiple war lives' account to be both most absorbing and most incomprehensible. Now please tell me, were you married during your nine former soldier existences, and if so, was your wife's name Doreen in each instance?"

"Yes!" the subject affirmatively replied. "Yes, I had been wed!" Pearson confidently reiterated.

"Was your wife the same Doreen to whom you're presently married?" the now-enamored psychiatrist asked. "Think carefully, for *this* matter is of utmost significance!"

"No! Each time it was a different Doreen with red, black, brown, or blonde hair!" the patient explicitly insisted. "But if I may add, each of my nine former wives was in her own way an intelligent, beautiful woman, that fact I am sure."

"Well, Jack, I've performed a bit of elementary math' in my head and have arrived at the statistic that, assuming that you were at least twenty-years old when you had been wounded at the battle of Bunker Hill, you've lived approximately two-hundred-and-fifty-years as you've already convincingly asserted. And according to my calculation estimates," Dr. Angelo DeMarco conjectured and maintained, "most of the time intervals between the various wars that you've chronologically cited were on the average in the range of twenty-five years apart. I've achieved arriving at *that* temporal mean average length by simply subtracting twenty-years from two-hundred-and-fifty, and then dividing the number two-hundred-and-thirty by nine!" the authoritative mind and emotion evaluator declared. "The basic arithmetic tends to support and justify your claim that you're born again every twenty-five years; mature to adulthood like any normal adolescent would, and then coincidentally, are injured or die in warfare, just about every standard generation. This uncanny recurrent sequence means that..."

"Means that I'm on a schedule to soon be wounded or die for the tenth consecutive time," Corporal Pearson completed his perceptive mentor's statement. "Oh my God! I think my brain's entering into a panic attack! I'm being overwhelmed by a weird-feeling, a definite death anxiety!"

"Listen carefully to my strict directions, Jack!" Dr. DeMarco imperatively instructed. "I'm going to count backwards from ten. When I reach the number 'one', I'll snap my fingers, and you'll slowly come out of your deep sleep, and then be as good as new. Ten, nine, eight, seven, six...."

* * * * * * * * * * * *

"Five, four, three, two, one...."

When Dr. DeMarco snapped his fingers, the office setting instantly became a thick dark fog, and the next thing that the psychiatrist knew, the mind expert was occupying a bunker surrounded by a wall of sandbags and that he and Jack Pearson were in Army uniforms nervously preparing for imminent combat. Plumes of dense smoke were billowing skyward in the background. Assessing the illogical situational anomaly, the alarmed and panic-stricken psychiatrist felt compelled to ask, "Jack, where the hell are we? What's going on?"

"It's now April of 2017, and we're on a plain somewhere in northern Israel, getting ready for the Battle of Armageddon! It's all very feasible and rational. The truths of Biblical prophecy must be fulfilled, you know!"

"What do you mean when you say that Biblical prophecy must be fulfilled? Are you totally insane or drastically inebriated?" the obviously incensed and apprehensive transported psychiatrist demanded a plausible explanation from his new-found companion. "Stop being so damned vague and evasive! Be more specific when answering me, Corporal Pearson!"

"It's all a matter of exact Cosmic Divine Inspiration that is actually quite ubiquitous throughout the entire Universe!" Jack endeavored explaining to the thoroughly-puzzled and perturbed mind doctor. "Believing is so much more vital to a human being than is the practice of abstract scientific thinking! Any avowed cynic or skeptic could engage in the simple act of doubting!"

"Your wife was right about your nonsensical verbalizations! Stop speaking this incessant, ludicrous gibberish of yours! Explain yourself before I lose my temper and get violent!" the now-terrified mind doctor loudly yelled like an asylum maniac.

"I really don't fear dying at this particular moment like you do!" Jack cryptically and enigmatically answered. "The laws of the Universe prescribe that a person must die ten-times to reach his or her ultimate destiny. After the final ninth reincarnation," the Corporal methodically articulated, "the individual's Karma has been finally attained upon rendezvousing a tenth time with the immortal Eternal Force. There's one thing I've neglected to tell you, Dr. DeMarco. I want you to know that I've actually died nine times and *not once* as you currently believe, you frivolous Fool!" Jack Pearson solemnly informed his fit-to-be-tied listener.

"Jack, I don't want t die!" Dr. Demarco shrieked.

"So, when we're both exploded into the hereafter, Dr. DeMarco, I'll be emotionally content traveling to my ultimate destiny, commonly referred to as Nirvana, because Dr., *my* final spiritual examination will have ended, and I will have then successfully passed the obligatory Karma test. Don't you comprehend what I'm expressing? My ten assigned life-and-death Earth cycles will have been finally satisfied. My restless soul will have finally achieved harmony with the Great Universe! When *you* die, you'll have to die nine more times!"

"But what about me?" the about to go berserk psychiatrist bellowed into the Corporal's serene-looking face. "What is to be *my* personal fate?"

"I've finally found you, Dr. Angelo DeMarco, as my gullible soul replacement, and you're now my foolish victimized substitute; you're futilely trapped in a three-century series of future life/death reenactments," the Army Corporal apprised his greatly dumbfounded Army Private counterpart.

"But Jack, that's *your* eternal status! Tell me more about what's going to happen to *me?*"

"As I've stated, you must die nine additional times, thereafter, that is, following your about-to-happen first expiration in order to fulfill your Eternal Karma. And then, after you eventually die nine additional times, as I certainly will have soon accomplished, you'll progressively become spiritually purified. Then, your troubled soul can finally exist in total tranquility with the Endless Universe," Jack Pearson candidly conveyed to his still-astonished and totally alienated, neurotic, army bunker mate. "Then and only then, Dr. DeMarco, you and your pseudo-science psychiatry, along with your immortal soul, will at last be accepted by the omnipotent Powers-That-Be. And after ten deaths, your total being will finally be integrated as One' with the truth and wisdom of the Supreme Cosmos! Oh God!" Jack joyfully exclaimed. "I just can't wait to die for the tenth and final time, and majestically reach my Ultimate Karma!"

"Triple Jeopardy"

Ever-vigilant FBI Inspector Joseph Giralo was quite fatigued from his grueling daily work schedule that involved apprehending major East Coast felony criminals, and now the veteran federal law enforcement official and his wife Gina were anxiously looking forward to a week-long bus excursion originating from the Senior Tours Bus Terminal on Route 9 in Cape May Court House, New Jersey. Upstate Michigan was the land tour's principal destination, and also its culminating tourist experience, the site of the famous and historic Grand Michigan Hotel, majestically occupying a picturesque ridge on tranquil Mackinac Island. The world-renowned vacation resort is ideally located midway between the mid-western state's Lower and Upper Peninsulas.

After boarding the huge white bus along with the other dozen bleary-eyed early rising passengers, Joe and Gina were ready to start their great adventure at precisely 5 a.m. on a mild September Saturday morning. The husband and wife sat impatiently in their soft blue seats and watched out the window as Mike the bus driver dutifully loaded the group's luggage into the modern deluxe vehicle's right-side storage compartment. The FBI Inspector seemed rather content coping with his "rooster time existence."

"It's great being a regular non-government civilian for the next seven days. And Hon, you just can't get any bus better than this one anywhere in Jersey," the somewhat relaxed man commented to his devoted spouse. "This is one of those new 'kneeling buses' that has an impressive spiral boarding entrance. I don't know if you had noticed it or not Gina, but the front steps had actually lowered several inches to allow us to conveniently get inside and then move up the aisle more easily. How long until our first rest stop? I could use some hot coffee to wake me up?"

"Well, Hubby, according to the itinerary I'm holding in my hand," Gina alertly answered, "we'll be stopping at the King-of-Prussia rest stop on the Pennsylvania Turnpike in about three hours. The local bus tour company had to team-up with a couple of other regional operations to fill-up this bus. Other passengers will be picked-up at the Shore Mall just outside Atlantic City, and later at the Wyndham Hotel on Route 73 in Cherry Hill," Mrs. Giralo prattled and informed. "Then it'll be across the Delaware River via the Betsy

Ross Bridge to the Neshaminy Mall where the remainder of the people will be picked-up along with our special tour guide."

"This trip looks like a real bargain costing only eleven hundred dollars a person," Joe Giralo reminded his very upbeat traveling mate. "Where are we staying the first night?"

"At a La Quinta Inn in an Ohio town called Macedonia."

"I hope we don't run into King Philip or his conquest-minded son Alexander-the-Great," Joe jested, as the vacationing FBI Inspector curiously stared through the passenger window and noticed Mike slamming shut the side luggage door. "This might sound stupid, but I've done more than my share of up-front combat with enough local *barbarians* during my thirty-year FBI career. I hope that folks traveling the busy Interstates in Ohio and Michigan don't think we're a part of a traveling high-jacked sequestered jury," the husband facetiously quipped.

"Why do you say that?" Gina asked, anticipating one of her spouse's incessant ridiculous jokes.

"Because on the side of the bus is painted the words Senior Tours, Cape May Court House," Giralo replied before giggling. "You know me, Hon. Always thinking about some aspect of the law and some oddball facet of the American justice system."

At eight a.m. (and on schedule) the bus rumbled into the King-of-Prussia rest area on the Pennsylvania Turnpike, and Joe and Gina stepped-out to enjoy some hot coffee and fresh doughnuts during their half hour stop. In the midst of their light conversation, Gina gave her loyal companion some background on what Senior Tours had planned for the week besides a "glorious three-night stay" at the splendid Grand Michigan Hotel.

"After the first night in Ohio at the La Quinta Inn, we'll be spending Sunday afternoon viewing the many exhibits at the Ford Museum in Dearborn, just outside Detroit," the excited wife reviewed. "Then, right next to the museum is Greenfield Village, a wonderful re-creation of the place, where Henry Ford had lived his childhood. I won't go into all the details of what's in the museum or inside the village, because I want to see how surprised you'll be when we view them. Our tour guide Julie told me five minutes ago that we'll be on our own for the entire museum and village explorations. Then next, we'll be staying the night at an area Ramada Inn before heading out to Frankenmuth in the center of Michigan."

"What's Frankenmuth?" the puzzled husband wondered and asked. "It sounds like a special gift the Three Wise Men brought to Bethlehem, or it might just be a distant relative of Victor Frankenstein. Or perhaps it's a gross mispronunciation of the dangerous monster's *mouth?*"

"No, Silly!" Gina corrected, revealing a cute grin upon her lips. "I read in the informative trip brochure that 'Franken' refers to the German people that eventually settled in central Michigan and that 'Muth' is a German word meaning courage, so together Frankenmuth means the bravery of the original German settlers. The place is a really neat Bavarian-style town in appearance, and I think you'll actually feel like you're in a Black Forest village rather than meandering-around in the middle of a Midwestern State."

"That all sounds pretty terrific and exactly what I need; a nice change of pace from our hectic New Jersey environment," Joe opined. "Now tell me, Dear. Did you bring along that new deck of cards of yours? I'm even willing to play a game of 'Phase Ten' to pass the night in Macedonia, that is, if there aren't any major baseball or football games on TV."

Julie promptly sauntered over to the Giralos' rest stop table and announced, "Bus leaves in five minutes! Mike's already had his standard two cigarettes and an extra-large cup of coffee, so the nicotine and the caffeine will keep him wide-eyed for the next two and a half hours until we reach western Pennsylvania and have a chance to view the beautiful Allegheny Mountains. After another casual rest stop," Julie continued her narrative, "it's then into Ohio, and finally off to rural Macedonia and supper at a Cracker Barrel Restaurant, followed by a restful night at the very comfortable La Quinta Inn. And after a decent continental breakfast just off the lodge's lobby," Julie concisely expressed, "Sunday morning it's off to Dearborn. Don't forget, Folks. Except for the nights at the Grand Michigan Hotel, you can only take your two carry-on bags into the several motels where we'll be staying."

"Thanks, Julie," Joe replied with a smile. "What does La Quinta mean in English? Is it a number?"

"No, but just like we have words for 'house' like 'home', 'abode', 'dwelling' and 'residence' in English," the knowledgeable tour guide stated and then paused to further emphasize her point, "La Quinta means 'country house' in Spanish and it's a synonym for regular words like 'casa' and 'hacienda'."

"Pardon my ignorance when it comes to foreign languages," Joe indulgently laughed as the FBI Inspector rose from his red plastic snack area seat. "But even a broken clock is right twice a day! Ha, ha, ha!"

* * * * * * * * * * * *

Late Sunday morning, Mike used his reliable GPS device to leave a very congested Interstate having plenty of infrastructure construction. And then, the man behind the wheel skillfully navigated his ultra-modern bus through downtown Detroit, heading west in the direction of Dearborn and the aforementioned Ford Museum and adjacent Greenfield Village. Since the outside temperature was approaching an unseasonably high eighty degrees, most of the bus entourage, including the smart-thinking Giralos, decided to amble through the village first, and then later enjoy the air-conditioning provided inside the immense museum.

Train tickets were purchased at the village's main station, and the New Jersey duo stepped aboard the third carriage car of the *Edison,* a small refurbished steam locomotive that had been manufactured during the past century. Gina explained to her somewhat-interested husband that one of Henry Ford's closest friends was inventor Thomas Alva Edison, so naturally, it made perfectly good sense that the train engine appropriately bore *that* particular name.

Most everyone riding the colorfully painted train cars decided to exit at the second depot stop, which amazingly was a full-scale re-creation of Michigan's legendary Port Huron Railway Station, where incidentally, a young Thomas Edison had become a twelve-year-old "news butcher" on a train owned by the then prominent Grand Trunk Railway. Young Edison was quite ambitious, and the lad sold newspapers, candy, peanuts, and various sandwiches on a popular rail route that ran from Port Huron all the way down to Detroit.

According to a brochure Gina had been reading, one day young mischievous Tom tried conducting a difficult chemical experiment in the baggage car, when a stick of phosphorus accidentally caught on fire. The appalled and angry conductor entered and roughly grabbed the boy, vigorously boxed Edison's tender ears, and then mercilessly kicked the non-penitent youth off the train at the next station. That particular ear abuse led to Edison being nearly deaf, but later in a separate railroad incident, another conductor on a slow-moving train helped Tom clamber aboard by lifting the adolescent up by the ears, thus additionally contributing to Edison's virtual deafness that regrettably accompanied him throughout the remainder of his curiosity-oriented life.

"Last year my class read a short story about the amazing Thomas Edison," elementary school teacher Gina Giralo recalled and related to her somewhat apathetic spouse. "The theme was that Thomas Edison had often said that he didn't mind being almost totally deaf, because the lack of sound afforded him the luxury of thinking and concentrating better. Edison really was quite a remarkable man."

"And I remember from a high school science class lecture that Edison had kept plenty of clocks on the walls and tables of his New Jersey laboratory, but none of them ever had the right time," the husband shared. "Soon, everyone on his staff working on their various projects forgot all about time and focused their attention on individual tasks at hand. Perhaps I'll remember to do a similar thing in my FBI office when I get back to Jersey."

Greenfield Village was indeed rather spectacular for the first-time visitors to experience. After stepping away from the realistic-looking Port Huron Railway Station, the New Jersey couple stopped their trekking for several minutes and enjoyed listening to the calliope music emanating from an enormous children's amusement carousel house, which was strategically situated towards the center of the spotless, clean-street village.

Other delightful surprises were seen and soon entered. One brick building was a facsimile of the original H.J. Heinz office and processing plant; another attractive edifice was a rendition of the Wright Brothers Store in Dayton, Ohio, and also several foundries had been meticulously erected inside Greenfield Village to show the tremendous economic "factory progress" that had been made during the great American Industrial Revolution.

And next, the two enamored visitors strolled around the grounds of Henry Ford's birthplace, a handsome white country house with a fine rotating windmill occupying the back yard. The eye-appealing property was quaintly situated next to a replica of Thomas Edison's gray laboratory building in Menlo Park, New Jersey, where marvelous inventions such as the phonograph, the light bulb, and the motion picture film projector had been conceived during the extraordinarily dynamic early stages of the twentieth century.

But the most truly wonderful aspect of anachronistic-looking Greenfield Village was yet to come. At a booth, the Giralos purchased tickets to climb into an authentic, well-maintained Model-T Ford that was still functioning as if it was a brand-new transportation machine. A fleet of fifteen Model-Ts of different designs (ranging through the years 1915-1927) was available to the visiting public. Every Model-T had a private chauffeur, and the knowledgeable drivers took captivated tourists on refreshing fifteen-minute rides all throughout the immaculate, cement-paved streets of absolutely incomparable Greenfield Village.

"Nothing at all like this unique attraction exists back in Jersey," Giralo noted to his wife. "I'm not exaggerating when I say that *this* inspirational ride is borderline sensational."

"Yes, Sir. the Model-Ts became obsolete in the late 1920s and the design was then followed by the upgraded more sophisticated Model-A Ford," eavesdropping Ben, the Model-T operator added to the dialogue. "Don't ask me why the early Fords are in reverse alphabetical order, because I can't answer that question. But it's a known fact that the Model-A definitely came into production after the Model-T became extinct."

"Regardless of the chronological order," Joe Giralo declared with an air of certainty evident in his tone of voice, "tell me now, Ben. Are the buildings here in Greenfield Village all miniature models of the original structures?"

"Actually, many of the main structures are the same size as the originals and have been carefully dismantled. And after being specially transported here, they've been gingerly reassembled stone by stone, brick by brick," Ben conveyed to his fascinated audience of two. "It was quite a colossal undertaking to say the least, but just like good old Henry Ford had achieved during his lifetime, the almost impossible engineering feats represented here in Greenfield Village could only be accomplished with extra diligence and perseverance. When you have a chance, be sure to walk through the several large machinery buildings where the theme 'machines making machines' is the key message."

"Positively incredible!" Joe Giralo evaluated and exclaimed. "*Special* is the only word I can think of to describe this pretty unbelievable place!"

After passing through the Main Pavilion's exit turnstiles, Joe and Gina strolled hand-in-hand like two newlyweds over to the nearby

Ford Museum, which also offered its guests many outstanding attractions. And after taking photos' of each other standing in front of the sentimental-in-appearance, famous Oscar Mayer Wienermobile, the rejuvenated pair swallowed-down delicious hot dogs at the adjacent Oscar Mayer food concession.

Other exquisite exhibits were visually enjoyed including a reproduction of a '50s Texaco gas station; an original Golden Arches McDonald's walk-up Restaurant advertising 15cent hamburgers; the actual Rosa Parks bus that was still in mint condition; a walk-in '50s diner, and the historic Presidential limousines of Franklin D. Roosevelt, John F. Kennedy, and Ronald Reagan. But besides the giant generators, turbines, tractors, airplanes, and powerful steam locomotives occupying strategic spaces, the main highlight of the Ford Museum (for the Giralos) happened to be the nearly two hundred classic American automobiles on display, the array including a vintage white Duesenberg; a terrific-looking Rolls Royce Phantom; a sporty red Jaguar Roadster; a fantastic Bugatti; several memorable Cadillacs and Packards, along with a contingent of nostalgic-looking, shiny '50s Chevy Corvettes and sporty Ford Thunderbirds.

"Did you see the rear seat of F.D.R.'s limo'?" Gina asked. "It had three buttons positioned on a back seat console, one each for NBC, ABC and CBS, the three dominant radio networks of the awesome 1940s!"

"Wow!" Joe exclaimed, showing his new-found exuberance. "President Roosevelt had a form of push button radio remote control several years before television had ever been invented. I suppose that those three useful network buttons were really high tech' state-of-the-art back in the Big Band, art deco days of the 1940s. Glenn Miller really had it right all along. This fabulous out-of-this-world Ford Museum has really gotten me out of my tedious work doldrums and 'In the Mood'."

* * * * * * * * * * * * *

Midway into the third day of scenic traveling, Mike steered his bus into the town of Frankenmuth, and the weary passengers all checked into their various rooms at the Drury Inn at 260 South Main Street. That evening, a tasty chicken and beer supper was enjoyed at the extra-large-sized Bavarian Inn, owned by the same family as the landmark Zehnder's Restaurant, situated across the street, which proudly promotes itself as the largest family restaurant in the entire United States. The waiters at the Bavarian Inn wore green feathered hats and knee socks with short pants, traditional German festival apparel known in and around 'Old World' Munich as 'lederhosen', while the pretty waitresses were garbed in attractive cotton dresses that were referred to as 'dirndl.'

But much to everyone's appreciation, after a delectable pastry/ice cream dessert had been served and consumed, the Jersey tourists re-boarded the dependable bus, and Mike drove the now-spirited delegation to the magnificent Bronners Christmas Land on the east end of Frankenmuth. Upon its nighttime arrival, the bus passed up and down a series of parallel lanes that featured a brilliant spectacle of flickering and blinking lit Christmas decorations: angels, elves, Magi, a North Pole setting, Bethlehem manger scenes, Santa Clauses, glistening snowmen, colorful giant boxed gifts, impressive toy soldier guards, and the like. The bus's radio was instantly tuned to a certain FM frequency, and everyone cheered when the thrilled passengers heard the loud refrains to "We Need A Little Christmas," "Here Comes Santa Claus", and "Frosty the Snowman," with the entire fantastic, circular lane route requiring three full songs to finally complete.

After a quick breakfast the following morning, the energized group spent several hours walking around downtown Frankenmuth, viewing and taking pictures of the elaborate Glockenspiel Clock, situated on the side of the alpine-in-appearance Bavarian Inn, with the very splendid apparatus chiming twelve times at noon. And simultaneously, the Giralos and their traveling party were treated to seeing character figures mechanically moving out, one by one, from the high-elevated clock, and then methodically reenacting a rendition of medieval history's legendary perfect pest exterminator, the classic "Pied Piper of Hamelin". Later that afternoon, Mike again conducted the forty-eight bus travelers to Bronners, the colossal-sized Christmas store that advertised itself as being open for business three-hundred-and-sixty-one days of the calendar year.

"This place is incredibly mammoth, at least ten-times as big as anything like it I've seen back in Jersey," Gina observed and stated. "Joe, this place Bronners claims to be the most prodigious Christmas paradise in the whole-wide world, and I believe that their assertion is without a doubt a hundred-percent true."

"Yes, and the only thing saving us from getting lost inside this phenomenal building are the gigantic overhead red and white ceiling signs that tell us what section of the store we're shopping in, ranging from area #1 to area #12. And Gina," Joe Giralo said. "I just got an idea. I think I'll get my office's two secretaries these matching Michigan State and University of Michigan stockings to hang from their fireplace mantels. The two schools are bitter rivals ya' know, especially during football season."

"And about a half an hour ago, I had seen some cute Christmas tree ornaments that I'd like to purchase. They're located over in Section 7," the wife indicated. "I had always thought that the Yankee Candle Christmas Shop we had visited in Connecticut on our last fall bus trip up to the Beacon Resort in New Hampshire was massive, but this whopping place is at least three times as big."

The Giralos lazily spent the remainder of the afternoon sampling various red and white wines (offered in plastic jiggers) at the town's St. Julian's Winery. And that evening, the couple played two games of 'Phase Ten' in the Drury Inn's 'Card and Recreation Lounge' with another husband/wife twosome they had met on the trip, Jim and Janice Heisler from Buena, a rustic South Jersey borough just south of Hammonton.

And finally, after indulging in a good night's sleep and partaking of the usual continental breakfast, the rested Jerseyites toting their various carry-on bags, climbed aboard the long white bus and then settled into their respective seats. Loquacious tour guide Julie Setzer provided her attentive audience with essential background about the Grand Michigan Hotel and picturesque Mackinac Island.

"The name Mackinac has a French pronunciation, and it's really sounded-out as the word *Mackinaw* would be enunciated in English," Julie educated her listeners over the bus's microphone. "Ironically, Mackinaw City is the town from which you'll take your ferry ride three-miles across the channel to Mackinac Island, having the same pronunciation, but obviously spelled differently. There're three ferry services shuttling people and goods back and forth from Mackinaw City to Mackinac Island: Arnold, Starr Lines, and Shepherd's Ferry."

"How far is the island from the famous Mackinac Bridge?" an elderly male senior citizen, seated in the back of the bus, hollered his question. "My uncle worked on that super five-and-a-half-mile long bridge way back in the mid-1950s."

"Actually, you'll be able to see the Mackinac Bridge from certain parts of the Grand Michigan Hotel property," Julie communicated over the bus's intercom. "The span is quite an engineering marvel. Now here's something fairly interesting I just thought of. The Michigan people that live on the state's Northern Peninsula are called Oopers, a name given by the residents living on the Lower Peninsula. And the folks living on the Lower Peninsula intentionally gave *them* that designation 'Oopers,' the term being a deliberate misspeak of the word 'Uppers'. Conversely," Julie lectured on, "the Upper Peninsula residents refer to their Lower Peninsula Michigan neighbors as 'trolls', probably referring to the fairy tale The Three Billy Goats Gruff, the children's story having a mean-spirited troll threatening the three crossing goats from below a bridge."

"I think the Mackinac Bridge goes over one of the Great Lakes," a gentleman sitting in the fourth row (right hand side) blurted-out. "Would you know which one?"

"Well, let me see now," Julie politely thought and answered. "The Mackinac Bridge divides Lake Superior on the left, and Lake Huron on the right. That is, presuming we're facing the Upper Peninsula. Yes, that's correct," the guide clarified. "Facing north, Lake Superior would be on the left, and Lake Huron would be viewed on the right."

"Do the locals call *us* tourists anything weird?" an inquisitive-but-vociferous woman in the central section asked Julie. "I mean, *we* at the Jersey Shore call summer tourists 'shoebies', because during the Great Depression, the day-tourists would come into Atlantic City on a train carrying their modest lunches on their laps in shoe boxes."

"Why yes!" Julie quickly acknowledged and laughed. "Tourists are referred to up here as 'fudgies', because there's a variety of at least thirty fudge shops selling their delicious sweet confections to visitors, both in the shops in Mackinaw City, and also in the many fudge stores on Main Street on Mackinac Island."

"How will our luggage get from the bus to the Grand Michigan Hotel?" the curious woman's apparently worried husband wanted to know. "I understand that there aren't any cars, trucks, or buses allowed on the island."

"You're right!" Julie concurred with a smile. "When the famous Grand Michigan Hotel was built back in the late 1880s, the island's town council passed an ordinance stating that no new-fangled, noisy horseless carriages would be allowed. So, from that day forward,"

Ms. Julie Setzer courteously explained, "the only way around Mackinac Island is by foot, by bicycle, or by horse and wagon, with many of the transportation carts looking like colonial-era stage coaches. During the peak summer months, around six-hundred-horses take people around Main and Market Streets, the island's two chief thoroughfares. The horses are usually in sets of two, but if you want to take a ride to the higher parts of the island, the horses will be in a team of three."

"But you didn't answer my question! How will our luggage get from the bus to the hotel?" the stubborn impetuous elderly fellow persisted as his perturbed wife gave him a dig into his ribcage with her bony elbow.

"Dock workers will take the luggage from the bus's storage compartment, put the pieces onto carts, and then carefully wheel the carts onto an awaiting Shepherd's Ferry. When the boat makes the three-mile trip across the bay to the island," Julie suavely conveyed to her traveling flock, "several horse-drawn wagons will be loaded with your suitcases. And I assure you, then your items will be safely delivered to the hotel, where you'll find your luggage in the hallway just outside your assigned rooms."

"I saw some postcards of a few wonderful houses on Mackinac Island, and the homes look like the bread and breakfast places in Cape May," Gina told Julie. "Many of the houses show a lot of external gingerbread designs."

"Yes, even the incomparable Grand Michigan Hotel flaunts a gorgeous Victorian appearance," Julie Setzer articulated through the bus's overhead speakers. "And the hotel's magnificent front porch overlooks a flower-laden terrace facing down towards the water. The famous porch is over six-hundred-and-fifty-feet long, the largest hotel porch in the world. And the Grand Michigan's spacious dining room easily seats seven-hundred-and-fifty guests for supper and breakfast. And Gentlemen," Julie purposely reminded her male passengers. "This next announcement is very important. You *must* wear a suit or formal jacket with a tie if you wish to be seated and eat supper in the resort's extraordinarily elegant main dining room."

"It sure beats Burger King!" vacationing FBI Inspector Joe Giralo whispered into Gina's ear, and then characteristically chuckled.

"And now," Julie proudly announced, "you'll be seeing the widely acclaimed 1980 movie *Somewhere in Time,* starring

Christopher Reeve and Jane Seymour. The film's a classic time-traveling adventure where a young playwright goes back in time to the early 1900s and has a dramatic love affair with an actress of *that* era, who had done stage performances at Mackinac Island's Grand Michigan Hotel. And a lot of the movie's scenes had been filmed on location, right at the Grand Michigan!"

* * * * * * * * * * * *

The scenic three-mile Shepherd's Ferry ride across the placid channel from Mackinaw City to Mackinac Island was both swift and invigorating for the picture-taking passengers aboard. A trio of two-horse pulled open-air carriages (capable of seating eighteen passengers each) met the eager tourists at the central Mackinac Island docking terminal. Another three wagons that had been differently designed to specifically convey cargo had six workmen assiduously loading-up the group's bulky luggage pieces, and after everyone was accounted for by Julie, the Giralos and their highly motivated traveling colleagues were soon riding down Main Street, featuring its many souvenir shops and casual eating establishments.

"Looks a little like a typical Jersey Shore boardwalk without any evidence of any boardwalk!" Joe instinctively quipped. "Julie was right! There're fudge shops galore here! And there were plenty more too, over in those tourist-trap shopping centers back in Mackinaw City. If we were to stay on this island paradise for a month, I'd probably weigh seventy-five more pounds than I do right now!"

"Stop being so cynical!" Gina coyly chided her all-too-garrulous husband. "Learn to relax and forget your eminent FBI identity for a few days! Look, Joe! The driver's turning the corner at the end of Main Street, and we're now going onto Market! And you just have to admire those stately Victorian mansions up on the high ridge overlooking the water! And just look at the beautiful architecture of that church steeple!"

Upon arriving at the regal-looking Grand Michigan Hotel, the New Jersey guests were warmly greeted by an employee/guide, who then led the awed group through the well-decorated and extra-large main lobby; through a beautiful green-draped oval-shaped sitting lounge, and next directly into the venue's sophisticated entertainment room, where orchestra music was played nightly after supper.

Various hotel speakers and guides then addressed the assembled visitors, describing and discussing in detail the myriad amenities available to guests; explaining the "no-tipping policy"; lecturing about the exotic botanical gardens surrounding the majestic edifice, and finally, a woman greeter enthusiastically elucidated about the hotel's inimitable Paul Bunyan outdoor swimming pool.

When the Giralos finally reached Room 132, their three pieces of luggage had already been delivered outside their door. Each of the hotel's three hundred and seventy guest rooms had its own sophisticated décor, and no two sleeping chambers were identical. And the window view of the property's flowers, shrubs, well-manicured lawns and gardens, along with an abundance of astonishing tree varieties, was indubitably stupendous, and none-the-less, extremely breathtaking.

"Joe, just look at the magnificent dark green drapes, matching mint-colored wallpaper, and accompanying light green, silk-cushioned-background above the bed's headboard," Gina marveled and gasped. "And the contrasting green and white table lamps, and the thick rich rug, match perfectly. I've read where this hotel has a separate interior decor for each room!"

"And besides, the bed's soft, and it seems more than adequate. When do we eat!" the less-intrigued spouse wanted to know. "My stomach's growling for some fine cuisine."

"Joe, did you see the framed caricatures of all the U.S. Presidents hanging along the wall down the first-floor corridor," the wife asked as she zipped open *her* Totes carry-on bag. "And just a couple of doors to our left is the Presidential Suite. I wonder if anyone important or famous is staying in it?"

"Maybe the President of Somalia, or the Yemen Ambassador to Cuba!" Joe pessimistically replied and then characteristically laughed. "I'm famished, Honey! Perhaps I won't be so sarcastic after I have the highly publicized five-course dinner!"

The patient wife totally ignored her mate's brazen attempt at demonstrating typical male negativity, so she shrewdly decided to change the subject. "Well, Honey. What did you think of the movie we had seen on the bus, *Somewhere in Time?*"

"I'd have liked the film a whole lot more if Christopher Reeve had fallen in love with a female in his own 1980s, and not with a lady in the year 1912," Joe criticized. "I mean, I think that Jane Seymour is an excellent actress, but quite frankly, I prefer TV reality shows to science fiction, fantasy time-travel love stories. I liked Christopher Reeve better when he played Superman."

"Have it your own way without the culinary magic of Burger King!" Gina Giralo wittily retorted. "You probably think that Oscar Mayer hot dogs are the greatest thing going since ancient man invented the fork and knife!"

"Now you're talking!" the FBI official on vacation bellowed. "Let's unpack our stuff and then get ready for supper in the main dining room. I can't remember the last time I wore a jacket and tie at a restaurant. Maybe a tuxedo at a wedding, but definitely not a suit and tie for dinner!"

"You'll have to start dieting when we return to Jersey," Gina diplomatically mentioned and predicted. "I don't want you getting diabetes!"

"But really and truly, I have to apologize, Honey! The filet mignon on tonight's menu is several levels above either a frankfurter or a charcoal-broiled slab of meat. But honestly, Gina. I don't know why they call the round things hamburgers," Joe Giralo awkwardly introduced his next comical remark. "Ham comes from a pig, and steak happens to come from a cow. The round food in a bun should rightfully be called 'steak-burgers', and not hamburgers!"

* * * * * * * * * * * *

The first full serene day on Mackinac Island (for the Giralos) was a rather nondescript pleasant one. After consuming a sumptuous breakfast in the hotel's nearly eight-hundred-seat main dining room, Joe and Gina ventured outside to partake of the early brisk Northern Michigan autumn air. The pair slowly descended wooden steps, leading them through the eye-appealing terrace area down to the massive Paul Bunyan Swimming Pool in order to inspect the many recreational facilities that were quite conveniently provided to accommodate the Grand Michigan's thousand or so catered-to, pampered guests.

Julie was standing outside the hotel's main entrance with her names' checklist clipboard, and at precisely ten a.m., three red and yellow painted horse-drawn carriages were ready to take the forty-eight New Jersey tourists on a "horizontal cross island journey" to the "Carriage House", where fifteen-minutes thereafter, a fleet of three-horse carriages was available to transport the delegation to the island's scenic higher elevations. There, the tourists could observe marvelous panoramic views of Lake Huron, along with snapping impromptu pictures of the natural rock "Arch Formation", located towards the island's summit.

Next on the itinerary was a tour of Fort Mackinac and nearby the dull white ramparts was the Governor's Summer Mansion, where James Heisler remarked to the Giralos, "Mitt Romney probably spent many of his youthful years there, since his father George was once the Michigan Governor."

The afternoon hours sped-by rather rapidly, as the Giralos and the Heislers casually meandered around parallel Main and Market Streets, doing light shopping at the sundry souvenir stores, and occasionally munching the irresistible fudge "free samples" randomly being offered on employee-held trays to sweet-tooth, targeted pedestrians. Pizza and Coca-Colas were purchased at a snack bar, but Gina warned Joe that he was limited to two slices, so that the weight-conscious food connoisseur would not spoil his upcoming five-course lobster tail feast back at the hotel.

After the sumptuous seafood-style dinners were consumed, the remainder of that Tuesday evening had the formally dressed Giralos and Heislers sitting on sofas in the expansive, color-coordinated lobby, and drinking cocktails while listening to an accomplished pianist playing a selection of popular 1940s and '50s melodies. And then after playing three fun-packed games of Phase Ten, the card playing couples retired to their respective first-floor rooms for the night. Everything was copacetic with the world, and FBI Inspector Joseph Giralo's mind was finally devoid of solving the plethora of illicit criminal activity, habitually plaguing American society.

On Thursday morning, Joe was suffering from a mild case of acid reflux, so the ailing epicure thought he would rest-up and recover from his brief malady inside Room 132, while his wife accompanied the Heislers on a walking tour of the hotel's majestic gardens. The trio's prime objective was viewing the property's many deciduous trees exhibiting their wondrous red, brown, and yellow autumnal hues. The husband had promised Gina that he would be feeling better after a few cups of "Room Service Coffee", and Joe also mentioned that she should not worry about his general health during her three-hour absence. Giralo picked-up a copy of the *New York Times* main stories that had been left under the suite's door, and feeling his newly acquired lackadaisical disposition, the calm vacationer waited for his pot of coffee to be routinely delivered by room service.

* * * * * * * * * * * *

At nine-thirty, a loud frantic rapping upon Room 132's door interrupted Joe Giralo's peaceful coffee consumption. The FBI man opened the portal, and the occupant was somewhat astonished to perceive the normally debonair suit-and-tie head hotel manager impatiently standing in the hallway.

"Mr. Giralo," the exasperated hotel executive said all out of breath. "I'm Giles Martin, the Grand Michigan's chief operating officer. May I come in?"

"Why of course!" the surprised Inspector replied, closing the door behind the unexpected visitor's entrance. "Is everything okay? You do appear to be more than a trifle alarmed!"

"I understand that you're an experienced inspector with the FBI. Our desk records indicate *that* much, Inspector Giralo. And I've already verified *that* formerly confidential information through our local police department, which incidentally also drastically needs your immediate assistance."

"Mr. Martin, exactly what is wrong?" the now thoroughly interested hotel guest asked. "What's of so much paramount importance and concern?"

"A most serious epidemic of colossal proportion has broken-out among the horse population here on Mackinac Island," panic-stricken Giles Martin boisterously disclosed. "Just about all of our six-hundred-horses are terribly sick with colic and influenza symptoms, and our town veterinarians are going crazy attending to all of the afflicted animals. And besides that," the agitated hotel manager impulsively expounded. "The entire transportation system on the island has been shut down. This is a colossal nightmare dilemma in progress, Inspector Giralo, an unimaginable worst-case scenario. And its basic origin, or should I say 'its real cause', *we* certainly find exceptionally baffling. That's why I'm here to both request and solicit your expertise."

"But Mr. Martin, by your vivid description, I'm not so sure that a genuine FBI crime has actually been committed here on this island," Giralo politely answered. "To be perfectly candid, I'm usually involved with kidnappings, ruthless murders, interstate prostitution,

380

and drug smuggling, money counterfeiting, along with major assassinations and multiple homicides performed in adjacent neighboring states. Horse epidemics might just be out of my law enforcement background realm, and the infections that you've depicted might just be a result of a bizarre-but-rare widespread contagion going on."

"The horses are biting their stomachs in response to the colic, and others inside their stables are nauseous and lethargic, apparently suffering from severe flu symptoms," the virtually delirious and animated hotel executive reported. "If you can't help us, truthfully Sir, I don't know who else can!"

"Well, Mr. Martin, what about the hotel's CEO? Is he around for me to interview?"

"He's away attending a national conference at the Greenbrier Resort out in White Sulfur Springs West Virginia, and quite confidentially," Giles Martin pontificated, "I'm afraid to divulge the exact magnitude of the current horse catastrophe to him!" the desperate and now-neurotic man-in-charge of daily operations ranted.

"Well, then, what about your Board of Directors? Can I consult with and interview them about this urgent horse matter?"

"Unfortunately, Sir, the Board is spending a week at the Hotel Del Coronado near San Diego where, off-the-record, they're doing a little espionage work checking-out *that* facility's various amenities including the food menu," the nervous and distraught hotel administrator reluctantly shared. "The group won't be back until next Monday, and I'm afraid to contact them about the bad news. But I'm sure they'll soon learn about the calamity from another source!"

"Well, Mr. Martin, how about your Corporate President? Is he to be found anywhere in Michigan?"

"This is all indeed very embarrassing for me to endure," the fit-to-be-tied, emotionally encumbered hotel executive apprehensively complained. "Our illustrious President is over in Dixville Notch, New Hampshire, and he's anonymously staying at the famous Balsams Resort while sizing-up the competition. Is there no compassion or rhyme or reason in this heartless world?"

Just then, Giles Martin's cell phone rang three times, and the man's anxiety level instantly heightened to its crescendo level. The hotel manager's facial expressions, along with his florid complexion, suggested to Inspector Joseph Giralo that the executive's secretary on the other end of the line was communicating additional negative news to the completely harried fellow.

"Mr. Giralo, I think I need to swallow-down at least a dozen aspirins. My secretary Ms. Gibson just informed me that the famous small photograph/portrait of Jane Seymour has been stolen from the downstairs Hall of History. And in addition," miserable Giles Martin continued his tale of woe, "I've recently learned that three priceless paintings from the mezzanine level art gallery have also been pilfered and nefariously replaced with authentic-looking counterfeits."

"I usually get involved with counterfeit money distribution, and if there's evidence or suspicion that these valuable heisted paintings have crossed state lines," Inspector Giralo qualified his complicated explanation, "then I'll be obligated to cut my vacation short and get immersed into cracking-open these new-found riddles of yours."

The usually composed and normally unfazed hotel manager's cell phone again rang, and the already besieged and flustered Giles Martin hesitated before finally responding to the three rings. Obviously, more horrible information was being transmitted to *his* ear, because the perplexed man's facial skin was gradually turning from red to purple. After ending the disturbing telephone call, the beleaguered and perspiring chief executive had more catastrophic developments to sadly convey to his now-fascinated listener.

"Oh my God, Inspector!" the chagrined, about-to-go-insane manager screamed while dramatically holding the sides of his head. "Duchess Priscilla from Denmark is staying with her cousin Princess Natasha two doors down from you in the newly renovated Presidential Suite. I feel like fainting and collapsing on the rug, Mr. Giralo. Their cache of diamond and sapphire necklaces and pendants, along with their emerald and ruby gemstone rings, have been mysteriously purloined from their room's safe. What an unprecedented career shattering nightmare I'm experiencing!" the extremely delirious gentleman related to his objective-minded Grand Michigan guest. "This entire sequence of events is absolutely scandalous, not only for me, but also for the respectable reputation of this distinguished hotel! It's unprecedented and horrendously devastating upon the long-honored history of *this* truly noble and esteemed establishment!"

"Okay, Mr. Martin. You've now overwhelmingly convinced me to personally and professionally intercede in your crisis!" Inspector Giralo declared. "I'll immediately notify my superiors in Washington of the problems here on the island. I strongly suspect that definite criminal activity is going on here; yes, bizarre occurrences that are evidently on the cusp of being suspiciously pernicious! The events you've just described have to be more than a series of peculiar coincidences! This complex puzzle now is much greater than a simple case of grand larceny!" Inspector Giralo firmly maintained. "The present circumstances absolutely warrant and justify my pledged Justice Department services! The Duchess and the Princess are both foreign dignitaries, who have inadvertently become felony victims. The fact that royal foreign aristocrats have been robbed now makes *your* very unenviable hotel plight into an important federal investigation matter!"

* * * * * * * * * * * *

Much to Giles Martin's utter astonishment, FBI Inspector Joseph Giralo showed-up without an appointment at the hotel director's office early on Friday afternoon, with the man-on-a-mission bearing some wonderfully propitious news. After being greeted by the somewhat relieved upper echelon executive, the highly skilled federal investigator orally delivered a most stunning exposition.

"Well, Mr. Martin. I've cracked your seemingly strange and inexplicable conundrum wide open. And I'm happy to tell you that the overall case has been solved."

"Please divulge what you know, and how you've managed to achieve your amazing results so quickly," Giles Martin reflexively insisted. "For example, what was the horse sickness hysteria all about? What culprit, or should I say *culprits,* were responsible for such a despicably cruel deed?"

"When you had first told me about the unusual colic and influenza epidemic affecting your Mackinac Island work horses, I immediately suspected that some sort of ruse, or should I say some sort of deliberate diversion had been set into motion," the experienced FBI sleuth remarked. "And when you later found-out about the missing Jane Seymour portrait being stolen from the Hall of History, and also found-out about the Duchess and the Princess's cherished jewels being burglarized, then those separate revelations confirmed my theory about a very clever cover-up horse malady canard being slyly enacted."

"Before you proceed with your discoveries, did you work alone on this case?" Giles inquired. "That prospect would seem to me to be a relevant part of the mystery riddle."

"Yes, Giles. I did have competent assistance," Joe Giralo bluntly answered. "FBI command in Washington assigned and dispatched a trio of fine men operating up here in Michigan to help me, Agent Arthur Orsi out of Flint, and Salvatore Velardi and Dan Blachford out of Saginaw. The three ambitious agents immediately drove up here to Mackinaw City and conducted comprehensive interviews with the local merchants, most of whom were proprietors and employees of shops on Central Avenue, on Huron Street, and in the Mackinaw Crossings shopping mall. Several conversations from trustworthy people at the Sweet Tooth Confectionery Store, at Joann's Fudge Shop, at the Michigan Peddler, and at the Mackinac Bay Trading Company provided *us* with key information that then led to the acquisition of essential clues and additional vital evidence. Once that specific knowledge had been gleaned and fed into our sophisticated national police data base computer system," Inspector Joe Giralo attested, "the rest of the well-conceived plot was quite easy to decipher."

Giles Martin demanded that Inspector Giralo slow-down his general recollection and precisely state the pertinent facts in their exact chronological order. The cooperative investigator promised to comply with the still-mentally disheveled manager's entreaty.

"Well, as I had already stated Giles," Joe Giralo proceeded with his sage analysis on a more personal basis. "Just as I had suspected, the abnormal horse epidemic was basically a creative canard to divert *your* attention from high level felonies that were in the making. Now Giles, I've noticed that most of your summer employees here at the hotel are from Jamaica and the Dominican Republic, and a few more from Haiti."

"That is quite true," Giles Martin readily verified. "The hotel annually closes for business in mid-October. Most of the imported summertime help then all return to their native lands, while the Island's working horses are transported to various farms in the Upper Peninsula for the winter. Only about five-hundred brave souls stay around on Mackinac for the extremely frigid, snow-laden months."

"Anyway, Giles, after I learned about the art collection counterfeit replacements and about the replica phony Jane Seymour portrait being exchanged for the original one, along with the snatched

384

jewelry from your royal guests staying in the luxurious Presidential Suite," Inspector Giralo keenly elucidated, "I immediately thought about your employees and about their countries of origin. A background check on various merchants across the bay over in Mackinaw City established that a certain art gallery dealer there by the name of Mortimer Benton had once owned a pawnshop in Montego Bay, Jamaica, and that Mortimer's eldest son Clyde…"

"Once was a lower management clerk here at the hotel, who had been dismissed two years ago because Clyde Benton had gotten into a heated dispute with my younger brother, Ted, *his* immediate boss at the time! We don't tolerate or allow insubordination to occur here! That's our strict company policy!"

"So, Giles, now we have two distinct motives: Aggrieved Clyde Benton wanted his revenge on the hotel management team, and diabolical Mortimer Benton loved the hotel's art collection, and ultimately schemed to steal its three most valued canvas treasures," the Inspector plausibly explained. "But don't you see, Giles? It was the missing and substituted for Jane Seymour Portrait that got me hot onto Mortimer Benton's trail."

"How did that narrowed-down pursuit come to be?" the still bewildered hotel administrator asked. "There are still several missing components to this rather confusing jigsaw puzzle!"

"Agents Orsi, Velardi, and Blachford had discovered over in Mackinaw City that Mortimer Benton was infatuated with *that* very desirable Jane Seymour portrait, ever since he had first cinematically viewed in 1982. And what later became *his* passionate obsession, Mortimer's favorite movie happened to be *Somewhere in Time*. In Mortimer Benton's conniving mind," Inspector Giralo revealed and then paused, "my hypothesis upon initial instinct was that nothing was going to prevent this scheming art gallery thug from confiscating and possessing that coveted Hall of History object. But then, I logically reasoned that the other art masterpieces, along with the opulent jewelry heist, would eventually be fenced, with the obtained money being used for desperate Mortimer Benton to pay off his huge gambling and loan-sharking debts, before the ruthless Detroit Mafia closed-in on their pathetic 'mark'."

"And I guess that since Mortimer Benton once owned a pawnshop in Montego Bay, Jamaica," Giles Martin surmised and expressed. "The slippery scoundrel, just like his volatile son, Clyde, the devious rogue was able to speak Patois, the language often used by the island's natives that had been handed-down from their colonial-era Jamaican slave ancestors, who didn't want *their* vindictive masters to understand what they were plotting or communicating. To the British colonists, the words in Patois all sounded like stupid gibberish."

"And since Clyde and Mortimer Benton both spoke this contrived native language, Patois, pretty fluently," Inspector Giralo eloquently concurred, "the reprehensible Benton thieves were able to bribe and persuade some of your hotel's less loyal employees to temporarily poison the island's horses; to snatch and replace the three expensive art works; to steal the precious jewels from the Duchess's Presidential Suite, and finally, to stealthily swipe and switch the notorious Jane Seymour Portrait inside the Hall of History."

"And naturally, a former pawnbroker would have access to unscrupulous trading fences and illicit underworld dealers, along with numerous nefarious-minded business connections that would be able to easily dispose of the artwork trove at a handsome profit and to also...."

"To also chop the brilliant diamonds, rubies, emeralds, and sapphires down to be dispensed with on the thriving global black market," Inspector Joe Giralo clarified. "Now also, Giles. I've learned that Mortimer's brother Nigel owns and operates an import/export business over in Alpena, thanks to the dedicated research of FBI Agents Orsi, Velardi, and Blachford. But I still need to dig deeper into Mortimer's strategy in order to excavate more salient facts that'll enable me to fully implicate Nigel Benton directly to Mortimer and Clyde's felonious Michigan activities."

"And I must say, that rather imaginative horse epidemic diversionary ploy really had us officials here on the island going on a frustrating wild goose chase, just as it had originally been designed by the wily perpetrators," Mr. Giles Martin concluded and orally conveyed. "For several days, pandemonium was rampant all over Mackinac. And, oh yes, Inspector Giralo. The Chief-of-Police just notified me a half-hour ago that a Jamaican room-cleaning maid he's described as a 'person of interest' is now under interrogation for her possible participation in the grand larceny royal jewelry theft caper."

"Yes, and I must admit, even the crafty crooks were surprised when the flu and colic epidemic proved to be more widespread than the plotters had ever anticipated or imagined," the very skilled Inspector nonchalantly verbalized to his most recent admirer. "And to add a new dimension to the confounding ugly mess, another

386

disgruntled former hotel employee named Milo Ransom has confessed to being a secondary co-conspirator in the elaborate crime scenario. Up to yesterday," Giralo informed Martin, "Milo had been employed as a maintenance crewman on Arnold Ferry Services boats, but after admitting to smuggling and transporting the jewelry, the original canvas paintings and the singular Jane Seymour portrait from Mackinac Island back to Mortimer Benton's art gallery in Mackinaw City, I'm sorry to report to you that *our* subordinate villain Milo Ransom is currently out of a job, and the adventurous lowlife is now on the local judge's docket and scheduled to be sentenced to a minimum of six months jail time."

"Most remarkable and extraordinary!" Giles Martin sincerely commended his veteran crime-fighting guest. "If it weren't for you coincidentally vacationing here at the Grand Michigan, *we'd* still be struggling with a mammoth mystery on square one!"

Just then, the elated manager's land-line phone rang, and Ms. Gibson stated over the desk speaker that Inspector Joseph Giralo's boss wished to converse with the new Mackinac Island hero.

"Hello, Joe! And may I add congratulations, too!" Chief D.C. Inspector Matthew Riley praised and complimented over the desk speakerphone for everyone present inside the hotel manager's office to hear. "My reliable sources have informed me that you've become a veritable champion of justice up there in Northern Michigan!"

"All in the line of duty, Sir. But quite frankly, I didn't expect all of the wild excitement to transpire in the middle of my late summer vacation! It's all been a little surreal, to tell you the candid truth! But the Duchess and Princess's gemstones have been recovered intact, and also, the stolen paintings from the hotel's art gallery, along with the original Jane Seymour portrait, are all now safely back in the possession of the rightful owners," Joe Giralo respectfully replied. "Honestly, Boss. Agents Orsi, Velardi, and Blachford did most of the difficult gumshoe groundwork investigation. But what's up Chief? Anything new that I should know about?"

"Well now, Joe," Giralo's no-nonsense, straightlaced superior driveled on. "Since your well-earned Michigan hiatus has been abruptly interrupted with the outlandish Mackinac Island crime spree adventure, I want you to know that I've received special permission to have your vacation at the Grand Michigan Hotel extended for an additional week, expenses all paid for by good old Uncle Sam. Such fine compensation couldn't have happened to a more deserving guy."

"Why that's positively wonderful news, Chief!" the very satisfied Inspector boomed into the telephone speaker. "My wife Gina is enamored with this place, and she'll be absolutely thrilled to be relaxing here for another seven days."

"And that's not all!" Chief Inspector Matthew Riley expeditiously vociferated. "As an added bonus reward, at noon a week from tomorrow, we've arranged for a limo' to pick-up you and Gina at the Mackinaw City central loading pier, and then, a hired chauffeur will drive the two of you down to a cute German town in central Michigan called Frankenmuth, where you'll both be treated to another free and fully paid week at a certain lodge; here it is on a sheet of paper sitting on my cluttered desk," Chief Riley stated as he fumbled through some irrelevant letters and memos. "It's called the Drury Inn. What do you think about those apples, Joe? Talk about living the 'Life of Riley!' Ha, ha, ha! Pretty neat stuff, huh?"

"Why, er yes, it is Chief!" the totally shocked and astounded FBI Inspector uttered. "I'm almost flabbergasted! My Uncle Manfred is from Bavaria, and I can't wait to tell him all about my good fortune, being able to hang out in a German town right here in idyllic Michigan! Thanks a million, Chief! I can't wait to relay the good news to my wonderful wife!" Click.

The following Thursday morning, Inspector Joseph Giralo was feeling a bit sluggish, suffering from mild indigestion. The FBI Investigator was all alone, sipping his morning coffee inside Room 132 when a loud knocking on his first-floor hotel room door interrupted the gentleman's intense reverie. Deja Vu! Standing in the hallway was the very distressed hotel manager.

"Mr. Giralo, a very terrible horse epidemic has just broken-out on the island!" a perspiring Giles Martin announced. "I've learned through our confidential records kept here at the Grand Michigan that you work for the FBI. It's a very urgent matter that I have to tell you about! Yes, a very serious emergency situation involving colic and influenza must be addressed! May I come in?"

About the Author

Jay Dubya is author' John Wiessner's pen name and also his initials (J.W.) John is a retired New Jersey public school English teacher and he had taught the subject for thirty-four years. John lives in southern New Jersey with wife Joanne and the couple has three grown sons. John is the creator of thirty-nine published books.

Jay Dubya has written adult satires *Fractured Frazzled Folk Fables and Fairy Farces* and *FFFF and FF, Part II. Black Leather and Blue Denim, A '50s Novel* and its sequel, *The Great Teen Fruit War, A 1960' Novel* and *Frat' Brats, A '60s Novel* are adult-oriented literary endeavors constituting a trilogy.

Pieces of Eight, Pieces of Eight, Part II, Pieces of Eight Part III and *Pieces of Eight, Part IV* are' short story/novella collections featuring science fiction, paranormal and humorous plots and themes. *Nine New Novellas* is the companion book to *Nine New Novellas, Part II, Nine New Novellas, Part III* and *Nine New Novellas, Part IV.* And *So Ya' Wanna' Be A Teacher* is a satirical autobiography describing the author's thirty-four-year educational career in American public schools.

Ron Coyote, Man of La Mangia is adult humor and the work is an imaginative satire/parody on Miguel Cervantes' Don Quixote, published in 1605. *Mauled Maimed Mangled Mutilated Mythology* is a work that satires twenty-one famous ancient tales. *The Wholly Book of Genesis* and *The Wholly Book of Exodus* are also adult satirical humor. *Thirteen Sick Tasteless Classics, Thirteen Sick Tasteless Classics, Part II, Thirteen Sick Tasteless Classics, Part III* and *Thirteen Sick Tasteless Classics, Part IV* are adult satirical rewrites of famous short fiction.

John has also authored a trilogy of young adult fantasy novels, *Enchanta, Pot of Gold* and *Space Bugs, Earth Invasion. The Eighteen' Story Gingerbread House* is a new collection of eighteen diverse and creative children's stories.

Jay Dubya likes '50s rock and roll music and he also enjoys pop' songs by the Beach Boys', Fleetwood Mac, the Eagles, the Rolling Stones, ELO, John Mellencamp and by John Fogerty. When not writing or listening to music, Jay Dubya likes watching 76ers basketball and Phillies and Yankees television baseball games.

Author Biography

Born in Hammonton, NJ in 1942, John Wiessner had attended St. Joseph School up to and including Grade 5. After his family moved from Hammonton to Levittown, Pa in 1954, John attended St. Mark School in Bristol, Pa. for Grade 6, St. Michael the Archangel School in Levittown for Grades 7 and 8 and then Immaculate Conception School, Levittown, Pa. for Grade 9. Bishop Egan High School, Levittown PA. was John's educational base for Grades 10 and 11, and later in 1960, the aspiring author graduated from Edgewood Regional High, Tansboro, NJ. John then next attended Glassboro State College, where he was an announcer for the school's baseball games and also read the nightly news and sports over WGLS, GSC's radio station.

John Wiessner had been primarily an English teacher in the Hammonton Public School System for 34 years, specializing in the instruction of middle school language arts. Mr. Wiessner was quite active in the Hammonton Education Association, loyally serving in the capacities of Vice-President, then building representative, and finally, teachers' head negotiator for a period of 7 years. During his lengthy teaching career, John had been nominated into "Who's Who among American Teachers" three times. He also was quite active giving professional workshops at schools around South Jersey on the subjects of creative writing and the use of movie videos to motivate students to organize their classroom theme compositions.

In addition, John Wiessner was very active in community service, being a past President of the Hammonton Lions Club, where he also functioned for many years as the club's Tail-Twister, Vice-President and Liontamer. John had been named Hammonton Lion of the Year in 1979 and in 2009 received the prestigious Melvin Jones Fellow Award, the highest honor a Lion can receive.

John also was a successful businessman, starting with being a Philadelphia Bulletin newspaper delivery boy for two-years in the late 1950s in Levittown, Pennsylvania. After his family moved back to New Jersey in 1959, John worked at his grandparents and his parents' farm markets, Square Deal Farm (now Ron's Gardens in Hammonton) and Pete's Farm Market in Elm, respectively. He later managed his wife's parents' farm market, White Horse Farms in Elm for three summers.

Also in a business capacity, for 16 summers starting in 1967 John Wiessner had co-owned Dealers Choice Amusement Arcade on the Ocean City, Maryland boardwalk and also co-owned the New Horizon Tee-Shirt Store for eight summers (1973-'81) on the Rehoboth Beach, Delaware boardwalk. In addition, "Jay Dubya" was a co-owner of Wheel and Deal Amusement Arcade, Missouri Avenue and Boardwalk, Atlantic City. And then, for 18 summers beginning in 1986, John had been the Field Manager in charge of crew-leaders for Atlantic Blueberry Company (the world's largest cultivated blueberry farm), both the Weymouth and Mays Landing Divisions.

After retiring from teaching in 1999, writing under the pen name Jay Dubya (his initials), John Wiessner became the author of 75 books in the genre Action/Adventure Novels, Sci-Fi/Paranormal Story Collections, Adult Satire, Young Adult Fantasy Novels and also Non-Fiction Books. His books exist in hardcover, in paperback and in popular Kindle and Nook e-book formats.

In January of 2022, John Wiessner (Jay Dubya) was nominated into Marquis Who's Who in America, and in April of that same year, was one of nine distinguished Who's Who in America members honored with receiving Lifetime Achievement Awards, all nine sharing a news article of recognition appearing in the Wall Street Journal.

Google: Jay Dubya books
Google: Walmart, Jay Dubya

www.ingramcontent.com/pod-product-compliance
Lightning Source LLC
Chambersburg PA
CBHW070745120726

47910CB00001B/173